D0387559

Swear by the Moon

Also by Shirlee Busbee in Large Print:

Midnight Masquerade

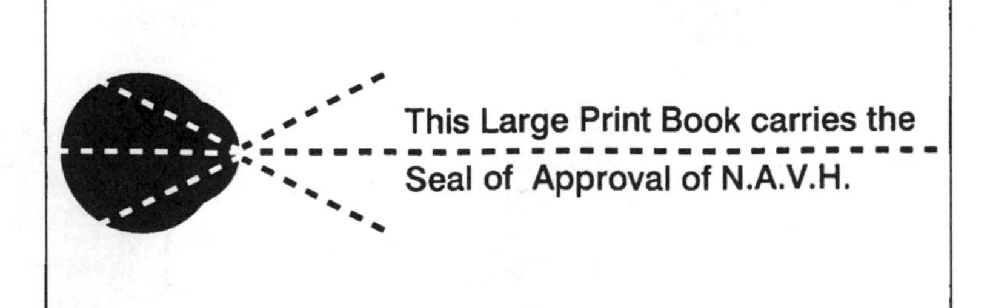

Swear by the Moon

Shirlee Busbee

Thorndike Press • Waterville, Maine

Published in 2002 by arrangement with Warner Books, Inc.

Thorndike Press Large Print Romance Series.

The tree indicium is a trademark of Thorndike Press.

The text of this Large Print edition is unabridged.
Other aspects of the book may vary from the original edition.

Set in 16 pt. Plantin by Myrna S. Raven.

Printed in the United States on permanent paper.

Library of Congress Cataloging-in-Publication Data

Busbee, Shirlee.
Swear by the moon / Shirlee Busbee.
p. cm.
ISBN 0-7862-4054-7 (lg. print : hc : alk. paper)
1. London (England) — Fiction. 2. Large type books.
I. Title.
PS3552.U7895 S94 2002
813′.54—dc21 2002018026

To a pair of dear friends who have often
made my life
simpler — and more fun!
PAULINE BRUMLEY, who always
brightens my day and brings me squash
from the garden that her husband, Ernie,
grows with that 'good stuff' he gets from us.

and

MARLENE BAUER, who for years
patiently answered my
frequent, "Who's that?" and who kept me
up on the latest gossip — and turned me
onto Weight Watchers — for that alone she
deserves ten dedications!

And as always, the love of my life,
HOWARD.

Prologue

Cheltenham, England
1788

The two small figures scurrying across the vast grounds of the estate of Lord Garrett, had anybody been looking, were clearly visible by the light of the full November moon. It was highly unlikely, at two o'clock in the morning, that anyone would have expected to see Lord Garrett's just-turned-seventeen sister, Thea, acting in such a clandestine manner. Which was precisely the plan.

A half-excited, half-nervous giggle escaped Thea as she and Maggie Brown, her maid, finally made it to the cover of the tall trees that encircled the grounds. The plan was not hers. Lord Randall had concocted it, and with all the naïveté of one so young and wildly in love for the first time, Thea had thought it a very clever plan. But then she thought every word that fell from Lord Randall's lips was clever. She had altered his plan only slightly, deciding at the last minute to let Maggie, who was training to become her personal maid, in on the secret.

She had known Maggie all of her life and had known that Maggie would support her in this momentous undertaking.

Maggie, just a year older than Thea, had been agog with terror and excitement when Thea had enlightened her about what was in the wind. It was, as Maggie had averred passionately this evening, "ever so romantic and thrilling" that Miss Thea and Lord Randall were flying in the face of family disapproval and eloping. Maggie thought it was too bad that Lord Garrett and Mrs. Northrop, Lord Garrett and Thea's mother, were so against the dashing Lord Randall. Hadn't it been Lord Garrett himself who had introduced Lord Randall to the family? Invited the handsome aristocrat to stay at the family estate, Garrett Manor, for weeks on end this past summer?

Only hours before, her huge dark eyes full of emotion, Thea had declared to the highly sympathetic Maggie that she would just *die* if she did not marry Lord Randall! Mama and Tom, Lord Garrett, just did not understand. They were being unreasonable to expect her to wait until the end of her London season next year before announcing her intention to marry Lord Randall. Why, that was *months* away! And as for their objections to the match, it was all nonsense! Her firm little chin had lifted. Pooh! What did she care that Lord Randall was older than she was? Or that her fortune was much larger than his? Or that he had a reputation of being a rake? Didn't rakes make the best husbands? Everybody knew that!

Tom was just being vexatious, Thea had declared roundly as she tossed various items to Maggie to pack, and Mama . . . Hadn't Mama been just a year older than Thea was now when she had married Papa? And hadn't Papa been known as one of the wildest rakes around? And hadn't he been nearly twenty years her senior? She didn't see why she couldn't marry a rake. Mama had married a rake, actually two rakes counting Mr. Northrop, whom Mama had married after Papa had been so foolish as to get himself killed when he, his horses and curricle had all gone over a cliff in Cornwall while he had been trying to win a drunken wager. And hadn't Mama married the much-gossiped-about Mr. Northrop two years later, a man who had been some fifteen years older than she? Having married two men so much older than herself and both with notorious reputations, how could Mama now be so cruel and unfeeling as to deny Thea her heart's desire? Mama just wasn't being fair! She would marry Lord

Randall. No one, not Mama or Tom, was going to stop her.

As they had hastily packed the bandboxes for the journey to Gretna Green, Thea had extolled Lord Randall's virtues, almost convincing Maggie that there was much merit in this runaway marriage and that Lord Randall was a paragon of virtue. Almost.

Maggie, flattered and awed by her sudden inclusion in the most exciting event that had ever come her way, had nodded in agreement with Thea's arguments. As Thea had said, Lord Randall was handsome. He was, according to Lord Garrett himself, a capital fellow. Well connected and with a comfortable fortune. It was true, as Thea had explained earnestly, that Lord Randall had lived a wild and even scandalous life, but he had sworn that all that would change once Thea became his wife. Besides, Thea had said airily, everyone knew that the gentlemen could do as they pleased. Why, even Tom was known to be a "hard goer" and was no stranger to the gaming table and was fond of his liquor. And didn't Tom keep a mistress in London? Thea wasn't supposed to know about *that,* but her young half sister Edwina, who had the nasty habit of listening at keyholes, had heard Mama scolding him about some little actress he had in keeping and Edwina had wasted little time in prattling to Thea all about it. Now how, Thea had asked scornfully, could Tom possibly object to her marrying a friend of his who acted just the same? Of course, Lord Randall had sworn that those days were past for him.

Caught up in Thea's enthusiasm, Maggie had agreed with her young mistress, but now that they had left the safety of the house and were on their way to the rendezvous with Lord Randall, she suddenly found herself full of misgivings. Lord Randall, she admitted as she followed Miss Thea's darting, slender form through the woods, was indeed much older than her young mistress. At thirty-three, he was even much older than Thea's brother, Lord Garrett, who had just turned twenty-one in August. And if the downstairs gossip was correct, Lord Randall was also a hardened gamester — one of the wild crowd that Lord Garrett had fallen in with lately. Mrs. Northrop had not been pleased about that! Nor that her only son was fast becoming as care-for-nothing as his late, lamented father had been in his heyday.

But none of that mattered, Maggie told herself firmly. Everyone knew that Lord Randall had taken one look at Miss Thea and had fallen in love with her. And Miss

Thea . . . Maggie sighed blissfully. Miss Thea had felt exactly the same way. And while Maggie might have reservations about Lord Randall's suitability for a young, innocent lady like her mistress, and the covert nature of their courtship, with snatched meetings here and there, it certainly wasn't up to her to question the actions of the gentry. As for betraying Miss Thea . . . why, she'd never be able to lift her head again!

None of the reservations that plagued Maggie even crossed Thea's mind. She was too excited, too intent on reaching Lord Randall's side, to question the wisdom of what she was doing. She was in love! Certain that Lord Randall, or Hawley, as he had asked her to call him, was the man of her dreams. With his smiling gray eyes, thick black hair, and tall, broad-shouldered form, he was every maiden's dream, of this she was positive. And to think *she* was the lucky one whom he had chosen to marry! A scowl crossed her gamine features. It was too bad of Tom to claim that it was her fortune that Hawley had chosen, she thought, as memories of her brother's pithy remarks floated across her brain.

Thea and Maggie suddenly burst from the woods and there, drawn up to the side of the road, was the curricle and pair right where he had said they would be: Lord Randall, tall and imposing in his greatcoat, was nervously pacing beside the restive horses. At the sight of Thea, her lively features framed by the hood of her purple-velvet cloak, a pair of overflowing bandboxes clutched in her hands, he left off his pacing and swiftly approached her.

Swinging her into his arms, he kissed her passionately, far more passionately than she had ever been kissed in her life, and exclaimed, "*Darling!* You are here at last. I have been in a fever of impatience — fearful that your tender heart would fail you at the last moment."

Flustered by the kiss and a trifle shy, Thea looked up into his attractive features. "I would let nothing stop me," she declared softly. "I promised you I would be here."

He smiled, his gray eyes glinting in the moonlight, his chiseled mouth curving with satisfaction. "I know . . . but I was fearful nonetheless. I would not blame you if you had decided that your family was right and that I was not worthy of you." His lashes dropped, and he glanced away. "I should send you back," he said manfully. "I am a selfish cad to take you from everything you know and love."

"Never say so!" Thea protested, her dark

eyes bright with emotion. "You are everything that I desire. Once we are married and they see what a wonderful husband you are to me, Mama and Tom will change their minds. You'll see."

His moment of doubt gone, he flashed her a melting smile and nodded. "I am sure you are right. But now we must be off before you are missed."

He tossed Thea up into the curricle and was on the point of joining her when he became aware of Maggie standing uncertainly by the side of the road. He frowned, the lines of dissipation in his handsome face suddenly pronounced.

An edge to his voice, he asked, "And who is this? I told you that no one was to know. No one."

"Oh, it is only Maggie," Thea said blithely. A faint blush, barely visible in the moonlight, suddenly crossed Thea's features. "I know that we are to be married, but I did not think it proper for me to travel alone with you all the way to Scotland. It would not be seemly."

"And where," he asked coolly, "do you expect me to put her and all those boxes and whatnot you have brought with you? As you can see, I have only a curricle for us."

Thea blinked. She had never heard that

tone of voice from him before and was not certain how to react. Maggie could have told her that the servants of Garrett Manor were very familiar with that particular tone and that it usually preceded a sound boxing of the ears.

Feeling that the strain of the situation was making him a bit testy, Thea sent him a dazzling smile. "Oh, we shall manage. Maggie and I can squeeze together — we are neither of us very big, and I am sure that you will find a place for everything."

"I see." The expression in his eyes was unreadable. Turning to Maggie, he muttered, "Since my wife-to-be brought you along, you had better get in." He glanced at Thea. "In the future, my dear," he said, "I would appreciate it if you did not make changes in my plans without consulting with me first."

In the silence that followed he made no attempt to help Maggie as she awkwardly clambered into the curricle. Making herself as small as possible, she squeezed gratefully next to Thea.

It was a silent threesome who traveled through the silvery moonlight. Lord Randall, wanting to put as much distance as possible between himself and the sure-to-be-infuriated Lord Garrett, set the horses at a spanking pace. The expression on his face did not invite conversation, and Thea, the first blush of excitement having vanished and Lord Randall's manner not very encouraging, found herself uneasy and a trifle let down. Maggie, remembering all the gossip amongst the servants who'd had the misfortune to run afoul of Lord Randall, was cowardly wishing that Miss Thea had not chosen her to partake in this particular adventure.

Garrett Manor was situated a short distance from the town of Cheltenham in Gloucester, nearly ninety miles northwest of London. Gretna Green, their destination, was on the border between Scotland and England, a considerable distance farther. They would be more than a few days on the road, even with Lord Randall driving at great speed. The hope was that by the time Lord Garrett and Mrs. Northrop discovered Thea's absence, the eloping couple would have an insurmountable head start.

Everything went well until midmorning, when one of the horses they had hired from the last inn threw a shoe and came up lame. Lord Randall, who had seemed to have gotten over his annoyance at Maggie's inclusion and had been gaily regaling the two young women with a politely risqué story about Prinny, King George III's heir and eldest son, muttered a curse and pulled the horses to a stop. A quick examination of the horse confirmed the lost shoe and the fact that they were going nowhere with any speed until the shoe was replaced, and possibly the horse, too.

Since they were on a rather deserted stretch of road, Lord Randall left the two women in the curricle while he rode the sound horse some miles back to the nearest village. It was nearly two hours later before they were once again on their way, and Lord Randall's surly manner had returned. Thea's attempts at conversation were met with either a cold silence or a curt reply.

Late that afternoon, when Thea suggested that they stop at the next posting inn so she and Maggie could stretch their legs and perhaps partake in some refreshments, he sent her a forbidding look that startled her. "You seem to have forgotten that it is urgent that we reach our destination before your brother overtakes us," he snapped. "I'll not have all my plans overturned just because you wish to sip some lemonade." And when they had swept past the posting inn with nary a check of the horses, the expression on his face had kept her protest unspoken.

As the posting inn disappeared in a cloud

of dust behind them, it occurred belatedly to Thea that her husband-to-be could be very charming . . . as long as everything was going his way, but let adversity strike . . . She peeped over at him as he drove, his attractive profile grim. This was a side of him she had never seen, never suspected. Of course, he was upset, she told herself charitably. The delay with the lost shoe had been costly, and it was imperative that they reach Gretna Green well ahead of Tom. Still, she did not think that it was necessary for him to be quite so ungracious. If not for themselves, they should have stopped for Maggie, she thought unhappily, after a glance at Maggie's tired features.

They had been on the road over fourteen hours and surely a half hour stop would not have spelled disaster, especially since their only breaks involved flying stops . . . Thea sent another look at Maggie's face. While it wasn't Maggie's place to complain, it *was* Thea's place to see that her servant was not abused. It was a family tradition that the Garretts took care of their own, and practically since birth it had been drilled into Thea's head that she was responsible for the well-being and care of her servants, actually of anyone of a lesser position than herself. Thea might be madly in love, but she was not unintelligent, and Lord Randall's utter disregard for her and Maggie's needs made her thoughtful and a little wary of the glamour with which she had viewed him.

A mile or so down the road, Hawley sent Thea an apologetic look. "I am sorry," he said. "I should not have been so abrupt with you. In my haste for us to be safely beyond your brother's reach, I have pushed all other considerations aside." He smiled winningly at her, his gray eyes crinkling attractively at the corners. "Of course, I shall stop at the next posting inn and you and your servant shall have all the lemonade you wish." Softly he added, "Will you forgive me, sweet, for being so anxious to marry you that I ignored all else? Even your simple needs? I swear I shall not do so again."

Thea's heart swelled. Of course, he was ill-tempered and snappish — he was terribly worried that Tom would manage to part them. Why, anyone would act the same.

Smiling sunnily at him, she nodded. "Mind," she said teasingly, "it must be the very next posting inn."

"Indeed it shall be."

Hawley was as good as his word, and they stopped at the very next posting inn. While Thea and Maggie were feasting in the private room he procured for them, he ordered a basket of food and drink to take with them on their journey.

Some minutes later, revived and re-freshed, they were once more on the road. As the miles sped by and more and more distance was put between themselves and possible pursuers, Hawley relaxed. The delay caused by the thrown shoe had been unfortunate, but he intended to travel on through the night. It was almost pleasant for early November, and the bright, clear moonlight made it entirely feasible. He smiled to himself. There was still a great distance before them, but Thea was as good as his bride right now.

That thought had hardly crossed his mind when there was a loud crack, and the curricle gave a wild lurch as the right wheel went spinning down the road. The horses reared and plunged at the sudden drag, the curricle nearly tipping over on its side without the support of the wheel. Thea and Maggie gasped and clung to each other as Lord Randall fought to keep control of the struggling horses.

Eventually he was able to bring the horses to a standstill and, a moment later, had leaped down from the curricle to survey the problem. The wheel was gone, the body of the curricle tipped precariously onto one side. A brief search revealed the wheel several yards down the road. The hub was completely cracked, which had allowed the wheel to break free of the axle. Hawley swore as he looked at the damage. It was unlikely he'd find a blacksmith who could fix the wheel at this hour. Provided he could even find a blacksmith. His expression unpleasant, he walked back to where Thea waited for him.

"Is it very bad?" she asked anxiously, her eyes filled with worry.

"As bad as it can be," he growled. Looking both ways down the road and seeing not so much as a farm cart, he sighed. "The last village we passed was several miles back," he said finally. "No doubt there is a posting inn or another village just ahead of us. I am afraid that I shall have to leave you alone again, my dear, and go see what help I can find." He glanced at her. "It may be dark before I return. The moon will be out though, so you will not be completely without light. Will you be frightened, if I leave you here?"

Thea shook her head. "No. Maggie and I shall be fine."

He helped the pair of them down from the unsteady curricle and, spreading a carriage blanket on the ground at the side of the road for them to sit upon, quickly unharnessed the curricle. Astride one of the horses, the other tied to a nearby tree and the curricle dipping drunkenly where they had left it, he prepared to leave. Looking down at Thea and Maggie as they sat on the blanket, he hesitated. They should be safe. He might be careless of others' comfort but even he did not like leaving two young defenseless women alone on a deserted stretch of road. "I would take you with me, but I shall travel much faster on my own," he said apologetically.

"Of course you will!" Thea said. She smiled at him. "Go. Go. Do not worry about us. We are country-raised, and the night holds no terror for us. We shall be quite all right. And do not fear we shall become chilled — Maggie and I both are wearing our heavy cloaks — we shall be quite warm." She stifled a yawn. Her lack of sleep was telling, and her eyes already drowsy, she added, "When you come back you shall no doubt find us sound asleep."

When Hawley returned, driving a rented farmer's cart, his temper was none too good. Even the sight of Thea and Maggie curled next to each other and asleep on the blanket did not lighten his mood. The village, more a small hamlet although it did boast an inn of sorts, had been a goodly distance down the road. By the time he had reached it and learned that it would be morning before anything could be done about his curricle, he had known that the elopement was in grave danger of coming to naught. They would have to stay the night, and he was certain that morning would bring Lord Garrett hot on their heels. His face tightened. He had come too far to be thwarted now — and the state of his finances made marriage to Thea urgent. This unforeseen patch of bad luck left him with no choice but to make it impossible for Lord Garrett to oppose the marriage.

If Thea noticed that Lord Randall was silent during the bone-jarring ride to the little inn where they would be staying the night, she said nothing. She was tired, hungry, and looking forward to sleeping through the night. This elopement business was all rather exhausting and not very romantic, she decided as she fought an enormous yawn.

Thea had not thought a great deal about what would happen when they reached the inn, but she was disturbed when she discovered that Maggie would not be sharing the room with her. Her expression troubled, she said to Lord Randall, "It is not necessary to procure another place for Maggie — she can share my bed. I will not mind."

"Ah, but *I* will mind," Hawley said with a smile. "I'll not have it bandied about that my wife is reduced to sleeping with servants. I have the care of you now, my pet, and it simply would not do."

"Oh," Thea said blankly, touched and yet strangely uneasy.

He smiled again and ran a caressing finger down her soft cheek. "Go to bed, my dear, I shall see to everything."

"What about Tom?"

His smile became fixed. "Do not worry. I have everything in hand."

Reassured and having seen for herself that Maggie was comfortable in the room she would share with the innkeeper's daughter, Thea climbed gratefully into bed. Wearing a demure cotton shift and the covers pulled up to her chin to keep out the chill of the November night, she lay there feeling rather small and uncertain.

The day had been long and tiring, but she found herself restless. The elopement was not proving to be quite as romantic and thrilling as she had assumed it would be, and Hawley's manner at times troubled her. Tom and her mother had both warned her against him, telling her to be careful, that he was not the charming suitor she thought him to be. Especially, her mother had pleaded, don't be fooled by a sophisticated air and a handsome face. They were going to be furious when they discovered that she had defied them, she admitted guiltily. Thoughts of home and her mother's disapproval and Tom's condemnation flickered through her mind. They had to be mistaken in their beliefs about Hawley. Despite his actions that day, Thea was positive that Hawley was going to be a wonderful husband.

The sound of the opening of her door had her sitting bolt upright in the bed, her eyes big and round with apprehension. In the light of the candle he held, she recognized Hawley and let out a sigh of relief.

Smiling shyly, she said, "It is very kind of you to come and check on me before retiring. As you can see, all is well." When Hawley made no reply but walked to the center of the room and set the candle on the small oak table, she asked, "Is your room nearby?"

"Not exactly," he said with a slight slur, and began removing his clothing. Tossing his coat on a chair, he sat down and began taking off his boots.

Thea could smell the scent of liquor

coming from him; that coupled with his faintly slurred speech was a clear indication that he had been drinking heavily in the time since she had last seen him. She had seen her brother, late at night, weaving and staggering through the house once or twice by accident, and she knew gentlemen under the influence of strong drink acted somewhat erratically — she didn't think she wanted to be around Lord Randall in such a state. Her eyes even bigger, her stomach feeling as if it were filled with ice, she fastened on what he had said, and stammered, "W-w-what do you m-m-mean?"

Removing the lace at his throat and wrists, he shrugged out of his shirt, and said, "Why, nothing, my pet." He looked across at her and the glitter in his gray eyes made her mouth go dry. "My room is not nearby because my room is right here."

"Here!" she squeaked, her eyes skittering away from his broad naked chest. "But it cannot be! You cannot stay here. We are not married."

He nodded. "I know. I would have preferred this to be done differently, but tonight's delay has made it necessary."

"W-w-what do you mean?" she asked, her heart thumping in her chest.

Gently, he said, "We are to be married, are

we not, my love?" And at Thea's cautious nod, he added, "I have no doubt that morning will bring your brother to our very door. We must make it impossible for him to part us."

Suddenly frightened and uneasily aware of what Hawley was implying, Thea frowned. She was rather innocent, and while she knew that when she and Hawley were married he would share her bed, she hadn't thought about that aspect of their marriage very much. Born and raised in the country, despite her station, she had a fair idea of what sharing Hawley's bed would entail — she just wasn't prepared for it to happen right now. And certainly not without marriage!

"You mean make love?" she asked in a small voice.

Hawley nodded. He walked to the bed and, sitting on the side of the bed, he took one of her hands in his. Kissing her fingertips, he said, "We would do it eventually, my love. We will just be anticipating our vows by a few days."

She was resistant to the idea. He could see that from her expression, and he bent forward, saying urgently, "Thea, it is the only way. Your brother will be here by morning. You know that he will tear you away from me."

Thea wouldn't look at him, a tight ball of panic fisting in her chest. What had seemed so romantic and dashing only hours before had taken on a sordid hue. She wanted, she discovered with horror, her mother. It suddenly dawned on her that she didn't really know this handsome man as he bent nearer and kissed her wrists. Those snatched meetings in the rose garden at Garrett Manor, the passionate missives that had been furtively pushed into her trembling hands, and the burning looks they had exchanged in the company of others had not prepared her for reality.

Miserably, she realized that those brief contacts were definitely not enough upon which to base a marriage. She had been, she admitted unhappily, in love with the novelty of it, the excitement of it; flattered and thrilled that such a handsome, urbane man had deigned even to notice her, much less declare himself utterly besotted by her. Her mother's and Tom's disapproval had only set the seal on her determination to elope with Lord Randall, to show them that they were wrong, that she was old enough to make decisions for herself, that she was not a *child* anymore. But now . . .

Thea swallowed and glanced around the small room. It was pleasant enough, neat and tidy, but it was foreign and strange to her, the furnishings worn and ragged. It was certainly not the satin-and-silk bower she had imagined for her wedding night.

Confused, her thoughts tumbling through her mind, she looked at Hawley. "Couldn't we just pretend? Just my being alone with you here is enough to ruin me. Wouldn't Tom agree that your marriage to me would satisfy honor?"

"Don't you want to make love with me?" he asked, his gray eyes fixed on her.

Her gaze dropped. The way he was looking at her made her feel naked — and frightened. "I-I-I don't k-k-know," she stammered. "I thought I d-d-did, but now I don't know."

His mouth thinned. It was what he had feared, why he had pushed her as far and as fast as he could. He had not wanted her to have time to think, time to consider what was happening.

"It is too late to change your mind," he said. "And I'll not have that brother of yours wresting you away from me and trying to cover this up — too much depends on our marriage."

Panic had spread through her entire body, and, struggling to free her hand from his grip, she said breathlessly, "Let me go. I want you to leave this room — now! We will talk in the morning."

"No, we won't. After tonight there will be nothing to talk about, my pet. The deed will be done."

He reached for her, and Thea shrank away, fighting to evade his capture. "Oh, please," she cried, "let me go."

"No," he said, smiling queerly, lust burgeoning within him. "You *will* be mine . . . my wife."

Pampered and petted all her life, sheltered and innocent as only the daughter of a powerful aristocratic family could be, Thea was beyond her depth — had been since the moment her brother had introduced Lord Randall to the family circle. She wanted only one thing at the moment, to wake up in her own bed at Garrett Manor and to know that this was all a horrible nightmare. Unfortunately, it was not, as Lord Randall's next actions proved.

Ignoring Thea's violent struggle to escape him, he bore her back onto the bed, his mouth crushing against hers. The taste of her sweet mouth and the thrashing of her slender body excited him, provoking the beast within him. Heedless of her fight to escape, he made short work of her cotton shift, the fragile material tearing easily beneath his determined assault, leaving her naked before him.

Lifting his mouth from hers, he glanced down at the pale, budding breasts, the nipples rosy and tempting. His breath hissed in his throat at the sight of her slender curves, and, cupping one breast, he took it into his mouth, sucking hard, biting the tip.

Thea arched up in pain, nearly mindless in terror and disbelief at what was happening. She blinked away frightened tears and pushed at his shoulder, simply wanting him to go away.

"Oh, please," she begged, "let me be — if you love me, you will not force me."

He glanced at her and smiled. "Of course I love you — and if you loved me, you would not deny me what I want most ardently."

She bit back a sob, her lashes spiky with tears. "I d-d-don't know if I love you," she admitted. "I thought I d-d-did, but you are frightening me."

"It doesn't matter — it is too late now to change your mind," he murmured, his hands roaming over her with shocking intimacy. She gasped and squirmed beneath him, and, glancing at her face, he wasn't surprised to see that she was blushing. So innocent. So untouched. And so very, very delectable.

"Shy, my pet? Don't be. Before I am through with you, you will not have a shy bone in your body."

He was wrong about that. By the time the light of dawn crept into the small room, Thea's humiliation and embarrassment were nearly palatable. She was painfully, mortifyingly conscious of her body, and she was very certain she had never loathed, would never loathe, anyone as much as she did Lord Randall.

All through the long night he had thwarted her frantic attempts to escape and had taken her against her will more than once, ignoring her cries and shrinking flesh. He had not been deliberately brutal — after all, as he had muttered hotly into her ear, his body plundering hers, he loved her. Intent upon his own needs and designs, he had simply taken what he wanted, done what he wanted, and it had not mattered that Thea had been stiff with revulsion and terror.

When he finally rose and, after a hasty wash in the water that had been provided by the tight-lipped landlord, dressed and strolled from the room, Thea had gathered her tattered bloodied shift around her naked body and curled into a small bundle of abused, shattered dreams. She didn't cry — she was beyond tears, had been beyond tears after that first painful intrusion of his body into hers.

Maggie timidly entered the room, not bothering to knock. There were few at the little inn who didn't know what had happened; the walls were thin, and Lord Randall had not been able to stifle all of Thea's tearful pleas. Maggie had known that something was amiss last night when Lord Randall had sent her away from her mistress, but she had not known just how amiss until she had been in the kitchen this morning and overheard the innkeeper and his wife talking.

Asleep at the rear of the inn, Maggie had not heard Thea's cries, but the innkeeper and his wife had, and they were most disturbed by the situation. They were a good sort, but they did not know Thea's identity, and it was unthinkable that they would have tried to interfere with a member of the gentry taking his pleasures with a maid — willing or not. Such things were known to happen, but they did not like it.

As Maggie had listened with growing horror, the wife, her features angry and resentful, had said to her husband, "I don't want them staying here another night. We are not that kind of place, and I don't care if he is a gentleman, I don't want to cater to his sort — no matter how much money he gave you. Disgraceful what he did. And I don't care what he told you — he as good as raped that poor child, and you know it. And her such a young little thing. What can her people been thinking of to let her go off with him?"

The burly innkeeper had pulled his ear. "Now, Bessie, don't carry on so, he said it was just a lover's argument, and that the girl is fine. It isn't our place to call him to account."

Bessie had sniffed and, spying Maggie's shocked face over her husband's shoulder, bustled away.

Breakfast forgotten, Maggie had flown to Thea's room. The bloodstained sheets and Thea's white, stunned features told their own tale.

Wordlessly Maggie helped Thea to bathe and dress, the innkeeper kindly sending up a large bucket of hot water and towels. By the time they left the room, Maggie was nearly frantic at her mistress's silence and lack of animation. Miss Thea was always chattering away, a smile on her face, but this pale, silent stranger bore no resemblance to her, and Maggie feared for her sanity.

Thea was quite sane; she just couldn't cope at the moment with what had been done to her, could not believe how horribly awry her life had suddenly gone. She was ruined. And now she would be compelled to marry the detestable creature that had brought her to that state. There was no other choice left to her, and her misery and pain were all the deeper for knowing that it had all been her fault. Her foolish, foolish fault for thinking herself in love.

At breakfast, Thea could not bring herself to eat. That she had to share the space with a smiling, expansive Lord Randall killed whatever appetite she might have had.

After enduring her silence for several minutes, Hawley said, "Oh, come now, pet, it is not so bad. I know that you were a virgin, but you will find that you will come to enjoy what we did." He smiled, that smile she had once thought so charming. "I know that I did."

Thea looked at him, blind fury churning in her breast. Her lip curled and she said, "Do not call me 'pet.' "

His face tightened. "And you shall not speak to me in that tone of voice."

"Will I not?" Thea asked, her spirit springing to life. "I will do, my lord, precisely as I please — after all, what can you do about it — rape me again? That is what happened last night, wasn't it? Rape?"

"Call it what you will," he growled, rising from the table and throwing down his napkin. "I only did what I had to do to ensure that your brother could not part us."

"But did you have to enjoy it quite so much, my lord?" she asked sweetly. "Did you need to take quite so much pleasure in my resistance?"

"You are overwrought," he said coldly. "I suggest that you remain here and try to come to your senses while I see about making arrangements for getting another wheel for the curricle."

His hand was on the knob of the door when the sounds of pounding hooves heralded the approaching hard-riding horsemen. He paused and looked back at her. "No doubt your brother."

Thea's bravado vanished. For Tom to find her there with this creature, for him to know what had happened last night, to face his gaze after he had warned her against Lord Randall, was the final shame and humiliation. She wanted to die.

The door to the room burst open, Lord Garrett's entrance knocking Hawley several steps backward. Magnificent dark eyes, so like Thea's, flashed dangerously. Lord Garrett, murder in his face, rushed forward, only to stop when he spied Thea.

The murderous expression faded, leaving his attractive features to show the strain of worry and sleeplessness he had endured. As he took in Thea's shattered look, his face softened, and, Hawley forgotten, he crossed the room to her. Kneeling before her, he took one of her cold hands in his, and said huskily, "Hello, Puss. You have given us quite a chase. But we have found you now and will take you home. Mama is most anxious to know that you are safe."

At his kind words, Thea's eyes filled with tears. "Oh, Tom," she cried, "I have been such a wicked person — but you must not blame Maggie. It is none of her fault — I made her come with me." Thea bit back a sob. "You must leave me here — I am ruined. Mama will not want even to lay eyes on such a sinful creature as I am. You will never want me near you. Nobody will. I can never go home again."

"Hush," he said, gently brushing back a lock of her black hair, black hair very like his own. "How can you say such a thing? There is nothing you could do that would ever change our love for you."

Two more gentlemen suddenly entered the room, their faces stern and anxious. Thea's mortification was even greater as she recognized her mother's brother, the Baron

Hazlett, and his eldest son, John. John was precisely one year older than she was; they shared the same birth date and were very close. For John and her uncle to be privy to her shame only made the situation worse.

Lord Hazlett closed the door behind them. He and John stood there, looking large and intimidating in their greatcoats, with their arms folded across their chests.

Keeping a comforting hand on Thea's, Lord Garrett glanced across to his uncle and cousin. "We shall need to procure a carriage for her and Maggie."

Lord Randall, who had remained silent, suddenly cleared his throat. Stepping nearer to where Lord Garrett knelt by Thea's side, he said, "That will not be necessary. Thea is going to be my wife. I shall have the care of her from now on."

In one movement, Tom was on his feet, the back of his hand striking Hawley violently in the face. "No, you won't," Tom said softly, the dark eyes nearly black with suppressed fury. "What you will do is leave this room and be glad that I have not killed you like the dog you are."

A muscle bunched in Hawley's jaw, and he controlled his temper with a visible effort. "Because we are friends, I shall overlook your actions," he said tightly, "but you are too late. I'm afraid that we, ah, anticipated our marriage vows last night. There is noth—"

Tom's fist smashed into Hawley's mouth. "Shut your filthy mouth!" Tom snarled, blood spurting from Hawley's lips as he reeled backward from the force of the blow. "Nothing you may or may not have done changes our plans to return Thea to her mother and her home." Contempt on his young face, Tom demanded, "Do you think that we would leave her to your tender mercies?" Tom's expression grew bitter. "I am ashamed that I ever called you friend, that I was ever so foolish and misguided to introduce you to my family. This is all my fault, and I shall have to live with that knowledge for the rest of my life."

"Oh, no, Tom," Thea protested, rising to her feet. "It is my fault. You must not blame yourself. I was stupid and foolish — I should have listened to you and Mama."

He glanced back at her. "No, Puss. The blame is mine. It was criminal of me, knowing what I did about him, to introduce you to him, much less to have invited him to stay at Garrett Manor." He shot Lord Randall a scathing look. "But I thought he was my friend, and I was arrogant enough to think that he would not dare try his tricks on *my* sister. I was wrong, and you have paid the price for my arrogance."

"I've had about all of this that I am going to take," Hawley snapped. "I have tried to make allowances for your strong emotions and your feeling of injustice, but there is not a damn thing that you or anybody else can do about it. Thea will be my wife."

"No, she will not," said Lord Hazlett, entering the fray. "We, the family, had already decided before we came in pursuit of you that this affair will go no further. Thea will come home with us, and you" — his fine lip curled — "you, my lord, can go to the devil!"

Hawley looked thunderstruck. This was a possibility that he had not considered. "Do you mean to tell me," he said incredulously, "that knowing she has been alone with me for over twenty-four hours, knowing that we have made love, that you intend to keep it quiet?"

Lord Hazlett nodded, his gaze full of dislike and condemnation.

Hawley gave an ugly laugh. "Oh, by God, this is rich! The girl is ruined, and you intend to hide that fact. And what," he gibed, "do you intend to tell a future suitor? That she is only *slightly* soiled? Only a little damaged?"

The words had hardly left his mouth, before Tom was at his throat. His fingers biting into Hawley's throat, he growled, "Silence! You are never to utter another word about this! I particularly never want to hear that you have even spoken Thea's name. Do you understand me? Speak her name, and I'll kill you."

Hawley was blind with rage. Hoping to come about without bloodshed, he'd forced himself to suffer the insults of this impudent puppy, but by heaven he would no longer. It was clear that he now had nothing to lose — without Thea's fortune financial ruin stared him in the face; all his plans and schemes had come to naught.

Hawley broke Tom's hold on his throat, and deliberately slapping the young man across the face, he said, "Name your seconds!"

Tom's eyes glittered, the imprint of Hawley's hand scarlet on his cheek. "Gladly."

"Tom! Are you mad?" demanded Lord Hazlett. "A duel is the last thing we want. If we are to brush through this without arousing a scandal, we must keep everything quiet."

Tom nodded reluctantly. He looked at Hawley. "Thea's reputation is worth more to me than the satisfaction I would gain from skewering you, my lord." Caustically, he added, "You'll forgive me if I refuse your challenge."

Balked at every turn, his pride battered and his future ruined, Hawley was spoiling for a fight. He needed someone to strike against, someone upon whom to vent his rage, and Tom was right in front of him.

"Coward?" he asked nastily.

Tom blanched. "Coward? You dare to call me a coward? You, who prey on the young and innocent?"

Lord Randall examined the nails of his fingers. "Well, I do not know what else to call a man who refuses a challenge."

Tom's hands clenched into fists. "I accept your challenge — if you will have my cousin act as your second, my uncle shall act as mine, and we fight here and now."

Hawley smiled. "Swords?"

"Swords."

Despite the protests and pleas of the others, neither man could be persuaded to back down. In a terrifyingly short time, the rules had been set and a space had been cleared in the room, the furniture pushed back against the walls to provide an area for the duelists. The gentlemen of her family tried to hustle her out of the room, but Thea would not budge.

Her eyes huge black pools in her white face, she said fiercely, "What difference does it make now? I know you are trying to protect me, but it is too late. I must stay. I must."

There was no dissuading her, and, after a helpless shrug, Tom turned away to face his opponent, who stood in the center of the cleared space. His blade kissed the tip of Hawley's. "En garde."

Both men had shed their jackets for freedom of movement, and the fight that followed was swift and vicious. It was clear from the onset that Hawley intended to win, delivering a furious onslaught that immediately drove Tom backward. Again and again their blades met and clashed, the deadly sound of steel against steel ringing in the small room.

The two men were evenly matched in height, but Hawley was more muscular and had far more experience, and Thea's heart nearly stopped a dozen times when it seemed inevitable that Tom would fall beneath Hawley's attack. Tom fell back time and time again from the expert thrust of Hawley's flashing blade, seeming only barely able to prevent Hawley from slipping under his guard.

It was silent in the room except for the

heavy breathing of the two combatants, the clang of their swords and the slide and stamp of their booted feet across the wooden floor. Arraigned against the wall, her uncle's arm clasping her comfortingly, Thea watched in silence, terrified by the violence she had caused.

The tempo of the fight gradually changed, Tom's flying sword working magic as his blade clashed against Hawley's, blunting Hawley's forward charge. A grim smile curved Tom's mouth as Hawley began to retreat, the sound of his blade singing in the air as he closed on his enemy, the flashing blade slipping beneath Hawley's guard to open a long rip along his shoulder.

The blood from the wound was crimson against the white of Hawley's shirt, and he seemed astonished that Tom had managed to strike him. Breathing heavily from his exertions, Tom stepped back reluctantly. His sword held down by his side, he said, "First blood. Shall we cry quits?"

"Never!" cried Hawley. His lips curled over his teeth in a feral grimace, he leaped toward Tom, his sword poised for Tom's heart.

Thea screamed, but Tom nimbly met the maddened charge and the fight began anew, everyone aware now that it would now only end in death. Tom fought steadily, his dark eyes intent, his young face grim, as he met every deadly thrust of Hawley's blade. As the minutes passed Tom once again gained ascendancy and compelled Hawley to retreat across the room.

Forced backward by Tom's attack, Hawley stumbled and fell against the table that had been pushed against one of the walls, the remains of the meal he and Thea had shared scattered across it. His blade locked with Tom's as Tom bent him over the table, he sought for a way to blunt Tom's attack. When their swords swung free, as Tom angled for the final thrust, Hawley's free hand suddenly brushed against the still-hot teapot from breakfast. In a mad rage his fingers closed around it and with an oath, he raised up and threw the contents into Tom's face.

Blinded, Tom staggered backward, dropping his guard as Lord Hazlett and John gasped in stunned disbelief at Hawley's dishonorable act. Before either could call a halt to the struggle, Hawley's sword sank into Tom's breast in one swift lunge. Tom groaned and sank to one knee, his hand clutching his breast, blood seeping from between his fingers.

Thea screamed and struggled free from

Lord Hazlett's grasp. But it was too late; Hawley's sword plunged again into Tom. Tom sagged farther, his dark head bent, as he fought back the black waves that lashed over him.

"Die, you damned arrogant puppy!" Hawley shouted, his face livid and ugly as he towered over Tom.

Tom lifted his head, and, smiling queerly, gathering all of his fading power, he thrust clean and true, his blade sinking deeply into Hawley's heart.

For an instant Hawley looked incredulous, as if he could not believe what had just happened — the next, he fell dead to the floor.

Thea flew across the room to Tom's side, and, his enemy vanquished, he slumped bonelessly into Thea's slender arms. His head cradled on her lap and his eyes closed, Thea stared in horror at the rapidly spreading blood across the front of his shirt.

"Oh, Tom," she pleaded. "Do not die, I beg you. It is all my fault. You must not die. You must not!"

Tom's lashes fluttered, and he looked up at Thea's tearful features. Running a finger down her tear-stained cheek, he said weakly, "Don't cry, Puss. It is not your fault. The fault was mine." A violent spasm shook him.

Almost in a whisper he added, "Not yours. Mine." And then his eyes closed, and he was still.

She held him near, her tears falling heedlessly. Mindless with grief and guilt, she rocked back and forth, clutching Tom's lifeless form to her breast, oblivious of the body of the man she was to have married lying only a few feet away.

Eventually Lord Hazlett was able to wrest Tom's body away from her. John's strong arms around her, she was urged toward the door, where the innkeeper and his wife crowded around trying to see inside the room. At the doorway, she took another glance at her brother's body, guilt knifing through her. Almost by chance her gaze fell upon Hawley's sprawled form. Hatred such as she had never believed possible curdled inside her. She would never, she vowed fiercely, believe the sweet words and promises of any man again. *Never.*

Chapter One

London
1798

Whistling softly to himself, Patrick Blackburne took the steps to his rented house on Hamilton Place, two at a time. It was a fine September morning in London, and having just come from a sale at Tattersall's, where he had bought a nice chestnut mare that had caught his eye, he was feeling pleased with himself.

Life had been good to Patrick. He had been blessed with a handsome face and form, as well as a fortune that allowed him to live where and how he pleased. Across the Atlantic Ocean from England, he owned a large plantation and fine home near Natchez in the Mississippi Territory. His father had been a rich, wellborn Englishman who had taken a respectable fortune and had made it a magnificent one in the New World; his mother, even more wellborn, was related to half the aristocracy in England and possessed a large fortune of her own. Patrick's father had died fifteen years ago and Patrick had inherited that fortune at the relatively young age of twenty-three; in time, since he was an only child, he would no doubt inherit his mother's fortune.

It could be argued that his mother, Alice, had abandoned Patrick at twelve years of age when she had decided she could no longer bear to live in the backwoods splendor of Willowdale, the Blackburne plantation near Natchez. Only England, London in particular, would suit her. Her husband and Patrick's father, Robert, had given a sigh of relief and had helped her pack, not about to give her a chance to change her mind.

It was known that theirs had been an arranged marriage and that they had been indifferent to one another from the beginning. Within months of the wedding, their indifference had turned to outright loathing, and Patrick, arriving almost nine months to the day after the wedding, had been born into a household that resembled nothing less than an armed camp.

Used as a weapon between the warring partners, Patrick had continually found himself in the middle of his parents' frequent and virulent battles. It had not engendered in him any desire for the married state and was the main reason he had reached the age of thirty-eight with nary a matrimonial prospect in sight.

His mother's rejection of Natchez and everything connected with it had hurt and confused him as a child. Patrick loved his home and thought the spacious, three-storied mansion at Willowdale to be comfortable and elegant. To this day, he still enjoyed tramping through the wilderness that bordered the plantation and had never quite understood why his mother detested everything connected with Willowdale and Natchez. When he was twelve, his mother's attitude had baffled him and, to a point, it still did, but he had learned to accept her contempt of a home and place that he adored, though her occasional comments about it could still cause a pang of resentment.

His parents' marriage, Patrick admitted, had been like trying to mate chalk and cheese, and neither had been really at fault. With his wife gone, Robert finally had peace and enjoyed his remaining years — never setting foot in England again for fear of coming face-to-face with his wife. As for Alice, she was wildly happy in England. These days she bore little resemblance to the miserable woman who had lived at Willowdale. Her relationship with Patrick was a trifle distant, more because he had grown up apart from her and had chosen to live the majority of the time at Willowdale. When he did come to England, she always greeted him with warm affection, and he enjoyed seeing her.

Patrick's mother was the last person on his mind this particular morning as he entered the house. Setting down his narrow-brimmed hat on the table in the foyer of the house, he frowned when he spied an envelope lying there, addressed to him in his mother's fine script.

Now what? he wondered. Surely not another ball that she wished him to attend? Since his arrival in England only two weeks ago, he'd already escorted his mother to a soiree; driven her on three different occasions around Hyde Park in his curricle; and endured an uncomfortable family dinner with her husband of just over a year, Henry, the tenth Baron Caldecott. Surely he had shown himself to be a dutiful enough son. Couldn't she now leave him to enjoy his own pursuits?

Sighing, he opened the letter, his frown not abating one whit as he read the missive. She wanted to see him this afternoon. Urgently.

A thoughtful look in his deceptively

sleepy gray eyes, Patrick wandered into his study. Now why would his mother need to see him urgently? Especially since he had just taken her for a drive around Hyde Park not two days ago and at that time she had been relaxed and carefree. Certainly there had been no sign that she had anything more urgent on her mind than what she was to wear to Lady Hilliard's ball to be held on Thursday evening.

Seating himself behind the impressive mahogany desk, he proceeded to write a reply to his mother. That done, he wrote another note, canceling the plans he had made with his friend Adam Paxton to watch a match at Lord's Cricket Ground on St. John's Wood Road. Naturally they had a friendly wager on the outcome.

At two o'clock, as requested by his mother, garbed in pale gray pantaloons, a bobtailed coat in plum, his dark gray waistcoat extravagantly embroidered and his cravat neatly tied above his frilled shirt, he mounted the steps of the Caldecott town house on Manchester Square. After giving his hat to the butler, Grimes, he walked through the grand hallway into the front salon.

His mother was seated on a sofa, her pale blue bouffant skirts dripping onto the floor.

A silver tea tray sat in front of her, and, as Patrick entered the room, she said, "Ah, precisely on time. I worried that I'd had Grimes bring me the tea too soon."

The resemblance between mother and son was not pronounced. Except for the fact that both were tall and had the same wide-spaced gray eyes and black hair, their features were totally dissimilar: Patrick was, to Alice's dismay, the very image of his father. It always gave her a shock when he first walked into a room, the sight of that firm, determined jaw and chin, the straight, bold nose, and arrogantly slashed black brows making her feel for a second that her first husband had come to drag her back to that godforsaken plantation, Willowdale.

After pressing a kiss to Alice's powdered cheek, Patrick seated himself across from her. Long legs in front of him, he watched as she poured tea and passed a cup to him.

"You are," she said a moment later as she stirred sugar and lemon into her own tea, "no doubt wondering why I wanted to see you."

Patrick inclined his head. His mother looked as regal as always, her hair arranged in an elegant mass of curls on top of her head; the wide silver wings at her temples one of the few signs of her advancing age.

For a woman who had just passed her fifty-ninth birthday in June, Lady Caldecott was very well preserved. The pale, flawless skin was only faintly lined, the proud chin was perhaps a bit fuller than it had been in her youth, and there was a delicate network of wrinkles that radiated out from the corners of her eyes. Still, she was a striking woman, her body slim and well formed, and Patrick wasn't surprised that Lord Caldecott had asked her to marry him. What did surprise him was that, after being a widow for so many years and considering her first foray into the married state, she had accepted him. What astonished him even more was that the marriage seemed to have been a love match, if the open affection he had noticed between Lord and Lady Caldecott was anything to go by. Truth be told, Patrick was puzzled by his mother's second marriage. Why would anyone, having escaped from the noose once, deliberately stick their head into it again?

Watching his mother as she stirred her tea, it occurred to him that she looked more worn and tired than he had ever seen her, and, for the first time, it crossed his mind that her demand to see him might have a serious overtone. He gave her a few minutes, but when she said nothing, seeming fascinated by the swirling liquid in her cup, he asked, "Mother, what is it? Your note said it was urgent that you see me."

She forced a smile and, setting down her tea untouched, admitted, "It is urgent, but now that I have you here, I do not know how to begin."

"At the beginning, perhaps?"

She made a face, her reluctance to proceed obvious. If he had not known better, Patrick would have sworn that his mother was embarrassed — she was certainly not acting in her usual forthright manner.

When several minutes had passed and his mother still remained silent, Patrick said, "Perhaps you have changed your mind about seeing me?"

She shook her head and sighed. "No — you are the only one I can turn to. It is just that I am . . . humiliated to have to explain to *anyone*, and particularly my son, the predicament in which I find myself."

There was such an expression of misery on her face that Patrick felt the first real stirrings of unease.

"I am your son," he said slowly. "Surely you know that you have no need to be embarrassed by anything that you tell me?"

Her gray eyes met his and she flashed him an unhappy look. "You're wrong there. I know that we have not always seen eye to eye . . . and I hesitate to tell you something that may lower your opinion of me."

Seriously alarmed, Patrick bent forward. "Mother, tell me! Surely it cannot be that bad."

"You're probably right," she said reluctantly. "It is just that I —" She stopped, bit her lip, and then, apparently steeling herself, she said, "I have to tell you something that happened over twenty years ago when I first left your father and returned to England." She hesitated, and color suddenly bloomed in both her cheeks. She cleared her throat and went on, "I was still a young woman, and I made the mistake of falling madly in love with another man. A married man of high degree." Her eyes would not meet his. "We embarked willy-nilly into an affair. The fact that we were both married and that he was a member of the Court made it imperative that the affair remain secret. I would have been utterly ruined if it had become public, and he, well, he would have been banished from the king's presence." She made a face. "George III is not known for his tolerance of adultery." She glanced across at Patrick. "Are you shocked?"

Patrick shrugged, not certain what he felt.

He *was* startled that his mother had had an affair, but not shocked. He was, after all, a gentleman of the world, and was privy to the various follies that people commit in the name of love — another reason why he avoided that state. Aware of his mother's silence, he admitted, "Surprised is more like it. But why are you telling me?"

Alice took a deep breath. "Because someone is blackmailing me about it."

"With what?" Patrick asked with a frown. "From what you have just told me, the affair was two decades ago — who would care now? Your former lover?"

She shook her head. "No, he is dead — has been for at least ten years." Her gaze dropped. "I wrote some letters. Some very explicit letters." Tiredly, she added, "The affair wasn't of long duration — less than a year, but it was intense while it lasted. And when it ended, when I came to my senses and realized that I was acting little better than some Covent Garden soiled dove, I simply wanted to put it all behind me. I told the gentleman that it was over between us and that I no longer wished to see him. He took it well — he had been a faithful and honest husband until I came into his life, and I am sure that our liaison caused him much soul-searching and anguish." There was a faraway look in her eyes. "He was an honorable man, and I think, as I look back on those days, that he was as horrified by our passion for each other as he was entranced. I suspect that he was secretly grateful when I ended it. At any rate, once we had parted, I never gave the letters a second thought." Her mouth drooped. "I certainly never thought that someone would try to extort money from me for their return twenty years later."

Despite his impassive expression, a dozen thoughts were jostling around in Patrick's mind. His mother's confession made him look at her differently, to see her not just as the unhappy figure of his childhood, the stately matron she had become, but also as a woman with needs and desires of her own. It was difficult to imagine her in the throes of an illicit, passionate affair, but he had her word for it that it had happened — and that someone was blackmailing her because of it. His mouth tightened. Now that was something that he would not allow.

"How were you contacted?" he asked, his heart twisting at the look of vulnerability on her face. He had never seen his mother look vulnerable before, had never thought she *could* be vulnerable, and he was conscious of a growing anger against the person who put that look on her face.

"A note was waiting for me," Alice said, "when I returned home from our drive on Monday in the park. I did not recognize the handwriting, but the contents alluded to the affair and the letters. Along with a demand for money for their return." She sighed. "It was very cleverly done — nothing was stated outright, but whoever wrote it knew of the affair and the letters and wanted to be paid to keep quiet about it."

"When and how much?" asked Patrick grimly.

"I have already paid the first installment," Alice admitted. "The sender knew that Henry and I were attending Mrs. Pennington's 'at home' that very evening. I was told to put a thousand pounds in my reticule and to leave it with my wrap when we arrived. When I got home, I looked inside my reticule and the money was gone. As promised, there was also one of my letters . . . just in case I had any doubts about whether the blackmailer actually had the letters." Her mouth thinned. "I burned it as soon as I was alone."

"Your blackmailer was clever — those 'at homes' are crowded affairs, with people coming and going all the time. Anyone could have slipped into the cloak room and taken the money." He shot her a keen glance. "Since only one letter was returned to you, it is obvious that this is to continue indefinitely."

She nodded. "I had hoped the one demand for money would satisfy them — foolish, I know. This arrived this morning."

"This" was another note that had been lying on the table beside the tea tray. Reaching over, she handed the folded paper to him. Swiftly Patrick scanned the missive.

"Two thousand pounds this time." He glanced at her, concern in his gray eyes. "Can you stand the nonsense? I can, if you cannot."

"Money isn't the issue — although it may become one, if these 'requests' continue and the price keeps doubling."

"Have you talked to Caldecott about it?"

Her gaze dropped. "N-n-no," she admitted after a long moment. When Patrick continued to stare at her, she stood up and took several agitated steps around the room. Stopping in front of him, she said fiercely, "I love Henry — very much. And he loves me. He thinks that I am perfect." She smiled ruefully. "I know that it is hard for you to believe, but he does." Her smile faded, that look of vulnerability that had so disturbed him returning. "No one has ever loved me as

Henry does. No one, not even that long-ago lover, has ever cared for me as deeply and sincerely as he does." One hand formed a fist at her side. "I would do anything to keep him from learning about this distasteful incident from my past. It is silly of me, I know, but I do not want Henry's image of me tarnished."

"Well, then," Patrick said quietly, "I shall just have to find your blackmailer and pull his fangs, won't I?"

Returning to her seat on the sofa, her gray eyes anxious, she leaned forward and asked, "Can you do that? Can you really find out who is behind this? And keep Henry out of it?"

"Don't worry about my esteemed steppapa," Patrick said dryly. "We don't move in the same circles — my activities on your behalf are not likely to come to his attention."

"I could wish," Alice said with a return of her usual tartness, "that you didn't move in those circles."

"Well, yes, I'm sure of that, but in this case, my raffish friends and cronies may actually be of help."

"You wouldn't tell anyone else about this, would you?" she asked, a hand to her throat.

Patrick looked at her and she visibly relaxed. Smiling apologetically, she said, "Of course you wouldn't. I was foolish even to consider such a thing. Forgive me?"

He nodded. Rereading the note, he frowned. "It would seem that he, and for the time being we shall assume it *is* a he, has decided that you are easy prey. I suspect that the demand for payment on Monday was simply to see if you would bite. Since you did, he now knows that he has you hooked. You can certainly count on receiving more of these."

"My feeling exactly, and why I asked you to call on me." She closed her eyes for a second. "I cannot believe at my age that I am being blackmailed for something that happened so long ago. It is ridiculous!"

"Do you have any idea who the blackmailer could be?"

"None. The recipient of the letters is dead — has been for a decade. There were no direct heirs. When he died the title, and everything else, went to his brother. His brother, incidentally, has also been dead, for a half dozen years or so. It is his brother's eldest son who now holds the title."

"Having told me what you have, don't you think you can trust me with your lover's name?" Patrick asked gently.

Alice grimaced. "It was the Lord Embry,

the Earl of Childress — the sixth earl. I believe you know his nephew, the current Lord Embry."

Patrick nodded. "Indeed, I do. And while he is up to every rig and row in town, I cannot imagine that he would be your blackmailer."

"And I cannot believe that his uncle did not destroy my letters when our affair ended."

"Mayhap he did not take your parting as easily as you thought?"

"You may be right," she agreed unhappily. "But since we must assume he kept my letters, why am I just now being blackmailed for their return?"

"The most obvious answer is that they have just now come into someone else's hands. But whose and how?" He frowned. "Embry may sail close to the wind, but I would never have thought he would stoop so low as to blackmail a friend's mother — and he *is* a friend of mine. Besides, unless the family fortune has suffered a dramatic decline, he has no need of more money — and I can't imagine Nigel pawing through the attics of Childress Hall, which is one of the few places the letters could have been and not be discovered before now."

Alice sighed. "I suppose you are right. It is

just so difficult to believe that after twenty years they have just resurfaced."

An arrested expression suddenly crossed Patrick's face. "What about his wife? Could she have had the letters?"

Alice shook her head. "No, she died about six months after the affair ended." Something occurred to her and she leaned forward intently. "Wait! He remarried a couple years after that. What was her name? Ah, I have it — Levina Ellsworth."

"You think that she might have kept the letters?"

"I can't imagine her doing so — there isn't a spiteful or mean bone in Levina's body. If she knew what was in the letters, she would be far more likely simply to give them to me."

"But suppose," Patrick proposed slowly, "she didn't know about the letters? Suppose they were in some old trunk that she had brought with her from Childress Hall after her husband died? I assume that after he died, she moved into the Dower House there?"

"I have no idea," Alice admitted. "Once the affair ended, I did not keep track of what was happening in his life — I wanted to forget about it, to pretend that I had never been so wild and foolish. The only reason I remember about Levina is because I knew her and felt sorry for her. She had little fortune, no looks to speak of, and her family treated her like a drudge. She comes from a large family, but her sisters and brothers always struck me as a bunch of rapacious ravens — their needs came first. What I remember most about Levina is that she is singularly sweet-natured. When I read the announcement of her marriage to Embry, I was pleased that she had made such a good match at her age." She looked reflective. "They would have been good for each other."

"Do you think she is still alive?"

"She could be — she was about ten years my elder, so it is not out of the realm of possibility."

"I think I should start with Levina's whereabouts," Patrick said, rising to his feet. "We shall assume that Levina unknowingly had the letters and that she took them wherever she went. And they stayed there until someone, for whatever reason, discovered them. With luck, she took them to the Dower House at Childress — I can easily cadge a visit out of Nigel."

"And this recent demand? What shall I do?" his mother asked.

Patrick's face hardened. "We shall have to

pay it, but I think I shall be the one to deliver the payment."

"Is that wise? Might it not annoy the blackmailer?"

Patrick smiled like a tiger. "Oh, believe me, I very much want to *annoy* our blackmailer!"

He glanced at the address where his mother was to have left the money tonight. "So you're to be there at ten o'clock this evening, eh? Curzon Street — rather a nice neighborhood for a blackmailer, don't you think?"

His mother shrugged. "I suppose so — if anyone lives at the address."

Patrick nodded as he rose to his feet. "Unless your blackmailer is a fool or very bold, I agree. It would be folly for him to have you come to his home — might as well send an announcement telling you who he is."

Crossing the room, he bent over and kissed his mother's cheek. "I suppose it would do me little good to tell you not to worry? That I shall take care of this for you?"

"Which only gives me another reason to worry," Alice said ruefully. Glancing up at her tall son, anxiety in her eyes, she added, "You *will* be careful? We have no way of knowing just how dangerous this creature may be. I could never live with myself if something happened to you because of my folly."

Patrick laughed. "Considering some of the risks I have taken merely for a mere wager, this will be a lark." He kissed her again. "Do not worry, Mama."

Taking leave of his mother, Patrick left the house and drove directly to Curzon Street. He was not surprised to find that the house named by the blackmailer was empty. It was a handsome Georgian mansion, very similar to several others in the same block, but his knock on the door aroused no reply or sign of any inhabitants. A brief conversation with a prosperous-looking gentleman descending the steps of the house next door brought forth the information that it was in the hands of a solicitor, who had been trying to lease it out for the past six months. The previous owner had died a year ago and the heir, a spinster of intermediate age, had no desire to live in London.

After obtaining the name of the solicitor, a Mr. Beaton, and his direction, Patrick thanked the gentleman and promptly went to pay a visit to the solicitor. Pretending to be in the market for a house to lease, in the company of Mr. Beaton's assistant, he was able to obtain entrance to the house. The interior, while spacious and well appointed, had the unpleasant, dank smell of a house long closed up and the dust-covered furniture loomed ghostlike in the dim light filtering in from the shuttered windows. A brief inspection of the three floors turned up nothing that gave Patrick any clue to the blackmailer's whereabouts or his identity. After promising to let Mr. Beaton's assistant know what he decided about the house, he went home to think.

Sitting in his study, his booted feet resting on the mahogany desk, he considered the situation for some time. No solution occurred to him, and he was bitterly aware that he could do nothing productive until tonight. In the meantime, however, he could see his friend, Nigel Embry. Since she was his aunt by marriage, Lord Embry would, no doubt, be his most likely source of information about Levina.

Telling his butler not to expect him until he saw him, he put on his hat and departed Hamilton Place once more. Luck was with him, and he found Lord Embry at the first place he looked; Embry House on Albemarle Street. In fact, Lord Embry was just stepping into his curricle when Patrick arrived. A congenial, amiable soul, Nigel would accept nothing less than for Patrick to park his own vehicle and to come for a ride in Hyde Park.

The news he obtained from Lord Embry confirmed his own suspicions: Levina had died in January. Her estate had gone to her nieces and nephews — as grasping a pack of money-grubbing Cits as Nigel had ever seen.

Having learned what he could for the present, Patrick settled back and enjoyed the ride, listening with half an ear to Lord Embry's pleasantries. At this hour, the park was crowded with various members of the ton, garbed in their finest and driving their most elegant vehicles. Since Embry knew everyone, and Patrick was very well acquainted with many members of society, their progress was slow as they stopped to talk to this person or that and nodded politely to others.

They were stopped at present, exchanging jests with several cronies, when the sound of a swiftly approaching vehicle made Patrick glance in that direction. A second later, a pair of long-limbed black thoroughbreds pulling a high-perch phaeton burst into view.

With nary a check, the crimson-clad driver of the phaeton expertly wove the horses through the crowded park. As the vehicle and horses swept by, Patrick looked at the driver to see if he recognized the damn fool who was driving at such a dangerous pace down the crowded thoroughfare. He was astonished to see that it was a woman. Her features were a blur as the vehicle raced by, and he was left with the impression of masses of black curls under a saucily tilted crimson hat, huge dark, dancing eyes, and a red, laughing mouth.

"Who in blazes," he demanded, "is that hoyden?"

"Ah," said Nigel, "I see that you have not yet had the pleasure of being introduced to the notorious Miss Thea Garrett."

"Not met Thea?" exclaimed the gentleman who was leaning against the side of Lord Embry's curricle. "Good Gad, man! She is the talk of England. Has been for the past decade — ever since that nasty business with Randall and her brother, Lord Garrett. Don't tell me you don't remember it?"

Patrick nodded slowly. "Of course. I remember now. The girl was ruined, and when her brother caught up with them, he and Hawley fought. Both men died, didn't they?"

"Indeed they did. Terrible scandal. Family tried to hush it up, but there was no help for it. I mean, two peers dead from a duel? Naturally the reason for the duel came out. No one talked about anything else for weeks on end."

"Can't believe you haven't met her before now," Nigel commented. "Must be that your trips to England didn't coincide with her stays in London. Of course, she wasn't in London — for years after the scandal she kept to the country with her mother and that half sister of hers, Edwina."

One of the other gentlemen said, "It is a damn shame that the scandal tainted her half sister's chances in the marriage mart. As I remember she was a lovely girl. Didn't the chit finally end up marrying some bounder four or five years ago?"

"Alfred Hirst," Nigel answered. "A nasty bit of goods, but related to enough of the ton that he has entrée in certain circles."

Patrick wasn't interested in Edwina Hirst. It was the crimson-mouthed, dashing driver who had caught his attention, and he brought Nigel back to that particular subject by asking impatiently, "But how is it that Miss Garrett is brazenly driving through Hyde Park amidst the cream of the ton? Has she no shame?"

Nigel laughed. "That's our Thea! She's taken her notoriety and turned it into a bloody asset! Proud as the Devil himself.

Doesn't give a damn if she's accepted or not — goes her own way, and these days, only the highest sticklers refuse to admit her to their homes. Besides, she's related to so many members of the ton, with a fortune to boot, that scandal or not, she is invited everywhere." He looked thoughtful. "Of course, the doors would shut in a blink of an eye if there was any hint that one of the gentlemen had gone so far as to lose his head and was considering marrying the wench."

"But didn't I hear something about Lord Gale developing a tendre for her last year?" asked one of the gentlemen. "Swore he'd marry her or no one."

Nigel nodded. "Caused a real dust-up. Family had a devil of a time before they were able to pack him off to the country."

"Why," Patrick demanded, "would any gentleman of breeding want to marry such a baggage?"

"Wait until you meet Thea," drawled Nigel with an infuriatingly smug smile.

Patrick shook his head. "I have no desire to meet the young woman."

Nigel's blue eyes gleamed. "A wager?"

"What sort?"

"That before we leave London for the winter, you'll change your mind."

"You're wasting your blunt. I won't."

"So, is it a wager or not?" prompted Nigel.

Patrick suddenly grinned, amusement glinting in his gray eyes. "Very well, if you want to lose your money, I'll take your damned wager. But I can promise you that I have no desire to meet Thea Garrett!"

Chapter Two

Unaware and uncaring that she was the topic of conversation in the group she had left behind, Thea concentrated on her driving. She knew she would raise eyebrows for driving at this speed through the park, but like so much in her life these days, she didn't really give a damn. Why should she? She was the notorious Thea Garrett, and people would talk about her no matter what she did — so let the gray-eyed stranger stare!

Her mind on other things, she left the horses and phaeton with the groom and entered the house on Grosvenor Square that she had bought four years ago, just after her mother's death. Pulling off her black-leather driving gloves, she nodded to her butler, Tillman, as she crossed the hallway, intending to head upstairs to change her clothes. When Tillman coughed politely and called her attention to a note that had arrived while she had been out driving, she made a face and picked it up from the silver salver where it had been lying.

Of course, she recognized the writer's

scrawl immediately and a hard glint shone in the usually smiling dark eyes. She asked Tillman, "Did he bring it himself or did he have it delivered?"

"He brought it himself, Miss." Looking uncomfortable, he added, "I followed your orders and would not let him inside — though it pained me to treat a member of the family in such a fashion."

Since Tillman had been with the Garrett family since before Thea had been born, she allowed him a great deal of license — which he considered his due as a loyal family retainer.

Cocking a slim brow, she murmured, "I do not rememberING seeing the name 'Hirst' anywhere on the Garrett family tree. Perhaps I am mistaken?"

Tillman drew up his small stature as tall as it would go, and said primly, "A family member by marriage, Miss — as you know very well."

Thea snorted. "Well, you can consider him a member of the family if you wish, but I do not." Crossing swiftly to the stairs, she said over her shoulder, "And under no circumstances are you to let that verminous creature into my house — not even if Edwina is with him!"

"*Miss!* Never say you would deny your

own sister entrance to your home?" he gasped.

"Half sister," Thea said as she strode up the stairs. "And I didn't say the door was barred against her — only her husband."

Reaching her suite of rooms, Thea tossed the gloves on her dressing table and sent her saucy crimson hat sailing across the room, where it landed on her bed. Seating herself with more haste than grace in a nearby chair, she ripped open the envelope and read the contents.

It was more of the same — another request, a demand really, for money. The sheer effrontery of her sister's husband amazed her. Having depleted a fortune of his own in four years of marriage, he had managed to make great inroads into Edwina's fortune, too.

It gave Thea no pleasure to admit that she had recognized Alfred Hirst as a fortune hunter from the first day that she had met him almost six years ago. None of her warnings, however, could dissuade Edwina, then eighteen, from marrying him. Thea had pleaded with her younger half sister not to marry Hirst, to wait until she was older, but Edwina, starry-eyed and madly in love with the handsome, sophisticated Hirst, would not listen. Thea saw goblins where there were none, Edwina had replied airily. Not all handsome older men were cut from the same cloth as Lord Randall. Thea was just jealous! And she always had been, Edwina averred, because Mama had married Papa and had left her and Tom to be raised by the Garretts.

Thea had been three years old when her father had died. She had been too young to have many memories of him and most of her ideas about her father had come from the reflections of others. Her mother's marriage to Mr. Northrop a year later and Edwina's birth a year after that, when Thea had been five, might have aroused resentment in someone else at the happy little family group the Northrops represented, but not Thea. She had been an amiable child and tended to accept without question the actions of adults. Besides which she had been fascinated by her new baby sister, and almost from the moment she had laid eyes on the blue-eyed cherubic baby, she had been filled with a feeling of protectiveness. Her mother had encouraged that feeling, wanting a bond between her two daughters, and Thea's devotion to Edwina had grown rather than dissipated throughout the years. She had never once been jealous of her younger half sister or resented the fact that her mother had made the choice to leave her and Tom with their aunt and uncle. She adored her aunt and uncle and had scant affection for her mother's second husband.

Northrop, a bachelor of long standing, had made it clear right from the beginning that he would not tolerate another man's children constantly underfoot. Tom and Thea, already settled with their aunt and uncle, had viewed Mr. Northrop with aversion — which Mr. Northrop returned in full measure. Even a simpleton could see that the situation was going to be intolerable. Consequently, after much soul-searching and many tears, the new Mrs. Northrop had agreed for Tom and Thea to stay at Garrett Manor and be raised by their father's younger brother and his wife. Mrs. Northrop was not a heartless woman, merely a practical one.

Tom and Thea had not had much contact with Edwina until after Northrop had died and it was discovered that he was deeply in debt. Desperately poor, Mrs. Northrop, along with eleven-year-old Edwina, had had no choice but to accept the generous offer of her former in-laws to return to live at Garrett Manor. Mrs. Northrop was fortunate the Garretts were so kind — the only thing left was a tidy little trust fund for

Edwina, to be dispersed when she married or reached the age of twenty-one.

It had been an awkward melding of families, and it had made Thea feel even more responsible for her younger sister.

After Tom's death and the resulting scandal, the two sisters were very close. It was only when Edwina grew older and realized the difference between her fortune and Thea's great one that her feelings began to change. It was during Edwina's London season, the year after Mrs. Northrop had died, that she began to actively resent her older half sister. Her dreams of taking London by storm unfulfilled, Edwina was convinced that it was the old scandal, Thea's reputation, that kept her from having the choice of grand suitors and being the belle of the ball. When Hirst began to court Edwina, Thea's sincere but misguided attempts to throw the rub in the way of his suit had only made Edwina more determined to marry him, and a growing chasm had developed between the half sisters. Thea had longed for her mother's calm, good sense in dealing with Edwina and mourned her passing.

At the time of Mrs. Northrop's death, Edwina and Thea and their mother had been living at the Dower House on the

Garrett estate. Thea had been happy at the Dower House, and if it had not been for her mother's death, she might still be living there today. But when Mrs. Northrop had died, the family had been adamant that it was unthinkable for her and Edwina, then only seventeen, to live alone, with no older person to guide them. Thea had protested, insisting that at twenty-two she was perfectly capable of running her own household, but Lord Garrett would not be swayed. A distant cousin had been pressed into service to live with the two young women.

Miss Modesty Bradford, possessing a small independence of her own, had been living happily in London when Lord Garrett had approached her, and though she thoroughly enjoyed Thea and Edwina and tried to adjust to the quieter pace of life, she had disliked the country. A brisk, tall, lean woman of forty-two, after enduring nearly nine months of bucolic boredom, Modesty wasted little time in convincing Thea that she could not, and *should* not, bury herself in the country forever. There was a whole world out there for her to see, and London was just the start. Thea resisted, but Modesty craftily put forth the one argument she could not withstand; there was Edwina to think of — before her mother's death, a London season had been planned for her when she turned eighteen. Was Thea going to deny her sister her moment of glory? Deny Edwina the chance to make a good, if not spectacular, match?

Thea capitulated. Move to London they must. And while Lord Garrett was perfectly happy for them to stay at the Garrett town house in London, Thea discovered that she wanted a place of her own, and since she had the fortune to do as she pleased, there was no gainsaying her. A year to the day after Mrs. Northrop's death, with Lord Garrett's approval, Thea had purchased the town house on Grosvenor Square, and she and Modesty and Edwina had moved in. Their year of mourning finished, Modesty and Thea immediately began to plan for Edwina's debut to society that spring.

Setting aside the letter from Hirst and thinking back on Edwina's first forays into society four years ago, Thea grimaced. It had been heady, painful, exhilarating, infuriating, exciting, and humiliating — for Thea. All the old scandal had been revived, and the whispers whenever she appeared in public nearly drove her back to the country. It had been Modesty, a glint in her fierce dark eyes, who had kept Thea's chin up and spine straight. Looking at her younger cousin after a particularly distressing outing, she had asked sharply, "Are you going to let a group of people you don't know, a group of people who don't know you, drive you from town with your tail between your legs? I thought you had more spirit, gel! They have no power over you — only you can *allow* them to make you miserable. What difference does it make that Lady Bowden looked down that long, skinny nose of hers at you? Or that Mrs. Rowland hustled that dreadful daughter of hers away from you at the party as if you had the plague? Are you going to let them rule your life?" Shaking a finger under Thea's nose, she had gone on sternly, "You have friends, titled friends, and a widespread family who will stand by you. Why should you care what petty-minded people think? The only wrong you did was to be young and foolish and to be bewitched by a blackguard and scoundrel. Wrong was done you, not the other way around."

Her eyes bright with tears, Thea had stared at Modesty's plain features. "I killed Tom," she had muttered.

"No! You did not kill Tom. Randall killed Tom." Modesty had given her a not unkindly shake. "And it is for Tom that you must not let all those old tabbies and cats send you running for cover. For Tom you must stand up and face 'em." Modesty had grinned at her. "As my father used to say, 'give 'em hell, gel'!"

With Modesty's backing, Thea had done just that, after a time, taking pride and delight in staring down the stiff-rumped old matrons and their equally disdainful daughters. It had not been easy, but for the past several years she had learned to carry her head high and ignore the gossip that swirled in her wake.

But if Thea had been able, for the most part, to ignore the whispers and sly looks, Edwina had not. Young, spoiled, and pampered, Edwina had been convinced that with her sweetly angelic looks, butter yellow curls, and sapphire blue eyes she would be much sought after and it would be only a short time before she was engaged to a wealthy member of the peerage. But she had suffered a distinct shock when it became apparent that, while happy to dance and flirt with her, no gentleman of high degree or great fortune was eager to align himself with the sister of Thea Garrett — even a half sister. And, of course, there was the matter of Edwina's fortune — it was not large. It was true that a fortune and family connections such as Thea possessed *might* have made some impecunious lord look the other way, but Edwina's portion was nothing so very magnificent, and she had no powerful connections — except through Thea.

When Alfred Hirst, so very sophisticated and a member of the Prince of Wales's set, had appeared on the scene and shown a definite interest, Edwina had been overjoyed. Hirst was well connected with a tidy fortune and, to hear him talk, he was a great friend of Prinny's. With visions of rubbing shoulders with royalty circling in her brain, Edwina had been convinced that he was the man she had been waiting for her entire life.

Thea was less than convinced. The fact that Hirst was thirty-five years old and a member of the Prince of Wales's rackety entourage did not recommend him to her. Prinny's friends were not always known for their respectability, and there was much gossip about his wild and raffish companions. Discreet inquiry by Thea revealed the fact that Hirst was badly in debt and was known to be hanging out for a rich wife.

Edwina would hear none of it, and she and Hirst had made a runaway match of it. With the deed done and painful memories of her own aborted elopement in the back of her mind, Thea tried to put a good face on it. But she had said too much in trying desperately to dissuade Edwina from marrying Hirst for the situation to be easy between them.

Thea picked up the letter from Hirst and reread it, sighing. She supposed she would have to meet him tonight and see what sort of new scheme he had now concocted to wheedle more money out of her. It wasn't, she thought as she stood up and began to undress, as if she had not already saved Hirst and Edwina from financial embarrassment. Not six months ago, she had paid off their debts for the third time in eighteen months. At that time, she had again made the offer to settle them in a nice little place in the country, with a small income, but had had her generosity thrown back in her face.

"Very well," she had said, "since you won't leave London, I'm afraid that I must say some harsh words." She had looked at her sister, her heart aching. "This is the third time that I have paid off your debts, mainly your husband's gambling debts, and deposited a sizable sum in the bank for you. I cannot continue to do so — especially if you make no effort to change your ways."

"*Will* not, you mean!" Edwina had said, her blue eyes glittering with temper. "I don't see why you have to be so selfish — you have plenty of money; you don't need it all. Alfred can't help it if the cards have been unlucky for him of late. It wouldn't hurt you in the least to share your fortune with me. Mother would want you to — you know she would."

"Edwina is right," Alfred had inserted, his darkly handsome face full of mockery. "I am sure Mrs. Northrop would be appalled to discover that you are not willing to help your sister in her time of need."

Thea had smiled sweetly at him. "I am perfectly happy to help Edwina . . . it is *you* that I object to helping. And since you are her husband and have control over her finances, and will proceed to gamble away any money I give her, I have no choice but to deny her." She had looked at Edwina. "And I will. Believe me. This is the last time. I will not pay his gaming debts again."

That unpleasant scene had taken place this spring, just before Thea had left for the country for the summer. She had returned to London only a few weeks ago for the "Little" Season, and she had had no direct contact from either Edwina or Alfred until now. She eyed the note again. Was she being a fool? Should she simply tear it up and let Edwina face the consequences? She bit her lip. No. She could not do that. If her family had taken that attitude toward her when she had needed them so desperately ten years ago, who knew what her life would be like today? No. She could not desert Edwina. She made a face. And that meant she could not desert Edwina's detestable husband either.

As always whenever she thought of the man Edwina had married, a wave of guilt swept over her. She was certain that, except for her shameful reputation, Edwina would have made the grand match she'd set her heart on. It was, she admitted sadly, her fault that Edwina was married to a man of Hirst's stamp. She had no choice but to meet with him and try to gain some sort of security for Edwina — it was what her mother would have wanted.

Thea was preoccupied at dinner that evening, and Modesty noted it. She waited until they were seated in the front saloon and Thea was halfheartedly reading a Minerva Press novel before she said anything.

Putting down her embroidery, Modesty asked, "What is it, my dear? You were very quiet during dinner and now you are positively scowling at that poor book. Is it so very awful?"

Thea glanced over at her affectionately. She didn't like to think of what her life might have been like if her uncle hadn't insisted that Modesty move in with her and Edwina. Modesty had not let her brood, and Modesty would not let her hide either. She owed this tall, bony, gray-haired woman a great deal.

Shaking her head, Thea said, "No, there is nothing wrong with the book — it is Alfred. He left a note for me this afternoon. He wants me to meet with him this evening."

Modesty's thin lips pursed. "I suppose he wants money?"

"His note did not say, but I cannot imagine that it can be anything else!"

"Are you going to meet him?"

Thea sighed. "I don't see that I have much choice. If I don't, Edwina is sure to suffer."

Modesty snorted. "I think you worry too much over that little Madam. She has known exactly what she was doing from the day she was born. Edwina will always land on her feet — have no fear of that!"

"I know you always thought that she was spoiled . . ." Thea grimaced. "And I'll admit that she is, but I cannot simply abandon her — it is my fault that she is married to the vile creature." Thea's hand tightened into a fist, and she said fiercely, "If only I had not been such a bloody little fool and fallen under the spell of a fortune hunter like Hawley Randall."

"And if you don't stop feeling sorry for yourself and quit blaming yourself for what happened a decade ago, you are going to let him have the final laugh," Modesty said bluntly, though her blue eyes were kind.

"I'm not feeling sorry for myself," Thea said, outraged. "Why should I? I have everything I could want: my own home, my own fortune, a circle of dear friends, and a family that loves me — what more could I want? But I *am* to blame for what happened. If it hadn't been for me — !"

"Now that's about enough!" Modesty said. "I know you feel guilty for what happened, but it wasn't entirely your fault. You were out of your depth. Randall took advantage of your youth and innocence, and it was simply tragic circumstances that your brother died — but it wasn't your fault! He chose to fight the duel with Randall. You couldn't have stopped him no matter what you did." Her face softened. "Don't you think you suffered long enough simply for being young and foolish?"

Thea smiled crookedly. "And stubborn. And headstrong. And reckless."

Modesty smiled back at her. "Yes, I agree you are all of those things, but so are many other people. It doesn't," she said tartly, "make you unique."

"Well, that has put me in my place, hasn't it?" Thea replied with a laugh, her dark eyes dancing.

"One hopes so, but I doubt it shall be for long — you being so very reckless and headstrong."

Thea laughed again and stood up. Crossing the room to where Modesty sat with her embroidery, she sank down on the sofa beside her. Hugging her, Thea muttered, "Thank you. I needed that."

"You certainly did," replied Modesty as she calmly started a new color of thread. She glanced inquiringly at Thea. "What are you going to do about Hirst?"

"I don't know. I suppose it depends on what he wants." Her lips quirked. "Rather, how much he wants."

Thea looked at the gilt clock on the mantel. "And I had better have the carriage brought 'round if I am going to make the appointment."

"Are you going alone?" Modesty asked with a little frown.

Thea nodded. "You forget that I am twenty-seven and no longer considered in my first blush — not that I ever had a first blush — Randall took care of that. Everyone in London already knows that I am eccentric and considered notorious — why would anyone question my going out to meet my brother-in-law? It is a respectable address, and I shan't be there long." She grinned at Modesty. "I'm taking the carriage and will have a coachman and groom with me. I promise to cause no scandal."

Once she was in the carriage, however, Thea wasn't quite as confident as she had appeared to Modesty. Giving her coachman instructions to stop in front of the number given in the note, she craned her head out the window and surveyed the street in both directions. It certainly looked respectable enough, but she wondered why Hirst had given her this address. He and Edwina lived in a very nice house on Bolton Street. Why couldn't they have met there? Because he didn't want Edwina to know about the meeting? But why not?

Uneasy and not certain why, Thea told the coachman to drive on. Settling back against the blue-velvet squabs, she considered the situation. She wasn't afraid to meet Hirst, was she? Of course not! Then why hadn't she gotten out of the coach and knocked on the door of the house? Because she didn't trust Alfred Hirst one little bit!

Wishing she had brought the note with her, to reread it, she sat there for several minutes as the coach bowled smoothly down the street, thinking about what she was going to do. Go home with her tail between her legs? Certainly not! Her full mouth twisted. Well, that left only one thing to do.

Rapping smartly on the divider between herself and the coachman, she gave him orders to turn the coach around and to park on the opposite side of the street, a few doors down from where she was going. After being helped down from the coach by the groom, she stood there a moment, wrapping her heavy purple-velvet cloak around her and taking particular care that the hood was securely over her head. She wasn't, she told herself, trying to disguise herself, it was just that there was no reason to flaunt her presence.

Thea crossed the street and stopped at the base of the steps that led up to the tall Georgian house. Except for a pair of flickering candles in the sconces on either side of the wide door, the place looked deserted, no light spilling out from any of the tall windows. Yet it was the correct address; the house number told her that.

Gripping her cloak tightly in one hand, she mounted the steps. Giving a sharp rap on the door, she waited with a pounding heart. When several seconds passed and nothing happened, she knocked again. Nothing. She was on the point of turning away, convinced that Hirst had been playing a jest at her expense, when the door behind her suddenly swung open.

"Ah, Thea, I hoped that it was you," Alfred Hirst said pleasantly. "Please come in. I am sorry that you had to wait so long, but I was busy in the back of the house."

Thea eyed her brother-in-law warily. He was smiling broadly, his bold blue eyes crinkling attractively, his thin lips pink and moist, his full face revealing nothing more than polite pleasure at her arrival.

Reluctantly Thea allowed him to usher her inside the house. When the door shut behind her, and he began to urge her to the back of the house, she stopped and asked, "What is the meaning of this? Why is it so dark? Why are there no candles lit, no servants around?"

Alfred chuckled. "So suspicious, dear sister-in-law. You have nothing to fear from me. This place belongs to a friend of mine and when I mentioned that I wished to meet, er, privately with a, ah, lady, he mentioned that he knew just the place. It is empty because it belongs to a relative of his who lives in the country and has no taste for the city."

Thea remained rooted to the spot, her heart hammering in her chest, too aware of Alfred's big, broad-shouldered form behind her. Swinging around, she demanded, "What is it that you have to say to me that could not be said in your own home? Or a more public place?"

He chuckled again, the sound of it making Thea's teeth clench together. Whether from fear or disgust she did not know.

"Don't tell me you're afraid of me?" he asked incredulously. "Come now, Thea, you have nothing to fear from me. We are allies. We share one goal — to see that Edwina is kept happy. Yes?"

"That much is true," she admitted. "The problem is that we have vastly different ideas of what it is that will make her happy."

He laughed and again urged her forward. "Not so very different. Not so very different, as you shall see. Come along now. I only want you to go to the study — a fire is lit; candles burning — if you look for it, you can see the light coming from beneath the door of the room. It will be much more comfortable than standing here in the dark."

Without a word, Thea marched toward the light she glimpsed, and pushing open the door, she walked into a charming room. A pair of silver candelabra lit the room; the walls were lined with crimson-, blue-, and green-bound books; yellow-chintz-covered, comfortable furniture was scattered about the room. A mahogany desk, its expanse broken by some paper and a quill and ink bottle, was at the far end of the room. A cozy fire burned on the hearth, the firelight casting a golden gleam over a pair of scissors near the edge of the desk.

Feeling a trifle less suspicious, Thea stood in the center of the room and watched as Alfred poured himself a brandy from a tray of liquors and glasses sitting on a long chest against one wall. Looking over his shoulder at her, he cocked a brow, but Thea shook her head.

Brandy in hand, he turned back to her, and murmured, "Won't you be seated?"

"I'd rather stand. What is it that you wanted to see me about? Money?"

He smiled, not a bit fazed. "Well, yes, my dear. It is."

"I told you how I feel. I haven't changed my mind."

He nodded. "Oh, I'm aware of that. I have a proposition for you — if you're interested?"

Her features shadowed by the cowl of the purple-velvet hood, her eyes dark pools in her white face, Thea muttered, "I can't imagine that any proposition of yours would find favor with me, but what is it?"

"How would you feel, if for a, er, certain sum of money, I promised to go away and never bother you — or Edwina — again?"

Thea frowned. "You mean you want me to pay you to stay away from her?" When he nodded, her lip curled. "I thought you loved her — isn't that what you claimed? That she was your heart's desire? That you adored her?"

He shrugged. "I may have in the beginning, but passion has a way of fading, and I can see now that perhaps it might be best for her if we parted."

"You'd break her heart?" Thea asked incredulously. "Desert her and leave her open to all sorts of gossip and whispers?"

"Well, what the hell else do you expect me to do?" he demanded, his cheeks suddenly flushed with temper. "Would you prefer that I stay by her side, and we both end up in debtor's prison? Because that's what is going to happen if you don't loosen the purse strings."

"Oh, you're despicable!" Thea said hotly, her eyes fierce and angry. "I don't know why I even came here!"

She swung away, intent upon putting as much distance between herself and Hirst as possible. He caught her at the door, his hand closing around her arm.

"You have to listen to me," he growled. "I need the money. I owe a great deal of money to people who will not take no for an answer. I *must* have it — and if it means I desert my wife in order to get you to pay the piper, by God, I will!"

Thea wrenched her arm away from him, her hood falling to her shoulders and her black hair tumbling in wild disarray around her furious face. "You dare! Keep your hands off me!"

Alfred stepped back and raised his hands. "I'm sorry — I forgot myself. But you have to listen to me. I have to have seventeen thousand pounds by the end of the week or —" He smiled bleakly. "Or Edwina will be a widow. Do you want my death on your conscience, too? Aren't two men enough for you?"

Thea ignored the jab. "Seventeen *thousand* pounds?" she burst out, her expression stunned. "That is a fortune in itself." It was indeed, since a gentleman could live off less than four hundred pounds a year.

"I know. The original amount was nothing near that, but the exorbitant interest those bloodsuckers demand has driven it skyward." He sat down in one of the comfortable chairs and buried his head in his hands. "I'm at my wits' end. I do not know what I am to do." He lifted his head and stared at her. "You must help! If not for me, then for Edwina."

"When I last paid off your debts, why was there no mention of this?" Thea asked with a frown. "Surely, you haven't gone in debt that much in just six months."

"I thought I could come around, but the damned cards —"

"You've been gambling? Trying to recoup your losses?"

"What the devil did you expect me to do?" he demanded. "You cut me off. I had to think of some way of coming about."

"It never crossed your mind to stop gambling? To practice a little economy?" Genuine shock was evident in her voice.

"No. Why should I?" he said. "One of the reasons I was willing to marry Edwina was because I knew she was your sister — her fortune alone would not have tempted me, but the Garrett wealth . . ." He smiled faintly. "Now that was something that made her nearly irresistible."

Disgust on her face, Thea regarded him, uncertain of her next move. She could not, she decided tiredly, be the cause of the death of her sister's husband — even though

Edwina would be far better off without him. But Edwina loved him, and Thea was committed to seeing that, to the best of her ability, Edwina was happy.

She stood there trying to think of a solution. His offer to leave Edwina for enough money was very tempting, but Thea knew she could never take such a questionable step — even though Edwina might eventually be much happier. It wasn't her decision to make.

"If," she said slowly, "and I am only saying 'if,' but if I were to pay this seventeen thousand pounds, what guarantee do I have that you will not come back to me in a few months with another tale of woe?"

He smiled with all the charm he was capable of. "I knew that you would not desert us! Edwina is fortunate to have a sister such as you." A look that made Thea distinctly wary came into his face. "You know, I should have married you. I have always thought that you were far more interesting than your sister. Do you think we could have made a match of it?"

Thea was only giving half her attention to him. For the last several minutes she had become aware of a feeling of unease. It wasn't just the natural unease she felt in the situation, but something else. The hair on the back of her neck prickled, and she had the unsettling impression of prying eyes.

She looked around but saw nothing to cause her alarm. The room was still pleasant and cheerful; the door through which she had entered was still half-open, the hallway beyond a black hole. She glanced discreetly about her once again, but her gaze came back to the half-open doorway, the feeling of being watched persisting. A chill went through her at the idea that someone might be standing in that darkened hallway spying on them.

It was silly, she knew, and though she stared hard at the half-open door, she saw nothing that confirmed her increasing sensation of unease. Concentrating intently upon her feeling that they were not alone, she was thoroughly startled when Hirst rose to his feet and, kneeling in front of her, took one of her hands in his.

Dropping a kiss on the back of her hand, he said huskily, "You haven't answered my question: Do you think I should have set my sights on you instead of that child, Edwina? If you do, I am sure that we could come to some arrangement between the pair of us."

The import of his words suddenly sank in and, nearly knocking him backwards in her haste to get away from him, Thea took several steps toward the door leading to the main hall. "Are you mad?" she cried, greatly agitated, horrified and repulsed both by his words and by his manner. "You are detestable! Why, I would rather embrace a leper than have you touch me."

An ugly look crossed his face. "Perhaps I shall have to change your mind," he said, advancing toward her.

Frightened as she had not been in a decade, Thea ran for the door, but he caught her, his hands closing brutally around her. Swinging her around, he jerked her next to him and bent his head to kiss her.

Memories of her night with Hawley Randall surging through her, Thea fought like a maddened creature, twisting and clawing. Like Hawley, Hirst was bigger and stronger, but Thea was no longer a shrinking, terrified virgin — she was frightened, but she was also gloriously, powerfully enraged. Ignoring the revulsion that choked her as his mouth caught hers and his tongue forced its way into her mouth, her fingers clawed at his arms, her teeth clamping down on his intruding tongue.

With a snarl, he flung her from him and she crashed into a small table near the doorway. As she scrabbled to keep her footing, her outstretched hand brushed against a heavy marble figurine that sat in the middle of the table. Regaining her balance, instinctively, she braced herself to meet his attack, her fingers clutching the figurine.

This time when he grabbed for her, she brought the figurine down against his temple with all her strength. He gave a funny little sound and collapsed at her feet.

Her breathing labored, her heart banging, she stared down at his fallen form, a thick rivulet of blood flowing from the wide gash on his head. He did not move. He simply lay there, and Thea stared at his still form, utterly petrified, the terrible knowledge that she had meant to kill him and that she had actually done it racing icily through her body. Dumbfounded, she looked at him, unable to believe what she had done. She had killed him. Dear God! She had murdered her sister's husband.

Chapter Three

Thea never remembered how long she stood there staring at Hirst's sprawled form on the floor, but finally something, some instinct for survival, made her move. She was aghast at what had happened, but the strongest emotion in her breast at that moment was a panicked urge to run.

The marble statuette still clutched in her hand, she turned, not even certain what she intended to do, when she heard a noise. Fear flooded through her and, unnerved and horrified by the situation, she could not even tell whence the sound came — from the hall or somewhere in the room behind her. She only knew that she had heard something: a thump, a scrape, perhaps a gasp. She couldn't tell. In the state she was in, it could have been all three, but it galvanized her as nothing else could have, and she bolted into the darkened hallway.

Intent only on escape, she fled through the shadowy house, almost crying with relief when her hand touched the crystal knob of the front door. Flinging the door wide, she catapulted out onto the stoop and right into the arms of the gentlemen who had just ascended the steps.

Strong hands caught her shoulders, and suppressing a scream, Thea gazed wide-eyed up into the dark, powerful face of a stranger. But not an utter stranger. She had seen him before and, even in her agitated state, she recognized him — it was the gray-eyed stranger from the park.

For a moment she stood there staring up at him, her raven hair swirling wildly around her shoulders, her eyes black with emotion, her face starkly white. Then she gave a gasp, muttered something incoherent, and tore herself from his grip. The statuette fell from her hand and clattered at his feet as she half ran, half stumbled down the steps, her cloak rippling darkly behind her.

She heard him call out, but heedless of the coach pulled by the team of spirited horses bearing swiftly down on her, she darted out into the road. Hardly aware of the snorting, high-stepping horses that swept by dangerously close to her slender form, Thea ran to the safety of her own coach.

Ignoring the startled glance of her servant, she scrambled into the vehicle and blurted out, "Home. *Now.*"

Obediently, the coachman did as she commanded. Feeling the comforting sway and bump of the moving vehicle, Thea sank back against the velvet interior, shaking uncontrollably.

She buried her face in her hands. *I killed him,* she thought half-hysterically. *I killed him — my sister's own husband — I struck him and murdered him!*

Patrick stood on the stoop, staring astonished at the spot where Thea had plunged into the street, wondering if he had imagined the whole incident. He gave himself a shake, knowing it had not been his imagination. Her shoulders had been warm and yielding beneath his hands, and he would never forget the stunning effect that white, taking face, huge black eyes, and crimson mouth had had upon him.

Even now he was still oddly breathless, could still remember the faint warmth that had radiated from her body . . . and the stark fear in her eyes. Thoughtfully, he watched the coach that had been parked on the other side of the street pull into the light traffic that cluttered the street.

Of course he recognized her: Thea Garrett. And what, he wondered, was she doing coming out of the house where he was to meet his mother's blackmailer? It crossed his mind that Thea could be the blackmailer, but he dismissed that thought as soon as it occurred. He could think of no connection between Thea and his mother's dead lover; more importantly, he could not even begin to name a reason why someone like Miss Garrett would stoop to blackmail . . . except perhaps for the thrill of it?

The coach disappeared out of sight, and Patrick momentarily dismissed the mystery of Thea Garrett and turned back toward the house. Staring at the blackened rectangle that greeted him, he studied it for a moment. Something had obviously sent Thea Garrett running like a startled fawn, but what? And was whatever had frightened her waiting for him? Or rather for his mother?

His mouth tightened. Someone, he decided, was in for a surprise. A tigerish grin crossed his face. And not a pleasant surprise at that! He strode purposefully forward, only to stop as his foot hit something. Bending down, he picked up the statuette that Thea had dropped. Curiouser and curiouser.

The statuette in his hand, he stepped gingerly through the opened doorway and noticed that there was a light piercing the blackness. Carefully shutting the front door behind him, he walked slowly toward the light.

Just outside the lighted doorway, he stopped and listened. Hearing and seeing nothing alarming, he looked into the room.

It was cheerful enough, with a fire crackling nicely on the hearth, but his eyes were immediately drawn to the body of the man lying on the floor, blood trickling from the nasty wound on his head. Patrick glanced at the statuette and was even less surprised to see a faint smear of blood on its base.

He studied the features of the man on the floor. He was aware that he had seen the man about town and that he probably knew him, but at the moment he could not call his name to mind. Was this his mother's blackmailer? And was the fellow blackmailing Thea Garrett? He doubted it. From what he had learned of Thea Garrett, there was little the public did not know about her. And since she seemed to care little what people thought, he would not have considered her a good prospect for blackmail.

He glanced again about the room. It was charming. Was it a love nest? Now that, he thought cynically, was far more likely. Had Miss Garrett come to meet a lover and had they fallen out? He smiled wryly. The lady must be a fierce mistress if the condition of the man on the floor was anything to go by. Having decided that he had a fair idea of what had happened, he put down the statuette and was on the point of checking how badly the man on the floor had been hurt when he heard a creak on the stairs behind him.

Patrick froze. Listening intently, he realized that someone had been stealthily using the staircase. But going up or coming down?

A sound came again from the stairs, and, stepping swiftly into the hallway, Patrick called out, "Halt! Who is it?"

Making no attempt to hide its presence, whoever it was bounded up the final few stairs to the upper floor. Cursing under his breath, Patrick took only time to grab one of the candles from a nearby candelabrum, then leaped after the shy visitor.

Reaching the top of the stairs, Patrick stopped, realizing suddenly that he had no weapon with him. Still, he had no choice but to search for whoever had been on the stairs. If the man downstairs was not the blackmailer, then whoever had been lurking on the staircase might very well be.

He glanced up and down the dark main hall, his candle illuminating only a small area around him. The gloomy shapes of furniture met his gaze, and he could make out the outlines of several doorways that faced the wide hallway.

Not relishing the prospect before him, he cautiously approached the nearest door and, holding the candle away from his body, slowly opened the door. Warily he glanced into the room, the wavering light revealing a room full of piled furniture, haphazardly covered with dust covers. He studied the contents for a long moment, wondering at the wisdom of poking around the shrouded furniture. If the other rooms were in the same condition, he had a long search in front of him.

Deciding to glance into the other rooms before committing himself to a more thorough search, he was on the point of shutting the door when his glance fell upon a huge mahogany wardrobe that sat against the far wall. Of all the furniture in the room, it was the one piece not hidden by a dust cover. In fact, on the floor in front of it lay what looked to be a large crumpled dust cover.

Thoughtfully, Patrick studied the wardrobe. It was certainly large enough to hide a person, and the discarded dust cover aroused his suspicions. He glanced around for something to use as a weapon, but nothing met his eye.

Grimacing, he approached the towering wardrobe. Body braced for trouble and holding the candle aloft, he flung open the right door of the wardrobe. There was a screech and, swathed in God knows what, a figure exploded out of the interior, a heavy brass candlestick in one hand.

Even though he'd been prepared to find someone hiding in the wardrobe, Patrick staggered backward, the violence with which the person erupted from the wardrobe nearly knocking him down. Before he could regain his balance, the attacker was on him, and he was struck a vicious blow on the head with the candlestick. He went down soundlessly, landing in an inelegant heap, the candle falling from nerveless fingers and rolling across the floor.

Patrick had no idea how long he lay unconscious. Eventually he stirred and gradually regained his senses, his aching head reminding him instantly of what had transpired.

Warily he opened his eyes. The room was dark, the doorway leading into the hall, faintly outlined by the light from downstairs. He sat up, suppressing a groan as pain lanced through his head. Reaching up, he touched the spot that ached the most and muttered under his breath when his fingers came away wet with what he knew was blood. He smiled without humor. It seemed to be the night for careless gentlemen to be hit upon the head. Giving himself a moment to recover, he rose to his feet.

Feeling a fool, he walked to the door and made his way downstairs. He moved carefully, on the alert for another attack, but he sensed that whoever had struck him was long gone. At the bottom of the stairs, he stopped, listening and looking around. Everything seemed the same.

He glanced into the lighted room near the stairs, his breath catching at the sight of the man sprawled half in and half out the doorway. He moved closer for a better look. His mouth tightened. Even from where he stood, it was obvious that the man was dead.

Stepping carefully over the dead man, Patrick wasted precious few minutes searching the room for any clue he could find. He found nothing. Nothing to identify the body on the floor, and more importantly to him, nothing that led to his mother.

After one last glance around, he slipped out the back of the house. No use risking someone seeing him leave the house, and he hoped to God that no one but Thea Garrett had seen him on the stoop of the house.

Thea had other things to worry about than the gray-eyed stranger she had collided with on the stoop of the house. Reaching home, she dismissed the servants and hurried up the stairs to her room. Flinging off her cloak, she took several agitated steps around the room, her thoughts chaotic.

Pushing back her tumbled curls with a shaking hand, she continued to pace, frightened and appalled by what had happened.

What in heaven's name was she to do? Confess that she had murdered her sister's husband? She shuddered. She was brave, but not that brave, and the instinct for survival was strong.

She closed her eyes, tears leaking from under her lids. She hadn't meant to kill him. She despised him, but she had never wished him dead. Away, yes. Out of Edwina's life, yes. But not dead. And certainly she had never planned to murder him. But would she be believed? If she told the authorities, would they understand? Or would she, after a horribly public trial, be found guilty and hanged?

Another shudder went through her. Dare she risk it? Wouldn't the truth save her?

A light rap on the door interrupted her thoughts, but before she could deny entrance, Modesty opened the door and walked into the room.

Modesty took one look at Thea's features

and immediately crossed the room to her side. Taking one of Thea's icy hands in hers, she demanded, "What is it? What happened?"

It would never have occurred to Thea not to tell Modesty. Modesty listened intently, saying nothing, and when she judged that Thea had told everything, she urged her to sit down on the bed.

Patting Thea's hands, she said, "I think a hot cup of tea, laced with a healthy dose of brandy, would be just the thing for you right now."

After ringing for a servant, Modesty walked back across the room and sat down on the bed beside Thea's forlorn figure. "It wasn't your fault, you know. He attacked you — you really had no choice." Modesty sighed. "It really is unfortunate that he died — I always said that he was an inconsiderate man. And look, he had just proven my point. Imagine letting himself be killed by a stupid little blow to the head! If that isn't just like him. Inconsiderate to the very last."

"I am very sure that he did not mean to be so inconsiderate," Thea replied dryly.

Modesty smiled at her, pleased to see that bleak look leaving her eyes. "Oh, you're wrong there. If he had planned it, he could not have been more inconsiderate."

A tap on the door took Modesty to the door, and after giving orders for tea and brandy, she rejoined Thea on the bed. Patting Thea's hand again, she said, "I would tell you to put it from your mind, but I know that you will not. You must not, however, allow it to plague you." She looked steadily into Thea's eyes. "You did not mean to kill him. It was an accident. A terrible accident to be sure, but an accident nonetheless." When Thea would have spoken, she raised an admonishing finger. "More importantly, there is nothing to be gained by you telling anyone else what happened. When his body is discovered, you will, if you are wise, be as surprised and astonished as anybody else."

Leaning forward, Modesty said urgently, "Thea, confessing what happened will change nothing. It will not bring him back and will only ruin your life. While I would hope that if the truth were known, you would not hang, you have to realize that being condemned to death is a very real possibility. Your contempt for him is well-known, and there would be those who would believe that you deliberately killed him — even though we know differently." Modesty's mouth tightened. "Alfred Hirst is not worth ruining yourself again . . . or dying for. You must see that." When Thea's expression did not change, she added, "Think of Edwina! She has just lost her husband. Must she lose her sister, too? Must she know, no matter the circumstances, that you killed her husband? She will need you now more than ever. Think of that whenever you are moved to confess the truth. In this case, the truth would do far more damage than simply keeping your mouth shut."

"But it seems so wrong — so cowardly," Thea muttered. "Oh, God! I do not know what to do. I killed him. I cannot deny it." Her eyes shut, and her hand closed into a fist. "But dear God, I did not mean to!"

"Of course, you didn't! You are no murderess! Nor are you a fool, and for now, I strongly urge you to keep your mouth shut — at least wait until his body is discovered. If your conscience continues to bedevil you, you can always come forward and confess at a later time. But right now, tonight, I want you to think about the scandal and disgrace such a drastic step would bring down upon not only your head, but those of the entire family."

Thea nodded miserably. "I have thought of it. I have thought of nothing else. I've caused one ugly scandal already in my lifetime and cost my brother his life. Believe me, I certainly would prefer to pretend that tonight had not happened." She glanced at Modesty's concerned features. "But it did happen. I did kill him."

Another tap on the door sent Modesty to answer it. Taking the tray from the servant, she shut the door behind her and, crossing the room, set the tray on a nearby table.

Pouring out a cup of steaming tea from the china pot and adding a generous dollop of brandy from the crystal decanter that had been set beside the teapot, Modesty brought it to Thea. "Drink this. It will make you feel better — at least momentarily."

Modesty was right. After several sips of the hot liquid, Thea could feel the terror and icy chill that had settled in her stomach easing.

Biting her lip, Thea glanced at Modesty, who was also partaking of the same beverage, with an even bigger dose of brandy in her cup. Thea smiled faintly. If the amount of brandy Modesty was consuming was anything to go by, Modesty was more worried than she had let on. A burst of love for her sometimes-astringent spinster cousin went through her. Modesty would stand by her . . . and understand and love her no matter what she did.

There was silence for several moments as both women drank their brandy-laced tea and thought about the death of Alfred Hirst. Neither came to any final conclusion.

Rising to her feet and walking to where the tray sat, Thea put down her cup. Turning back to face Modesty, she said unhappily, "I think for the time being that I shall do as you suggest and say nothing. As you said, I can always confess."

Modesty sighed with relief. "Thank goodness! I knew that you were a sensible gel."

Thea made a face. "Why does being sensible make me feel like a coward?"

"Because you are not a fool — you know you killed him, but you also know that it *was* a tragic accident — not something you planned or had even considered doing. Remember too, that you were protecting yourself. It was not your fault — the blame lies with Alfred. Which is also why you are taking the wisest course." Her blue eyes warm and worried, Modesty added urgently, "Thea, you are doing the right thing. You *must* believe that! Nothing can be gained by your confession. It will not bring him back, nor change a thing. All it would do would bring further shame and disgrace to you and the family — and might very well lead to your execution. Edwina is going to suffer enough; she does not need to know that you killed her husband. No one does." She hesitated, then asked quietly, "I assume that no one else does know that you were there?"

That tight, pinched look returned to Thea's face. "Unfortunately," she said heavily, "someone else *does* know — remember I told you about the man I collided with as I was leaving the house."

Modesty uttered a decidedly unladylike curse. "I had forgotten about him. Are you positive that he recognized you?"

"I'm positive that he got a very good look at my face — and if he doesn't know who I am now, he soon will — especially since it appears that he is a member of the ton. He was with Lord Embry and his crowd when I saw him in the park."

"Hmm. Perhaps if we left town early and retired to the country until the spring, he wouldn't remember you, if you were to meet at a later date?"

Thea shrugged. "It's possible. But I suspect that Nigel told him who I was — you know what a gossip he is." Sourly, she added, "Of course, we will have a perfectly legitimate excuse to go to the country — Hirst's death. I suspect that Edwina will not want to remain in London — she certainly will not be attending any balls or other entertainment for several months."

"Well, there you have it! I shall tell the servants first thing in the morning that we are packing and retiring to Halsted House for the winter."

Halsted House was the country estate Thea had purchased just two years ago. While Modesty much preferred London, there were times that Thea simply could not bear the noise and bustle a moment longer and would escape to the country, to Halsted House. She loved Halsted for another reason: it was located not five miles from Garrett Manor, and living there, tramping through the three hundred acres that went with the estate, brought back all the happier moments of her childhood. Modesty's suggestion was tempting, but a thought occurred to her.

"Shouldn't we wait until after we are informed of Alfred's death before we begin packing?" Thea asked.

Modesty looked vexed. "Of course. I can be such a fool sometimes." She stood up, and said decisively, "Well, we can settle nothing more tonight, and we will just have to wait until the news of his death is brought to us before we put our plans in motion."

A sudden rap on the door had both

women exchanging a frightened glance. Taking a deep breath, Thea called out, "Yes, what is it?"

The door opened and Tillman's bald head appeared as he peered around the door. "Miss, I know it is very late, but there is a gentleman downstairs, who insists upon seeing you. I told him that you were not receiving visitors," he complained, "but he persisted." Walking into the room, he handed her a folded piece of paper. "He said that you would want this and that he would await your reply."

How she kept her features schooled, Thea never knew. Taking the paper with as much enthusiasm as she would have a live cobra, she opened the note and read it. Ignoring the fear that stabbed through her, she crumpled the note and said coolly, "Tell the gentleman that I shall be down in just a moment. Show him into the blue saloon — offer him refreshments if he wishes."

Tillman looked offended. "Very well, Miss, if you say so, but if you want my opinion —"

"I do not!" Thea said sharply. "Now do as you have been ordered."

Muttering, Tillman withdrew.

Thea glanced at Modesty. "It is the man I collided with as I left the house. He wants to talk with me."

"Should you meet with him alone? Should I come with you?"

Thea thought a moment, then shook her head. "No, I had better see him by myself." She smiled bitterly. "If I am to be exposed and condemned to hang, I do not want you involved. For the moment let him think that only he and I know what happened."

Her most haughty expression on her face, Thea entered the blue saloon a few minutes later. Telling herself that he could not *prove* that she had even been out of the house tonight — her servants were loyal and would never give her away — Thea had decided that her best course, right now, was to deny everything and keep denying it.

Shutting the door behind her, she confronted the tall, gray-eyed stranger. Attacking immediately, she began crisply, "And what is the meaning of this unwarranted intrusion? I do not know who you think you are or what you hope to accomplish, but I'll not have you berating my servants and forcing your way into my home this way. I've a good mind to send for the Watch."

"Perhaps you should . . . considering what happened at Curzon Street this evening," Patrick drawled.

Thea's breath caught painfully. "And what," she demanded, "do you mean by that?"

Patrick had to admire her poise if not her manner, and under different circumstances, he would have enjoyed sparring with her. But not tonight. And not at this moment.

"I think you know very well what I mean," he said, his gray eyes steadily meeting hers.

Thea bit her lip. He did not appear to be a person who bluffed easily, but she had no choice but to continue on the path she had chosen. Her chin lifted, and she snapped, "It is very late. Even at the best of times, I have no taste for games, and I am afraid that you are trying my patience. I would suggest that you leave."

Across the width of the pleasant room that separated them, Patrick studied her. She was tall, but not as tall as he had first thought, and for a young woman with such a sordid past and wild reputation, she seemed oddly innocent and vulnerable. The two times he had seen her previously had been so brief that he had been left with only a fleeting impression of flashing dark eyes and a soft crimson mouth. Reality did not change that impression much, her eyes were still just as dark and compelling and that red mouth . . . He frowned. Dalliance was *not* the reason for his visit, but he could not pretend that his only interest in her had to do with the dead man in the house on Curzon Street.

From his very first sight of her in the park, though he would have denied it, he had been aware of a spark of interest. He hadn't understood it then and certainly did not understand it now. Knowing what he did about her, Patrick had expected to meet a calculating harpy — a harpy with whom closer acquaintance would kill whatever appeal she had aroused within him. Instead he was confronted with a slender, fairy-faced creature who looked as if she might have just left the schoolroom only a few years ago. She was also, he admitted uneasily, by far the most taking female he had seen in a very long time — if ever. To his alarm, he found those wide, eloquent eyes and intriguing features much, much too attractive.

Still frowning, he said, "And that is your last word?" When she remained silent, he added, "If you take this attitude you may leave me with no alternative but to give evidence to the magistrate."

Her façade crumpled just a bit. Not meeting his gaze, Thea studied the pale blue and cream pattern of the rug that lay upon the floor.

She was in a terrible quandary. She dare not let him lay evidence, and yet she was terrified of admitting that she had reason to fear such an action by him.

Patrick watched her, wondering if she knew how appealing she appeared as she stood before him in her simple gown of delicately spun rose-colored silk, her features hidden by the curve of the lustrous dark hair that tumbled around her shoulders. He had come prepared for battle, determined to wrest the truth out of her — no matter how brutal he had to be. His problem was that the reality of his opponent did not match the picture in his mind of a scheming, hard-hearted little harlot.

Sighing, Patrick said, "I doubt you'll believe me, but I honestly do not want to cause you trouble. I simply want to know why you were there, what happened, and the identity of the dead man." A coaxing note in his voice, he added, "I swear to you that anything you tell me shall remain between us. We might even be able to help each other."

"Why should I trust you? Why should you help me? You're a stranger — I don't even know your name."

Patrick smiled, a singularly attractive smile, the corners of his deceptively sleepy gray eyes crinkling. Bowing with exquisite grace, he murmured, "Allow me to introduce myself: I am Patrick Blackburne, late of the Mississippi Territory in America."

"That tells me nothing," Thea muttered, not willing to respond to his undeniable charm. Charming men in her view were particularly devious and dangerous — Hawley Randall had taught her that over a decade ago!

Patrick straightened, his smile fading just a little. "Perhaps the name of Lady Caldecott is more familiar to you? She is my mother. The Baron is her second husband."

"Of course I know Lady Caldecott — everyone does," she admitted faintly, her heart sinking. Good God! Lady Caldecott — one of the most imperious society matrons in all of England, and this man was her son. Of all the gentlemen in London that she could have seen on Curzon Street tonight, Thea wondered despairingly, why did it have to have been him? If he even breathed a word to his mother about her presence there tonight, it would be all over London in a matter of hours. Ruination and scandal, possibly execution, stared her in the face.

Patrick arched a brow. "Well? Does that make me a trifle more trustworthy?"

"Not very," she admitted. "I saw you with Lord Embry today, which means, I assume, that you are an intimate of his." Her voice hardened. "And Lord Embry and his cronies are as wild and scapegrace a band of fellows one can meet. Being friends with him does not raise you in my estimation."

Stung, Patrick snapped, "And I suppose your reputation is so spotless?" It was an unfair jab, and he knew it as soon as the words left his mouth.

Crossing to her, he grasped one of her hands, and said, "Forgive me! That was uncalled-for and ungentlemanly."

Slipping her hand from his, she smiled bitterly. "You have no reason to apologize — I know my reputation."

He glanced at her keenly. "And is it all deserved?" he asked softly.

"It doesn't matter," she said, stepping away from him, suddenly aware of how very attractive he was with his black hair and dark, handsome features. It had been a long time, in fact not since Hawley Randall, that she had met a man who aroused anything within her other than wariness or indifference. But there was something about this tall American that inexplicably pulled at her, something about him that made her conscious of him in a way she had thought never to feel again, and she was at once unnerved and distrustful.

Once she had established a safe distance from him, she looked at him, her expression troubled. "This conversation is gaining us nothing. I'll grant you that you probably mean well, but I have nothing to say to you. I suggest that you leave."

Patrick stared at her, disturbed by how disappointed he was that she would not trust him, but not surprised. After all, she didn't know him, and under the circumstances he didn't blame her. But he had to have her help. Whoever was blackmailing his mother had used the same Curzon Street house where Thea had been and a man had been murdered. Whether she or the dead man had anything to do with his mother's plight he didn't know, but at the moment, Thea Garrett was his best chance of discovering the identity of the person who was demanding money from his mother.

Patrick pulled on his ear, his expression wry. He wanted her help, but there was only one way he could think of to get it, and he would have preferred not to reveal the only card that he held. Especially since he wasn't positive of her reaction to it. It could tip the scales in his favor, and then again, it could allow her to escape. He studied Thea a moment longer. From the stubborn tilt of that determined chin and the set of her mouth, it was obvious that she wasn't going to budge an inch. Blast!

Uneasy of his considering gaze, Thea said, "Mr. Blackburne, I do not mean to be rude, but I've asked you now several times to leave. Won't you please do so and save both of us an embarrassing scene?"

Patrick sighed. "I sympathize with your situation — I really do, but I'm rather in a pickle myself — you could help me." His eyes held hers. "We could help each other."

"I'm sorry, but your problems are really none of my concern," Thea said stiffly, desperate for him to leave but frightened of what he might do when he did leave. Deny, deny, and *deny,* she reminded herself, but heaven knew it was increasingly difficult. Her nerves felt as if they had been flayed with fire, and the strain of the night was telling on her. How much longer she could maintain her composure she didn't know — the American was very appealing and when he offered help, she was almost frightened enough to take it — which frightened her even more. Trusting her fate to a man was not something she had contemplated for ten years — Hawley had taught her too well. But the American touched something within her . . . he aroused a shocking desire within her *to* trust him. Feeling vulnerable in a way she had not thought possible, she hesitated. Dare she risk it? Could she trust her own instincts? She dithered, torn between trusting . . . and not. In the end, mistrust won. She wanted him gone — aware that every second he remained increased the chance that she would throw caution to the winds and break down and tell him everything — and that shocked her most of all. It would be fatal to give him a weapon, to trust him with the truth. Oh, but it was tempting to do so — particularly when those gray eyes urged her warmly to do just that.

Not meeting his gaze, she forced herself to say, "Please leave."

Patrick took a turn around the room, stopping in front of her. Quietly, he said, "You've no reason on earth to trust me, but I implore you to do so."

Her dark eyes searched his. Even now, with her decision made, she was astonished at how very much she wanted to believe in him, to tell him what he wanted to know, but she shook her head. "I'm sorry," she muttered, "but you ask too much."

"Would it help," he asked softly, "if I told you that you didn't kill him?"

Chapter Four

Thea gaped at him. "But that's not true," she blurted out. "He was dead, I tell you! Dead when I left him." Suddenly realizing what she had said, she clapped a hand over her mouth and stared at him, her eyes wide and horrified.

Clasping her shoulders, Patrick shook his head. "No. You did not kill him." He smiled wryly. "Hit him hard enough to give him a damned painful headache when he awakened, that you certainly did, but you did not kill him."

"Are you certain?" she asked almost in a whisper, torn between terror at having so foolishly blurted out a confession and the fierce hope that he was telling the truth, that she had *not* murdered Alfred.

Gently turning her toward a blue-velvet sofa, his voice warm and coaxing, he said, "May we sit? This is going to take some time."

She nodded and allowed him to guide her across the room. Seated beside him on the sofa, her hands tightly fisted in her lap, she demanded, "Tell me! Tell what you know."

"Don't you think it only fair that you tell me something first?" Patrick asked reasonably. "Such as the name of the gentleman I first found lying unconscious on the floor?"

Relief poured through her. She had not killed Alfred! She had only knocked him senseless — thank God! But she could not quite believe it, and after the terrors of the night, she desperately needed the American to confirm his statement. Bending toward him, her eyes fixed painfully on his face, she asked urgently, "Are you telling me that he is alive? That I did *not* murder him?"

Patrick grimaced. "No and yes."

Thea jerked back. "What do you mean? What sort of answer is that?" Her gaze narrowed. "Are you playing some sort of wicked jest on me?"

"No. Absolutely not! What I'm trying to tell you — and badly at that — is that the gentleman was unconscious when I first laid eyes on him." Annoyed at the sorry figure he had played that night, he quickly told her of the person lurking on the stairs and his own bout of unconsciousness. "When I finally regained my senses," he ended ruefully, "and staggered back down the stairs, the gentleman you had knocked unconscious was still lying there, only now he was dead. But not," he added hastily, as Thea's breath caught audibly, "from your blow to his head. Someone had stuck a pair of long-handled scissors into his throat."

Thea blenched, the huge dark pools made by her eyes and her slim black brows the only color in her face. She remembered the scissors; they had been on the desk. And someone — the person she had sensed watching? had used them to murder Alfred. At that thought even her lips paled.

"Someone *else* murdered him?" she got out shakily. "But why? And who?"

Patrick knew the moment the possible identity of the murderer occurred to her. She shrank away from him and looked at him, with horror and dawning suspicion.

Patrick shook his head. "No, I did not kill him — I don't even know his name, so it is highly unlikely that I had any reason to kill him. And if I did, why would I come to you? You were obviously convinced that you had murdered him — which gave me a perfect alibi. Why would I come here and disillusion you?" He glanced at her, and said softly, "You didn't kill him — I can attest to that fact if necessary. Neither did I kill him — I swear it. Having, hopefully, relieved your mind of those worries, don't you think it only fair that you tell me his name?"

Thea bent her head, biting her lip. Dare

she trust him? He wasn't, she reminded herself, asking for much, only Alfred's name. He already knew a great deal — the most damaging of all that she had been at the house on Curzon Street and thanks to her own unruly tongue that she had thought she had left Alfred for dead. What he said made sense; if he had murdered Alfred himself, he'd had no reason to seek her out. Aware of all that, it seemed silly to hold back Alfred's identity.

Sighing, she muttered, "His name is, was, Alfred Hirst. He was my sister's husband."

"Ah, I see, your brother-in-law," he drawled, his very masculine mouth curving with faint distaste. "Keeping it in the family, were you?"

She flashed him a look of contempt and snapped, "You, sir, have a decidedly nasty mind. I did not meet him for some sort of tawdry assignation! I leave that sort of disgusting behavior to gentlemen of your ilk!"

"Touché," Patrick murmured with a wry smile.

Ignoring his comment and surprised by an urge to smile back at him, she said stiffly, "I disliked Alfred intensely — he was nothing but a common fortune hunter — but I did not want him dead." Rising to her feet, she murmured, "It is very late. I appreciate your kindness in relieving my fears that I may have accidentally killed him, but I cannot see that we have anything else to say to each other."

Patrick leaned back into the plump blue-velvet cushions as if he were settling in for the night. "It is not quite that simple," he drawled. "Someone murdered your brother-in-law — doesn't that bother you? Don't you want to know who it was? Or even why?"

Her lip curled. "You must not have been listening to me — I detested him — I would not have wanted him dead, but I cannot say that I am sorry that he is dead."

"Well, I'm afraid that it is not that simple for me." He shot her a hard look. "Do you really expect me politely to take my leave and toddle off into the night — with both of us knowing that a man has been murdered?"

"I can't," Thea said tightly, "very well go and report his death — not without answering some extremely embarrassing questions."

"I agree and I sympathize. To expose oneself to public scrutiny would be most unpleasant, but unless you're willing to be honest with me, and help me discover what went on tonight, that is precisely what will happen."

"What do you mean?" she asked sharply.

"You know very well what I mean," Patrick answered. "I had my own reasons for being there tonight. Stumbling across a murder was not one of them. However, since he was murdered while I was lying upstairs knocked senseless, I feel some compunction about his death."

"You wouldn't if you had known him," Thea muttered.

"That may be true — I did not recognize him, but his name is not unknown to me — I remember it from previous visits to England. His reputation, even among the wildest rakes and bloods, was not good."

"And you still feel compunction?"

"Perhaps," Patrick admitted with a smile, "compunction is the wrong word. I find the knowledge downright insulting that he was murdered almost under my nose." He leaned forward, his features suddenly intent. "I want very badly to know who murdered him and why. Don't you?"

Thea glanced away from that compelling gray gaze. She did want to know, but she also wanted to put the matter behind her. She had not killed Alfred. Someone else had, and she would have liked very much to pretend that it was none of her business. But she could not. The question of who had killed Alfred would always haunt her, and she was curious enough to want to know *why* he had been murdered, if only for her sister's sake.

Not quite ready to cooperate with the tall American, she swung back to stare at him, and demanded, "Why were *you* there? How do I know that you are telling me the truth? How do I know that you aren't trying to embroil me in some devious plan?"

Patrick grimaced. "Ah, now there you have me. I'm afraid that I cannot tell you. It is not my secret to reveal."

"But I'm supposed to tell you why I was there?" Thea demanded, outraged.

"Well, I would appreciate it if you did," he said, with a sudden teasing gleam in his eyes.

"I'm sure you would," she answered tartly, a faint hint of amusement creeping into her own gaze, her generous mouth almost curving in a smile.

The change in her face was remarkable, and Patrick felt as if he had been punched in the gut. She wasn't beautiful in the conventional sense — her mouth too wide, her nose a trifle long, and that jaw and chin, while enchantingly molded, far too determined for the insipid ideal that was currently the rage in England. Patrick, however, was certain that he had never seen a more fascinating creature and was positive that he had never beheld another woman who appealed to him as much as this slim doe-eyed female of notorious reputation. He shook his head as if to clear it, wondering if the blow to his head had damaged his brain.

"Is something wrong?" Thea asked, a little unnerved by his stare.

"Uh, no, I'm fine," he muttered, annoyed with himself for straying from the matter at hand. Sitting up straighter, he said, "I know you don't trust me — you have no reason to trust me, but whether you like it or not, we're in this together. Someone else knows that we were both at that house tonight. Now whether the murderer was working with Hirst and they had a falling out, I don't know. I do know that I most sincerely need your help. Can't we please work together on this?"

It suddenly dawned on Thea that he really was a very attractive man, his skin much darker than the average Londoner's, his thick raven hair neatly tied at the back of his neck with black-silk ribbon. His features were finely honed, as if someone had taken a block of granite and carefully and elegantly chiseled the high brow and cheekbones, the sleekly arrogant nose, and the long, mocking mouth. He was, she admitted with a thump in her chest, very handsome. Too handsome, with that wicked-angel face and broad-shouldered, slim-hipped powerful body — oh, she had noticed, she'd just tried not to think about it. He was far, far too handsome. Far too confident and charming. And probably not to be trusted, she thought bitterly, even as she felt her will weakening. Not because of his masculine attributes, she reminded herself fiercely, but because she was scared, tired, and couldn't see much point in maintaining her aloof position. Too much of what he stated was true. It made sense that they work together — even if she didn't trust him.

She sank down on the sofa beside him, and asked warily, "What do you want to know?"

"Why you were there tonight."

Sighing, she said, "He'd sent me a note, requesting that I meet him there alone." She glanced ruefully at Patrick. "He needed money — he always did. He'd made serious inroads into my sister's fortune and wanted me to tow him from the River Tick again." She made a face. "I knew from the beginning that he was a fortune hunter, but Edwina, my sister, would hear nothing bad about him. She was," she said cynically, "convinced she was madly in love with him and she would do nothing but marry him."

"From your tone, I gather you do not think highly either of the married state or love."

She sent him a sardonic look that sat oddly on that elfin face. "Mr. Blackburne, if you know my reputation, then you know that I have good reason to doubt protestations of love." A bleak expression crossed her features. "Because I once believed a charming scoundrel's sweet words, I ruined myself and my brother died. As for marriage — I am sure that it is possible for there to be a 'good' marriage, I just have seen few of them. Edwina's to Hirst was certainly not a good marriage. *She* may have thought so once, but I have spent too many evenings with her crying her heart out to me because he had been unfaithful to her *again* to believe that she still feels the same. Equally unforgivable, I know for a fact that his gambling and spendthrift habits have brought her to the brink of ruin. Her fortune was not princely, but it was certainly a comfortable one — one that should have, if managed correctly, been more than adequate for both of them to enjoy a pleasant life with few worries."

He nodded, astonished at how deeply her

words touched him and by how much he would have liked to argue in favor of love and marriage with her. Not very many months ago he would have toasted and heartily applauded her attitude. But having seen the love that existed between his friend Tony Daggett and Tony's wife, Arabella, having observed firsthand the happiness their marriage gave them, he'd begun to question his long-held aversion toward love and marriage.

"I see," he said, irritably pushing aside his rambling thoughts. "If it was only money he was after, why didn't he simply come to your house and ask for it? That would seem the logical thing to do."

She smiled thinly. "Several months ago, when I last rescued them from their embarrassments, there was a rather, er, acrimonious exchange. I had not spoken to either one of them since that time. I had also refused Hirst entrance to my home — he knew he would be denied my presence."

"You wouldn't let him into your house, yet you went and met him under such clandestine circumstances?"

Thea looked away, thinking of how much simpler life would be if she had given in to her first impulse and tossed Hirst's note away. Reluctantly, she admitted, "I know it sounds specious, but at the time, I felt it best to go ahead and meet him and find out precisely what it was that he wanted." Wryly, she added, "It seemed an easy solution — I knew that if I did not meet with him, he would continue to importune me — embarrassingly so. It may not make sense to you, but I just wanted to meet him and be done with it."

"And that was all he wanted? Simply money? Wouldn't he have stood a better chance for success to have sent your sister to ask for it? I gather you are fond of her."

"Oh, yes. He's known all along that I seldom deny Edwina anything. In fact, tonight, he admitted that one of the reasons he married her was because he'd figured that not only would he have her fortune to dally with, but that mine would always be there for a reserve." She smiled bitterly. "And to a certain extent he was right — I have expended great sums on them these past few years. And, of course, both of them swore each time it would be the last. But my patience had run out and I knew, painful though it would be, that the only way to help Edwina to see him for what he was, was to let her bear the consequences of her own actions. I know that sounds pompous and heartless, but I was at my wits' end. I could not allow him to run through my fortune, too." Her face hardened. "And he would have, if I'd been fool enough to let him."

Patrick frowned. "He said nothing else? Except to demand money from you? Nothing that would point to him being in danger?"

Thea started. Her gaze flew to his. "Oh. I had forgotten. He *did* say something about being in danger, about Edwina being a widow if he did not pay someone seventeen thousand pounds." Her forehead wrinkled as she tried to recall that conversation. "It was, I think, a long-standing debt. I believe from what he said, that he had borrowed the original amount from moneylenders, and that their charges and fees had caused the debt to soar astronomically." Her voice dropped. "Do you think that they killed him?"

"I don't know," Patrick admitted. "And I'm inclined to think not — moneylenders are in the business of making money, and killing Hirst would not be good for business. Beating him severely or breaking a limb or two would be their tactic to bring home the point that it wouldn't be wise not to pay them, but to kill him . . . I don't think so." He shrugged. "But anything is possible. Perhaps someone wanted to send a message to others of Hirst's ilk who are being laggard in paying. I don't know."

It occurred to Patrick that Hirst's death might have nothing to do with whoever was blackmailing his mother. It could have been, he thought grimly, a coincidence that Hirst had chosen the same spot chosen by the blackmailer to meet with Thea. From the agent he understood that the house on Curzon Street had been on the market for months; it was possible that half of London knew that it was unoccupied. Getting a key would be a simple matter. It could have been just chance that had brought him and Thea to the same address tonight. But he didn't think so. It was too much of a coincidence. So did that mean that Hirst was involved with the blackmailing scheme? That he had a partner and that Hirst's partner had murdered him? But why? A falling-out? Perhaps.

He slanted a glance at Thea, struck again at how vulnerable she looked. Nothing like a woman who had "notorious" attached to her name. He could think of far more appropriate words to describe her, he thought, words like *appealing*, *enchanting*, and *desirable*. Oh, yes, he admitted, as his eyes drifted to her generous mouth, *desirable* would be at the top of his list, very, *very* desirable.

Feeling his gaze upon her, Thea looked up, and their eyes met and held. She could not look away from his intent stare, her heart beginning to thump in thick, painful strokes.

Sexual awareness crackled in the air between them, both of them physically conscious of the other in a way that had been absent only seconds before. Thea was stunned by the powerful emotions that burst through her, terrified of their force and import. She could not, she thought, horrified, be *attracted* to this man. After Hawley, she had sworn that she would never allow herself to feel anything approaching the heedless excitement and heady wonder that had marked her first disastrous foray into love. And yet there was something about Patrick Blackburne. . . .

Leaping to her feet, Thea stammered, "Um, as I m-m-mentioned earlier, it is v-v-very late. I suggest that we discuss this matter further after we have both had a chance to think about it."

Patrick knew a skittish filly when he saw one, and it was obvious, whatever was happening between them, that the young lady viewed the situation with as much enthusiasm as she would a descending horde of wild Indians. Smiling wryly, he rose to his feet.

"Of course, you are right. Since tonight's events are to remain secret between us, shall I arrange a public meeting for us?"

"Y-y-yes, that would be much better," Thea said with relief. He seemed very big and intimidating as he stood in front of her. Vibrantly aware now of him as an extremely virile, attractive male animal, she wanted him gone. Somewhere far away from her until she could gather her unruly thoughts.

He bowed with exquisite grace. "Very well then. I shall take my leave."

Patrick reached for her hand, intending merely to drop a polite kiss upon it, but the instant his fingers closed around hers, he felt as if he had grasped a bolt of lightning. His very skin seemed to sizzle, and when he brushed his lips across her flesh, he was positive that his lips came away seared.

Thea snatched her hand away from him, and from the wide-eyed expression in that dark gaze, Patrick knew she had felt something very similar. Shaken, they stared at each other speechless and then, as if waking from a trance, Patrick blinked, and muttered, "Good evening. I shall look forward to meeting with you again."

Thea nodded, certain that if she tried to speak, she would only babble utter nonsense. Once the door closed behind him, she sank down onto the sofa, staring blindly into space.

What had happened between them at the

end? It had been, she thought dizzily, as if she had been swept up in a thunderstorm and dazzled by too-close contact with the raw power of lightning. She shivered, her skin still tingling where his lips had brushed against her hand. It was, she decided, a most exciting and pleasant feeling. And she very much feared that the feeling could become addictive.

The sound of the opening of the door brought her gaze in that direction, and she smiled as Modesty entered the room.

"I kept away as long as I could," Modesty said. A faint blush bloomed in her cheeks. "And like some silly housemaid, I'll admit that I peeked over the banister at him when he left." She raised a brow. "He is a very handsome man, isn't he? Who was he? And what did he want?"

Thea quickly explained the situation to Modesty. Her eyes glowing with relief, Modesty sat down beside Thea, and, squeezing her hand, said, "Oh, thank goodness! I felt certain that you could not have killed Hirst, but you seemed so positive that I am afraid I allowed myself to be carried along in your wake." She beamed at Thea. "Isn't it wonderful? *You* did not kill him."

"Somebody did," Thea replied dryly.

"Well, yes, and it really is too bad, but none of our concern, now is it?"

Thea made a face. "That was the attitude that I initially took, but Mr. Blackburne convinced me that I was wrong to feel that way." She glanced at her cousin. "Don't you want to know who killed Hirst and why?"

Modesty sighed, and her lower lip twitched. "I suppose so. And I suppose for Edwina's sake we should want to know the truth. She is going to take his death hard — especially the manner of it, and unless the murderer is unmasked, she is always going to wonder who murdered him and why. And I suspect that those questions will, no doubt, bedevil us, too."

"So you don't think I was wrong in agreeing to help Mr. Blackburne?"

"No, although I have to confess I can't see that you are going to be much help to him. You told him everything you know — which we can't say for him." Frowning, Modesty asked, "He never said what business had taken him there tonight?"

Thea shook her head. "No."

"Well, that doesn't seem like a very fair partnership, does it? Perhaps when you next meet with him he will be more forthcoming."

Thea shrugged her shoulders. "Perhaps." A huge yawn suddenly overtook her.

Modesty rose to her feet. "Come along

now. In bed with you — you've had a very stressful night to say the least, and tomorrow will be even worse, once news of Hirst's death is brought to Edwina."

"I wonder if she will turn to us," Thea mused. "She might even be more hostile toward us with Hirst dead than she was when he was alive." Thea bit her lip. "She might even blame me for his death. Not even knowing the part I played tonight, I'm afraid that she will feel that if I had helped them financially, he wouldn't have been at the Curzon Street house and consequently wouldn't have been murdered." Slowly climbing the stairs, she smiled bitterly. "And she'd be perfectly correct. If I hadn't told them I was cutting them loose, they would have come to me and, eventually, I would have relented and given them money again and Alfred wouldn't have been at that house tonight."

"You don't know that," Modesty said firmly, her blue eyes glinting. "Alfred Hirst was a greedy man. He still might have tried to bleed you for more money. And how," she asked, as they reached the upper floor, "do you know that you were the *only* one he was trying to raise money from? He might have been putting the touch on any number of individuals."

Thea looked startled. "Oh! I hadn't thought of that."

"Well, you should have! Now get into your bed and no more beating yourself up for something that wasn't your fault. Hirst," Modesty said firmly, "was a scoundrel, and I, for one, am not the least bit saddened that he is dead."

Patrick wasn't saddened either, but neither was he pleased. Hirst's death only complicated the issue for him. Complicated it in ways that he had not foreseen. And Thea Garrett was very definitely a complication.

Having reached his own house and having dismissed his butler, Patrick had gone upstairs to his rooms. After tossing aside his dark gray coat, he poured himself a brandy from the tray of refreshments that had been left for him and wandered around his bedroom, a frown wrinkling his brow as he considered those last moments with Thea Garrett.

It had been a very long time, if ever, since he could remember a woman arousing the emotions within him that he had felt tonight. Some of them were more than familiar — desire certainly. She was, after all, a very attractive young woman, but it wasn't *just* desire that she awoke in him, and that had him worried. He was conscious of a feeling of protectiveness and a simmering anger against the man who had made her so wary of love. Those emotions were bad enough, but what really had him frowning was the fact that she was smack in the middle of a murder that might be connected to whoever was blackmailing his mother.

Patrick took a long fortifying swallow of the brandy, thinking over what he was going to tell his mother tomorrow. Probably, he thought with a faint smile, as little as possible. Certainly nothing about his own ignominious part in the evening's events. And definitely nothing about Hirst's murder — there was no need to alarm her. And he definitely wasn't about to mention Thea Garrett's presence. His mouth twisted. Again, no reason to alarm his mother, and she would be, he admitted, very alarmed if she even suspected how attracted her only child was to a young woman with a tarnished reputation.

Patrick wondered about that reputation. After seeing Thea in Hyde Park, the first moment he and Nigel were private, he'd gotten all the ugly details about her past. And some current gossip, such as the fact that, while she didn't exactly go out of her way to cause gossip, she didn't care a fig what people said about her.

"You remember old Rivers?" Nigel had asked, naming a wealthy, infamous roué, notorious for his seduction of the unwary. When Patrick had nodded, Nigel had gone on, "She befuddled him so badly that he actually offered for her. She laughed in his face and tossed him out on his ear." Nigel looked thoughtful. "Funny thing though — Lord Gale wasn't of that ilk — nice young man, wealthy, handsome, suitable, and I can't say that I ever heard of her throwing out any lures to him. Tried to discourage him from what I saw, but he was totally enthralled — wouldn't take no for an answer. Seems to me that there was some gossip that she was the one who got his family to convince him to leave London — and her. Don't know if I believe it or not, but it's possible. I do know that she seems to relish sending some pretty shameless libertines skulking away with a flea in their ear."

A rueful smile on his face, Patrick had said, "Well, I have to confess to a bit of admiration for her tactics. Few people would dare to show their faces in polite society after the sort of scandal she endured — and she not only shows it, but doesn't seem to give a damn what people think. And as for her seeming to relish the discomfort of some shameless libertine, who can blame her after what happened? I certainly do not."

Bending a sharp eye on Patrick, Nigel had added, "You best be careful — she has slipped under the guard of some of the most marriage-wary fellows that I know. Take care you ain't among 'em."

Patrick had looked startled. "Good God, you don't think that I would fall under her spell, do you?"

Nigel had smiled and looked wise. "One never knows, my friend, one never knows."

Recalling Nigel's words, Patrick's frown grew blacker, and, tearing his thoughts away from Thea Garrett, he began to consider just what he was going to tell his mother in the morning. That subject kept his mind occupied until he was in bed. Then, as if determined to ruin what was left of the night, Thea's fairy features loomed up in front of him. To his disgust, he found himself making excuses for her and wanting fiercely to believe that she was precisely what she appeared to be; a charming damsel he very much wanted to know more intimately. Extremely intimately.

The visit with Lady Caldecott went well the next morning. She was disappointed that he had little to report and thought it strange that the blackmailer had failed to appear.

Seated across from her, nattily attired in a dark blue coat of superfine and yellow nankeen breeches, Patrick murmured, "As I mentioned, it could have been simply a ploy on his part to see precisely what you would do. While I did not see him, I am sure he knows that I came in your stead. That has, no doubt, given him food for thought."

"Well, yes," his mother said uncertainly, looking anxious. "I'm sure that it has. You don't think that your presence might have annoyed him?"

Patrick shrugged. "Anything is possible. I only know that there was no one at the house besides myself — and I waited for nearly an hour after the appointed time and no one appeared." Inwardly Patrick winced; lying to one's mother, even as an adult and for her own good, wasn't easy. He soothed his conscience by telling himself that while it was an outright lie that no one else had been at the house, he *had* waited for over an hour. What he hadn't mentioned was that he had been unconscious for most of that time. He stood up. "Until you hear from him again, there is little I can do about your blackmailer but follow up on the information I learned from Nigel. Nigel said that his aunt Levina died in January and that it was her family, the Ellsworths, who took most of her private papers and belongings away. I shall start with them."

"Ellsworth?" murmured a new voice. "Do we actually know someone by that name, dear?"

Alice stiffened. Flashing a glance at her son, she turned and smiled warmly at the tall, slender gentleman who had quietly entered the room. Lord Caldecott sent a benign smile at his stepson, and, settling himself down languidly on the sofa beside his wife, remarked, "I thought that I knew all of your friends, my love, but I don't recall their name being among them. Surely it is not that encroaching family that poor Lord Talbot married into? The eldest daughter as I recall." He frowned slightly. "If it is the same family, I think one of the sons married the daughter of Lord Bettison — gaming debts you know."

Lord Caldecott had, in his youth, been undisputed leader of the fashionable set, and signs of this could still be seen in the exquisite arrangement of the Brussels lace at his throat and wrists and the impeccable cut of his pale blue jacket and elegant fit of his dove gray breeches. Unlike many of his friends, at the age of sixty-two, he owed his full head of silver locks to no artifice — every carefully arranged hair on his head was his own. He was, even at his age, a handsome man. Beneath slim brows, his eyes were an icy blue and his features patrician. Lord Caldecott professed to be a brainless fop, but those who knew him well knew he was precisely the opposite.

Patrick knew him to possess a sharp intellect, and he was uneasy at Lord Caldecott's entrance into the scene. Smiling, Patrick bowed, and murmured, "Good morning, my lord. It is a pleasure to see you."

Lord Caldecott looked abstracted. "Yes, but didn't we just see you earlier this week, my dear boy?"

"Surely, you cannot object if my son comes frequently to call upon me?" Alice queried.

Lord Caldecott smiled sweetly and patted her hand. "Why of course not, my love — you know I would deny you nothing that would make you happy. I was merely trying to remember if it had been earlier this week that I had seen your son."

Lord Caldecott lifted the quizzing glass that hung around his neck by a white-silk ribbon. Looking sleepily at Patrick, he asked, "Were you leaving, dear boy? Going to find those, ah, Ellsworth people, weren't you? Some family friends, perhaps?"

"Not exactly," Alice said hastily, and went

on to babble about Levina Ellsworth, who had married into the Embry family, having been an acquaintance of hers. "I only recently heard that she died, and Patrick was telling me that her nieces and nephews, the Ellsworths, were her heirs." She glanced helplessly at Patrick. "Wasn't that it, my dear?"

"Yes, precisely," Patrick drawled, wondering just how much his esteemed stepfather had overheard and what he knew about the blackmailing of Lady Caldecott. He met Lord Caldecott's limpid blue stare and felt a stirring of unease. Despite his vague air, the man never missed a trick. So did he know about the blackmailing? And if he did, why hadn't he said something to his wife? Secrets of his own? Secrets that had a bearing on the blackmailing of his wife? Patrick's eyes hardened. Was it conceivable that Caldecott was brazen and desperate enough to blackmail his own wife?

Taking his leave a few minutes later, Patrick decided that before he did anything else, he was going to institute a discreet inquiry into the finances of Lord Caldecott. His face grew grim. The last thing he would want to do was destroy his mother's marriage. So what was he going to do if suspicion pointed at her husband?

Chapter Five

Thea spent a restless night. She woke Thursday morning tired and listless. The previous night's events didn't engender any desire to leap from bed and greet the day. Eventually she did rouse herself and, after a light breakfast of coffee and toast in her room, she descended the stairs as the tall clock in the foyer rang out the half hour. She glanced at it, startled to see that it was already eleven-thirty.

It took Thea only a few minutes to find Modesty. She was standing before an arrangement of late-blooming lilies and roses, staring at the flowers. She glanced over her shoulder at Thea's entrance, and said, "Well, this is probably the last of them until next year. I shall miss having their sweet scent in the air."

Thea sent her a perfunctory smile and walked around the handsome room before stopping to stare out of one of the long narrow windows that faced the street. She stood there for several minutes, not really seeing the horses and carriages that clattered past the house.

Wandering over to one of the sofas upholstered in a fine straw silk, she sank down. She looked at Modesty, who had seated herself a moment before in a dainty channel-backed chair near the sofa.

"What are we going to do?" Thea asked, her expression troubled.

"There is nothing that we can do for the moment," Modesty replied. "Until we receive word of his death, there is nothing that we can do but wait."

Thea jumped up and took several strides around the room. "I have never been very good at waiting — especially not for something like this! It is like waiting for the sky to fall."

"Surely not that dramatic, my dear."

Thea sighed. "Probably not. It is just that I feel so helpless. I cannot even go to Edwina and be there to offer her comfort when she learns that he is dead." She glanced back at Modesty. "She will come to us, won't she? You don't think she will think that I would turn my back on her at a time like this? Perhaps I should have a note delivered indicating that I wish to end this silly estrangement between us?"

"Absolutely not!" At Thea's mulish expression, Modesty said, "Don't you see how suspicious that would look? After months of estrangement, you suddenly write her on the very day she receives the news that her husband has been murdered. It simply will not do."

"Oh, I know you are right, it is just that I cannot bear doing *nothing!*"

"If you had done nothing in the first place," Modesty said dryly, "you wouldn't be in this position."

Thea made a face. "You're absolutely right about that, too, and believe me, that thought has crossed my mind."

"So," Modesty said, deliberately bright, "are we going to Lady Hilliard's ball tonight? We did send our acceptances."

Thea looked aghast. "Modesty! We cannot go to a ball with Edwina's husband newly dead."

"But we don't know that he is, dear," Modesty said gently. "And until we do, we must go on as we would normally. Which means attending a ball for which we have already written our acceptance."

"Must you always be right?" Thea asked, half-exasperated, half-mocking.

Modesty smiled. "Well, I do try, my dear, I do try."

Thea laughed reluctantly and made an effort to talk of something else. She succeeded fairly well, and on the surface no one would have guessed that anything more than the Hilliard ball was on her mind. But inwardly, she was braced for a blow. As the day went on, she started at every sound, and whenever Tillman entered the room she turned an anxious face his way, convinced that he came to tell her that Edwina had arrived with the devastating news that her husband had been murdered. By the time she had gone upstairs to dress for the ball, her head was aching, and her stomach was frozen into a knot.

Why had they heard nothing? she wondered. Surely Hirst's body had been found by now and Edwina apprised of that grisly fact? Was the estrangement so deep between them that her sister didn't feel that she could come to her?

Anxious, uncertain, and dreading the evening ahead, Thea descended the stairs once more, hardly aware of the bell-skirted pale yellow silk gown her maid, the ever-faithful Maggie Brown, had helped her to put on. The gown had tiny puffed sleeves, and the rounded low-cut bodice was edged with a profusion of delicate lace. Maggie had also arranged Thea's gleaming black hair into a saucy topknot of curls that begged to be tugged loose by a masculine hand. A few wispy curls framed her fairy features, and no one looking at her, seeing the speaking dark eyes and rosy mouth, would ever guess of the turmoil hidden behind the charming façade.

Modesty was also handsomely garbed. Her gown was far less daring but obviously made by a skilled hand and of a rich plum shot silk. A black-silk shawl was draped around her shoulders, and a necklace of small but fine pearls adorned her neck. Her thick, gray-streaked hair had been decorously arranged in a gold-netted chignon at the nape of her neck, and she looked precisely what she was — a fashionable older woman of independent means.

The ball was every bit as dreadful as Thea had feared. As she laughed and chatted with friends and relatives, she tried not to think of Hirst's body lying on the floor of the Curzon Street house or her sister's pain upon learning of his death. As far as Thea was concerned he had been a wretched man and she could not regret his death — only the manner of it. But Edwina, she reminded herself unhappily, had loved him, and her heart ached for her sister.

The Hilliard ball was very successful. The magnificent ballroom had been decorated with pale yellow roses and waxy, white gardenias grown in the greenhouses of the

Hilliard country estate, the scent of the gardenias perfuming the entire room. The company was all the first stare; the clothing worn by the guests was an ever-changing sea of gorgeous silks and satins, the ladies glowing in the pale rose, blue, and cream shades of their gowns. The gentlemen were handsomely attired too, with their carefully tied white cravats and cutaway dress coats of embroidered silk in hues of burgundy, dark blue, and dark gray. Pale, tight-fitting breeches revealed many a shapely masculine leg — or not, as the case might be. The hired musicians played wonderfully, and liveried servants in black bustled about with enormous silver trays of refreshments. To drink there was lemonade, punch, port, and a vast array of wines, and to nibble upon there were small pastries filled with shrimp, chicken, and veal and crystal bowls full of bonbons and dainty almond and lemon tartlets.

But Thea could have been standing in the middle of a dung heap for all the pleasure the sights, sounds, and scents gave her. As far as she was concerned, the evening was simply to be endured; she was merely marking time until she and Modesty could take their leave.

Upon their arrival, Modesty had sought

out several older matrons and widows of her acquaintance and, having been greeted with happy enthusiasm, was settled in their midst. Thea had no doubt that she was passing away the evening gossiping, smiling, and observing the amusing antics of the younger guests with her many friends. Thea had friends, too, and she usually enjoyed herself, talking and laughing with several young, dashing matrons and a couple of equally young, but decidedly sophisticated, widows.

Despite the decade-old scandal and the gossip and rumor that swirled in her wake, she was, these days, welcomed in most houses of the ton. But Thea never quite forgot that she owed her return to the reluctant bosom of society to her family — they had worked unceasingly on her behalf to help her regain a measure of acceptance. She had been fortunate to be related by blood or marriage to two barons, a countess, and a duke, as well as possessing a fortune of her own; all of which had made her partial redemption possible.

Of course, she was well aware that she had not been totally absolved of her crimes, and there were people who still oh so very politely avoided her company. Innocent young ladies and eligible young men had always been, and still were, carefully kept from her vicinity. When she became aware of what was going on, those actions used to hurt her, but no longer. The stratagems employed by some parents to keep their innocent little doves and pups from coming under her wicked spell now brought a wry smile to her face. Occasionally, goaded by an imp of mischief, under the very noses of those helpless guardians, she would deliberately charm members of this protected and coddled set. But her conscience would all too soon make itself felt, and she would relieve the anguish in the parental breasts by gently and swiftly ending the tête-à-tête before any harm was done. She was never deliberately cruel.

Thea had managed to pass the evening well enough. She had danced a few of the country dances with her cousin, John, and a couple of his friends, and had spent part of the evening laughing with other friends and acquaintances. The ball was already half-over when a particular friend of hers, Lady Elizabeth Roland, came up to her.

Lisbeth, as Lady Roland had insisted that Thea call her moments after they had first met three years ago, looked nothing like one would expect a widow of some years' standing to look. A year older than Thea, she was a tall, stately creature with laughing sea-green eyes and a mass of riotous silvery-fair hair. Lady Roland was considered very dashing by many of the older, stuffier members of the ton, which of course had instantly endeared her to Thea. They had spent many a pleasurable hour together thinking up horrid fates for the top-loftiest members of society and laughing at the foibles of those who considered themselves leaders of fashion. Both were reckless and had little respect for convention. Theirs had been an instant and natural affinity, both of them considered "not quite the thing" and both having enough family connections and fortune to thumb their pretty little noses at all who looked at them askance.

Thea had just sent John and his friends on their way and was thinking of finding Modesty to beat a retreat for home, when Lisbeth came up to her.

Flouting convention, Lisbeth was wearing a lovely gown in a brilliant shade of emerald green. The silk skirt was so narrowly fashioned that it clung to her long legs, and the bodice was cut daringly low and revealed a tempting amount of her magnificent bosom. Lisbeth had no compunction about shocking society.

The sea-green eyes were sparkling, the silvery hair was pulled back into an artful cascade of curls, and a mocking smile was on her generous mouth when she swam up to Thea's side. They exchanged greetings and Lisbeth took a long look at her friend.

Affectionately pinching Thea's chin, she asked, "What is the matter, pet? You look positively hagged tonight. Don't tell me that that wretched brother-in-law of yours has been causing trouble again."

Thea nearly jumped out of her skin, and only by the greatest presence of mind did she prevent herself from telling Lisbeth how very right she was. Forcing a smile, she glanced at Lisbeth and muttered, "I think I have a headache. I was just on the point of going to look for Modesty when you appeared. Are you having a good time?"

"Hmm. Probably. I'm almost positive that with this gown I've managed to offend at least two old pussies and given them enough scandal broth to keep them happy for weeks," Lisbeth replied, those intelligent green eyes not moving from Thea's face. She gave Thea's arm a little shake. "And you are not going to put me off that easily. I know you too well. Something is wrong. What is it?"

Thea smiled at her. "Nothing. Really. I am just not feeling quite the thing tonight.

Nothing for you to worry about."

"And why don't I believe you?"

"Because you are a naturally nasty, suspicious woman?" Thea asked sweetly, amusement glimmering in her eyes.

"Hmm, there is that," Lisbeth readily agreed, an enchanting little dimple appearing in one cheek as she smiled at Thea.

Apparently abandoning the present topic, Lisbeth sent a glance around the handsome room. "Lady Hilliard is to be complimented on managing to have such a large turnout considering how many families did not return to London this fall for the Little Season." She looked at Thea. "Are you and Modesty going to remain in London? Or are you going to Halsted House for the winter?"

Thinking of Edwina and the mourning period Hirst's death would require, Thea said, "We shall probably go to Halsted House. In fact, I think we may be leaving shortly."

"Aren't your plans rather sudden? I thought you intended to remain in the city until the first of November?"

Thea shrugged. "I find that London has begun to pall for me. I shall look forward to being in the country once more."

Lisbeth gave a vague reply, her restless gaze suddenly stopping. "Oh, my," she purred, "I wonder who that devilishly handsome gentleman is? I don't recall seeing him before."

Thea glanced in the direction of Lisbeth's gaze, her heart leaping as she caught sight of Patrick Blackburne. His mother, Lady Caldecott, was at his side, and it was obvious that they were heading toward her and Lisbeth.

Lady Caldecott, looking none too pleased after greeting both women, said stiffly, "May I present to you my son, Patrick Blackburne. He is visiting from America."

Introductions were made, and Thea had to admire Patrick's adroitness in choosing such a very public arena for their supposed first meeting. She also could not help admitting that he looked very handsome in evening dress. His coat was of a rich burgundy silk, his face very dark and riveting above his dazzling white, discreetly tied cravat. His breeches were of cream silk and fit his long legs admirably. But then he had, Thea admitted reluctantly, admirable thighs and calves.

Lisbeth certainly thought so, the gaze she fixed on him almost laughable in its blatant appraisal. She had all but undressed him with her green eyes, and Thea was surprised at the jolt of jealousy that flashed through her.

Uncomfortable with her thoughts, Thea put on a smile, and asked brightly, "And how are you enjoying your visit to England so far, Mr. Blackburne?"

A mocking gleam in his gray eyes, Patrick replied gravely, "It has had its, ah, interesting moments — not at all what I expected."

"And what," fairly crooned Lisbeth, "did you expect?"

Patrick glanced at her, amusement quirking his lips. "Certainly not what I have found." His gaze slid back to Thea's face, and he said softly, "Definitely not what I expected."

Lady Caldecott almost snorted, but spying an acquaintance, she said, "If you will excuse me, I see Lady Blanchard and wish to speak with her for a few minutes."

Patrick was hardly aware of his mother's departure, his gray eyes taking in with pleasure the picture that Thea presented. Last night he had thought her attractive, but tonight . . . Tonight she was dazzling in her yellow-silk gown, and he was conscious suddenly of a stirring of something more than passing interest.

Lisbeth looked from one face to the other and grinned to herself. *Well, well. Who would have thought it?* She didn't know precisely what was going on, but it was obvious, to her at least, that there was something at work between Thea and the intriguing Mr. Blackburne. Any thoughts she might have had for the handsome American promptly vanished. Lisbeth did not believe in poaching, and it was clear, for the first time in her memory, that Thea regarded the gentleman with something more than her usual contempt.

Deciding that she was *de trop*, she murmured a polite good-bye and glided away. Neither Thea nor Patrick seemed to be aware that she had departed.

His gaze fixed on Thea's face, Patrick said, "You look very beautiful tonight." He hesitated, then asked, "You have heard nothing? By your presence here tonight, I presume that nothing has been discovered."

He began to urge her toward the edge of the room, and a second later, they had stepped out onto the terrace. It was cooler out there, the black sky brilliant with silvery stars. A few couples could be seen wandering down the lanternlit walkways of the small London garden. The terrace was relatively private and nearly deserted except for two gentlemen smoking cigars at the far side.

"You presume correctly," Thea said in a

low voice, vividly conscious of Patrick's warm skin beneath her hand, which lay on his arm as he walked by her side. "It is possible that my sister has been notified and has chosen not to tell me, but I cannot believe that she would not come to me in the face of such a tragedy."

"Since I don't know the young lady, I cannot comment." He sighed. "Until his death is made public we can do little but wait."

Thea's face turned up to his. "Do you think that once his death is known that we will learn something new?"

They had stopped strolling and were standing in the deep shadows at the far side of the terrace. The cigar-smoking gentlemen had returned inside, and there was no one else in sight.

Becoming aware of how isolated they were, though the laughter and sounds of the ball could be heard coming through the thrown-wide French doors that led to the terrace, Thea was suddenly nervous. The fact that she found Patrick attractive made the situation all the more unnerving.

Some of her nervousness must have communicated itself to Patrick. A hint of amusement in his voice, he said, "I promise that I shall not pounce upon you. And if it is your reputation you are worried about, I assure you that it is perfectly permissible for us to converse quietly here together — at least for a few minutes."

In the shadows, Thea flushed. "Perhaps with another woman such would be the case, but you have forgotten that I am the 'notorious' Thea Garrett." She glanced at him from beneath her lashes. "You asked your mother to introduce us, didn't you? And she didn't want to, did she?"

Patrick grinned, his white teeth flashing in the darkness. "No, she was not happy about my request. But then, she has just about given up the notion of ever seeing me married, and the fact that I expressed an interest in *any* young woman won her over."

Thea flushed again. Stiffly, she asked, "And did you tell her that you were 'interested' in me?"

"Not exactly. I merely mentioned that I wished to know who the ravishing creature in the yellow gown was. The rest was simple."

Even knowing that he had had to give his mother some reason for their introduction, Thea felt a wash of pleasure at his words. Did he think she was ravishing? Telling herself not to be a silly goose, she wrenched her thoughts away from such a foolish path.

Patrick startled her by lifting her chin with a firm hand. Staring down into her wary features, he said softly, "And you are, you know. Ravishing. In fact, too ravishing for your own good."

She looked up at him, her breathing suddenly constricted. "Wh-what do you mean?" she managed, her eyes very wide and wondering.

His head dipped. Against her trembling lips, he muttered, "Why, only that any man of good red blood could not resist you."

He kissed her. His mouth was warm and soft against hers, the softness surprising her, making her want to melt into that very softness. Gently that mocking mouth teased hers, arousing emotions and sensations she barely remembered. Lost in the awakening wonder of the moment, conscious only of the seductive pressure of his lips, she was hardly aware of his arms closing around her. It wasn't until she felt herself swept next to his muscled length that she realized several disturbing things at once. First of all, that he had been kissing her a very long time; secondly, that she was enjoying it far too much; and thirdly, that if the rather large bulge that jutted so stiffly near her thighs was anything to go by, Mr. Blackburne was unmistakably and thoroughly aroused.

Most astonishing of all, she was also aroused, aware of her body in a way that she hadn't been in a very long time — if ever.

Galvanized by the knowledge of where such dalliance could lead, Thea wrenched herself away from him. Humiliated by her own weakness, angry with herself, she snapped, "I do not appreciate your attempt to seduce me. Did Nigel put you up to it? Was it a wager between you?"

His own breathing rather ragged, his lower body aching in a way he had not thought possible, Patrick fought to regain his senses. Furious with himself for his loss of control, stung by her words, Patrick snarled, "Neither Nigel nor a bloody wager had anything to do with what just happened between us — and I resent your accusation that I would stoop so low."

A cynical smile curved her mouth. "Well, you wouldn't be the first gentleman who thought to try his hand at seducing me — or had a wager on the outcome."

Innocent of such reprehensible action for probably the first time in his life, Patrick was outraged. "I have not," he said stiffly, "made wagers about young ladies since my callow youth. And I have learned and lived to regret that I ever did."

"Oh, really?"

Memories of certain rather disgraceful wagers he had made in the past flashed through his mind, including the most recent one involving an introduction to Thea herself. He grimaced. He couldn't even swear that he had never made a wager concerning her.

Suppressing a curse, he muttered, "A wager had nothing to do with what just happened between us. I warned you that you were too ravishing for your own good."

"Oh, it was *my* fault?" Thea asked incredulously.

"No, dash it, it wasn't! I merely meant that I found you much too appealing to resist." He threw her a look of resentment. "It will not," he said grimly, "happen again."

"One hopes not — not if we are to work together," Thea said serenely. His admission that he found her appealing soothed her ruffled feathers — at least it did until it occurred to her that he could simply be plying her with empty compliments. She'd heard enough of them whispered in her ear by unscrupulous gentlemen bent on seduction these past few years to last her a lifetime. Yet, despite all the reasons why she shouldn't believe that he was sincere, she wanted to believe that he had spoken the truth — a desire that she had not experienced so far. Which made him, she realized unhappily, very dangerous for her peace of mind.

Deciding to beat a retreat, Thea turned and was walking toward the opened doorway when a woman's laugh came wafting out into the darkness. She knew that laugh, and she stopped as if she had been turned to stone.

Edwina? But it couldn't be! Not even Edwina would be brash enough to attend a ball on the very day she learned of her husband's death!

Quickening her stride, she hurried inside, stopping in stunned incredulity when she spied the laughing lady. It *was* Edwina, looking absolutely delectable in a stunning gown of gossamer silk the exact sky-blue shade of her eyes. Her guinea gold hair was fashionably arranged in delicate little curls that framed her lovely features. Laughing and coyly hiding behind her painted silk fan, she was enchanting.

It was clear from the expression on the face of the young man that was by Edwina's side that she had certainly enchanted him. Watching as Edwina expertly plied her fan and fluttered her lashes at the gentleman, Thea's lips thinned. The little fool! What game did she think she was playing? Did she want to be totally ostracized by the ton?

Thea started forward, intending to hustle Edwina away from the ball in the shortest possible time, when she felt a steely grip on her arm.

"Don't," Patrick said.

"What do you mean?" Thea hissed. "It is Edwina. Hirst's wife — widow. She should not be here tonight."

He quirked a brow. "Are you positive that she knows of her husband's death? It is possible that his body has not been discovered yet — have you considered that? And if his body has not yet been discovered, how are you going to explain your knowledge of his demise, hmm?"

Thea froze. She hadn't considered that possibility, and it made far more sense than for Edwina to fly in the face of society and blithely attend a ball with her husband newly dead. Another dreadful thought crossed her mind.

Looking at Patrick, she asked uneasily, "Do you think that he is still just lying there? That no one but we know that he is dead?"

"Someone else does — the murderer, or have you forgotten that?"

Taking a deep breath, Thea muttered, "How could I? You certainly seem to take great delight in reminding me of that unpleasant fact."

Patrick smiled winningly down at her. "No, my dear, I take great delight in you — not your brother-in-law."

Flustered, Thea glanced away, her eyes unexpectedly meeting Edwina's. For a nerve-wracking moment, she thought Edwina would snub her, but with a toss of her curls, Edwina walked up to her.

The sky-blue eyes full of resentment, Edwina said, "Good evening, sister dear. Are you enjoying the ball?"

Thea mumbled a reply, all the things she had wanted to say to Edwina turning into a mass of jumbled, incoherent thoughts in her brain. Fortunately, there were introductions to be made and by the time everyone knew each other's names, Thea had her wits back in hand. At least she hoped she did. Each time she looked at Edwina she could not help thinking of Alfred's body lying on the floor of the house on Curzon Street. It was all she could do not to blurt out that horrible news.

The gentleman hovering at Edwina's side was Lord Pennington, a shy young man who had inherited his father's title eighteen months previously. Thea had seen him on the London scene the past few months, but while he had been pointed out to her, she had never been introduced to him. Since his visit to London this past spring, he had been considered a matrimonial prize of the highest order. He was wealthy, good-looking, very nice mannered, well connected and with a charming shyness that instantly endeared him to every matchmaking mama's heart; it was no wonder that his obvious fascination with Edwina Hirst was causing all manner of dark looks to be sent their way.

Unhappily aware of those looks and aware, too, of how easily Edwina's reputation could be linked to hers, Thea's one thought was to escape — and if possible take her sister with her. But when she made some comment on the fact that it was late and that she was thinking of leaving and invited Edwina to join her, she was balked.

"Oh, no," cried Edwina prettily. "It is too early to leave now." She fluttered her eyes at Lord Pennington, who blushed. "I have promised Lord Pennington the next country dance. You would not have me treat him rudely, now would you?"

Pennington stammered that he would not expect his wishes to be held above those of her sister's, but Edwina tapped him with her fan, and murmured, "Silly boy. As if I would deny myself the enjoyment of dancing with you to listen to my stuffy sister lecture me." She looked at Thea. "For that is what you will do, won't you?"

It was Thea's turn to stammer, and she was saved from sounding like a fool by Patrick's intervention. Having taken an accurate reading of the delectable Mrs. Hirst and having decided that it was Thea that needed protection and not the lovely little minx with the blue eyes, he drawled, "I don't believe that I have had the pleasure of meeting your husband, Mrs. Hirst. Is he here tonight?"

Thea's mouth nearly flew open, but by the greatest exertion of control, she managed to keep it shut. She gazed at Patrick's bland features, undecided whether to be shocked or pleased.

"No, Alfred is not here tonight. In fact, he is not even in the city." She smiled at Lord Pennington. "Actually, I don't expect him back for several days. He told me yesterday morning that he would be away for a few weeks." Demurely, she added, "I just don't know how I am to get about London without a masculine escort. I really don't like to go out, especially at night, without a gentleman at my side. So many awful things can happen to a poor woman alone."

Lord Pennington nearly fell over himself

as he stammered. "B-b-be honored t-t-to escort you until your h-h-husband returns."

"Oh, would you?" Edwina said. "It is so very kind of you to offer." Glancing at Thea, she said, "You see, I even have a proper gentleman to squire me about. There is no reason for you to worry about me."

Thea was aware of an unsisterly urge to smack Edwina's face, but she mastered it. Honing in on the only part of the conversation that interested her, she asked, "Did Hirst say where he was going?"

Edwina looked thoughtful. "Devonshire? Wiltshire? Or was it Leicestershire? Do you know, I can't remember?" Her brow furrowed. "Now let me think. Ah, I have it, before he left yesterday, just in case I needed to reach him, he wrote a note for me with his destination and the name of the people he would be staying with. Shall I find it and let you know where he was going?"

Thea would have very much liked to say yes, but caution held her tongue. The last thing she wanted was for Edwina to start wondering why she was curious about her husband's destination — especially since she and Hirst were on unfriendly terms.

"No, no, that won't be necessary," Thea said weakly. "I just wondered."

Since there was nothing else to be gained

from further conversation, and it was obvious that Edwina wished her in Coventry, Thea and Patrick wandered off in another direction. The calculating look in Edwina's eyes when she had gazed at Patrick troubled her. Edwina was a married woman. It was bad enough, Thea thought, that Edwina was flirting so shamelessly with poor Lord Pennington, but surely she wasn't considering casting her net for someone like Blackburne?

"Well, that answered one question, didn't it?" Patrick said as he walked at her side.

Thea sighed. "Indeed it did. It makes me feel queasy to think that while his wife is here laughing and enjoying herself, confident that her husband has gone somewhere in the country, he is actually lying dead in an empty house just a few streets away."

"It is strange that his body has not yet been discovered," Patrick murmured as he deftly guided Thea toward the edge of the crowd and a modicum of privacy. "I vaguely remember the house agent mentioning that they have someone look in at the place every day to make certain that nothing is amiss — rats, broken windows, house thieves, and the like. And while it is possible that a day is skipped now and then . . ." He looked thoughtful. "I wonder if . . ."

When he said nothing more, Thea looked sharply at him. "You wonder what?"

"I wonder if he is still lying there."

Thea's eyes widened. Hardly aware of the chatter and press of people around them, she turned to him, and said urgently, "He must be! He couldn't just get up and walk away."

"No, but someone could have moved his body."

"Merciful heavens, why?"

Patrick's eyes met hers. "To keep his death a secret."

Thea opened her mouth, then shut it with a snap. A determined expression on her face, she plunged into the crowd.

"Where are you going?" Patrick demanded as he kept pace with her.

"I'm going to find my cousin Miss Bradford, then she and I are going to take our leave from Lord and Lady Hilliard and go home." She threw him a challenging look. "Then I am going to the house on Curzon Street to see for myself precisely what is going on."

Chapter Six

Oblivious to their surroundings, Patrick caught her upper arm in an inescapable grip. "Are you mad?" he demanded.

"Ah. Patrick, my friend, here you are," drawled a well-known voice.

Patrick groaned. Meeting Nigel's twinkling eyes, he muttered, "Yes, as you can see, here I am."

Lifting his quizzing glass, Nigel took a long, leisurely look at Thea. "And with Miss Garrett, too, I see."

Patrick cursed the capriciousness of fate. Of all the people he did not want to meet at this particular moment, his very good friend Nigel Embry headed the list. Not only would Nigel tease him unmercifully, but he was an inveterate gossip. Before midnight half of London would know of his association with Thea.

"Yes, with Miss Garrett. Mother introduced us earlier this evening," Patrick said coolly.

"Ah."

"And what," Thea demanded, "do you mean by that?"

Patrick grinned down at her. "That, I believe, my dear, is my line." One black brow arrogantly lifted, he cast a challenging glance at his friend.

Nigel looked innocent. "Why, nothing, my friend, nothing at all." Looking beyond Patrick's shoulder, he said happily, "Here comes Paxton." He glanced at Thea. "I don't believe that you have met Blackburne's friend, Adam Paxton. It will be my pleasure to introduce you to him."

If Adam was surprised to find Thea Garrett with Patrick, he gave no sign. The light from the huge crystal chandeliers gleamed on his tawny head as he bowed politely and made the appropriate remarks. He stood as tall as Patrick; once the introductions were behind them, his golden brown eyes met Patrick's, and, from the glint in their depths, Patrick knew that he was in for a vast amount of raillery when his friend got him alone.

The four of them stood there talking for a moment, then Thea said brightly, "Well, if you gentlemen will excuse me, I must be on my way." She glanced at Patrick and Paxton. "It was pleasant to meet both you gentlemen this evening. Perhaps I shall see you again around town." When Patrick started forward, his intention to accompany her plain, she smiled even more brightly, and murmured, "Oh, no, sir. I would not take you from your friends." The smile took on an impish cast. "I am positive that you all have much to talk about. Good evening."

Having had the ground effectively cut out from beneath him, Patrick could only watch impotently as Thea sailed away. He saw her approach a well-dressed, older woman, and, a second later, both ladies were headed toward their host and hostess.

"Think that's her cousin and companion, Miss Modesty Bradford," Nigel said helpfully, when he saw the direction of Patrick's gaze. "Family had Miss Bradford come and live with Miss Garrett and her younger half sister, Edwina Northrop, after their mother died. When Edwina married Alfred Hirst, Miss Bradford stayed on with Miss Garrett."

"I know," Patrick said flatly, sending his friend a decidedly unfriendly look. A thought occurred to him. "You know nearly everyone in society," he said slowly. "Did, er, do you know Hirst?"

Paxton snorted. "Of course he does. We all do. Hirst hangs around on the edges of our group. Puffs himself up to be a blood-and-guts goer, but doesn't have the bottom to be a true sporting fellow — whether the sport is gambling or horses. He's a sluggard."

"After he married the Northrop chit," Nigel added, "flashed a lot of money around, gambled heavily, but hasn't either the head or fortune for it." Nigel frowned. "Think the bloodsuckers have their hooks in him deep. Pity." Nigel looked around. "Don't see him here tonight." He raised his quizzing glass. "See his wife though. Chit is making eyes at young Pennington. Bad ton."

"And Pennington is such a green 'un, he'll no doubt be taken in by those innocent blue eyes of hers," Paxton said wryly. "If you will excuse me, I had better go rescue the young fool before he ruins himself."

Patrick stared in astonishment as Paxton's elegant form disappeared into the swirling crowd. "Why does he feel obligated to rescue Pennington?" he asked, his bewilderment obvious. Paxton was not known for his altruistic nature.

"Cousin, several times removed. Great-aunt or grandmother or some old family tabby coerced him into keeping an eye on the boy." Nigel grinned. "Has proved most amusing at times watching one of the most notorious rakes in London guiding a young innocent through the pitfalls."

"Well, if anyone should know the pitfalls, it would be Adam," Patrick replied dryly, his gaze surreptitiously following Thea's progress through the ballroom. She and Miss Bradford had just taken their leave from Lord and Lady Hilliard and were heading toward the main hall. If he could shake loose of Nigel, he could catch them before their coach was brought 'round.

"I believe that I win the wager," Nigel said with a gleam in his blue eyes. "Think you owe me five hundred pounds, my dear fellow."

"Five hundred! I don't remember an amount being named."

Nigel coughed. "Thing is, dear fellow, we didn't, but five hundred is a nice round number, don't you think?" When Patrick stared at him, Nigel smiled sweetly, and murmured, "Of course, if it is too steep for you . . ."

"Damn you!" Patrick said with a laugh. "You shall have your five hundred by morning. And now if you will excuse me?"

Thea was feeling satisfied with herself when her carriage eventually deposited her and Modesty at their town house. She had slipped right out from under the haughty nose of Mr. Patrick Blackburne and in a very few minutes she was going to discover for herself what was going on inside the Curzon Street house. With that in mind, she requested the coach to wait for her.

Modesty raised her brow at this command, but said nothing until they were inside the house. When asked about the waiting coach, Thea smiled, and Modesty had to content herself with asking about the tall, dark gentleman who had stuck so tenaciously to Thea's side during the latter part of the ball. As they ascended the staircase and entered Thea's bedroom, Thea brought her up to date, including Edwina's presence at the ball.

Modesty was not the least interested in Edwina. "So that is Patrick Blackburne, hmm?" she murmured. Sending Thea a birdlike look, she added, "My glimpse over the banister last night informed me that he was handsome, but until I saw him this evening, I didn't realize how really very handsome he is."

"As if *that* has anything to do with Alfred's murder!" Thea said crossly, ringing for Maggie. While she waited for Maggie's appearance, she yanked off her dainty satin slippers, and said, "I intend to go back to that house tonight and see Alfred's body for myself." Her lips thinned. "Or not."

"Good Gad! Are you mad? If you are seen

and recognized, it would be disastrous."

"I intend to be disguised. No one will know it is me," Thea said quickly. "Please, do not worry. I have a plan."

Modesty looked skeptical, but before she could say more, Maggie appeared.

Maggie Brown had changed little in the decade since that night when Thea had so blithely slipped out to meet Lord Randall. The brown eyes were more cautious, shrewder, the sturdy form taller, but just as sturdy, and her hair, neither brown nor blond, no longer swung wildly about her shoulders but was neatly caught in a bun at the back of her head.

Maggie had hardly entered the room before Thea said, "Didn't you tell me that when the attics at Garrett Manor were being cleaned this spring an old trunk of Tom's clothing was found?"

Not liking the sparkle in her mistress's dark eyes or the shimmer of excitement that seemed to radiate from her, Maggie said grudgingly, "Yes, there was." Speaking with the familiarity of a servant who knows her worth, she added, "If you will recall, I told you about it then — you refused to let your uncle dispose of the contents and insisted that nothing would do but that he immediately send the trunk to you in London."

Thea smiled. "Am I such a trial to you, Maggie?"

Maggie's face softened. "Now, Miss, you know the answer to that." Her eyes narrowed. "There are times, however, when you get a maggot in your brain and turn us all on our heads. I hope this is not to be one of those times." When Thea only laughed, Maggie cried, alarmed, "Miss! What sort of mischief are you up to now?"

Thea made a face. "Nothing for you to worry about. Now tell me: Where is the trunk at this very minute?"

Knowing there was no swaying Thea when she was in one of her moods, Maggie shrugged, and said, "Upstairs, in the attic — you refused to look at it, once it arrived. Shall I have one of the footmen get it for you?"

Thea nodded.

A few minutes later, the women were standing in front of a leather-bound trunk. Thea's light mood had disappeared, and Modesty had to glance away from the expression on Thea's face as she stared down at the trunk.

Thea seemed frozen, and several minutes passed before Modesty said gently, "Perhaps you have changed your mind?"

As if waking from a nightmare, Thea

started and shook her head. "No," she said. "I haven't any choice. I must know for myself what is happening in that house." After taking a deep breath, she knelt before the trunk and carefully undid the straps that held it closed.

She had thought that she was prepared for what was inside, but at the sight of a spotted waistcoat and wide-brimmed hat that she remembered Tom proudly wearing only a week before his death, her eyes grew misty. She bit her lip to hold back the sob that rose in her throat.

Blinking furiously at the tears that threatened to fall, she gently, almost reverently began to search through the trunk for the items she needed. It was a painful process, each piece of clothing bringing back memories of her brother, but as the minutes passed, an odd calm came over her. She couldn't explain it, but it was almost as if Tom stood by her side, almost as if she could hear his voice in her ears, telling her softly that it was all right, that she *should* remember the things of his life, not the manner of his death. There was, she realized, no need to cling to these physical reminders of his life — her memory of him, of their childhood and the simple delights and sibling battles they had shared, was as bright and precious as if it had only been yesterday.

It was difficult nonetheless to paw through Tom's belongings, the sight of each garment and the memories those odd pieces of clothing aroused bittersweet. Eventually, though, she found what she wanted and, taking those items out, gently shut the lid, her fingers lingering for a moment on the top of the chest.

Staring at the chest, she finally asked, "What should I do with it?"

Maggie said quietly, "My brother's youngest son would be most grateful to own such fine garments — despite their age. He is handy with his needle and hopes to become either a valet or a tailor. He would like them very much."

Thea nodded. "See that they are delivered to him."

When Maggie and the chest, hefted onto the shoulder of a brawny footman, had departed, Thea immediately began to change her ball gown for the masculine attire. Modesty helped, though her lips were pursed in disapproval.

"This is madness, you know," Modesty said, as she tied a creased black stock around Thea's neck.

The clothes smelled faintly musty, the

scent of the lavender in which they had been packed floated on the air. Although they had been neatly folded and put away carefully, there was no hiding the various creases and folds that marred the fabric, but since Thea did not intend to be closely examined by anyone, it didn't matter.

When she finally looked at herself in the cheval glass she was not displeased. The clothing was a decade out-of-date, but it would suffice. Tom had been leanly built, and the leather riding breeches fit Thea's feminine legs very nicely, especially her firm derriere. His white-linen shirt was large for Thea's slimmer build, but the waistcoat Modesty had quickly nipped in at the back hid that fact. The less-than-perfect fit of the jacket could not be disguised, but since the jacket was one Tom had worn as a stripling, it fit better than it might have. Footwear had presented a problem, but she had solved that by putting on a pair of her own riding boots.

Observing herself in the glass, Thea saw a tallish, slim youth garbed acceptably, if not in the first stare of fashion. Her ringlets had been dispensed with, and her hair had been ruthlessly pulled back into a respectable queue. After removing the unfashionable buckle on the low-crowned, wide-brimmed hat that had been on top of the clothing in the trunk and placing it on her head, she was satisfied with the picture she presented.

Turning to look at Modesty, she cocked a brow. "Well?"

Modesty snorted. "You'll do — provided no one takes a closer look."

"I don't intend for anyone to take a closer look. I intend to get into that house and out as quickly as possible."

There was one last item she planned to take with her. With Modesty on her heels, she went downstairs to the library. Walking over to the mahogany desk, she opened the bottom drawer and pulled out an old dueling pistol — it had been her father's and then her brother's.

Modesty's eyes widened, and she gasped at the sight of the pistol and the cool efficiency with which Thea examined the pistol and calmly loaded it. "Thea!" she exclaimed. "What are you thinking? If your task is so dangerous that you need to be armed, I absolutely refuse to have anything to do with this madcap plan of yours!"

Thea grinned at her, the dark eyes dancing. "It is not *precisely* dangerous — I am merely following one of Tom's precepts: play or pay." Her face hardened.

"And someone will pay if they attempt to trifle with me tonight."

Eyeing the pistol with misgiving, Modesty asked, "How well do you know how to use it?"

"Tom taught me years ago — we used to have shooting matches when we were bored," Thea said. "It has been a while, but I think that if I had to use the pistol that my aim would not cover me with shame."

The pistol safely stowed in the big inside pocket of her jacket, Thea squared her shoulders and prepared to leave the house.

Clearly unhappy with the situation, but unable to stop her headstrong young cousin from carrying out her plan, Modesty made one last attempt to dissuade her. Dogging Thea's heels, she followed her out into the main hallway and muttered, "Don't tell me that you are walking alone to Curzon Street at this time of night!"

Thea laughed. "Dear Modesty, I would never affront your sensibilities by trying anything so outrageous. I had the coach wait, remember?"

"I'd rather you did walk alone tonight than for you to do what you plan," Modesty said testily.

Kissing her cousin on the cheek, Thea said, "Stop fretting, my dear. I shall be home before you even realize that I am gone."

Only when the coach pulled to a stop several houses down from her destination did Thea question the wisdom of what she was about to do. If she were caught alone, abroad and garbed in men's clothing at this time of night, no amount of family pressure would be able to save her from complete ruin. The gossip and speculation would be horrendous. Her uncles, aunts, and any number of cousins had worked very hard to bring her a measure of redemption, and she, most desperately, did not want all their efforts to have been for naught. Creating a new scandal seemed a shabby way to repay their past kindness.

Yet she had to know what was inside that house. Was Hirst's body still lying there? Or had it been moved? If it had been moved, who had done it, when, and most importantly, why?

She had been, she admitted, too happy, and perhaps gullible, simply to take Patrick Blackburne's word for what had transpired that night. She needed to see for herself the actual state of things — and the longer she waited, the more doubts would fill her mind.

Not giving herself a chance to think further, she leaped down from the coach. Telling the driver to wait, she quickly walked the short distance to her destination.

No flickering light brightened the doorway this evening, and as she stood there, her hand prepared to grasp the door latch, it occurred to her that the door could very well be locked. Muttering to herself for not having thought farther ahead, she grasped the latch and pushed.

The door swung open. In the dim flickering light shed by the few streetlamps that lined the street, the entrance yawned like a black cavern. Uncertain whether to be pleased or frightened by the ease with which she had opened the door, Thea stood there hesitating. She did *not* want to enter that uninviting blackness.

The choice was taken from her when, out of the darkness, a powerful hand suddenly closed around the front of her jacket and yanked her inside. A hand was clasped over her mouth, and she was held tightly against a big muscular body.

The door was slammed shut with a careless shrug of her captor's shoulder, and Thea found herself in a darkened, deserted house, held captive by a stranger. Her heart banging in her chest, fright coursing through her, she feared that she was going to disgrace herself by fainting dead away.

A warm chuckle in her ear made her stiffen, and as he took his hand away from her mouth, Patrick murmured, "I didn't mean to frighten you, sweet, but I had to get you inside — the longer you dawdled about the more likely it was that someone might notice you."

"Dawdled!" Thea hissed, and brought her heel down sharply on his foot. Ignoring his yelp, she went on, "I was *not* dawdling!" Straightening the front of her jacket, she muttered, "I was merely assessing the situation."

"Forgive me," Patrick said, the thread of laughter in his voice making Thea bristle. "I thoroughly misunderstood the situation."

"I'm pleased that you find the situation so amusing," she said coldly, aware that her heart was still beating swiftly but that its rapid beat was not caused by fear. Quite the contrary: she was excited by Patrick's presence and vastly annoyed with herself for being so. The interior of the house was pitch-black, and the darkness, the knowledge that they were all alone, created a sense of intimacy that Thea found pleasurably disturbing — which bothered her all the more.

Stiffly she asked, "What are you doing

here? I thought you would still be at the ball."

"I'm sure you did," he answered, putting a hand in the small of her back and urging her through the blackness. "After I extricated myself from Nigel, I took my leave of our hosts and got here as fast as I could." The hint of laughter was back in his voice. "You didn't think I would let you have all the fun, did you?"

Ignoring him and the jumble of emotion his touch gave her, Thea said crossly, "Can't we light a candle? I cannot see my hand in front of my face."

"Certainly, if you wish to announce our presence . . . and since I doubt that is your intention, we will simply have to feel our way toward the back of the house."

His words made sense. Grumbling, with Patrick at her back, Thea fumbled her way to the room where she had first met with Hirst. The thought of tripping over Hirst's body in the dark made her stomach lurch, and she was inordinately grateful when they made it safely inside the room and Patrick had shut the door behind them.

A moment later, he had lit a candle. Holding it aloft, he glanced at her, a delighted smile curving his handsome mouth at the sight she made in her boy's garb. The gray eyes traveled leisurely down her long, shapely legs, and Thea was not certain whether she was insulted or gratified at the expression gleaming in their depths.

"You are inventive, I'll grant you that," Patrick finally said, putting down the candle on the nearby table.

"Thank you," she replied, her voice dripping with sarcasm. She looked around, frowning. One thing was instantly obvious, there was no sign of Hirst — alive or dead.

"There is no body; so is he alive or did you move his body?" she demanded, glaring at Patrick.

Patrick was frowning as he glanced carefully around the room. "I had no reason to move his body and yes, he was dead. Very dead." When Thea looked skeptical, he said, "He was lying faceup, right there in front of the desk; the scissors were in his throat."

Thea looked faintly ill. Glancing away from the spot Patrick indicated, she said, "When I left him, he was lying over there — by the doorway."

Patrick nodded. "I know. That is how I found him when I first came onto the scene. It was only after I came back down the stairs some time later that I found his body lying in front of the desk. It is apparent, that your brother-in-law must have regained his senses — no doubt while I was upstairs being knocked unconscious. And while I was unconscious, he must have come to and struggled with whoever killed him. That's the only explanation I can come up with."

Thea regarded him in the faint light of the one candle. "Rather a convenient explanation, isn't it?"

Patrick smiled, and there was something in his smile that made Thea aware of just how tall and powerful he was . . . and how very private and isolated they were. He slowly walked toward her, and only by the greatest effort was she able to keep from turning tail and running from the room. Stopping mere inches from her, he tipped up her chin with one finger.

His eyes holding hers, he said gently, "You really shouldn't antagonize me, my sweet. I am on your side, you know."

Ruffled and bitterly conscious of the leap of her pulse at his touch, she jerked her head away, and asked crossly, "How do I know that? Why should I trust you?"

He grinned, a grin that made his eyes dance and was at complete variance with his earlier expression. "Ask yourself this: If you distrust me so much, why are you here alone with me? Why didn't you scream and run for your life the instant I let you go? You can't have it both ways, sweetheart. Either you trust me or you don't." His grin vanished, and turning her face back to him, he asked, "So which is it?"

"Damn you! I have to trust you — I don't have any choice," Thea said, her dark eyes rebellious.

Satisfied with her less-than-gracious answer, Patrick let her go, and murmured, "Indeed you don't. And having settled that question, let us turn our minds to what happened here last night — in particular Hirst's body."

They spent several fruitless minutes searching the room but discovered nothing that gave them any clue or path to follow. Even a close examination of where Hirst's body had last lain revealed no sign of the terrible crime that had been committed. Thea was just as happy. Finding a patch of bloodstained rug was not high on her list of pleasant discoveries.

Flopping herself down in a decidedly unladylike fashion in one of the chairs near the desk, Thea said dispiritedly, "What I can't figure out is why move his body? What purpose does it serve?"

Patrick, his hips propped against the edge of the desk, his arms folded over his chest, regarded her with a faint smile. "Well, for one thing, it prevents discovery of the crime by the authorities. It may even be," he concluded, "that his body was moved, hidden to give the murderer time to accomplish some task that Hirst's death would prevent."

Thea shrugged. "Possibly. Edwina said that Hirst had told her, actually he left a note for her, that he would be gone to the country for a few weeks. She is not the least concerned about his whereabouts."

"Which might not be a bad thing. Until we know more, it is probably just as well that as few people as possible are asking questions about the whereabouts of Mr. Hirst."

Thea gave a little shudder. "I don't know if I like us being the only ones, except for the murderer, knowing that he is dead."

Patrick nodded, his eyes on her expressive face.

Thea jumped up and took a nervous step around the room. "This is all rather beastly, isn't it?" She glanced back over her shoulder at him. "Are you ever going to tell me why you were here last night?"

"Probably," he answered with a crooked smile. "But, at present, the secret is not mine to tell, so you shall have to control that curiosity of yours for a while longer."

Thea snorted. "Well, this has all been a

waste of time. We've learned nothing — except, of course, that someone has taken his body." She frowned. "Where would they have put it, I wonder?" An idea occurred to her. "Shouldn't we search the house? Perhaps his body is still here, hidden in one of the other rooms."

"Are you so certain you really want to find a corpse?"

Thea made a face. "No, but I cannot bear not knowing — as much for Edwina's sake as my own. It is unkind to watch her blithely going on her way, knowing that her whole world has changed." Thea bit her lip. "She may be young and foolish, but she loved him. She will suffer when she knows of his death."

Patrick pushed away from the desk and walked up to her. Laying a comforting hand on her shoulder, he said, "Isn't it kinder to let her live in her dream world for the time being? Grief will come soon enough."

Thea nodded. Looking up at him, she asked, "What do we do now?"

Patrick sighed. "Your suggestion that we search the house was not a bad one. I think we should at least make certain that his body is *not* still in this house." He looked at her. "I suggest that you remain here while I make a quick inspection of the premises."

Thea shook her head. "No, thank you. I would rather find a corpse with you by my side than stay in this room all by myself." She shuddered slightly. "He was murdered here; I'd rather not remain in this room alone."

Patrick shrugged.

Shielding the flame of the candle, he turned and led the way from the room. Thea followed closely behind his tall form, admitting wryly that she felt very safe in his presence — and that inexplicably, she trusted him. As you trusted Hawley? taunted a sly voice in her brain. She gave herself an irritated shake. Of course she didn't trust him as blindly, as wholeheartedly, as innocently as she had Hawley! She would have been a fool to do so. She had learned too well from that experience the ways of men, and while all men were not utter cads — the men in her own family were proof of that — many, most, she amended, had to be viewed with a jaundiced eye. So while she did trust Blackburne, it was a wary, watchful trust.

Lost in her thoughts, she was unaware that Patrick had stopped. She barged solidly into him and then had to clutch at him to keep from falling.

He turned. "Surely, my sweet, if you wish to embrace, it would be much more enjoyable if we faced each other."

"I certainly don't wish to *embrace* you!" Thea muttered, flustered by the incident and the mocking smile that lurked at the corner of his mouth.

"Hmm, pity," he murmured, and turned away again.

There was little conversation between them for the next several moments. The upstairs windows were tightly shuttered and so they were able to prowl around the entire upper floor without the worry that the light of the candle would be seen from outside. The search proved disappointing. Except for the room where Patrick had been attacked and one other, all of the other rooms were depressingly empty. They spent a longer time in the two rooms with the ghostly draped furniture, satisfying themselves that the dust covers hid only furniture and not a body. Patrick commented on the fact that the room where he had been attacked did not look any different; the wardrobe door still hanging open, the dust cover lying in the same position on the floor that he remembered.

Both of them were convinced that there was no reason to search the third floor of the house, but in the interest of thoroughness, they did so. The rooms were all rather small — and empty.

While not looking forward to finding a corpse, as they descended the stairs from the second floor, Thea confessed that she was somewhat disappointed with the results of their examination.

Patrick grinned down at her as she walked by his side. "Well, we haven't surveyed the ground floor. Perhaps, we shall find his body in the kitchen — all nicely laid out in the pantry."

Thea shot him a look. "Aren't you taking this entire affair a bit lightly?"

Patrick's expression grew hard. "Not at all," he said in a voice that made Thea glad he had stated that he was on her side.

Due to concern about their light being seen from outside, they were extremely cautious as they moved around the ground floor. With Patrick's comment in mind, Thea heaved a sigh of relief when the kitchen, the large pantry in particular, revealed no sign of Hirst's body.

The search of the downstairs took them quite some time. While the upper floors had been virtually empty of furniture, such was not the case with the ground floor. Every room seemed to be stuffed with furniture. Gingerly removing dust cover after dust cover, fearful that at any moment she would find Hirst's body, Hirst's decomposing body, she thought with a lurch of her stomach, Thea was extremely glad when their self-imposed task was completed.

They returned to the room where the murder had occurred. Seated once more before the desk, Thea said in half-disappointed, half-relieved tones, "Well, we know where his body *isn't*."

Regarding his boots as he lounged once more against the desk, Patrick muttered, "I agree — but it doesn't help us very much." He frowned. "Moving the body was a dangerous thing to do. It would seem to me that the smart thing to have done would have been to leave it here to be discovered at will."

"Except, as you said earlier, there must have been an imperative motive for it to have been taken from here and hidden." A terrible thought occurred to her. "What if we *never* find his body?"

Patrick grimaced. "That's a distinct possibility — unfortunately. I think that there is one thing that we can do though — you have to visit your sister and find out exactly where Hirst said he would be staying. Perhaps his stated destination will provide some sort of clue for us."

It was Thea's turn to grimace. "Edwina is

going to wonder why I am so interested in her husband's —." She stopped, not needing Patrick's sudden motion for silence; she had heard the shutting of the front door as clearly as he had.

They both stood up, looking at each other. Patrick cast a swift glance around the room, his gaze lingering on the elegant three-paneled silk screen in the corner. Grabbing Thea's arm, he blew out the candle, thrusting it into her hands, and whispered, "Hold on to that, will you?"

The room was now in utter blackness, and not waiting for Thea's answer, he dragged her across the room, crowding with her behind the silk screen. There was little space behind the screen, and Thea's back was jammed against Patrick's solid form, his arms wrapped in front of her, holding her tightly to him.

"Not a sound," he muttered, as they listened to the steady progression of footsteps heading directly, it seemed, to the room in which they were hiding.

From the heavy step, it was clear the person was male and knew precisely where he was going. As she listened breathlessly to his advancement, in Thea's mind there was only one question: Was this the person who had murdered Hirst?

Chapter Seven

The opening of the door made Thea shrink closer to Patrick. Their intimate positions did not bother her at all; she was very grateful for his solid warmth at her back and his strong arms wrapped securely under her breasts. Clutching the snuffed-out candle tightly in her hands, she held her breath, waiting for the person who stood in the doorway to make the next move.

He stood there for what seemed a long time to Thea, but in reality it was only seconds, then they heard him walk into the room, apparently shutting the door behind him. Even knowing that Patrick was with her, Thea was apprehensive — it could be a murderer standing just inside the room. The suspense was nearly killing Thea, and she almost sighed with relief when a faint light broke the blackness on the other side of the screen. He must have lit one of the candles that had been on the table near the door. From her position behind the screen, she could see a faint wavering light, but there was no way that either one of them could risk revealing their presence by peeking around the screen and seeing who it was that had entered the room.

From the sounds of his movements, it was obvious that he was familiar with the room. He walked quickly toward the desk . . . and the Chinese screen that hid Patrick and Thea, but at the last moment, he swerved and it sounded like he was walking toward the row of books that lined the nearby wall.

Intensely aware of Thea's slim form, particularly the firm buttocks pushed tightly into his lower body, Patrick fought to keep his mind on the matter at hand and not the distinctly erotic sensations her nearness aroused. As much as Thea, he was conscious that the person on the other side of the screen could very well be the man who had murdered Hirst, and more importantly to him, his mother's blackmailer. Violently ignoring the warm flesh flattened against him, he considered stepping out from behind the screen and confronting the new arrival.

Several things prevented him from doing so, not the least of these being Thea's presence. He would do nothing to place her in greater danger than she already was, and he had no way of knowing precisely how the mysterious arrival would react to being suddenly confronted. For himself, he was prepared to take the chance, but he could not risk bringing harm to Thea. Yet he could not simply stand there and miss an opportunity to learn *some*thing about the person who had entered the room.

His gaze fell to the narrow crack in the screen where two of the sections met. Dare he look out?

Thea must have been thinking the same thing, because the thought had hardly crossed his mind when she bent forward and carefully placed her eye to the crack.

She could see very little, the narrowness of the crack severely limiting her view, and except where the candlelight fell the room was in shadowy darkness. Breathlessly she waited, hoping the person holding the candle would come into sight.

It was frustrating to be able to see so little, but eventually she was rewarded by the sight of a jacket-clad arm. She watched as the owner of the arm fumbled with several books, tossing them aside, some falling to the floor. Reaching into the space he had made, he scrabbled around for a second, then gave a satisfied sound as he brought out a small packet from its hiding place. Thea could not see precisely what it was he held in his hand, but it seemed to have been the reason for his trip to the house. He turned away, and she caught a glimpse of a broad masculine back as he began to walk toward the door.

Thea didn't stop to think. The mysterious visitor might be Alfred's murderer; he had obviously returned to retrieve some important article and, having found it, was going to depart. She saw no reason not to confront him, especially not when she knew she had a loaded pistol in her pocket.

Thrusting the candle into Patrick's astonished grasp, she yanked out her pistol. Darting out from behind the screen, she leveled her weapon at the retreating man, and yelled, "Halt! Stop or I shall shoot!"

At the sound of her voice, the gentleman stiffened and almost simultaneously blew out the candle he carried. The room was plunged into darkness. Realizing that her actions might have been a trifle precipitous and that in the dark she would have no chance of hitting anything, Thea stifled an unladylike curse.

There was nothing stifled about the curse that came from Patrick as he lifted her bodily out of his way and rushed past her in the darkness. Thea's ears burned, especially at the decidedly venomous phrase — "interfering goose-brained hoydens."

The next few seconds were chaotic. The

visitor ran from the room with Patrick hard on his heels, Thea gamely bringing up the rear. The trio, one after the other, dashed down the black hallway, their feet hitting the floor with resounding thuds. No one was making any effort to be quiet.

The chase led to the back part of the house, and it was clear to Patrick that his quarry was hoping to reach the tradesmen's entrance near the kitchen. Once there, it would be a simple task to disappear into the alley.

Heedless of the objects that might be in his path, Patrick increased his speed, nearly overrunning the other man in the dark. Wasting little effort on finesse, he leaped for the man and they both went down in a heap.

It was an ugly struggle, the intruder fighting savagely to wrest himself free of Patrick, Patrick equally determined to hold on to him. They rolled and twisted, their grunts heavy in the air as flying fists connected with solid flesh.

Thea, following closely behind Patrick in the darkness, fell right into the middle of the tangled masculine mass. She went down with a gasp, the pistol flying from her hand. She had no way of knowing which man was which, but she weighed into the fight with fierce determination. She had to help Patrick.

The writhing mass fought viciously in the blackness, painful gasps and moans revealing the damage that was being done by flailing fists and well-aimed kicks. After suffering a knee to her chest, a cut lip, and an elbow in her eye, Thea managed to get both arms around the intruder's neck and squeezed for all she was worth. He was much stronger than she had expected and despite her efforts to choke him, he would not stop using his fists against Patrick. Furious and frightened, Thea brought her teeth into play and bit down as hard as she could on his ear. He roared and reared up, almost falling over backward. She hung on like a bulldog and bit down even harder, her slender arms tightening even more around his neck as she used every ounce of her body to throw him completely off-balance.

It worked, and together they went down in a heap, with the intruder on top of her, her arms still locked around his neck, his weight crushing her into the floor. She heard Patrick scrambling to his feet and releasing her savage hold on the man's ear, she caught her breath enough to cry out joyfully, "I have him! I have him!"

"No, goddammit!" Patrick growled from above her. "You have me, you little fool!"

Several things happened at once: the intruder took to his heels; Thea jerked her arms from around Patrick's neck as if she had just discovered she was clasping a cobra, her mouth forming a large dismayed "O;" and Patrick surged out of her slackened grasp.

The sound of a slamming door rang out through the darkness. Silence descended. The intruder had escaped.

Patrick and Thea sat on the floor in the dark, the silence stretching out. After a few seconds as the silence grew distinctly uncomfortable, thinking it prudent, Thea scooted a little distance away from Patrick and stood up. A moment later, she heard him rise to his feet. He didn't say a word, and the silence became unnerving.

"Um, I thought I was helping," she finally muttered. "I thought he was you . . . I thought I was stopping him from hurting you."

Patrick lit the candle he had stuffed into his pocket before he had charged past Thea. In the weak yellow light they regarded each other.

Both wore signs of the battle. Though the entire incident had lasted mere minutes, quite a bit of damage had been wrought. Glumly Thea wondered how much of it they had inflicted upon each other.

Uneasily she looked at Patrick, thinking that he was really rather large and intimidating as he stared at her over the wavering flame. His hair was wildly tumbled, his beautiful jacket was askew, his cravat half-undone, and he had a bloody slash over one eye and a dandy bruise forming on one lean cheek. He looked disreputable and, she thought foolishly, rather endearing. She knew an impulse to brush back those raven locks that fell across his forehead and kiss that bruised cheek.

Thea looked little better than Patrick. Her clothes were as disheveled as Patrick's, in fact one of the shoulders of her coat had been torn and her shirt hung free of the breeches at one side. Most of her hair had managed to stay in its queue, but wisps of black hair curled in untrammeled splendor around her face. The cut on her bottom lip had stopped bleeding, but the lip itself was slightly swollen, and if Patrick was any judge, she was going to have a magnificent black eye.

"I really *was* trying to help," she said defensively when he just continued to stare at her, the expression on his face hard to read. "I thought I was choking the intruder — not you. I thought —"

"No," Patrick said disgustedly, "you

didn't *think*. You simply leaped willy-nilly out from behind that screen, brandishing your pistol — thereby ruining any opportunity we may have had of following him or of finding out his identity — without, I might add, him being any the wiser."

"I didn't brandish the pistol," she muttered, glowering up at him.

"Ah, forgive me. I must have been mistaken." He looked at her politely. "And how would you describe your actions?"

Belatedly aware that she had acted without thinking and . . . *un*wisely, Thea was prepared to shoulder the blame for the fiasco that had befallen them. It was her fault. She knew that. She should not have been so quick and so eager to confront the intruder, and the dismal end to the evening could be laid squarely at her feet. Feeling chastened and guilty, she glanced over at his set face. He didn't look particularly angry, although he was clearly displeased — and she couldn't blame him for that. Reluctantly, she admitted that she'd made a mess of things. But with the best intentions, she thought virtuously. She *had* meant to help, and if she had tackled the right man, they would have captured the intruder. Patrick was right, however; she had ruined their chance to find out discreetly who the intruder was and where he had been going. She studied her feet for a moment, consumed with guilt and regret. If only, she thought miserably, she would learn to think before she leaped. She risked another glance at his face and sighed. She would really rather he railed at her than speak to her in those icily polite tones.

Watching her expressive face, Patrick could almost read every thought that crossed her mind. He was very aware that she regretted what had happened, but he was also aware that he didn't ever want to feel again the sheer fear that had flooded him when she had darted out from behind that screen. For all she had known the intruder could have been armed and have turned and fired at her in a split second. She could have been badly wounded . . . or killed. Something cold and painful coiled in his gut at the thought of this dark-eyed, beguiling, and equally infuriating little minx lying lifeless on the ground. He had never felt so helpless and full of stark terror in his life as he had that moment, when he realized how swiftly he could have lost her.

He took a long slow appraisal of her, an unwilling smile beginning to tug at the corner of his mouth. She looked a perfect disgrace. Her hat was gone, lost in the scuffle, and garbed in boy's clothing, her eye rapidly blackening and her lip swelling, she looked and had proved herself to be as notorious as her reputation. He had always considered himself a man of good breeding, and her actions and appearance should have aroused nothing but disgust in the breast of any gentleman of good breeding. He shook his head. Disgust was the last emotion in his breast when he looked at her. No, he admitted ruefully, disgust was not among the emotions that flooded through him. Appreciation of her misguided courage, yes. Amusement at the situation, yes. An odd-placed tenderness was there too, and as for desire. . . . Oh, yes, desire definitely churned in his breast . . . and loins.

Aware that proof of his desire was swelling rapidly and would soon be obvious, Patrick turned away. "Come along," he said, ignoring his baser emotions. "I doubt that there is any reason for us to linger here now."

Taking only a second to scoop up her pistol from the floor, Thea followed behind his broad-shouldered form. Uncertainly, she asked, "I know that we will probably not learn anything else, but shouldn't we examine that bookshelf more fully before we leave? You didn't see him do it, but he took something from behind some of the books — perhaps we might find something he left behind."

A close examination of the bookshelves revealed nothing but some mouse droppings and a layer of dust, and Thea was thoroughly disappointed. Her lip drooping, she allowed Patrick to urge her away from the room.

"You'd have thought that we would have found *something*," she muttered, as they approached the entrance of the house.

"I think we found quite enough for one evening," Patrick said dryly, as he opened the door and took a careful look outside.

At this time of the evening, there was little traffic and he hustled Thea out of the house and down the steps to the street. A moment later, they were climbing into Thea's coach.

"At least," he said grimly as he settled back against the velvet squabs and the coach began to move, "you had enough sense to bring transportation."

"I am not," Thea said haughtily, still smarting from her less-than-stellar performance that evening, "a *complete* fool."

Smiling in the darkness, Patrick murmured, "Actually it was very plucky, if misguided, of you to come to my rescue. I thank you for your good intentions."

"Don't patronize me," Thea said crossly. "I acted a perfect fool, and you know it." She sighed. "I did not mean to ruin things, I just wanted to stop him from leaving."

"Don't repine on it — there'll be other chances."

"Do you think so?" she asked, leaning forward, trying to see his expression in the darkness as he sat across from her.

He shrugged. "Since we do not intend to abandon our endeavors, it is a logical conclusion that sooner or later, our paths and those of our mysterious intruder will cross again." He grimaced. "And I hope with a better outcome."

"I wonder what was in that little packet that he took from behind the books," Thea mused. "It wasn't very big. It was flat and I think folded. Letters, perhaps?"

Patrick had a fair idea that the packet might very well have contained his mother's letters, but he wasn't about to share that bit of speculation with Thea. It was dangerous enough for her to be snooping around her brother-in-law's murder and disappearance without adding blackmail into the mix. Especially since the blackmail had nothing to do with her.

He frowned. Or did it? Or rather, how much, if anything at all, did Alfred Hirst's murder have to do with whoever was blackmailing his mother? Were the two events connected? The place of Hirst's death certainly seemed to lead one to that conclusion. But was it the right one? Or was it simply one of those incredible coincidences?

Patrick doubted it. He did not like coincidences. So. Were there actually two blackmailers? Had Hirst been one of a pair? Had Hirst's meeting with Thea been personal business? Business Hirst had intended to have finished long before Lady Caldecott's expected arrival? And Hirst's murder — the falling-out between partners?

He had no time for further introspection; they had arrived at Thea's town house. A few moments later, he was sitting in a small, charming room, decorated in shades of cream, blue, and gold, where Thea's cousin, Modesty Bradford, had waited anxiously for her young relative's return.

Modesty had not been the least perturbed by his unexpected appearance in her home at an unseemly hour, or their disreputable state. Patrick's impression was that very little indeed would perturb Miss Bradford. Introductions had been made; refreshments served by a disapproving, bald-headed butler; and Patrick was currently lounging in a large overstuffed chair that fit him very well; a half-consumed snifter of brandy was held in one hand. Thea had just finished up with a recital of their adventures.

"Well!" breathed Modesty, torn between envy and horror, "this is certainly developing into something far more than any of us expected." She glanced at Patrick. "I don't suppose you will tell us why you were at that house originally?"

Patrick smiled faintly and shook his head. "I cannot — it is not my secret."

Modesty regarded him thoughtfully. Instinctively she trusted him, and she knew a great deal more about him than she had let on. More importantly, from her point of view, he was the first gentleman outside of male relatives whose company Thea seemed to endure with something other than impatience and contempt. She found it highly interesting that Thea appeared to be tolerating his intrusion into such an intimate family matter. Patrick's actions were equally interesting, and Modesty wondered if she was the only one who found it curious that he had not immediately reported the murder of Hirst, but had instead imposed, there really was no other word for it, himself upon Thea. Of even more interest to her was the fact that he seemed not to be the least repulsed by Thea's reputation or her less-than-proper behavior. Tonight, she thought, had certainly been a good example of that! She had always known that it would take an exceptionally astute man to look beyond the scandalous stories surrounding Thea and see the warm, generous woman behind the façade. Was Patrick Blackburne that man? He might very well be, and that conclusion pleased her.

"So now what do we do?" Modesty asked, discreetly observing the interplay between Thea and Patrick.

"There is very little that we can do," Patrick replied, gazing into his brandy snifter. "Thea's description of the intruder does not give us very much to go on."

"Can I help it if, from what I saw, he just looked average?" Thea demanded. "It is not my fault that he was not a giant with flaming red hair."

Patrick chuckled, and Modesty smiled at Thea's comment.

Thea shot them both a disgruntled look and stood up. Ignoring their presence, she began to pace around the room with that restless energy that was such an innate part of her. She made a striking figure. Her hat had been lost at some point during the evening; her torn jacket had been discarded;

and her shirt had been retucked into her breeches. At first glance, she looked a stripling and yet, not.

From beneath heavy-lidded eyes, Patrick watched her, and it occurred to him that the boy's disguise would not have fooled anyone who might have looked closely at her. Blessing Providence for darkness and a largely deserted street, he found his thoughts drifting dangerously as he observed the gentle sway of her slim hips. The white shirt was too large for her, but even so, as his gaze shifted, he was able to discern the soft outward thrust of her bosom as she moved about the confines of the small room. Feeling his breeches suddenly tighten, he cursed his unruly body and deliberately set his thoughts down a different path.

"Are you certain there was nothing about the man that would help us identify him?" Patrick asked.

Thea shrugged. "I told you; I only saw his arm when he reached behind the books, and then his back when I came out from behind the screen. What I did see of his dress appeared to be of good quality — it wasn't something a macaroni would wear, but it didn't look to be the garb of a commoner either. His jacket was dark brown — tobacco-colored — and fit him well." She frowned. "He wore breeches, buckskin, now that I think of it, and boots. I had the distinct feeling that he was a member of the quality. His hair was neatly cut and dark — not black, brown probably." Sighing, she threw herself down onto the sofa beside Modesty. "As for height, I told you; he was not tall, neither was he short. He didn't appear, at least from the rear, to be very thin or very fat. We could, no doubt, pass him on the street and find him quite unremarkable."

"Do you think he is the person who murdered Hirst?" inquired Modesty, looking from one discontented face to the other.

Patrick shrugged.

Thea grimaced.

Silence fell.

"Well," said Modesty eventually, "since there is nothing further we can do tonight, I shall bid you both good night." She rose to her feet and extended her hand to Patrick.

Patrick had also risen to his feet. Bending gracefully over Modesty's slim hand, he bid her adieu. Loosing her hand and straightening, he said, "I should be on my way. The hour is late, and I am sure that both of you would like to retire to your beds."

"Don't be ridiculous," Modesty said forthrightly. "Considering the events of the evening and all that you know of our affairs, I feel that you are quite one of the family. That said, there is no reason for you to rush off." A twinkle in her blue eyes, she said, "I am sure that you and Thea have more to discuss — especially your plans to expose this villain. Normally I would not feel comfortable leaving Thea alone in the company of a man of your reputation —" At Patrick's uneasy look, Modesty laughed. "My dear sir, I may be considered an ape-leader, but I am not unaware of the doings of society — especially those of our more, er, rakish members." When his expression grew even more uneasy, she added, "Yes, I am afraid that your reputation is well-known to me." The twinkle grew more pronounced. "I suppose I should confess that while I have never met *you*, I have been acquainted with your mother for years. She has spoken of you often — even your more disreputable, ah, escapades."

Uncertain whether to laugh or curse, Patrick chose the former. Laughing attractively, he murmured, "And that confirms what I have always suspected, Mother *does* indeed have the most effective spy network known to man!"

"And eyes in the back of her head where you are concerned, young man," Modesty said with a chuckle.

They were in perfect charity with each other. Patrick escorted her to the door. Shutting it behind her, he turned to look back at Thea. She was still on the sofa, her breeches-clad legs now curled underneath her, and those incredible dark eyes on his face.

Uncertain of his emotions when it came to Miss Thea Garrett, he regarded her speculatively.

"What?" Thea asked sharply. "Why are you looking at me that way? I *told* you that I did not deliberately attack you."

"I'm sure that you did not," Patrick replied equitably as he strolled back to his chair. Seating himself, his long legs stretched in front of him, he shook his head. "We are, I am afraid, at a standstill. I doubt our fellow will return to the Curzon Street house. Hirst's body is gone — God knows where — and our visitor apparently got whatever he came for. There is no reason that I can see for him to come back."

"I wonder what it was that he took," Thea muttered. "If he is the same person who murdered and hid Hirst's body, and it is logical that he is, why didn't he take it then? Why risk coming back?"

It was a good question, one that Patrick

could not answer. He had several ideas, but none that he wished to share with Thea. In fact he wished most vehemently that she were well out of it — which was, he admitted sourly, exactly the opposite of what he had felt barely over twenty-four hours previously. He had hoped that she, by way of the departed Hirst, would lead him to whoever was blackmailing his mother. Presently that hope seemed to be dim at best, nonexistent at worst.

Tonight they'd discovered that Hirst's body had been removed, and who knew where or when it would surface. It was true, they had also nearly caught the mysterious stranger who had entered to remove an equally mysterious packet. For Patrick the packet was not mysterious at all — he was convinced it contained his mother's letters. It galled him to think that the bloody letters must have been there the entire time and that if only he had searched more diligently last night he would have been able to lay them in his mother's hand that same evening. Of course then he wouldn't have had reason to further his relationship with Thea . . .

His gaze fixed on Thea's expressive face, he was forced to concede that a great deal had changed within the past twenty-four hours. And most of that change had to do with the infuriating, equally enchanting creature seated across from him.

He now dismissed her reputation out of hand. Hawley Randall had always sailed a little too close to the wind for his liking, Patrick thought with contempt. And while he considered himself as wild and reckless as any member of the rakish society to which they had both belonged, seducing innocents, even with marriage in the end, had never appealed to him. Having met Thea, it appealed even less, and he found himself wishing, with uncharacteristic bloodthirstiness, that he had been the one to end Hawley's life. He smiled grimly. And that, he confessed, was probably the most unnerving thing of all — he had never considered a woman worth risking one's skin for, yet here he was, longing to cross swords in her defense, and with a dead man at that!

"Why are you smiling?" Thea asked abruptly.

Patrick shook his head. "Nothing you would understand — I'm not even certain that I do myself." Rising to his feet, he added, "The hour is late. I think that we will all be able to consider this evening's events more clearly after a night's sleep." Taking her hand in his, he urged her to her feet.

"May I call upon you tomorrow?"

A trifle breathless at his nearness, Thea stared up into his face. Curious, she asked, "If I said no, would you stay away?"

He smiled, his gray eyes laughing at her. "Now what do you think?"

"I think," she said acidly, "that you do precisely as you please."

"Ah, that rare thing — an intelligent woman."

"And you are that all too common thing — a rude, overbearing brute," Thea said tartly, a sudden smile lurking at the corner of her mouth.

Later he told himself it was the lateness of the hour, the strain they had been under, and that damned beguiling almost-smile of hers that caused him to lose his head. The current of sexual awareness had been flowing between them all evening, the kiss they had shared at the ball only intensifying its power. There was much about his dealings with Thea Garrett that left him feeling confused and uncertain, but he knew one thing — he wanted her. Instinctively, his grip on her hand tightened, and he pulled her into his arms. His lips found hers, and he kissed her.

Her mouth was soft and surprised, her body warm and supple as he crushed her against him. She felt wonderful, slim and womanly. The boy's clothing was oddly exciting, particularly when one of his hands dropped and he fondled that firm rear end, covered only by thin, tightly stretched leather.

Desire, sharp and urgent, slammed through Thea. Powerless to fight against the forces unleashed within her, she offered no resistance as his kiss hardened and deepened. Trembling with shock and excitement, escape was the last thing on her mind as she unashamedly savored the taste and texture of him, the blunt demand of his mouth and hands. Swept along by a storm of emotions she could not fight, even when he made her frankly aware of his readiness, she remained compliant and acquiescent in his embrace.

All of his senses enslaved by the woman in his arms, Patrick effortlessly plucked Thea up in his arms and, his lips never leaving hers, carried her to the sofa. Slowly he lowered her slim body to the sofa and knelt beside her. His head lifted, and they stared at each other.

Thea's mouth was red and swollen, her dark eyes wide and unfocused as she stared up into his passion-hard face. This, she realized hazily, was how she should have felt with Hawley, full of longing and eager for what would happen — not frightened and fearful. For the first time, she truly *wanted* a man. What she felt in Patrick's arms was no silly, innocent schoolgirl's half-understood dream of romance, and she knew finally with the right man just how powerful the yearning to mate could be. Helplessly, her fingers reached up to trace the contours of his lips, a sharp claw of pleasuring raking through her when he gently bit and suckled at her fingers.

Her touch had been tentative, but it reacted powerfully on Patrick, and his mouth hungrily claimed hers once again, his fingers making short work of the fastenings of her shirt. Shoving the opened garment aside, he cupped one small breast, and whatever remnant of sanity he possessed vanished. He *must* have her or he would go mad!

Thea gasped at the touch of his hand on her breast, arching up with pleasure. She had never experienced anything as exciting and thrilling as Patrick's lovemaking, and she was unabashedly eager for more.

It was the mundane clatter of crockery in the hall that brought them both abruptly back to reality. The butler was right outside and would soon be knocking on the door.

Passion doused effectively as a plunge into icy water, they sprang apart.

Cursing under his breath, Patrick yanked Thea upright and, closing her shirt, ruthlessly shoved the tails back into her breeches. Thank God, he thought with fervency he had not felt in years, that events had not gone further. A sophisticated man of the world, even he boggled at the thought of being found so boldly *in flagrante delicto.*

A tug at his cravat was all he had time for before there was a soft knock on the door.

Thoroughly rattled, Thea was astonished at how normal her voice sounded as she hurried to the door and opened it.

"Miss Bradford thought you might want further refreshments," replied Tillman, standing before her with a silver tray full of various pieces of china. His disapproving expression made it clear that he suspected what had been going on in the room.

"That won't be necessary," Thea said. "Mr. Blackburne was just leaving." She glanced back at Patrick, the dark eyes she fixed on him both pleading and demanding that he agree.

"Indeed, I was," he muttered, walking to the door where Thea stood rigidly. Taking her trembling hand in his, he kissed it. "I shall come to call tomorrow."

Thea nodded, not trusting her voice.

A moment later, Patrick was standing outside in the cool night air, wondering if he had indeed gone mad. How else to explain what had happened — his mouth twisted at what had very nearly happened tonight.

Shaking his head at his own folly, he stepped to the street. He did not understand precisely what was going on, but tonight had proven one thing to him: He was dangerously and utterly besotted by the notorious Miss Thea Garrett.

Chapter Eight

While Thea and Patrick were picking themselves up off the floor of the Curzon Street house, the intruder, packet clutched in one hand, had been half-stumbling, half-running in a blind panic through the twisted alley at the rear of the fine homes. It took him several moments to realize that his attackers were not chasing after him.

Gasping for breath, he finally leaned against one of the buildings and took a few minutes to regroup. As long as he lived he never wanted to experience the thrill of fright that had gone through him when he had heard that voice order him to halt. That even one person had been lying in wait for him had been bad enough, but that *two* people had been in the house trying to trap him was terrifying. Who had they been? And how had they known that he would be there that night? The how would have to remain unanswered for the time being, but the who he could see for himself — if he moved swiftly.

Slipping onto the main street, he hurried down its length, soon taking up a position almost directly across from the house where he had been attacked. Hiding himself in a convenient narrow walkway between two of the handsome buildings, he waited, his eyes fixed intently on the doorway of the house across from him, the packet still held in his hand.

The light from the few streetlamps cast a fitful yellow glow, providing little more than small golden pools of illumination amidst the darkness of the night. He realized immediately that it would be impossible to recognize his attackers from that distance and in the poor light, so resigned himself to having to follow when they left the house — provided they had not done so already.

He was not a brave man and would be the first to admit it, and when the door to the house across the street appeared to be opening he shrank deeper into the hiding place provided by the walkway. It was then that he discovered that he was not the only person concealed in the walkway.

As he moved deeper into shadows, he came up hard against the solid form of another person. His nerves already shattered, he gave a half-smothered shriek and leaped away, only to stumble wildly over the other person's judiciously placed boot. He began to fall, his arms flailing madly as he fought to keep his balance. There was no stopping his fall, and his head slammed against the brick wall of the building, and then again on the hard cobbled walkway where he finally landed. He was knocked senseless. The packet went flying out of his hand to land on the ground near his unconscious form.

"Oh, dear," murmured his companion in the walkway. "I do hope that you are only unconscious and not dead." A brief check of the man on the ground reassured him that he would not have murder on his conscience. Stepping over the prone body, the newcomer watched as the two figures hurried down the steps and toward the coach waiting several doors away.

When the coach had driven past him, he stepped back into the walkway and lit the small candle he carried with him. Spying the packet, he picked it up, regarded it thoughtfully, and put it safely into the inside pocket of his coat. Rather fastidiously he turned the face of the unconscious man toward his candle, recognizing him immediately.

"Ah," he said. "It is always a pleasure when one's suspicions are confirmed." He hesitated a moment, not happy about leaving the fellow in such a vulnerable position. But there was nothing for it — he didn't want to be here when the gentleman regained his senses. It would be so very awkward.

Standing up, he sighed. "I am sorry, my friend, but I really must be on my way. I trust you wake safely, with nothing more than a headache." He blew out his candle and, after taking a long look up and down the street, stepped boldly out of his hiding place.

It was several moments later, as he relaxed before the cheery fire in his study and sipped a snifter of brandy, that he was finally able to examine the packet. Opening it, he discovered that it contained a half dozen or so letters, written in a feminine hand. Reading the passionate outpourings of the first letter, his brow lifted. How very, very interesting.

His gaze fell to the signature, and he smiled. "My, my, my," he murmured with a smile. "What fun I shall have with these."

Rising to his feet, he walked to a large gilt-framed portrait of some long-dead ancestor and, moving it aside, disclosed a safe behind it. Taking a small key from his waistcoat pocket, he opened it and put the letters inside. Locking it, he replaced the picture and returned to his seat by the fire.

Watching the flames, his fingers steepled in front of him, he considered how best to use the letters.

⋆ ⋆ ⋆

A storm blew into London during the early hours of the next morning, and Thea woke to a day that looked as violent and unsettled as she felt. Even after bathing and dressing for the day, the turbulent mood had not left her, but at least the black eye Patrick had feared from last night's activities had not materialized. There was, however, the faintest suspicion of bruising — which she told herself could be passed off as caused by a restless night. Thea shared breakfast with Modesty; while her cousin conferred with the cook, she retreated to the room where she and Patrick had shared that astonishingly passionate interlude. Looking out at the rain-lashed street below her, Thea frowned.

She had sworn never to fall for the charms of another man, and here she was, on the verge of actually *liking* a man she had no reason to trust. She sighed. But then, she thought with a start, she had no reason *not* to trust him either. He could have caused her great grief and embarrassment any number of times since she had first run afoul of him, but he had not. Nor did he seem to have any notion of doing so. She didn't quite know what to make of him.

She turned away and wandered about the

pleasant room, oblivious to the sounds from the street, her mind on the disturbing Mr. Patrick Blackburne. Unaware of the passing time, she was startled when the door was suddenly flung open several minutes later and Edwina stood there.

Thea stiffened. Certain that Hirst's body had finally been discovered, she gathered herself to console the young widow. But Edwina, she realized suddenly, did not look distressed. In fact, garbed in a fashionable gown of blue muslin, golden ringlets framing her lovely face, she looked particularly charming. She certainly did not appear to be grief-stricken, so it could not be the discovery that she was a widow that had brought her. Yet why else would she be there? Had Edwina finally come to her senses and concluded that it was time to end their estrangement? Treading carefully, Thea said, "Edwina! My dear, what are you doing out on a foul day like today?"

"I had to see you," Edwina said breathlessly, her blue eyes fixed on Thea. "I was a perfect beast to you last night! I came to apologize." Smiling uncertainly, she added, "Oh, Thea, you do not know how much I have missed you. Please do not let us fight anymore! I was so happy to see you at the ball — even if I did not act it." She glanced away. "I was so afraid that you would snub me, and when you did not, I acted like a silly goose." She looked back at Thea. "Please tell me, dear sister, that you do not hold my petty manners last night against me. I want this silly estrangement between us to end."

Thea's heart swelled. Holding out her arms, she said, "Oh, dear, dear Edwina, you do not know how I have longed to hear you say those words."

Edwina flew into her outstretched arms, and for several moments there were tears, sniffled apologies on both sides, and, finally, watery smiles between the half sisters. Wiping her eyes with a dainty lace handkerchief, Edwina sank down onto the sofa, and said, "I am so happy that we have put the misunderstandings behind us. These past months had been positively grim! At least a dozen times I nearly came to call upon you to beg you to forgive my actions the last time we were together." Edwina made a face. "I acted a perfect brat. Worse, I was wrong and I know it — and foolish, too." She looked down at her lap, her expression sad. "My pride would not let me admit the truth." Her gaze met Thea's. "I realize now, in fact I've realized it for several months, that I never should have married Alfred. You were right about him — everything you said was absolutely true, but I could not bring myself to admit it — especially not to *you!*"

Modesty sailed into the room at that moment, ending the confidences. Her brow raised, she regarded Edwina. "Well!" she finally said. "Tillman said that you were here with Thea, but I wanted to see for myself." Crossing to Edwina, who had risen at her entrance, Modesty pressed a kiss onto her cheek. "Welcome, child. You have been away from us far too long."

Edwina threw her arms around Modesty, and cried, "Oh, cousin, how I have missed you! I have just been telling Thea what a fool I have been." Her blue eyes full of contrition, she added, "Will you forgive me?"

Modesty patted her cheek. "Of course, my child — it will make Thea very happy to have the troubles between you soothed. Now sit down and let me ring Tillman for refreshments."

The ladies settled themselves, conversing only lightly until after Tillman had taken Modesty's orders and returned with a silver tray groaning with all sorts of tiny cakes and biscuits, as well as a tall pot filled with coffee and another with tea. Once Tillman had departed, the ladies served themselves.

It was only when Modesty sank back into her chair, idly stirring her coffee, that conversation focused on the subject uppermost in her and Thea's minds. Taking a sip of her coffee, Modesty asked, "And where is that errant husband of yours? Do not tell me that he has abandoned you?"

Thea waited tensely for Edwina's reply, holding her coffee cup in a death grip.

Edwina smiled wryly. "He said he was staying with friends of his in Salisbury." She shrugged. "For all I know, he may be holed up with a mistress here in the city."

Modesty and Thea exchanged a glance. Putting her cup down, Modesty asked carelessly, "Did he by any chance mention the names of those friends?"

Edwina frowned and looked from one face to the other. "Why are you so very interested in Alfred? Thea asked almost the same questions last night." Her gaze sharpened. "Is there something you are not telling me?"

Modesty shook her head. "Of course not, my dear. I was merely curious if he was staying with anyone we know." She smiled and took a sip of her coffee. "I have several friends who reside in Salisbury — it wouldn't be so surprising that we know someone in common."

Her suspicions alleviated, Edwina smiled, albeit bitterly. "I doubt that Alfred knows anyone that you do. He is not, as Thea tried to warn me, very respectable, and, lately, that fact has been made abundantly clear to me." A faint flush stained her cheeks. "The Hilliards' ball is the first social event given by a leading member of the ton that I have been invited to in ages." She laughed. "It has been so long since I have attended any outing with that sort of cachet attached to it that I was determined to go, even if Alfred had died!"

Thea jumped as if stung, and it was only the death grip she had on her cup that kept her from spilling the contents. "Edwina! What a terrible thing to say," she finally got out.

Edwina grimaced. "I know. It wouldn't have been very Christian or proper of me, but I don't think I could have helped myself." She looked at Thea. "You do not know what these past months have been like. Alfred and I have done nothing but argue and scream at each other." Her lower lip trembled. "He has said some terrible things to me and hurt me badly — there were times that I actually hated him." She gave a self-conscious laugh. "Forgive me! I did not mean to come here and pour my troubles out in such a blunt fashion."

"Of course you are forgiven," Thea said

quickly, fresh resentment against Hirst burning in her breast. "And we are your family — your troubles are our troubles. We could never turn away from you." It was Thea's turn to look self-conscious. "Just think what would have happened to me if the family had turned their backs on me. You have brought no scandal down upon our heads or caused the needless death of someone you loved — you only had the misfortune to be young and in love with the wrong man."

Modesty's expression tightened at Thea's words. The dear little fool! Didn't she realize that the same could be said of her? Thea could forgive Edwina, but not herself. Modesty held back the comment she would have liked to make, and instead asked, "What do you mean to do, Edwina? Will you leave him? Live separately from him? Divorce is something that will not be easily condoned."

"I have not thought that far ahead," Edwina answered. Flashing them both a smile, she added, "My only purpose this morning was to mend my bridges with you and Thea."

"Well, you have done that," Thea replied warmly. "And we will speak no more about it. Modesty and I are delighted that you came to us this morning."

Modesty said nothing, merely picking up her cup and taking a sip.

The conversation became desultory for a while, the three ladies jumping from subject to subject as fancy took them. It was over an hour later that Edwina stood up and said, "I must go. I have promised Lord Pennington that he may escort me to the museum this afternoon."

Thea burst out laughing. "The museum?" she asked. "You?"

"I have decided that it is time that I improved my mind," Edwina said loftily, then ruined it by giggling. "I know, I cannot believe it myself. But he begged me to accompany him, and I could not hurt his feelings — especially not after I encouraged him so boldly last night." At Thea's expression, she said, "I know. I know. It is my own fault. I should not have been flirting so obviously with him." She sighed. "Sometimes it is very hard to behave oneself, isn't it?"

Thinking of her own escapades last night, escapades that were far worse than merely flirting with a susceptible young man, Thea's warning words died unspoken. Instead she nodded, and said, "Indeed it is. It seems that things one really wishes to do are precisely the things that one cannot do."

"Rules are what gives society order," Modesty murmured. "Without them, life would be utter chaos."

A gleam entered Edwina's eyes. "Well, I for one, think that chaos might prove to be extremely interesting."

Before Modesty could make the reply that hovered on her lips, Tillman knocked and entered the room. "Mister Patrick Blackburne has come to call," he said sourly.

"Then show him in," Modesty said before Thea could deny him — just in case her niece had been so inclined. She wasn't giving Thea a chance to snub the most fascinating gentleman who had crossed their path in many a day.

Patrick entered the room only seconds later, and Modesty had the distinct impression that even if Thea had tried to deny him, it would have been to no avail. There was something about him, something about that firm jaw and steady gaze, that indicated he was a man who was seldom denied anything he wanted. Taking another sip of her coffee, Modesty settled back to be entertained.

Greetings were exchanged, and Patrick was offered some refreshments. He selected coffee and, standing before the small fire that burned on the hearth, sipped his beverage and made small talk with the three ladies.

He looked very handsome in his dark blue form-fitting jacket and equally snug-fitting breeches as he stood there, and surreptitiously Modesty watched the interplay among the three younger people. Edwina's boldly flirtatious manner brought a frown to her forehead, and she could have kicked Thea for sitting there and letting the younger woman dominate the conversation.

Despite her manner, Edwina was curious about Patrick's presence. As well as anybody, she knew that her half sister normally avoided the male of the species. If Blackburne had been an elderly male friend of the family, Edwina would not have thought twice about his visit, but he was *not* elderly, nor as far as she could tell, a long-standing acquaintance. So what had brought him here? Speculatively she glanced from Thea to Patrick. Hmmm.

"How long do you intend to be in England, Mr. Blackburne?" Edwina asked. She flashed her loveliest smile. "Having just met you, my heart will be quite broken if you tell me that you are leaving soon for that barbarous country of yours. London has so many . . . pleasures to offer. Do say that you will be here for several months."

Patrick looked at Thea as she sat beside Edwina on the sofa. The contrast between the two siblings could not have been greater. Thea was dark and vital; tall and slim. Edwina was blond, small and curvaceous, and she exuded sexual promise. The tilt of her golden head, the pout of her lips, and the sensual glitter in her eyes told him plainly that she would not be averse to knowing him in the most intimate way possible.

There was a time, and in the not-too-distant past, that he would have returned her overt signals, but that, he thought ruefully, was before his path had crossed that of the notorious Thea Garrett. He found his usual taste in petite blondes had vanished, and these days his liking, nay, his fascination ran to slender dark-eyed wenches and one vibrant, outrageous little wench in particular.

His gray eyes on Thea's averted face, he said slowly, "I do not know when I shall return home. It all depends upon the outcome of a, er, business venture I am currently involved in." Because he had been watching her, only he saw the slight stiffening of Thea's shoulders. Almost purring, he added, "But that aside, I have a far more important reason for delaying my return to

Natchez. I have discovered, you might say, that London not only holds many pleasures, but it also has its treasures. I've a good mind to take one of those treasures with me when I leave."

Modesty beamed at him. "Excellent!" she exclaimed. "I suspected that you were a man of good sense. Your words have just proven it."

The corner of his mouth kicked up, and he lifted his cup in a silent toast. "And you, my dear lady, are far too astute for your own good!"

In perfect understanding they smiled at each other.

Annoyed that he ignored her lures and feeling as if she had missed the first act of a play, Edwina said with forced brightness, "Well, I am happy that you are enjoying your stay in London."

His smile deepened as Thea glanced up at him. "Oh, I am," he said softly. "I am indeed."

That Thea was the object of his interest was obvious, and Edwina's mouth thinned. Rising to her feet, she said, "Well, I must be on my way." She made one last attempt. Smiling warmly at Patrick, she added, "I have my coach. Perhaps I could give you a ride somewhere?"

"I appreciate your offer," Patrick said smoothly, "but I must decline. Thank you very much."

Edwina dutifully kissed Thea and Modesty, and, her irritation apparent, flounced from the room.

The door had hardly shut behind her before Patrick said, "I fear that I have upset the lady."

"Probably," Modesty replied. "But it will do her good. She has been petted and spoiled all her life. It is time that she learns that she cannot have everything that she wants."

"She is very young," Thea said defensively. "And it is true that she has been dreadfully indulged, but that is because she is so beautiful." Looking at Patrick, she said earnestly, "She has such a natural charm and warmth that one just naturally wants to please her. She cannot help being a trifle spoiled."

Modesty snorted.

A twinkle in his eyes, he said to Thea, "If you say it is so, my sweet, why then it must be so. I certainly will not argue the point that she is very beautiful. Too young," he continued as the twinkle died from his gaze, "to be a widow."

Modesty put a finger to her lips and, to

Patrick's mystification, stood up and walked to the door. Opening it, she stuck her head out and glanced up and down the hallway.

Shutting the door behind her, she resumed her seat. Looking at Patrick, she explained. "One of Edwina's less charming traits is her habit of listening at keyholes. She is a terrible snoop and not above eavesdropping should the notion take her." Her mouth quirked. "And unfortunately the notion seems to take her quite frequently."

That Thea wanted to refute Modesty's words was obvious, but they were too true, and she asked instead, "What do we do now? We still don't know where Hirst's body has been hidden . . . or why." A guilty look crossed her face. "And last night made it unlikely that we will learn anything else at the Curzon Street house."

"I agree," Patrick said. He had thought a great deal about what had happened, and one thing was obvious to him; there was no longer any need or reason for Thea to be involved in whatever was going on. Her initial involvement had been because of Hirst; with Hirst not only dead, but his body missing as well, her part ended. Since he was satisfied that she'd had nothing to do with the blackmailing of his mother, her usefulness to him in that connection also ended. One might almost think that it was time to cut the ties that had brought them together. He smiled faintly. Almost. He had the strong premonition that hell would freeze over before the feelings that bound them together could be severed. But it was going to take, he admitted wryly, some very tricky maneuvering on his part to convince his prickly darling of that fact.

With that in mind, he said, "I was going to suggest a drive in Hyde Park this afternoon, but the weather has unfortunately killed that idea. Perhaps I could escort you and Miss Bradford to the theater tonight? And arrange a late supper for us?"

Thea glanced at him with a puzzled frown. "But how will any of that help us find Alfred's body? We have learned nothing that would indicate that Hyde Park or the theater has any connection to Hirst's death."

Modesty's eyes lifted heavenward. She knew that Thea was an intelligent young woman, but sometimes she doubted it. The child was a babe when it came to gentlemen — no wonder that rogue Hawley Randall had found it so easy to convince her to run away with him.

"You're correct: Hyde Park has nothing to do with Hirst," Patrick admitted.

Her brows knitted in a frown, Thea asked, "Then why should we go? We are involved in finding out who murdered my brother-in-law, nothing more. Besides, everyone knows that I am a ruined woman; if you are seen to seek me out, if I am seen riding in Hyde Park with you, there will be gossip and ugly speculation." Thea bit her lip and glanced at the floor. "I do not mean to be unkind, but for your good, you would be wise to avoid my company."

Patrick sighed. Looking at Modesty, he asked, "May I have a moment alone with her?"

"Certainly!"

And before Thea could blink, Modesty had deserted her, shutting the door firmly behind her as she left the room.

Puzzled, Thea looked at Patrick. "What do you have to say to me that cannot be said in front of her? Have you both gone mad?"

Patrick crossed to her in one step and pulled her into his arms. "No, sweetheart, she is not mad," he said, "but I certainly am . . . for you." His mouth came down hard on hers, and his arms tightened around her.

Startled, by both his words and action, Thea stood pliant in his embrace, and, to her bewilderment, all of her senses sang into life. Magic enveloped her, and she lost herself in the sweet power of his kiss, the intoxicating sensation of his strong arms holding her against him, and the honeyed warmth flooding through her.

Her arms closed round his neck, and she kissed him back, reveling in her own boldness, in her pleasure at the touch of his lips on hers. He smelled good, too, she thought with pleasure, as she pressed nearer to him.

He kissed her a long, long time, and when he finally lifted his mouth from hers, Thea was breathless and starry-eyed.

Staring tenderly into her dazed features, he murmured, "Now do you understand?"

Thea came back to earth with a crash, all of her old suspicions rising up within her. She stepped warily out of his embrace and put a prudent distance between them. Sick inside, afraid of his answer, she asked, "Are you trying to seduce me? L-L-Like Hawley did?"

Patrick smothered a curse. What he wouldn't give for two minutes alone with Hawley!

The gray eyes hard, he demanded, "Is that what you think of me? That I am like Hawley?"

Thea shrugged. "N-N-No, not exactly. But what else am I to think? You know my reputation." A flush stained her cheeks.

"Gentlemen usually have only two reasons for seeking me out: to win a wager or to try their hand at seduction."

Furious with his entire sex, Patrick struggled to keep from smashing his fist into the wall. Would he ever be able to get past her mistrust of men? A well-founded mistrust, he admitted with a wince, some of his own actions in the past starting to haunt him. It was clear his courtship was going to be a rocky one and that he would have to proceed with great care.

"Perhaps," he said gently, "I had a different reason — have you considered that?"

Thea frowned. What other reason could he have had? Of course, she thought miserably. She should have guessed. *He wanted her for his mistress!* Her first instinct was to slap his face and order him from the room, but she hesitated. Would it be so very terrible to become his mistress? She was ruined anyway — no decent man would offer her anything *but* the sort of relationship Patrick apparently had in mind. Other men had alluded to the same thing, and she had sent them smartly on their way, but there was something about Patrick that she found nearly irresistible. . . . Unhappily she admitted that she wanted to be in his arms, that she wanted to learn all those intimate things she had not learned from Hawley . . . Dare she risk it? Dare she risk the scandal, if their liaison was discovered? No, she could not put her family through that again. But it wouldn't be the same, a sly voice argued in her mind. She was no young innocent maid running away to be married to a man she thought she loved. She was older now, her reputation already stained. She had far more license and freedom these days and had no doubt that Patrick would arrange for them to meet very, very discreetly. . . .

She glanced at him uncertainly. "You want me to become your mistress, that's it, isn't it?"

Patrick smothered a curse, and, his face hard, he demanded, "And would you be willing to become my mistress, if that is what I want?"

Faced with the actual offer, Thea dithered, knowing that her answer would change her life forever. Common sense dictated that she toss the offer back in his face, but the desire to know fully the pleasures to be had from his lovemaking and her own impetuous nature worked against her. Not giving herself time to think, or change her mind, she blurted out, "Yes — if you w-w-want me."

He turned away, his hands clenching into

fists. Staring at the fire he considered disillusioning her about his intentions, but he wondered if it would be wise. Convinced of her own notoriety, of her own damaged state, he had the unpleasant notion that if he were foolish enough to explain that he had a more honorable proposal in mind, she would turn him down in a flash. And banish him from her presence — and all for his own good, of course.

The anger slowly left him as he watched the red-and-yellow flames on the hearth. She was willing, at least at the moment, to become his mistress, and it was highly unlikely that she would consider any other offer from him. If he forced the issue, demanding that she marry him, she would no doubt send him on his way. Certain that she was acting in his best interest, she would shun him at every turn — which would make his wooing of her a trifle difficult.

He shook his head in frustration. She was willing to be his mistress — a position any other lady of her standing would view with outraged horror — and he suspected her agreement would not last very long. The dangers of being his mistress would dawn on her quickly — probably as soon as he left the room and she had a moment to think. But perhaps he could us this momentary weakness to his advantage? He meant to marry her, but if she thought differently, until he had the plans for their marriage firmly in place, did it matter?

Turning back to her, he said quietly, "I *do* want you, sweetheart — more than you know." He crossed to her, and taking her hand in his, he dropped a kiss on it. "I shall be honored."

Thea took a steadying breath, pushing aside her doubts and an odd pang of disappointment. This was what she wanted, she told herself firmly.

"When?" she asked simply.

Patrick stared at her, his expression unreadable, wondering if she knew precisely how completely she was putting her fate, her future in his hands. Swearing never to give her cause to regret her decision, he pulled her into his arms. "Soon, my pet," he said against her mouth. "You will be mine, just as swiftly as I can make suitable arrangements."

Chapter Nine

Patrick was thoughtful as he left Thea's town house several minutes later. He had made no definite plans with Thea concerning what she thought would be their new relationship. The morning's conversation, however, made it imperative that he move swiftly.

Pushing those thoughts from his mind, he began to concentrate on identifying his mother's blackmailer. A call on the solicitor handling the Curzon Street house seemed his only choice — going back to the house would accomplish little, but perhaps he could learn something new from Mr. Beaton.

Patrick did learn something new. The house was no longer on the market — the owner, the country spinster, Miss Martha Ellsworth, had decided not to sell it, but was deeding the property to her nephew — Thomas Ellsworth.

Patrick asked, "Would that be the same Thomas Ellsworth whose aunt, Lady Levina Embry, died earlier this year?"

Startled, Mr. Beaton exclaimed, "Why, why, yes it is. Never tell me it is such a small world that you know the young man?"

Patrick smiled. "I do not know him . . . let us just say that I know 'of' him. He is married to Lord Bettison's daughter I believe?"

"Yes, he is, as a matter of fact."

Taking his leave from Mr. Beaton, Patrick next called on his mother. He was fortunate to find her home alone.

Greetings were exchanged, and he imparted what he had discovered from Mr. Beaton. Seated across from Lady Caldecott in a dainty rose-satin chair in the cozy room in which he had found her, he said, "Stretch your memory, Mama. You mentioned Levina's sisters and brothers — was one of them a spinster who lives in the country? A Miss Martha Ellsworth?"

Puzzled, Lady Caldecott shook her head. "I don't believe so. In fact, I am almost positive that she did not — her sisters names were Anne and Cecilia — I do not recall their married names. And it was Levina who was the spinster in the family until she married Lord Embry. Oh, wait!" She frowned. "Let me think. It seems to me that there is something . . . Ah, I have it!" She leaned forward. "Levina's brother, Thomas's father, married a cousin, also named Ellsworth, and I believe that *she* had a sister who was a spinster."

Patrick regarded her with awe. "Is there no one's family tree that you do not have in that charming head of yours?"

"Of course not!" Lady Caldecott said. Amusement leaping into her fine eyes, she murmured, "I never keep track of the very common."

Patrick laughed. Rising to his feet, he walked over and bent down to kiss her soft, scented cheek. "I do not know what I shall do with this new information, but do not worry about your blackmailer — just let me know if he makes further demands."

He took his leave a few minutes later. As he walked away from his mother's home, he considered his next step.

Deciding that until he knew the address of Mr. Ellsworth's domicile an interview with him could wait, Patrick spent a busy afternoon making arrangements of his own. He dined with his friends, Lord Embry and Adam Paxton, at a favorite tavern of theirs on Gerrard Street, and it was only when they were savoring a final glass of port that he brought up the subject of Thomas Ellsworth.

Setting down his glass, Patrick asked, "Do either of you know where I might find Thomas Ellsworth?"

Nigel regarded him closely. "Seems to me

that you are taking an uncommon interest in the Ellsworth family these days. Didn't you just ask me about them the other day?"

"Guilty," Patrick answered lightly, "but I am not so much interested in the family as I am in Thomas in particular."

"Why?" asked Adam.

"Oh, let us say that I am just curious," Patrick murmured, his gray eyes deceptively sleepy.

Lord Embry snorted. "Call it what you will, I don't like it. Don't like Ellsworth, either, or that cousin of his, Hirst. A devilish handsome pair of rogues, but bad 'uns. Heard some gossip that the pair of them have been as thick as thieves lately. You don't want to know either one of them — especially not Ellsworth. Fellow's a bounder. *Not* good ton — even if he did marry that poor squint-eyed daughter of Bettison's. Not our sort." He shook a finger at Patrick. "Ain't like you to be so interested in that kind. You are up to something, my friend."

Ignoring Embry's last comment, Patrick quirked a brow, and asked, "What do you mean, 'not our sort'? Lord knows that we have done our share of carousing and whoring — half of London complains that our reputations are distinctly *dis*reputable." He smiled ruefully. "My own mother among them. And don't forget — Thomas Ellsworth's aunt was certainly wellborn enough to marry into your family."

"Didn't say the Ellsworths didn't have some good blood in them — said Thomas and that cousin of his, Hirst — no matter *who* they marry — ain't our sort."

Adam broke in. "I think," he murmured, "what Nigel means is that Ellsworth and Hirst are, ah, not quite the thing. It is true that branches of the families are respectably connected. And it is true that Hirst married the little Northrop chit and that Ellsworth married into the aristocracy. But it is also common knowledge that Hirst made a runaway match of it — much against the family's wishes, and that Bettison only offered his daughter's hand to cancel the debt he owed Ellsworth — a large wager between them that Bettison lost." Adam grimaced. "It was unlikely that the wench would ever make a better match, and Bettison was eager to be rid of her. More to the point, there are rumors that Ellsworth and Hirst have been helping gull green 'uns just up from the country in one of the more notorious hells off Pall Mall." He grinned at Patrick. "We may gamble and whore, my friend, but ruining youngsters too green to know any better has never been one of our vices."

"I agree. Thomas Ellsworth does not sound like a very savory fellow," Patrick said, concealing the start Hirst's name had given him, "but I have, er, business with him."

"You won't have far to look for him," Nigel grumbled, recognizing that stubborn look on Patrick's face from old. Reluctantly, he muttered, "Lives a few blocks or so up the street from where we are sitting right now."

"Thank you," Patrick said, his gray eyes laughing at Nigel, "and now if you gentlemen will excuse me, I must go pay the noxious-sounding Mr. Ellsworth a call."

Pushing aside speculation about the connection between Ellsworth and Hirst for the time being, Patrick found the address with little effort. The house was substantial, and even in the faint yellow light of the streetlamps, he could see that it was also handsome. It also appeared deserted. No light from behind shuttered windows gleamed out into the street, and a closer inspection revealed that the knocker had been taken down — a sure sign that the family was not in residence.

He knocked anyway, and after several moments was rewarded by the sound of activity behind the stout oak door. He rapped the door again with his walking stick, and a second later the door slowly creaked open.

A scrawny man of indeterminate age stood before him, a short, spluttering candle held in one bony hand. "What do you want?" the fellow demanded. "Family's gone to the country."

Putting forth his most charming manner, Patrick was eventually able to learn that Mr. Thomas Ellsworth had unexpectedly left just that morning for his country estate in Surrey — Apple Hill. "Said he ain't coming back to the city until the spring."

Patrick dropped a few coins in his hand and thanked him for the information. Suspicious that Thomas Ellsworth was his mother's blackmailer and, no doubt, the fellow he and Thea had tangled with the previous night, Patrick turned to walk down the steps. Was Ellsworth also the person who had murdered Hirst? It certainly seemed feasible. His mind on Ellsworth and Hirst, he had only taken half a step when he collided with a burly gentleman hurrying up the steps.

The man apologized. "Forgive me, sir! Had my mind on something else and didn't see you. Never let it be said that Yates is a rude fellow. Very sorry to have knocked you about that way."

Patrick flashed him a swift encompassing glance, taking in the merry blue eyes and ruddy features. Yates? Who was he — and did his presence have any bearing on Hirst's murder and his mother's blackmailer? Deciding it might be interesting to see what happened, Patrick accepted his apologies and went on his way . . . slowly. Slow enough so that he heard the gentleman's exchange with the surly servant.

"I know Tom's gone to the country," the newcomer said, when the servant had finally opened the door. "But he won't mind if I come in and leave him a note for when he returns. Now move aside, you old maggot, and let me in if you know what is good for you — and your master."

There was a threat of menace in those last words that Patrick found fascinating. He would have to ask Nigel if he knew a fellow named Yates.

His expression thoughtful, Patrick walked away from the Ellsworth house. Events, he thought, were beginning to move. Ellsworth's dash to the country seemed suspicious, and the news that Ellsworth and Hirst were related, partners in the disreputable business of cheating youngsters too green to know better out of their money, was a missing piece of the puzzle. Had Ellsworth and Hirst also been partners in the scheme to blackmail his mother? He rather thought so. And Hirst's murder, was it Ellsworth? Had they had a falling-out and fought, with Ellsworth killing Hirst? It fit with what Patrick knew. The disappearance of Hirst's corpse bothered him, and while it seemed logical to hide the crime if Ellsworth had murdered Hirst, he had to know that Patrick had seen the body. So why hide it? Ellsworth could not have known that he would have his own reasons for not immediately reporting the murder. No conclusions came to him as he wandered back to his lodgings. The whole situation was like a burr in his breeches — he could not ignore it, but neither could he wrench it free.

Tackling the problem from another angle, he wondered why Ellsworth, and he was certain it had been Ellsworth, had come back to the house for the packet Thea had seen the intruder take last night. Why not take it at the same time Hirst's body had been removed? He shook his head. Puzzles within puzzles.

That Saturday afternoon as Thea prowled around a small saloon decorated in sunny shades of yellow and apricot, she admitted that there were a few dark clouds on her horizon. As Patrick had suspected, she had begun to have reservations about her agreement to become his mistress and to realize all the dangers and pitfalls that lay in front of her. She had been trying all day not to think about them, but they were not easily banished. When Patrick finally came to take her away for their first assignation, she was going to have to lie to Modesty, and that knowledge filled her with guilt. Modesty trusted her, and she was going to repay that trust by lying to her. The debt she owed her family preyed even more heavily on her mind. Without the support of her family, she would have never survived the gossip and scandal that had swirled around her a decade prior. She owed her present acceptance by most members of the ton to them and their loyalty, and the knowledge that she was deliberately putting herself once more in scandal's path finally made her realize what a foolish thing she had done to agree to become Patrick's mistress.

Her soft mouth tightened. Oh, but she was the biggest fool in nature! Once again, she had allowed herself to be mesmerized by a handsome face with a facile tongue. Would she never learn?

Thea had been alone in the small saloon, and a fierce scowl marred her features when

Modesty wandered in.

Modesty took one look at Thea's face, and said as she seated herself in a chair covered in pale yellow damask, "I do hope that I am not the cause of that expression on your face."

Thea shook her head, the scowl vanishing. "No, I am. I am such a giddy goose sometimes."

"Oh really?"

Thea nodded. "Once again it seems that I have let my common sense be overruled by stolen kisses and strong arms. You would think that after Hawley I would have learned something. I am a fool."

"Ah. And you have now changed your mind about those, er, stolen kisses and strong arms."

Thea looked curiously at her cousin. She was not an unhandsome woman and in her youth must have been comely, if not a beauty. "Did you never long for a man's kiss?" Thea asked.

"Oh, indeed, I did," Modesty answered, her eyes twinkling. "And there was one particular youth when I was twenty with whom I shared many a stolen embrace." Modesty sighed, her expression far away. "We planned to wed, but he died . . . and that was the end of that."

Thea looked at her, appalled. "Never again? You never met another man who moved your heart?"

Modesty smiled and shook her head. "No, I am afraid not. There were a few others that I might have married, but by the time I had finally put my grief behind me, I discovered that I valued my independence more than I did the title of 'wife.' "

Thea sank down onto the floor beside the chair where Modesty was sitting. Her spring green gown billowing around her slender body, she laid her head on Modesty's knee.

Modesty reached out and gently caressed the thick black hair. "What is it, chicken? What bedevils you so?"

Her dark eyes full of misery, Thea glanced up. "Oh, Modesty! I am so confused. I actually agreed to become his mistress."

Modesty did not need the "he" identified. Her hand never stopping in its gentle stroking, she asked, "Is that what you want? To be his mistress?"

Thea hesitated. "I don't know. I only know that when I am with him, the world and everything in it seems so much more exciting and thrilling. And when he kisses me, I can think of nothing but how wonderful it is to be held by him . . . to be kissed by him."

"And what about your heart? What does

your heart tell you?"

Thea looked startled. "I don't know. I —"

Modesty leaned forward and, lifting Thea's chin, she asked, "Do you love him, child?"

Thea bit back a sob. "Oh, Modesty, I fear that I do!" Unable to sustain the kindness in Modesty's gaze, she buried her head in Modesty's lap and muttered, "What am I to do? I'm afraid to trust my heart — look where it got me last time. And I cannot disgrace the family again — oh, but I do want him."

"And becoming his mistress is the only avenue open to you?"

"What else is there?" Thea asked in a gruff little voice. "I am ruined — everyone knows that! No gentleman would want to m-m-marry me."

"Are you so certain? Perhaps you did not give Mr. Blackburne a chance. Perhaps he feels as you do. Have you thought of that?"

Thea's head jerked up. "Oh, don't be silly! Even if he did l-l-love me, I would not marry him." The dark eyes burned fiercely. "I would never bring shame upon someone I loved, and if I were foolish enough to marry him, *if* he even wished to marry me, he would soon grow to hate me. I am a ruined woman — everyone knows that! My reputation will always follow me, and, in time, any man I married would learn to despise me and regret his moment of insanity. If I suspected that Patr . . . Mr. Blackburne was developing tender feelings for me, it would be my duty to repulse him — to give him such a disgust of me that every feeling of affection would die. It is either that or I send him away and refuse to speak or acknowledge him in any way. It would be the only way to save him from making a dreadful, dreadful mistake." She looked away and sighed. "No, marriage is not for me."

Modesty regarded her for a long time. "You are certain?"

Thea nodded. "Yes," she replied, her voice tight and determined. "I will not be responsible for another person's unhappiness. I killed Tom and brought shame on our family — even Edwina's disastrous marriage is my fault. If I had not . . . I could not bear to disgrace the family in such a fashion again." Thea stood up. "Which is why I must write to him and tell him that I have changed my mind and that I cannot become his mistress."

After Thea went upstairs to write her note to Patrick, Modesty sat for several minutes staring into space. A not-so-honorable plan occurred to her. Telling herself that her motives were pure, if not her methods, she considered it from all angles. She sighed. It would be risky, but in view of Thea's determination to continue to punish herself for what had happened in the past and refuse marriage — no matter how eligible the suitor or what her heart dictated — Modesty felt she had no choice. She grimaced. In fact, it would be just like that dear little fool to make a totally inappropriate match just to show everyone that she *deserved* nothing better. Her mind made up, Modesty stood and went upstairs to write her own note to Mr. Blackburne . . . and several more besides. Putting all the notes in Tillman's hands a short while later, she gave him strict instructions: they must all be delivered as soon as possible.

If Patrick was startled to receive two notes Saturday afternoon from the ladies residing at the Grosvenor Square house, he gave no sign of it. He read Thea's note first, relieved and not exactly surprised that she was crying off. As he suspected, she could and did delight in tweaking society's nose, but she was not about to flout one of its most stringent rules. She might sail close to the line, but she was not about to cross it. He smiled. His darling was much more conventional than she realized.

Laying Thea's note aside, he broke the seal on Modesty's missive and read the contents, his brow lifting as the import of what she had written became clear. Her plan was tempting and, he admitted, probably the only way that he was going to gain Thea's hand. But, oh lud, Thea would be furious! And he wouldn't blame her. Dare he risk it?

He mulled the situation over for most of the remainder of the afternoon. Was Modesty's scheme so very different from his own? It was certainly a delicate situation. He reread Modesty's note again, his heart sinking. If he were fool enough to offer for Thea, she'd turn him down flat — of that he had no doubt, and Modesty's note confirmed it. Thea herself had come to her senses and had put paid to the notion of becoming his mistress — which was going to make her skittish in his company in the future and view any attempt at courtship, no matter how subtle, with even more suspicion. He sighed. His dark-eyed little darling was really making things rather difficult for all of them.

Unhappily he wrote his answer to Modesty's scheme. The reply he sent back consisted of one word: No.

Modesty read his reply and shook her head. Despite his reputation, Patrick

Blackburne was really too honorable for his own good. She sat down and wrote another missive. Giving it to Tillman with the same instructions as her earlier notes, she waited anxiously for an answer. She had not long to wait. And this time, she got the answer she wanted.

Having answered Modesty's note, Patrick immediately wrote to Thea telling her that, while he was disappointed by her decision, he perfectly understood her feelings. He hoped that she would still allow him to call and squire her about the city from time to time. Thea replied promptly: As long as he understood that there could never be anything between them but friendship — she would be pleased to have his company now and again.

He grinned as he read Thea's prim little note on Monday morning. If she thought that it was only friendship between them, she was deluding herself! And if she thought he could keep his hands off her, she was mad!

Putting Thea out of his mind for the moment, Patrick turned his thoughts back to Ellsworth. One thing was clear: He was going to have to call upon Mr. Ellsworth in Surrey.

Glancing at his engagement calendar, he

realized that a trip to Surrey would have to wait until Wednesday or Thursday — he had a social obligation that he could not in all politeness put off, dinner at his mother's on Tuesday evening; she had been particularly insistent that he be there.

Briefly he considered leaving within the hour and returning in time for Lady Caldecott's dinner party tomorrow night. A quick look at the clock and the weather outside put that notion out of his head. It was already approaching noon, and it had been raining steadily all morning. He made a face. Driving willy-nilly through pounding rain, fighting muddy roads, was not a favorite pastime of his. Ellsworth could wait.

Concluding that his dark-eyed enchantress needed some time to deal with their new arrangement, Patrick put off calling upon her, although every instinct demanded that he do so. She dominated his thoughts, and if he were not so painfully unsure of the outcome, he might have found the situation amusing. Here he was, reputed to be a rake among rakes, but he discovered that, where Thea was concerned, he was as vulnerable and uncertain as the greenest moonling in love for the first time.

Patrick looked startled. In love? A smile spread slowly across his hard face. By gad!

So he was! And the creature who had captured his black heart (if gossip was to be believed) was none other than the notorious Thea Garrett. Patrick laughed aloud. It was fitting, he thought, a rake and a lady of scandal. Oh, what a pair they would make. He could hardly wait for Tony and Arabella to meet Thea. They would be, he felt sure, charmed.

Patrick had not expected to enjoy the dinner party given by his mother and had resigned himself to an evening of boredom. Needing to bring her current with what he had discovered, he arrived early to have a few moments' private conversation with her before the guests began to arrive.

Lady Caldecott looked regal. Her hair was dressed with pearls and diamonds, and in a dark blue satin gown discreetly trimmed in spangled lace, she appeared every inch the aristocrat she was.

Mother and son spoke briefly in her boudoir, Patrick confirming all he had learned and explaining his intention to call upon Ellsworth as soon as possible.

Her eyes anxious, Lady Caldecott asked, "You think that he is the man who has been blackmailing me?"

"Either that or in partnership with the

fellow who did the actual blackmailing."

Lady Caldecott hesitated. "There have been no more demands. Perhaps we should simply let matters rest for the time being? Might we not let sleeping dogs lie? I do not want you to put yourself in any danger." Her hand rested on his arm, her eyes fixed on his face. "You are my only child. I have never been a demonstrative woman, nor able easily to speak of what is in my heart, but I love you, my son, and if anything were to happen to you —" Her voice caught. She smiled, albeit mistily. "As I grow older I find that I am increasingly sentimental."

There had been a time when Patrick had viewed his mother as merely a cold society matron. It had only been recently that he had begun to see the woman behind the polite façade. Because of the blackmailer, he had spent more private time in his mother's company than he had in decades. He was aware, as he had not been previously, of her warm affectionate nature, and knowing that she had once loved unwisely and impetuously, he saw her very differently. Her vulnerability to the blackmailer and her plea for help had aroused all his protective instincts and had brought to life a corner of his heart he had thought closed to her.

Touched by her words, Patrick kissed her

scented cheek. "It must be a family failing," he said, "for I find that as the years pass, things I would have once dismissed as unimportant begin to take on paramount importance. Having your affection is one of those things." His expression soft and unguarded, he murmured, "I love you, Mama — and I shall try not to get myself injured."

Her anxious look did not disperse, and Patrick smiled, his gaze bright with laughter. "You know me, Mama — I have fought my share of duels and taken part in more than my share of dangerous pranks and not come to harm. As you once said yourself — the Devil looks after his own. Do not worry over me."

"Now why," she inquired dryly, "do your words fill me with greatest alarm?"

He grinned and kissed her cheek again. "Do not worry, Mama. All will be right — I swear it. Now shall we go downstairs and await your guests?"

Resigned to a tedious evening, Patrick was delighted when he discovered that Modesty and Thea were among the guests of Lady Caldecott's very exclusive dinner party. He had been conversing, that is, listening to the elderly Lord Markley drone on about the wild and disrespectful youth of the day, when a flash of brilliant color caught his eye.

He gazed across the width of his mother's large drawing room, his heart leaping when he spied Thea, looking ravishing in a gown of burgundy silk, exchanging greetings with Lord and Lady Caldecott. Accompanied by an older couple whom he did not recognize, Modesty and Thea were talking to his mother and stepfather. From the smiles and animated conversation, it was obvious, even if Modesty had not already alluded to it, that his mother and Modesty were more than just social acquaintances. Lady Caldecott also greeted the tall handsome man and his plump little wife with more than just social politeness. Patrick was suddenly very curious about them.

Leaving Lord Markley in mid-complaint, Patrick closed the distance between himself and the group near the double doors of the drawing room.

Bowing politely, he greeted Thea and Modesty and waited for his mother to introduce the other couple.

"Ah, you have never met Lord and Lady Garrett, have you, my dear?" Lady Caldecott murmured with a smile at her son. "Allow me to introduce you to them — they are Miss Garrett's aunt and uncle having come up from the country to London to stay for a while. I consider them some of my dearest friends. We have known each other for years."

Introductions were made, Patrick sizing up Thea's uncle and recognizing immediately which side of the family Thea's dark, speaking eyes had come from. Lord Garrett had the same almost black eyes and a way of looking at one that made Patrick think immediately of Thea.

"It is a pleasure to meet you both," Patrick said, bowing over Lady Garrett's little hand. "I hope your visit will be most enjoyable."

Lady Garrett's kind face blossomed with a warm smile. "Oh, so do we! It is such a pleasure finally to meet you — your mother has spoken so often of you, but we always seemed to have been in the country when you have been visiting London."

"We have not seen each other for several months and have much to gossip about," Patrick's mother said. "While we are catching up, why don't you introduce Miss Garrett around? I do not think that she knows many of the other guests."

Since he had already been considering ways to cut Thea out from the pack, Patrick positively beamed at her. "It will be my pleasure." And with Thea's hand resting on his arm, he whisked her away.

The five older people spoke for several moments before Lord and Lady Garrett were hailed by an old friend and wandered off to join him.

Freed at last to watch Thea and Patrick, Modesty and Lady Caldecott did so. Lord Caldecott watched, too, a little frown creasing his forehead.

When neither one of the ladies seemed inclined to speak, he asked, "Er, do you think that this is wise, my dear?"

Lady Caldecott looked pensive, her thoughts on the woman she had been decades ago, a married woman who had embarked on an adulterous affair. With her own history weighing on her conscience, how could she hold Thea's past against her? Heaven knows if the affair had come out, she would have been as ruined as Thea. Who was she to look down her nose or cast stones?

"Wisdom has nothing to do with it. I have longed for Patrick to marry for more than a decade," Lady Caldecott said, "and Miss Garrett is not only the first woman he has ever shown any inclination to marry, she is the *only* one." She looked wistful. "All that really counts is Patrick's happiness, and if she makes him happy, then I shall be happy." She smiled at Modesty. "Besides, Thea is related to one of my dearest friends — how could I be against such a union? It may not be the match I might have hoped for him, but then *he* may not be the match her family might have wanted for her either!"

"Well, yes, all that is very true," Lord Caldecott murmured, "but what about her past? Doesn't it trouble you?"

Bristling in defense of Thea, Modesty snapped, "Her family and fortune are more than respectable. And as for the scandal — it was a decade ago. My poor lamb did nothing wrong — other than to believe the words of a scoundrel!" She glared at Lord Caldecott. "And you would do well to remember that your stepson is no angel!" She shot an apologetic look at Lady Caldecott. "I know that he is your son, Alice, and I would never say anything to hurt you, you know that. Half of what I know of him has come from you, and you would be the first to admit that the word 'angelic' could never be applied to him."

"No, it could not!" Lady Caldecott agreed, amusement lurking in her fine eyes. "As his mother, I would be the first, regrettably, to admit *that!* He has been wild, reckless, stubborn to a fault, and high-handed. His actions have often driven me to despair, and as the years have passed the thing I despaired of most was that he would ever marry — or that if he did, it would be to someone totally unsuitable." She glanced again at the younger couple as Patrick was introducing Thea to Lord Markley. A soft smile played around her lips. "Thea will do very well for him. Very well indeed."

Having done his duty and introduced Thea to his mother's guests, Patrick decided he could now please himself. But before he could do as he longed, and abduct Thea out from under the noses of some of society's highest sticklers for a private moment, Thea suddenly stopped, and exclaimed, "Why, that is Uncle Hazlett! How wonderful!"

Leaving Patrick to follow behind her, she crossed to where a compact individual in a superbly cut dark blue coat was talking with Lord Garrett. Rushing up to the gentleman, Thea gave him a swift kiss on his cheek.

"Uncle! I did not expect to see you here tonight."

Lord Hazlett smiled. "Why not? Lord Caldecott and I have known each other for years." His eyes twinkled. "You are not the only one, my dear, who can make a bustle in society. How have you been these past weeks?"

Before Thea could reply, Patrick walked up and bowed politely to Lord Hazlett. "My lord. How are you this evening?"

Patrick knew Lord Hazlett slightly, and it surprised him to learn that he was Thea's maternal uncle. But then it shouldn't have — the aristocracy for all its power was actually very small when compared to England as a whole.

Dinner was announced, and for the time being Patrick gave up any idea of a moment alone with Thea. His handsome mouth twisted. Ah well, it was probably for the best. She was keeping him at arm's length, and any sudden move by him would probably send her bolting to Modesty's side — or one of her uncles. He sighed. He would have to move slowly. Unfortunately, patience had never been his strong suit.

Patrick might have been in a more cheerful frame of mind if he had known how very hard it was for Thea to keep him at arm's length. Every time she glanced at him, her heart began to beat in a most unseemly fashion. He was so handsome. And charming. And tall. And exciting. And oh, just everything. Had she been an utter fool to decide not to become his mistress?

A little frown marred her forehead. Perhaps he hadn't really wanted her for a mistress? After all, he had taken her refusal without a murmur of protest. Surely if he had wanted her, he would not have given in so easily? If he had *really* wanted her for his mistress, wouldn't he have tried to change her mind?

She shot him a perplexed look and blushed charmingly when he glanced up and caught her staring at him. He smiled, such a warm, inviting smile that Thea's toes curled in delight in her satin slippers. She was definitely a fool! A fool for having denied herself the pleasure of his lovemaking.

Patrick was thinking something very similar as his gaze traveled appreciatively over her flushed features and the slim, white shoulders revealed by her gown. She was everything he wanted, and his body stirred with blunt desire. He sighed. No, patience was definitely not one of his virtues!

The long dinner finally came to an end. There were fifty guests scattered about the length of the linen-draped table — Lady Caldecott's idea of a "small, intimate" gathering of dear friends — and Patrick wondered what she would have called a large dinner.

Watching his mother rise from her place

at the head of the table, he almost groaned. The dinner had been tedious enough, but now the ladies would withdraw and he would be denied even the sight of Thea's enchanting face across the table from him. He would have to drink at least one glass of port with the gentlemen before escaping the dining room.

A smile on her face, Lady Caldecott lightly tapped a spoon against her crystal glass. When the guests all looked her way, she said, "I have an announcement to make — one that makes me very happy and one that I despaired of ever being able to make."

She smiled warmly at Patrick and an awful suspicion suddenly burst through him. He cast a swift glance at Modesty and her demure expression sent a chill along his spine. Oh, lud! They were for it now!

"I wish at this time to announce the betrothal of my dear son, Patrick, to the very charming Miss Thea Garrett. A notice has already been sent to the *Times* and will appear in tomorrow's newspaper." With nary a pause, she closed the trap. "The haste with which their wedding has been planned might seem unusual, but as so many of our friends and acquaintances have already left the city for the winter, there is no reason to delay. Do not forget — the demands of my son's plantation in America limit the length of his stay in England. I believe that he plans to leave for America in a few weeks — taking his bride with him. They will marry, by special license, this very Saturday." She sent a satisfied smile down the length of the table, passing quickly over Patrick's rigid features and Thea's blank ones. "All of you are invited. Lord and Lady Garrett have already agreed to allow my husband and me to have the wedding and reception here." Lady Caldecott beamed. "Isn't it wonderful!"

Chapter Ten

"You are the most underhanded, perfidious, *wicked* person I have ever known!" Thea exploded the minute she was alone with her betrothed. "How could I have trusted you? You lied to everyone — even your own mother. How could you? I thought that I had met the blackest-hearted beast in nature when Hawley Randall betrayed me, but *you — !*" Words failed her, and she shut her mouth with an audible snap that made Patrick wince.

In the shadowy darkness of the coach taking them to Thea's London residence, Patrick could not see Thea's features clearly, but he had no doubt of her feelings. He grimaced. He didn't blame her for feeling as she did either. His mother and Modesty had neatly boxed them in, and while he knew that he was innocent of all the crimes his seething bride-to-be laid at his feet, it was unlikely that she would believe his protestations to the contrary.

At least she had waited until they were alone to vent her rage, Patrick thought, and for that he was thankful. And she had not publicly contradicted his mother's announcement — for which he was even more grateful. He wanted to marry Thea. He intended to marry Thea. And while he would have wished to have arranged things in his own fashion, he was not above taking advantage of the situation. His mother and Modesty might have sprung as neat a trap as he had ever seen, but he had no inclination to escape from it. Not when he shared it with the dark-eyed virago who had captured his heart.

"You are vile!" Thea declared. "Vile and unprincipled and I will *not* marry you! Not even if you were the only man in the world. Not even if — !"

"Yes, you will," Patrick murmured, and plucked her from her seat across from him in the coach.

"Let me go!" Thea gasped, struggling to escape from his firm clasp. "Who do you think you are? Unhand me this instant, you blackguard."

She was a bundle of vibrating outrage, but Patrick effortlessly settled her on his lap. He sympathized with her feelings, but whether they liked it or not, they had been well and truly trapped by as clever a pair of conspirators as he had ever met. No amount of rage or fury was going to change things, and

Thea had to realize that they were going to have to make the best of things. They would marry. On Saturday.

Stilling her efforts to free herself from his grip, he asked, "Would you believe me, if I told you I had nothing to do with what happened tonight? That my mother's announcement came as much as a shock to me as it did to you? Would you believe that my mother and Modesty put their heads together and duped both of us? That I am as innocent as you?"

Thea flashed him a look. "No," she snapped. "And you are reprehensible to try to blame two of the kindest, finest women I know for your own duplicity."

Patrick sighed. He didn't think she would believe him, but it had been worth a try. "What do you want me to do, sweetheart?" he asked. "Shall I write the *Times* and inform them that the announcement is a mistake? That my mother lied? Have a retraction printed? Would you like that? It should cause at least twice the storm of gossip the news of our betrothal will cause. Perhaps you like being the subject of gossip?"

Thea drew in a furious breath. "Of all the wicked things to say! Of course I do not want to be the topic of gossip. After what I went through, you think I *like* notoriety? Are you mad?"

He smiled. "Only for you, sweetheart. Only for you."

Thea glared at him, not believing him for a moment. But she was very aware of him and wished she wasn't. She wished she found him as vile and repulsive as she claimed. But she didn't. Worse, she was conscious of him in a way that made her distinctly uneasy. His firm thighs were beneath her buttocks, his arms were holding her prisoner, and his mouth was only inches above hers. She was *very* aware of that mouth, memories of its touch, the sweet sensations it aroused, curling through her. Oh, blast! He had her emotions in a tangle and at this moment, she hated him. He had tricked her. Deceived her. Inveigled his poor mother and dear Modesty into a plot to help with his nefarious designs — and then he tried to blame them!

Her chin lifted imperiously. "Why should I believe you? I know that you don't want to marry me — you wanted me for your mistress." She gasped as a thought occurred to her. "You did this because I wouldn't become your mistress!" Her eyes narrowed. "Revenge! That's why you are doing this. Because I changed my mind about becoming your mistress, you are taking revenge by forcing me to marry you."

Patrick smothered a laugh. Only Thea would believe that there was something more honorable about becoming his mistress rather than his wife.

"Are you certain you don't want to think about that a little longer?" he teased. "Most women would be pleased by a marriage proposal."

Thea crossed her arms over her chest. "As I recall," she muttered, "you did not propose to me. At least not marriage."

His lips quirked. "Very well then." His head dropped and his lips brushed hers. "Miss Garrett, will you do me the very great honor of becoming my wife? Please?"

Thea's heart nearly leaped out of her throat at the touch of his mouth on hers, and her stomach felt as if it had dropped right down to her toes. But she was not going to let him distract her — no matter how pleasurable. Her lips tingling from his light caress, she gathered her scattered forces.

Sitting as far away from him as space, and his arms, would allow, she replied with relish, "Absolutely not!"

"You have cut me to the quick, sweetheart," Patrick said. "But I am afraid that you have no choice — even if all the guests at my mother's tonight could be sworn to silence, there is, you see, that damnable notice to the *Times*."

Thea stared at him for several seconds, her thoughts in chaos. Would it be so very bad being married to him? In her heart she knew the answer to that question, and while she was wildly attracted to him, it did not change the fact that she mistrusted him and did not understand his motives. That someone like Patrick Blackburne would actually want to marry her never crossed her mind — despite the intervening decade and her seeming acceptance back into the bosom of the ton, she never forgot that she was a ruined woman and that she had caused her brother's death. She did not know how to judge Patrick. Her reputation did not seem to deter him . . . and her reckless antics, such as the trip to a certain house on Curzon Street, had not seemed to give him a distaste for her. Was it her reputation that drew him? Was he using her to thumb his nose at society? Did he think her past would make her a complaisant wife, willing to turn a blind eye to other women in his life?

Feeling sick inside, she glanced out the window of the coach. She did not like the direction of her thoughts, but nothing else made much sense. Everything inside of her rebelled at thinking him so jaded, so calculating, but she could not deny that he had tricked her into marriage — for whatever reasons. It was all suddenly too much for her. Her emotions were tearing her apart, her heart leaning one way, past experience another. Two things were inescapable: He appealed to her in a way she could not explain, and though she was angry and resentful of it, tonight's announcement in a room full of the leaders of the ton and the dreaded notice in the *Times* sealed her fate. She would marry Patrick Blackburne.

Bleakly she said, "I cannot disagree with what you say. My family appears to be elated with the match, and I would do much to please them." She shot him an unfriendly glance. "Even marry you."

"As long as you marry me," Patrick muttered, ashamed of the exultation that flooded him. She would be his wife, and he would woo her and seduce and demand that she love him. And when her heart was won, why then, he would lay his own at her feet. Full of anticipation of the battle he would wage to win her love, he swept her against him and his mouth caught hers. He kissed her with all the hunger he had kept at bay, with all the longing that was within him.

Thea stiffened in his embrace. She was in no mood to be wooed, certainly not for dalliance, but her body, her heart, had other ideas. As his arms tightened and his kiss deepened, desire stirred and sprang to life within her, and all thought of resisting him fled. She loved him — wretch that he was! With a half sigh, half sob, she flung her arms around his neck and pressed ardently against him, returning his kiss.

She was sweet and yielding, her lips soft and willing, her taste intoxicating, and Patrick took all that was offered. Like potent wine she went instantly to his head, his breathing becoming ragged and the ache between his legs suddenly unbearable.

Heedless of the swaying coach, of its approach to the house, Patrick kissed her with growing passion, his rigid member pressing insistently against her buttocks, the soft swell of her bosom burning into his chest. He had to touch her. Had to.

His hand grazed her breast, cupping it gently before continuing its downward journey. The folds of her silk skirts impeded him only slightly, and he groaned when his hand finally slipped beneath the fabric and met the bare flesh of her leg.

Giddy and dazed, Thea clung to him, the sensation of his warm hand caressing her leg sending delicious thrills through her. When he clasped her thigh and kneaded its gentle contours, she gave an incoherent exclamation. Nothing had ever felt this way. Nothing. She ached everywhere. She wanted him to touch her everywhere. Most of all, she ached and yearned for him to continue his explorations. When he did, when his seeking fingers finally touched the thatch at the junction of her thighs, a shudder tore through her. Beset by unfamiliar emotions, Thea squirmed on his lap, the sensation of his swollen shaft rubbing against her bottom adding to the tumult inside of her.

"Your legs, sweetheart, part them, let me touch you," Patrick murmured against her mouth, urging her backward.

Drunk with sensation, Thea obeyed. How could she not? Every nerve and sinew in her slender body wanted this magic to continue. Her mind and body were united in one long yearning ache, but Patrick's touch, as he parted and petted the delicate flesh hidden by the thick curls, only made the ache worse, and she shuddered again. He was driving her mad, she thought dizzily, panting and twisting under his exploration. Suddenly one of his fingers slipped inside of her, and she almost screamed with delight.

The most primitive, demanding feelings rose up within her, shaking her, making her aware of the naked hunger that coursed through her body.

She wanted him. Trembling and uncertain, she kissed him repeatedly, her fingers clenching and unclenching in his thick, dark hair, her body inviting his caresses.

No less a prisoner of his emotions than Thea, Patrick groaned at her provocative actions. He wanted nothing more than to join them together, to unleash the passion that clawed through him, but he was painfully aware that there was no time. Oh, but there was time, a part of his brain conceded, for him . . .

He almost did it. Almost pushed Thea down onto the seat, almost freed himself and sought relief between her soft thighs. But he did not. There was a part of him, the sane part, that did not want their first joining to be a tawdry affair swiftly done on the seat of a coach. No, not only did he not want their first time together to be in these circumstances, he wanted time, time in which to give her pleasure, time in which to teach her the joys that could be shared by a man and a woman.

That thought had hardly crossed his mind when the carriage slowed to a stop. Swallowing back an urge to howl in frustration, Patrick regretfully removed his hand from beneath Thea's skirts and set her upright on the seat across from him.

"I am afraid," he muttered, "that we shall have to postpone our mutual pleasure for another time. You are home."

Thea stared blankly at him. Her body still on fire, the desire he had provoked still dominating her every thought, it took a moment for reality to return, and as it did, shame and mortification flooded her.

Suddenly frantic to escape him, before Patrick could divine her actions, she dived for the door of the coach and wrenching it open, sprang down from the coach. When Patrick would have followed her, she held up one hand.

"Don't," she said in a shaken voice. "I do not want your company. Leave me alone."

His lips tightened. "That is going to be rather difficult don't you think, since we are engaged to be married."

Thea bit back a sob, overwhelmed by the entire situation. "Leave me alone," she repeated. Picking up her burgundy skirts, she flew up the steps and disappeared inside.

Smothering a curse, Patrick sank back down onto the coach seat. Opening the divider between the interior and the coachman, he growled, "To White's."

Let down near the entrance to the club, Patrick walked up the steps and entered. He had been a member of White's since his father had put his name up for admission in what seemed a lifetime ago. Since the evening was still early by the standards of him and his friends, Patrick wasn't surprised to find Lord Embry, Adam Paxton, and a half dozen or so other acquaintances gathered around one of the gaming tables.

He watched the play for several minutes before catching Lord Embry's eye. Motioning his need for private conversation, he waited until Embry could excuse himself. Paxton caught the exchange and lifted his brow. Patrick made a face. A moment later, Paxton, too, threw down his cards and left the table.

Flanked by his two friends, Patrick headed for a quiet corner. When the three friends were seated and had been served glasses of port by a servant in black knee breeches, Patrick said, "I have an announcement to make. Once I have made it, I intend to get very drunk. Are you with me?"

"Why, I should be delighted to get drunk with you," Nigel replied. "I have not been thoroughly foxed for at least three days."

Adam smiled and lifted his glass in Patrick's direction. "It sounds like a pleasant way to pass the evening."

Patrick took a long swallow of his port. Looking at his friends' expectant faces, he said, "I want you to be among the first to know — I'm going to be married — soon. The notice will be in the *Times* tomorrow morning. The wedding will be Saturday afternoon — at m'mother's." A smile crossed his face at the stunned expressions of Embry and Paxton. "You'll be pleased to know that my bride-to-be is Thea Garrett." At Nigel's gasp and Paxton's pop-eyed stare, Patrick grinned.

When Paxton and Embry continued to stare at him as if he had suddenly sprouted horns and snorted fire, he murmured, "Congratulations are in order, you know."

"By Jove!" Nigel sputtered. "Have you gone mad? I warned you about her. Didn't you listen to a word I said?"

His expression warning his two friends to tread with care, Patrick said, "You would do well to remember, my friend, that you are talking about the lady I intend to marry . . . need I say more?"

Nigel blanched. Nigel considered himself a brave soul, but it would take a braver soul than he to leave himself open to the prospect of facing Patrick on the dueling field.

Patrick's skill with both pistol and sword was very well known.

Paxton cleared his throat. "Ah . . . how did this come about? I don't recall that you were, er, courting the lady."

Patrick smiled and sipped his port. "I have been, believe me. And I shall be the first to admit that my, uh, courtship has been most unusual. But the lady is won, and I intend to marry her."

Nigel's gaze sharpened. "You're in love with the chit!"

"I fear so," Patrick replied, with a twinkle in his gray eyes.

"It's a love match?" Paxton asked, not quite ready to believe what he had just heard.

Patrick nodded. "Very much so." He grimaced. "Although, at the moment, the lady would probably prefer to bury me than to marry me."

"Aha!" exclaimed Nigel. "I warned you." At the look Patrick sent him, he clapped his mouth shut.

"Marriage on Saturday, eh?" Paxton inquired. At Patrick's nod, he added, "Then I suggest that we find someplace less respectable where we can become disgustingly drunk."

"My thoughts precisely," Patrick replied.

* * *

While Patrick and his cronies were at White's, Thea was in her bedchamber, being helped to undress by Maggie. Thea didn't really need any help, but Maggie would have been offended if she had spurned her services, and so she endured having Maggie do things for her that she could have done very easily herself.

Maggie noticed that Thea's features looked strained and that her mistress was unusually silent. When Thea was finally wearing a fine lawn nightgown and settled amidst a pile of pillows on the bed, Maggie hesitated to leave her.

Standing beside the bed, she asked, "Is there anything else I can get you, miss? Perhaps a hot drink?"

Thea shook her head. "No thank you, Maggie. I am fine. Go to bed."

Maggie hesitated, and Thea waved a hand at her. "Go."

After Maggie had left the room, Thea sat there in her bed, wondering at the whims of fate. In the terrible aftermath following Hawley's and Tom's deaths, she had been certain that she would never love again. She had sworn during those anguish-filled days that she would never trust a silver-tongued devil again. Knowing that she was utterly ruined and that the world knew it, too, she had resigned herself to never marrying. Certainly she had never thought that a suitable gentleman would ever *want* to marry her. She sighed. At the moment, she couldn't say that Patrick *wanted* to marry her — a twisted need to pay her back for refusing to become his mistress might be driving him.

Her thinking was not as convoluted as it appeared — there were men, and she had known several, who went to incredible lengths to avenge themselves of even the tiniest slight. It was not impossible that Patrick was of that ilk.

She frowned. He had never shown any sign of being petty-minded, but then one never knew. Certainly, she did not know him well. She sighed again, her expression morose. No, she did not know him well, but what she did know she found very, very appealing and attractive.

She was aware of Modesty's arrival home, having heard several minutes earlier the faint sounds of the door to Modesty's rooms opening and shutting. As the evening at the Caldecotts had drawn to a close, Thea learned that it had been arranged for Lord and Lady Garrett to bring Modesty home in their coach. Since it was unlikely that Modesty would not want to talk about the night's events, Thea braced herself for a visit.

She had not long to wait. A soft rap on the door came next, and wearing a sumptuous amber dressing gown of silk and lace to cover her nightgown, Modesty stepped into Thea's bedchamber.

Shutting the door behind her, Modesty crossed the room and, settling on the edge of the bed, said, "I was hoping that you had not yet gone to sleep. I was quite delighted when I saw the light coming from beneath the door of your room." Picking up Thea's hand, she clasped it lightly. "Well, chicken," she said with a smile, "it was certainly an eventful evening, wasn't it?"

Thea smiled wanly. "Indeed it was." She sent a look of inquiry to Modesty. "Were you as bowled over as I was?"

Modesty glanced down at her lap. "Not exactly," she admitted. "It has been obvious, to me at least, that Mr. Blackburne was quite taken with you."

Thea sighed. "He wanted me for his mistress, Modesty, not his wife."

"If that was the case, then what was tonight all about?"

Thea made a face. "I don't know. I only know that when Lady Caldecott made her announcement, I was stunned. Marriage had never been even mentioned between

Patrick and me." A flicker of suspicion in her gaze, she demanded, "Did you know about it? And my uncles? Did everyone but me know what was planned?"

Modesty appeared astounded. "Thea! How could you think such a thing? Do you think I, er, we would sink to such depths . . . that your family would coerce you into marrying someone you didn't want to? I must confess that I find this conversation most disturbing. Are you telling me that you *don't* wish to marry Mr. Blackburne?"

"N-N-No," Thea confessed, "not exactly."

"Then what?" demanded Modesty. "Aren't you the young woman who only days ago admitted to me that you loved him? Have your feelings changed?"

Thea shook her head, looking confused and miserable. "I do love him. I just do not understand how one minute he is willing for me to become his mistress and the next, without so much as a by-your-leave, he has it announced that we are to be married on Saturday! Without causing a terrible scandal, I have no choice but to marry him." Uncertainly she began, "You don't suppose that he could be thumbing his nose at society or trying to get back at me for refusing to become his mistress?"

Modesty's brows flew up. "Of all the ridiculous ideas I have ever heard! A gentleman of Mr. Blackburne's stature would not stoop so low. Besides, doesn't it seem a rather, ah, desperate step to take, for such a slight?"

"I suppose you are right," Thea admitted. "But you must agree that it was the most underhanded thing of him to have his mother make that announcement this evening without even asking *me* whether I wanted to marry him or not! That was arrogant and unprincipled."

Her cheeks suddenly blooming with color, Modesty said, "Er, perhaps, he didn't dare take a chance that you would be high-minded and refuse him." Hastily she added, "Refuse him for all the wrong reasons, of course. He may have thought that giving you no other choice was the only way he could bring about your marriage."

Puzzled, Thea looked at Modesty. "And you think it is honorable, what he did?"

Modesty cleared her throat, looking decidedly ill at ease. "I wouldn't call it, er, honorable, but it was not *dis*honorable after all." She brightened. "You might say that it was expeditious!"

"It was certainly that," Thea said dryly.

Modesty patted her hand. "Don't brood

over it, dear. Just think, on Saturday afternoon you are going to marry one of the most eligible gentlemen in London. We have much to arrange and plan for before then." Modesty put a finger to her lip. "A wedding gown must be procured immediately. We shall have to prevail upon our favorite dressmaker to put aside all her other patrons' demands for a few days." She beamed at Thea. "Oh, isn't it exciting? You are going to be married!"

Despite her gloomy state and her mistrust of Patrick's motives, some of Modesty's enthusiasm began to rub off on Thea. A queer little spark of excitement billowed in her chest. She was going to be married! To Patrick Blackburne! There were, she admitted with a dreamy smile as she remembered his flashing smile and those moments in the coach, a few advantages to such a match.

Thea woke the next morning to discover that nearly everyone in the polite world had read the announcement of her impending nuptials and had come to call. She and Modesty had barely finished their breakfast and settled in the morning room to discuss plans before callers began to arrive. To her astonishment, Thea found herself basking in the approval of some of the most powerful leaders of society. She was fawned upon and petted and exclaimed over and viewed her suddenly exalted position with wide-eyed bewilderment. The early callers ranged from a genuine friend such as Lady Roland, thrilled by the news, to members of her own family such as Lord and Lady Garrett, Lord Hazlett, and her favorite cousin, his son, John. Thea had little doubt that the family was here as a sign of solidarity, signaling to the world that *they* did not think the haste and circumstances of her imminent marriage the least peculiar. A lump formed in Thea's throat, and she vowed that her reckless days were over — she would never embarrass or shame them again.

The fact that polite society had forgiven all was apparent when Lady Jersey, the Prince of Wales's current mistress and one of the patronesses of Almack's, swam into the room. Sitting down on the sofa beside Thea, Lady Jersey purred, "Dear, dear Thea, how wonderful for you! I was so elated when I read the announcement this morning. It is a shame that that charming rascal Patrick is determined to wrest you away from us so soon and not even allow you time to plan a proper wedding. Oh, but it is so very romantic, don't you think?"

Thea nodded, flashing an amused glance to Lisbeth, who sat across from them in the crowded morning room. In addition to the early arrivals, the room was now filled with dozens of fluttering women, from dashing fashionable matrons to simpering young ladies — their formidable mothers in tow. Even Patrick's friends Lord Embry and Adam Paxton had come to offer their congratulations. From the wince Nigel gave when one of the young ladies laughed rather loudly in his vicinity and the slightly green cast to Paxton's face, Thea suspected that they, and her betrothed, had spent the previous evening becoming thoroughly foxed. She hoped Patrick was suffering dreadfully.

Tillman, and a hastily-pressed-into-service footman, were gliding about with trays of refreshments, performing just as if this were a normal occurrence. The superior expression on her butler's face told Thea that he was enjoying himself.

Sipping a cup of coffee, Thea cast a bemused glance about the room, not quite able to believe that she was the cause of all this beaming goodwill. Of course she was smart enough to realize that it was *who* she was going to marry that had aroused all the curiosity and excitement — that and the fact that her betrothed was the son of one of the bulwarks of society, Lady Caldecott.

Watching the reactions of the company

when Lady Caldecott arrived a half hour later, Thea hid a smile. Sweeping grandly into the room, her fashionable blue gown fluttering around her ankles, Lady Caldecott smiled with satisfaction at the crowd before her. With all the haughty charm of a sovereign greeting her subjects, she nodded to this one and that as she made her way to Thea's side. Pressing a warm kiss onto Thea's cheek, she murmured, "My dear child! How are you bearing up under all this scrutiny?"

Thea grinned. "It is the most amazing thing! They all seem to like me."

Lady Caldecott chuckled and, glancing around, said softly, "And they are prudent to do so — otherwise they will have to deal with me."

Thea giggled. "Do you know that there are times that your son sounds remarkably like you?"

"What a charming thing to say," Lady Caldecott replied with a twinkle in her eyes. "Now tell me, have you and Modesty decided who is to sew your gown?"

Modesty and Lisbeth wandered over and there was a spirited discussion of the merits of several well-known dressmakers currently working in London. Patting Thea's hand, Lady Caldecott said, "I was never blessed with a daughter . . . I hope that you will allow me to guide you in this matter." She smiled gently. "And allow me to pay for your gown. It will give me such pleasure."

Thea was never certain afterward how it came about, but she found herself meekly agreeing to Lady Caldecott's request. Lady Caldecott, having accomplished what she had set out to do, rose to her feet. "Leave everything to me, my dear."

Gradually the crowd dispersed, and the newcomers became fewer and fewer. The last of them had just departed, leaving Lisbeth, Modesty, and Thea to sink back into their chairs in exhaustion, when Edwina erupted into the room.

Her blue eyes stormy, she strode into the room, and, tossing a copy of the morning *Times* onto Thea's lap, she demanded, "Is that true? Are you going to marry Patrick Blackburne?"

Modesty and Lisbeth exchanged a look, both of them straightening in their seats.

Taken aback by her sister's entrance, Thea blinked, and admitted, "Yes, it is. I am to marry him on Saturday."

Edwina sucked in her breath. "Why, you sly thing! You compel me to marry a nobody like Hirst and then you snatch a wealthy, well-connected gentleman for yourself!"

"That's enough, Edwina!" Modesty snapped. "No one compelled you to marry Hirst. You insisted upon it — despite Thea's pleadings to the contrary. You should be happy for your sister's good fortune."

A pout upon her pretty face, Edwina sank into a nearby chair. "I am happy for Thea," she insisted in a tone that gave the lie to her words. "It just doesn't seem fair," she complained, "that Thea should be the one to make the grand match in the family. I always wanted to marry someone like him — and I would have if it weren't for that dreadful scandal Thea caused." Edwina fluffed her golden curls. "Everyone has always said that I am much prettier than she is, and besides — I don't have her reputation."

Edwina's words cut deep, and the glow that had surrounded Thea vanished. Edwina's vanity had always been difficult for Thea to understand and excuse, but she had always blamed herself for much of it. After all, she had helped spoil Edwina, and the child was young — and lovely.

Lisbeth made no excuses. It was her oft-stated opinion that Edwina Hirst was a spoiled, headstrong, selfish little witch. A fighting gleam in her sea-green eyes, Lisbeth murmured, "Pretty is as pretty does, and as for a reputation . . . I wouldn't be too certain that yours is spotless."

Edwina glared at her. "What do you mean? Who is talking about me? Is someone spreading lies about me?"

"Not that I know of," Lisbeth returned carelessly. "But I would be careful, my pet, that you do not earn the reputation of being a spoiled brat. Or a woman who makes a cuckold of her husband — and I don't mean with Lord Pennington."

"How dare you!" Edwina exclaimed, leaping to her feet. Glancing at Thea, she demanded, "Are you going to let her speak to me that way?"

The urge to soothe Edwina's ruffled feathers was instinctive, and yet Thea hesitated. She might overlook and make excuses for many of her sister's childish and arrogant actions, but she was not blind to them. As much as she did not want to admit it, there was enough of a ring of truth about Lisbeth's words to make her say, "Your argument is with Lisbeth, not me." Stiffening her sudden resolve to allow Edwina to fend for herself occasionally, she added, "As you have told me often enough — you are a grown woman, a married woman, and quite old enough to make your own decisions. If you are offended by Lisbeth's comments, *you* settle it."

Edwina's pretty mouth dropped open unattractively, and she could not have been more astonished if Thea had spit on her. Modesty looked away, biting her lip, the faintest of smiles creasing her cheeks.

Lisbeth glanced approvingly at Thea. "Well done, my dear. I wondered how much longer you were going to put up with her antics."

Edwina gasped. Looking from one face to another and seeing that there was no help to be found, she jumped to her feet. "Well! If you feel that way, there is no reason for me to stay any longer." Stomping to the door, she rushed out of the room.

Thea half rose to her feet, but Modesty's firm grip on her arm kept her in place. "Let her go," Modesty murmured. "Everything you said was true. It is time that she learns to curb that tongue of hers and begins to think about the effect of her actions on other people. For too long Edwina has only thought of herself and what she wants."

Thea smiled unhappily. "I know, and it is my fault. I do not want to be too harsh on the child."

"She is not a child," Lisbeth said. "And you are doing her no good by your misguided coddling." Lisbeth rose to her feet. Pinching Thea's cheek affectionately, she added, "Be happy, sweet — you deserve it. I look forward to dancing at your wedding on Saturday."

The room seemed very quiet after Lisbeth had departed. Modesty and Thea looked at each other.

"This morning has been rewarding," Modesty said, "but you know, I am glad to have peace descend upon us — at least for a while."

Thea smiled. "Incorrect it may be, but me, too!"

Tillman knocked and entered. He was holding a silver salver almost overflowing with calling cards and notes. "Would miss care to go through these now, or shall I set them away for later?"

Thea shrugged, and after Tillman had left, leaving the salver with them, she and Modesty began the very gratifying task of reading the messages and reliving the morning's triumphs.

Thea found the note halfway through the pile. A smile on her face, she opened it and began to read the contents. Her shocked gasp made Modesty look up in alarm.

Her features ashen, her eyes great black pools in her white face, Thea handed the note to Modesty. Quickly Modesty scanned it, her mouth tightening as she read:

I know what you did and I have the evidence to prove it. If you wish my continued silence, you will follow these instructions precisely. Tell no one. If you go to Bow Street, I shall know and make plans accordingly. If anyone interferes with any of the steps I have set forth, I shall expose you.

There will be a black hackney waiting at the entrance to Hyde Park this afternoon at thirty minutes past five o'clock. The hackney will be empty. The driver knows nothing. Leave nine thousand pounds in small notes in a satchel on the seat of the coach. Do not make any attempt to follow the hackney — if you do, it shall go ill for you.

Chapter Eleven

It was later that day when Lady Caldecott finally climbed the steps to her own home. She'd been very busy on Patrick and Thea's behalf and was pleased with her efforts. Upon leaving Thea's town house, first on her agenda had been a visit to her favorite dressmaker. When she had left the discreet little shop, after two hours of intense discussion, she was confident that her son's bride was going to look positively ravishing on Saturday afternoon . . . and that the gown *would* be ready. From there she had called upon a half dozen of the most powerful female leaders of the town and had oh, so, politely cultivated their support for Patrick and Thea. All in all she felt very satisfied.

Upon entering her home, she ordered a tea tray and settled comfortably in her blue sitting room, prepared to spend a pleasant afternoon planning for Saturday's event. The Lords Garrett and Hazlett had indicated their willingness to handle all aspects of the wedding, but Lady Caldecott had politely brushed their offers away. This was to be her show. And when Lady Caldecott let it be known, ever so sweetly, that she had certain plans in mind, wise people usually found it agreeable to demur to her, er, wishes.

Her butler entered, and along with the silver tray covered with tea things, he also presented his mistress with all the cards and notes that had arrived while she had been out. Idly picking through the piles of cards and reading the names of some of the well-known members of the aristocracy who had come to call, her last doubts about the gamble she and Modesty had undertaken eased. Hastily planned the wedding might be, unorthodox it undoubtedly was, but it *would* be a success — she would see to it.

She had just taken a sip of her tea and was on the point of pushing the heap of cards away for later, more leisurely, contemplation when a folded note caught her eye. Picking it up she broke the seal and read the contents.

I have the letters. They make fascinating reading. If you wish their return, wear the Caldecott pearls to your son's wedding on Saturday. However, if you wear the Blackburne rubies, I shall know what to think . . . and make other plans.

Her fingers trembling, Lady Caldecott reread the note at least a dozen times. Her first impulse was to write to Patrick, demanding his presence, but she hesitated. Her son was to be married in less than four days; she was not going to have him involved in her troubles at a time like this.

Her lips twisted. It was bad enough that she and Modesty had sprung their trap on Patrick and Thea — even if they had had the couple's best interests at heart — to add to Patrick's troubles at this time was unthinkable. She would not let her worries distract her. No. She would wear the bloody pearls and see where it led. There would be time enough to tell Patrick what she had done after the wedding. In the meantime, she would wear her pearls — she had planned to wear them anyway, and the Blackburne rubies would have clashed dreadfully with the puce gown she had selected to wear on Saturday.

Lord Caldecott wandered in, looking very handsome in his dark gray jacket and black breeches. His silvery-fair hair was brushed back from his patrician brow, and his sky-blue eyes were tender as they rested on her. Lady Caldecott's pulse jumped at the sight of him. She had never thought to love this deeply, this profoundly, and the powerful emotions this one man aroused in her bosom still astounded her. Even more astonishing — he seemed to feel exactly the same toward her.

She was always happy to see him, but his presence just now was particularly soothing to her. For a while, in his company, she could push aside all her worries and fears, forget for the moment that there was a blackmailer hounding her and that her dear son was risking his own safety to find the culprit. The days ahead were going to be busy and full, and she was determined not to let anxious thoughts ruin it for her — or her son.

"Hello, my dear," Lord Caldecott murmured, as he leaned over and kissed her on the mouth. "You are looking very beautiful this afternoon." He smiled. "And very, *very* pleased with yourself."

He seated himself beside her and it was only after she had poured his tea and he had taken a sip that he set his cup down and said, "It seems that you and your friend, Modesty, are to be congratulated. Mind, I did not think you could bring it about, but it seems that your gamble paid off. Everywhere I went today, no one could talk of anything else but your son's impending nuptials." He smiled. "I did my best at my various clubs to scotch any speculation about the announcement and the hastiness of the wedding."

Lady Caldecott beamed at him, gratitude warming her breast. "As I knew you would," she murmured with a teasing glance.

He chuckled. "You know me too well, my sweet." His gaze became intent. "You hold my happiness in this little hand of yours," he said, picking up that member from where it lay on the sofa between them. "You know," he added softly, "that there is nothing I would deny you — remember always, my sweet, that I will do everything within my power to keep you safe and happy." He grinned. "Even if it means helping you hoodwink society about your son's sudden marriage."

Deeply moved, Lady Caldecott laid her head on his shoulder. "You are too good to me."

He kissed her. "And you are everything I ever dreamed of in a wife." They kissed again.

Lord and Lady Caldecott were enjoying their tea, when Patrick rapped on the door a few minutes later.

"Good afternoon," he said as he entered and walked across the room to stand in front of the hearth. "I hope that all is well with both of you."

Lord Caldecott murmured something polite and, putting down his cup and saucer, stood up. "Very well, indeed. After last night," he said with a mocking glint in his eyes, "I am sure that you have much to discuss with your mother — so I shall leave you to get on with it."

"Coward," murmured Lady Caldecott, over the rim of her cup.

Lord Caldecott glanced at her. "Indeed not, my dear — prudent."

Once her husband had departed and Patrick had declined her offer of refreshment, she looked up challengingly at her son as he stood in front of the hearth, one arm resting on the white-marble mantel. "Well?" she demanded. "Are you very angry at me?"

Patrick smiled, albeit caustically. "Why should I be when you have given me the one thing I wish above all else — Thea as my wife."

His mother regarded him closely, unable to discern anything from his dark, shuttered features. His words gave her hope that he was not too furious with her, but she could not tell for certain. Patrick had never been easy to read. She took a breath, and murmured, "I must say that you are taking it better than I had expected."

"And you, dear Mama, are bloody lucky

that the scheme you and Modesty hatched last night did not explode in your faces," he said. "Tell me what would you have done if I had risen from my seat and denied your announcement . . . or Thea had?"

"We were, I'm afraid, counting on surprise . . . and the feelings we suspected you have for each other to win the day." She cocked her head to one side, and, a question in her eyes, she said, "And it worked, didn't it?"

"Beautifully," Patrick replied, a grin spreading across his face. "I could not have arranged it better." He sent her a warning look. "But I would not try such a trick again. Next time it might be you who are surprised — unpleasantly."

She nodded. "Yes, I'm aware of that, and if the matter had not been so urgent and necessary, we would never have taken such drastic steps." She leaned forward. "You know that I only want your happiness. When Modesty wrote to me and explained the situation, we could see no other way — for both you and Thea. Will you forgive me for acting like a doting mother?"

"You have won this hand," he conceded, "and I have no ill will toward you — in fact, you may say that you have my gratitude — a bit grudgingly, but gratitude nonetheless."

He flashed her a narrow-eyed stare. "But I would warn you — in the future, no matter how, er, urgent or necessary you think a thing to be — do not meddle in my affairs."

"Oh, of course not," replied Lady Caldecott meekly. "Why, such a thought would never occur to me."

Patrick burst out laughing. "Don't try to bamboozle me with that meek as milk look either!" He paused, a speculative glint leaping to his gray eyes. "I wonder . . . never tell me that the pair of you also have plans for our honeymoon."

"Well, it did occur to us," Lady Caldecott began with suspicious carelessness, "that with the rush and everything that you might not have . . ."

While Patrick was having that discussion with his mother, Modesty was doing her best to prevent Thea from making what she felt was a mistake. Despite all of Modesty's arguments and pleading to tell Patrick about the note, Thea refused to be swayed. Her expression fixed and stubborn, Thea said, "I will not involve him or anyone else in this. It was my foolish insistence that I meet Hirst alone that put me in this position in the first place. It is up to me either to get myself out of it or pay the price." She threw

Modesty an anguished look. "You must understand!"

"I understand all too well that you have an unlimited capacity to blame yourself for all the ills that have ever befallen mankind," Modesty snapped. "How do you even know the note refers to Hirst? His name is not mentioned, and remember — according to Patrick, who was also there that night, you did not kill Hirst. You struck him, knocking him senseless, but you did not kill him, so what do you care what the note says?"

"Because the person who wrote the note is obviously the one who hid Hirst's body."

"And? What does that have to do with you? At least his death would be known." For the first time Thea looked undecided, and Modesty pressed forward. "If presenting the body to the authorities is what the blackmailer is alluding to, wouldn't that be a good thing? It will be hard on Edwina, but the fact that her husband is dead, murdered, has to come to light sometime. Wouldn't it be better that it is sooner than later? Is it fair to let Edwina continue to believe her husband is alive and visiting friends somewhere in the country, when we know very differently?"

Thea was clearly torn by Modesty's arguments. Hesitantly, she said, "The note mentioned 'evidence.' What if this person really has some sort of evidence to connect me to Hirst's death?"

Modesty sighed. "Thea, listen to yourself! You did not murder Hirst. You did not hide his body. Why play into this person's hands? If you are foolhardy enough to give in to this demand, it will only be the first of many — you have to know that! You didn't kill Hirst, why should you care what some cowardly opportunist thinks?"

Modesty's argument was beginning to sound more and more sensible to Thea. There was another reason why her resolve was beginning to weaken: She had realized that all of her troubles stemmed from having gone to see Hirst *alone* . . . was she on the brink of compounding the situation by doing the same rash thing again? She looked thoughtful. And did someone know her reactions so well that they were counting on her acting in such a reckless manner . . . again?

Thea took several steps around the room, her hands clenched into fists, her chin held at a pugnacious angle. She did not like being manipulated — it was bad enough that Patrick was manipulating her, but she was damned if she was going to let a stranger control her like a puppet.

She looked over at Modesty. "You have won. I will ignore the note."

"Oh, my dear, you are making a wise decision," Modesty said earnestly. "I just know it."

Thea wasn't entirely convinced, but she was willing, for the time being, to follow Modesty's urgings.

Worn out from the morning's constant flow of visitors, as well as the previous night's excitement, both ladies were looking forward to a restful afternoon. Patrick's arrival a short while later put an end to that idea.

Dispensing with Tillman's efforts to announce him to the ladies, Patrick strolled into the room where the ladies were sitting. He looked, Thea decided, far too handsome and self-assured for his own good. One would have thought that after the events last evening — both at his mother's house and in the carriage — he would have at least had the decency to appear somewhat diffident. But no. He walked into the room, *her* sitting room, like a conquering king and behaved as if she should be delighted to see him. Which she was, if the sudden flutter in her stomach was anything to go by, but which had nothing to do with the situation!

He greeted Modesty first, and they exchanged a moment's conversation. Turning to Thea where she sat in an overstuffed chair near the window, his gray eyes teasing, Patrick brushed a warm kiss across her wrist. "I trust that you slept well, my dear."

"Of course," she said. "Is there any reason why I shouldn't have?"

"Well, usually, upon becoming engaged," he said with a smile, "young ladies are rather excited about it."

Despite her best efforts to wrest it away from him, he still held her hand in his, and she glared at him. He grinned, and Thea's wayward heart beat a little faster.

Not knowing what to expect, she had dreaded this first meeting after their abrupt parting the previous evening, but if his manner was anything to go by, she need not have worried. He was being his usual irritating self. She tried again to free her hand, but, with a mocking gleam in his eyes, he kept a firm hold on it.

As she gazed up into that hard, dark, handsome face, particularly that wide, smiling mouth, a small tremor of carnal awareness slid down her spine. Memories of the passionate interlude that had taken place in the coach flashed through her mind. Those intimate, erotic things he had done to her last night had never been far from her thoughts, and she was horrified to realize that she would very much like for him to do those same things again — soon.

Furious with her weakness, her jaw set. "I am not, if you will recall, a *young* lady. You cannot have forgotten that I was once on the verge of marriage."

"I would take issue with you on the young part, and as for the other . . ." Patrick lifted her hand to his lips and gently bit one finger, sending a stimulating shock through her. "Being on the, er, verge of marriage to another man is nothing like being engaged to *me*." He kissed the tips of her trembling fingers. "Remember that, won't you, sweetheart?"

Indignation roiled in her breast, but she contented herself with jerking her hand away from him and saying stiffly, "With the announcement in the *Times* this morning, I assure you, it is rather difficult to forget."

"Excellent! I wouldn't have it said that my bride *forgot* to attend her own wedding."

"You have nothing to fear, sir," Thea muttered, "having been part of one ugly scandal, not even to thwart you would I leave my family open to that sort of gossip and speculation again."

Gently he said, "I never doubted it, my dear."

"Was there some particular reason that you came to call?" she asked with a stony expression on her face.

"Actually there was — besides wishing to see my charming fiancée for my own selfish reasons, I have come at the behest of my mother," he said. "She apologizes for her high-handed methods, but she has made arrangements with her dressmaker for you to come in for a fitting this afternoon at four o'clock. She trusts that you will forgive her — and not find it terribly inconvenient to make the appointment. I came in the Caldecott carriage and shall escort you there."

"That won't be necessary," Thea replied. "I am sure that if you leave me the dressmaker's name and direction, Modesty and I shall have no trouble finding it."

"Actually, I think it would be best if Patrick did escort you to the dressmaker," Modesty said quickly. The blackmail threat was in her mind, and she didn't quite trust Thea's resolution in the matter. "And while you are gone, I shall visit with Lady Caldecott and see how she is coming along with the arrangements for the wedding."

Patrick looked at her, a gleam in his eyes. "More plotting, my dear Miss Bradford?"

Modesty appeared flustered, and a distinct blush stained her cheeks, but she met his gaze, and asked, "Plotting?" Her eyes opened very wide. "Why, whatever do you mean, sir?"

She held her breath waiting for his answer, counting on the fact that he seemed to have accepted the situation and, more importantly, bore her no ill will, to bring her safely about. Still she breathed easier when he chuckled, bowed extravagantly, and murmured, "I believe this round goes to you, Miss Bradford."

Modesty dropped her lashes, a small smile playing at the corner of her lips. "Your mother warned me that you had a most, er, peculiar manner about you — I see what she means."

Aware of Thea's puzzled expression and not wanting her to think too deeply about the situation, Modesty glanced at the gray-marble clock on the mantel. Noting the hour, she stood up, and said, "It is nearly time for your appointment. Shall I have Tillman bring you your russet-silk pelisse? Or would you prefer the blue-velvet one?"

With the ground cut out from underneath her, Thea gave in gracefully. "The russet silk, please."

There was little conversation between Patrick and Thea while they waited for

Tillman to bring the pelisse, or during their ride to the dressmaker's establishment on Bond Street. Thea was too conscious of what had happened so recently in this carriage and far too aware of Patrick's broad form seated across from her to utter anything but the most inane comments. She decided she preferred silence to silliness. But with no conversation between them to distract her, her thoughts wandered, and too easily she recalled his kisses, the feel of his hand on her breast, and the deliciously erotic slide of his warm fingers up her thigh. A languid heat curled in her belly, her breasts tingled, and her mouth suddenly ached to be kissed by him again in that same hungry manner.

Patrick was just as aware of Thea and just as aware of what had nearly happened the previous night. So aware in fact, that by the time they had traveled a mere block, he was as hard as a rock and wondering how he was going to step down from the carriage without everyone in sight knowing precisely what was on his mind. He moved uncomfortably, trying to convince his unruly member to behave. He forced his thoughts onto the mundane and was relieved when they reached the dressmaker's address that his designs were deflated.

But the thoughts that had bedeviled them both did not quite go away, and even when Thea was being greeted and fussed over by Mrs. De Land, she was always aware of Patrick lurking in the background. Patrick was no less conscious of Thea. Unknowingly his gaze caressed her, a hungry light springing to those heavy-lidded eyes as he watched her confer with Mrs. De Land.

Mrs. De Land's establishment was considered one of the best in all of London, and her clientele came exclusively from the wealthy, titled class. While it was her skill with design, color, and fabric that brought the wives and daughters and sisters of the gentlemen to her shop, it was her discretion that brought the gentlemen themselves with their high-flyers and mistresses. Mrs. De Land's dressing rooms were noted for being private and spacious, with comfortable chairs and tables; refreshments were even served. But most notable of all was the soft, wide sofa in each room, which served as a resting place for young damsels during a long complicated fitting and a place where randy protectors could, if the mood so took them, swiftly sample the charms of their latest lady love.

Shown into one of the dressing rooms, Thea waited for Mrs. De Land to return with a sample of the fabrics and the drawing of the design Lady Caldecott had chosen for her. There was a mulish cast to her features as she waited, the sensation that she was being propelled willy-nilly down a path not of her own choosing growing stronger by the moment. It was her wedding. And her gown. Surely at least *that* decision should be hers!

When Mrs. De Land returned with a swath of lovely figured white satin and a bolt of palest rosy gauze for the overdress, Thea's resentment vanished, and she applauded Lady Caldecott's excellent taste. The design chosen was precisely what she would have selected herself — demure without being girlish. The high-waisted gown consisted of a bouffant skirt topped with a square-cut bodice, which would be trimmed with a profusion of Brussels lace, as would the tiny puffed sleeves. The filmy overdress of pale rose gauze would save the gown from being considered plain and also still any tongues that might have objected to Thea wearing white on her wedding day.

The fittings did not take very long, Mrs. De Land and her assistants quickly measuring and cutting a pattern as they went.

While Thea was being seen to, Patrick was enjoying a glass of port and reading a copy of the racing news in one of the private waiting rooms, well away from the main portion of the shop. Mrs. De Land was, after all, *very* discreet. It would never do for a wife to arrive for a visit and discover her husband already there . . . with his mistress.

Thea's visit did not take long. Once the measurements were done and she had approved of the material and design, there was nothing else to be done. After pointing out the urn of warm water for her use should she wish a brief wash and accepting Thea's refusal of further help, Mrs. De Land departed. Left alone, Thea did not begin to dress immediately, but instead, wearing only her chemise beneath the pale yellow silk robe that had been provided, she poured herself a glass of lemonade from the pitcher that had also been provided and stared into space.

She was so confused. She felt trapped and elated at the same time. She was going to marry Patrick, of that there was little doubt, but there was a stubborn part of her that wanted to expose her impending marriage for the deceitful sham that it was. She sighed and absently sipped her lemonade.

She wanted, she realized with a start, for Patrick to love her. She already knew that she loved him and that it was a far different emotion from the one Hawley had aroused in her innocent, young breast so many years ago. Hawley had been an infatuation, she could see that now, but Patrick . . . Patrick was everything she had ever dreamed of in a man, in a husband, and on Saturday she would marry him, but his motives worried her. He wanted her — *that* was plain enough — but was it enough?

She stood up and put down her glass. It was going to have to be enough. And remembering those torrid moments in the carriage last night, her heart thumped.

Thea had just untied the sash of her robe, when there was a tap on the door. "Yes?" she called out. "Come in."

When Patrick appeared in the doorway, they were both stunned by the sight of the other one — Thea, because she had been expecting Mrs. De Land, and Patrick, because the sight of Thea garbed in only a chemise and a half-opened, soft silk robe sent a missile of sheer lust right through him.

For a long moment they stared at each other, Thea's mouth half-parting and her breath coming faster, Patrick frozen in the doorway. His eyes were locked on her, especially the rapid rise and fall of her bosom, enticingly displayed between the lapels of the robe and her low-cut chemise.

The small, intimate room was suddenly filled with tightly leashed emotions, powerful, primitive emotions that fought for freedom. Raw desire floated in the very air between them, and Patrick felt his body's instant reaction; he was erect and ready, the scalding pressure in his loins demanding release. Thea was as helplessly enthralled as he; the sweet ache of anticipation swirled through her, her blood racing and her body yearning for his touch.

Without thought Patrick locked the door behind him, another sign of Mrs. De Land's excellent discretion, and slowly walked toward Thea. There was both question and demand in his gray eyes as his gaze searched hers. Thea could not look away, could not hide that she felt the same electrifying hunger.

His hands closed around her shoulders, and his mouth snared hers. The touch of his lips on hers was like a torch to summer-dry straw, instantly combustible, and Thea shuddered as her whole body turned to fire. Patrick's kiss was not gentle, but Thea reveled in the almost bruising pressure, in the blunt force of his tongue exploring her mouth. Each stab of his tongue, the very scrape of his teeth on her bottom lip sent a shock of dazzling desire shooting through her. Mindlessly, she pressed closer to him, hunger for more clawing through her.

Her arms went around his neck, and she kissed him back as passionately, as boldly as he was kissing her. Nothing mattered, only that she be in Patrick's arms and that he continue to wreak this carnal magic upon her.

They were melded together, seeking mouth to seeking mouth, breast to breast, thigh to thigh. Thea could feel every ridge and muscle in his body . . . especially the rock-hard shaft that rubbed so insistently against her stomach. A shiver went through her at the knowledge that if all else was wrong between them, at least they had this . . . this incredible wizardry of the senses.

His hands slid to her hips, and he moved her lazily against that solid rod, exciting them both, arousing both of them unbearably. Somehow his jacket was discarded, his cravat askew and his shirt half-unfastened; her pale yellow robe fell to the floor, pushed impatiently aside by Patrick's searching fingers.

Patrick found that for which he was searching, his hands cupping her breasts, pulling down the chemise so that they fell into his hands like ripe, sweet peaches. He could not resist tasting, and when his mouth left hers, Thea was consumed with disappointment, disappointment she hardly remembered when his lips closed around one hard nipple. He suckled and bit lightly at that sensitive flesh, sending naked pleasure streaking through her, pleasure that streaked unerringly to the blooming ache between her legs. She moaned, her head falling back, as she offered herself to his ravening mouth.

Blind with passion, his own blunt demands driving him, Patrick urged her backward, following her body down as she fell upon the green-satin sofa. He feasted on her breasts, kneading them, pulling on the nipples with his fingers, then using his mouth on them. She was fire and silk under his lips and hands, her response intoxicating him and making him nearly mad for their joining.

Thea's blood ran thick and warm in her body, every inch of her skin seemed to be on fire, but it was the loveliest fire she had ever experienced, and she wanted more, wanted this fire to burn hotter, brighter.

She had her wish when his hand slid up her thigh and he touched her, really touched her between her legs. She went up in flames at the first gentle brush of his hand against those tight little curls, and she trembled from the force of the emotions that racked her. Her hands clenched his hair and she arched up when he parted her thighs and stroked and explored that soft, secret flesh. She was wet and hot and achingly ready for his probing caress, the sensations he aroused by his blunt invasion, the slick slide of his fingers against her satiny flesh, forcing her toward the edge.

He could not wait. As awkward as a boy with his first woman, he fumbled at the opening of his breeches, groaning when his erection sprang free. Kneeling between her thighs, he slid his hands beneath her buttocks, positioning her to accept him. The brush of her crisp thatch against the tip of his shaft was exciting, but nothing as exciting, as mind-explodingly sweet as sinking inch by inch into her tight, slick sheath.

They were joined, their bodies one, and Thea lay beneath him in stunned compliance. She had wanted this, but wanting had not prepared her for the ecstasy of the moment. Though she was crushed beneath him, her body invaded, impaled by his, it was magic. Wizardry. It didn't matter that he was still half-dressed, that her chemise was pushed up around her waist like some servant girl's, or that her breasts had been dragged free of that same chemise, or even that this was taking place on a sofa in a dressmaker's shop. All that mattered was that he was in her arms, that his body possessed hers, that his mouth worked its dark power on hers. . . .

Patrick shuddered at the sweet sensations that rifled through him as he lay embedded within her. Her flesh clung so firmly, so tightly to his that he feared he might have injured her.

With an effort he tore his mouth from hers. Gazing down into her dark eyes, he muttered, "Did I hurt you, sweetheart? I did not mean to."

Thea shook her head, her dazed expression filling him with tenderness. He kissed her, kissed her so gently and tenderly that Thea thought her heart would burst.

The shake of her head was all the answer he needed. His mouth swooped down on hers, his hands tightening on her hips as he began to move, his body thrusting into hers.

Desire and heat welled up within her, the feel of his body on hers, the taste of him on her tongue, hurling her into a brilliant world of stunning sensation. It was a world shared only by the pair of them, the sweetness of their joining, the power of the emotions that drove them, blotting out everything but what they were feeling, what they were doing to each other.

Thea writhed beneath him, moaning her delight when he lifted her hips to deepen his possession, to fill her more fully. Suddenly she clutched his shoulders, her fingers digging into him as a sensation akin almost to pain gripped her. She twisted wildly, seeking succor from the sweet, sweet pain that grew and tightened within her. It was unbearable; she wanted it to end; she wanted it to go on forever, and just when she was certain she could not stand the pleasure/pain another second, ecstasy, ecstasy such as she had never envisioned, erupted through her. The world blurred, and there was only that incredible explosion of pleasure shattering her into a thousand pieces.

Patrick knew the instant she found release, her inner muscles clamping around him, milking him, and pitching him headlong into the same dazzling universe of pleasure.

Chapter Twelve

It was several moments before reality returned. Limp and astounded, Thea lay there on the green sofa. Nothing in her life, particularly the ugly night she had spent with Hawley, had prepared her for the pleasure of Patrick's lovemaking.

She felt weak, so relaxed that she could hardly move. Patrick was not in much better shape — he slid bonelessly from her body to sprawl beside her on the wide sofa. He kept one arm flung across her as if he needed to keep her anchored at his side and could not help himself from brushing soft, lazy kisses across her cheek and the corner of her mouth.

Eventually, reality did intrude, the faint knock at the door galvanizing both of them. Feeling foolish and for a brief, paralyzing second like a schoolboy caught in a scandalous endeavor by the headmaster, Patrick leaped upright. Brushing back his disordered locks, he closed his breeches, refastened his shirt, and did what he could with his cravat. It all took him but a moment, a moment in which the enormous stupidity of his actions raked across his mind.

At the sound of that knock, Thea jerked into a sitting position, fumbling with her chemise as she tried to right the wrongs done by Patrick. Rattled, she struggled to regain her composure — and to obliterate all signs of what had just transpired. It was hopeless — the scent of their lovemaking lingered in the air, her hair hung in a tangled mass around her shoulders, and she knew that her mouth was red and swollen from Patrick's kisses. And while Patrick had shrugged back into his jacket, there was just something not quite right about his attire . . . something that Mrs. De Land's knowing eye would spot in a moment. Humiliation scalded through Thea.

Frantically, she gathered her scattered wits, and by the time there was a second rap on the door, after a horrified glance at Patrick, she managed to mutter, "Yes? Who is it?"

Mrs. De Land's voice came muffled through the door. "Is everything all right, my dear? It is Mrs. De Land. Is there anything I can help you with?"

Choking back a hysterical urge to giggle, Thea said, "No. No. Everything is fine. I shall be out in a moment."

"Very well, my dear," replied Mrs. De

Land. "If you need any help, there is a bell-pull in the corner. Just pull it, and someone will come to your aid."

An uncomfortable silence followed Mrs. De Land's retreat.

Unable to look at Patrick, Thea turned her back to him and wrapped the yellow-silk robe protectively around her body — a body that still hummed with pleasure and still felt the warm, heavy imprint of his upon it. Her shoulders stiff, she said, "Will you please leave — I would like to dress . . . before Mrs. De Land returns again."

Not the novice that Thea was, Patrick could see the humor in the situation, even if he cursed his reckless part in it. He had not felt so young and green in many a year as he had at the sound of that knock, and he could never remember a time, even in his indiscreet salad days, that he had been found in such a compromising position. If it weren't for Thea's acute embarrassment, he might have laughed at what had happened, but eyeing her rigid back, he was certain that if he did not want his head separated from his shoulders, he had best keep his amusement to himself.

"Thea, my love," he began softly, "I am sorry for having put you in this invidious position. I am normally not so precipitate in my lovemaking, nor so thoughtless and careless. I should have known better, and I cannot apologize enough for causing you any embarrassment."

Patrick came to stand behind her. Placing his hands on her shoulders, he dropped a warm kiss at the junction of her neck and shoulder. "Do not fret over it, my sweet — we are to be married in just a few days and, despite polite society's protestations to the contrary, we will not be the first couple to have anticipated their wedding vows."

Thea swung around to face him. "And that is supposed to make me feel better?" she asked.

"No, it is to make you understand that Mrs. De Land's interruption was merely untimely, not catastrophic, and to make you understand that what we did was not so very terrible." His eyes searched hers. "What happened was my fault — I should have known better, but I wanted you — badly, and I could not help myself." He smiled wryly. "Regrettably, where you are concerned, there are times that I cannot trust myself to act as a gentleman."

"You have *never* acted the gentleman with me," Thea muttered, thinking of that passionate kiss at the Hilliard ball and their tangle with the intruder at the Curzon Street house.

He smiled, his eyes crinkling at the corners. "No, I never have, have I? When I am with you, I am afraid that every precept of gentlemanly behavior I have ever learned flies out of my mind. It is a good thing that we are to be married on Saturday — a long engagement would nigh kill me."

Thea's head snapped up. "And, of course, we must only consider your needs, mustn't we? You and Hawley have used me for your own ends."

His smile faded. "Is that what you think? That I am so base and selfish that it is only my wants that concern me? That I am like Randall?"

Her chin lifted. "Why wouldn't I think that?"

A muscle jumped in Patrick's jaw. "I am surprised that feeling as you do about me, you are willing to marry me."

"I do not have any choice," she ground out.

"Yes, there is that," Patrick drawled, fighting to keep a tight rein on his own rising temper. "And, of course, after what happened just a few minutes ago, our fate is sealed, isn't it?" At her blank expression, he added grimly, "You could become pregnant."

Thea's mouth dropped open — that thought never having occurred to her. Too well did she remember her terrible anguish a decade ago, that not only had she been responsible for the deaths of two men, but that she might be forced to suffer the humiliation of bearing Hawley's bastard child. The possibility that she had put herself in that same position a second time brought a bitter taste to her mouth. She could not believe that she had been so stupid and reckless . . . again. With Hawley she'd had no choice — what had passed between them had been rape, Hawley determined to give her no escape from marriage to him — no matter what her wishes had been.

Her breath sucked in sharply, and she gazed at Patrick with dawning suspicion. Had he done the same thing? She could not pretend that she had not been a willing partner in their lovemaking, but might Patrick's carnal assault been rooted in something other than passion? It was an ugly thought.

"Is that why you made love to me?" she demanded. "Are you behaving as Hawley did — compromising me to ensure that I marry you on Saturday?"

Patrick stared at her in appalled anger. Smothering a curse, he snapped, "Your opinion of me is most gratifying!" He took a step nearer and, grasping the lapels of her robe, jerked her next to him. His gray eyes black with fury, he snarled, "If you were a man and had dared to say such a thing, I would kill you. Since you are merely the woman I am condemned to spend the rest of my life with, I shall content myself with a warning — do not *ever* impugn my honor again."

Letting go of her lapels, with an almost contemptuous motion, he pushed her from him. Spinning on his heels, he stalked to the door. Glancing over his shoulder, he said icily, "I shall await you in the front parlor."

Uncaring if anyone saw him, he slammed from the room and walked in swift, angry strides down the wide corridor. His jaw was set and he was conscious of a strong desire to smash something. That she believed him so base!

Thea stared at the closed door for several seconds, stunned by his barely controlled rage. It seemed, she thought uneasily, that she had insulted him. Her mouth tightened. He deserved it. Condemned to spend his life with her, was he? Ha!

It was a stiffly polite pair who rode to Grosvenor Street together. Patrick escorted her into the house and, with a curt farewell, departed, the rigid set of his shoulders and the cast to his jaw declaring that he was furious.

Thea told herself that she had nothing to feel guilty about — if he chose to be insulted by some plain speaking, that was his difficulty. *She* was the one who had right on her side.

Cloaking herself in righteous indignation, she managed to endure a quiet evening at home listening to Modesty burble over with wedding plans and a restless night during which sleep escaped her. She woke Thursday morning tired and with a headache. A long bath and a light breakfast of scones and jam, followed by several cups of strong coffee, made her feel better.

An hour later a note from Mrs. De Land arrived, requesting a fitting as soon as it could be arranged. Thea and Modesty had been sitting in the morning room when Tillman brought in the note.

Hearing its contents, Modesty's brow rose. "Good heavens, the woman must have worked her needlewomen all through the night!"

"I'm certain she did — the wedding *is* Saturday, in case you have forgotten," Thea muttered.

Modesty shot her a look, her expression

troubled. "Is there anything wrong, my dear?"

Thea made a face and shook her head. "No. Probably just bridal nerves." She laughed with little humor. "Fortunately, I shall not have long to suffer them."

Modesty was on the verge of speaking when the door to the morning room was flung open and Edwina burst into the room. Her lovely face pale and frightened, she sped to Thea's side.

Sinking down onto the sofa beside Thea, she cried, "Oh Thea! You must help me. You simply *must!* I do not know where to turn."

"What is it?" Thea asked, alarmed by Edwina's manner.

Edwina took a moment to compose herself. Her golden head bent down and her hands knotted into fists in her lap, she said, "There is this dreadful fellow, Mr. Yates. He is an awful man, and he forced his way into my house this morning and demanded that I pay him seventeen thousand pounds! He said that Alfred owed him and that if he wasn't paid by Monday noon, he would take action." Her voice dropped to a whisper, "He threatened that if Alfred knew what was good for him, there would be no more delays . . . not if he wanted his pretty wife to remain that way."

Thea's arms closed around her sister's shoulders, and she pulled Edwina's trembling form next to hers. Across the distance that separated them, her eyes met Modesty's as they both remembered that Alfred had demanded the same amount from her the night he had been murdered. Recalling his air of fright, Thea thought that for once it seemed that Alfred had been telling the truth. He *had* been desperate, and it had obviously been no act.

Edwina was sobbing into Thea's shoulder, and Thea's heart was wrung. "Hush, sweet, hush. Do not fear — I shall not let any harm come to you. Mr. Yates shall have his bloody seventeen thousand pounds."

Modesty's lips tightened, but she remained silent.

Edwina's head lifted, a smile shining through the tears. "Oh Thea, I prayed you would not desert me. I was so frightened — I did not know where to turn — you were my last hope."

"Yes, yes, I am sure that is true," Modesty commented, "but what about that husband of yours?" Since Edwina didn't know of her husband's death, Modesty was curious if she had even made the effort to contact him.

"Did you think to write him to tell him what happened? It is his debt, after all, not your sister's."

Edwina's smile dimmed. "N-n-no, I didn't." Looking perplexed, she asked, "Besides what good would it do? Alfred doesn't have any money, you know that." And added, as if it explained everything, "He gambles."

Giving Edwina a brief hug and following Modesty's lead, Thea said, "But we do need to talk to Alfred, my dear. I cannot continue to pay his debts every time he gets into a bind. And I will not have you threatened and frightened this way. We must find a permanent solution."

"But there is no solution," Edwina wailed. "We are not wealthy like you, and Alfred is always going to gamble — as he explained it to me, it is in his blood, he cannot help himself. And unless you *do* continue to help us, or he dies, or I inherit a fortune, I can see no way to change the situation."

A trickle of unease went down Thea's spine. For the first time she looked at Edwina with less than blind adoration. There had been something so cool and unconcerned about the way she had said "unless he dies, or I inherit a fortune," that gave her pause. Edwina didn't know that her husband was already dead, but she had to have realized that under normal circumstances Alfred's early demise was not likely — he had been disgustingly robust. Had the thought of ridding herself of a compulsive gambler and ne'er-do-well husband already crossed Edwina's mind? Or that all of her difficulties would vanish if her sister were to die and she inherited a large fortune?

Feeling chilled, Thea's arm slid from Edwina's shoulders. She gave herself a mental shake. What rot! Edwina loved her and, despite being spoiled and inclined toward selfishness, would never wish for her death.

Ashamed of herself, she pressed an affectionate kiss onto Edwina's cheek. "Well, I think you would make a dashing widow, my dear, but please don't make any wagers on my dying unexpectedly anytime soon."

Edwina's eyes widened, and she looked shocked. "As if I would! What a horrible thing to say."

"But not impractical," Modesty said mildly. At Edwina's outraged stare, she added, "You were the one who mentioned inheriting a fortune — Thea's is the only one you could remotely lay claim to."

"Well, yes, but, but, I wasn't really thinking about what that really meant." She flashed Thea a smile. "I would never wish evil on you."

"I know you wouldn't," Thea replied, "but I fear we are straying from the subject. What are we going to do about your situation after I pay off the threatening Mr. Yates on Monday? If you would only *try* to economize, you could live pleasantly on your own fortune." She looked sternly at Edwina. "This really will have to be the last time that I rescue you from Hirst's debts, my dear. Not only because I wish it to be so, but do not forget that I shall be married on Saturday. From then on, my husband will hold sway over my fortune — I may have to account to him on my expenditures, and Pat — Mr. Blackburne does not impress me as being the sort of gentleman who will allow his wife's relatives to batten down on her — or him."

"That's an awful thing to say!"

"It may be," Modesty interposed, "but there is a great deal of truth in it."

"I'm sure that Mr. Blackburne would not want Thea's sister to be thrown into debtor's prison," Edwina said, looking distinctly unhappy. She sighed. "I know, I know, I am being selfish — I suppose that I shall just have to try to be more frugal. Although how I am to control Alfred's gambling I have no idea."

"My offer of a house in the country and a settlement to ensure you a comfortable, if not elegant life is still open," Thea murmured.

Edwina hesitated, took a deep breath, and said in a rush, "Perhaps it *is* time that I consider that offer."

Thea beamed at her. "Oh, darling, I know that you will be happy once you are settled in. Living in the country will not be as exciting as London, but there is great enjoyment to be gained from a bucolic life."

Edwina did not look convinced, but for the first time she appeared to be thinking about it. "I suppose you are right and, at the moment, it seems to be the only solution." She sighed. "Oh, but I shall miss London — the shops, the soirees, and the bustle that abounds." She made a face. "I do not think that Alfred will be very happy in the country."

Knowing full well that Alfred's happiness was not something that need trouble them any longer, Modesty said, "Well, I'm sure that he will adjust — and since there will be no gaming hells nearby, he might even learn to curb his gaming habit."

Edwina's expression revealed her doubts about that happening, but she nodded, and said, "Perhaps you are right." She glanced at Thea. "Did you have any particular place in mind for us?"

"No, not exactly . . . Have you visited any area *you* like?"

Edwina shook her fair head. "If I cannot live in London, it doesn't matter where in the country I live."

Thea hesitated. "If I remember correctly," she finally said, "there is a very nice property that might be obtained not far from my own Halsted House in Gloucestershire."

Edwina still looked doubtful, but she admitted, "Alfred should like that — he says that it is prime hunting country."

"Er, yes, I am sure that he will find it very enjoyable during hunting season," Thea mumbled, feeling guilty.

Exchanging an uncomfortable glance with Modesty, she pulled a face and found herself hoping, not for the first time, that Alfred's body came to light soon. Keeping Edwina in the dark about her husband's death seemed cruel, yet what else could she do? She could hardly say, "Oh, by the way, I happen to know that Alfred is dead, murdered. Unfortunately, his body seems to have disappeared, and I have not the faintest idea where it is. Or who took it. Or why." No. She wasn't about to say something that ridiculous.

Her unhappy thoughts came to an abrupt end when Modesty looked at the clock, and said, "Since we seem to have settled matters for the time being, I would suggest that you order the coach sent 'round. It is nearly time for the fitting of your wedding gown with Mrs. De Land."

"Mrs. De Land is making your wedding gown? How thrilling!" Edwina exclaimed. "She is far too dear for me. You're very lucky to be able to afford her."

"Actually it is not your sister who is paying for the gown," Modesty said crisply. "Lady Caldecott insists that it is to be a gift from her to her new daughter-in-law." She sent Thea a look. "And it is not wise to keep Mrs. De Land waiting."

Edwina surged to her feet. Looking particularly appealing, she said to Thea, "Oh, may I come with you? I have never dared to even enter Mrs. De Land's establishment. Please say that I may?"

"Of course, you may," Thea said. "And afterward, why don't you return here with me? After all, we have much to discuss."

Edwina agreed, and in happy accord the two sisters prepared to leave. Modesty watched them as they walked out of the room, wondering if Edwina would wheedle a gown of her own out of Thea. Not, of course, to wear at the wedding on Saturday — but perhaps, as a consolation gift for behaving so sensibly? Yes. That was precisely the tack Edwina would try, Modesty decided with a shake of her head. The child was spoiled, and Thea, with her generous heart, did not help matters.

About the time that Thea and Edwina were leaving for Mrs. De Land's establishment, Patrick was awakening in his town house on Hamilton Place. The night his engagement to Thea had been announced, despite his professed intention to do so, he had not managed to drink himself under the table with his friends: he had been already too intoxicated by the knowledge that Thea would be his wife to need further stimulation. Such had not been the case the previous night.

Furious at the sharp exchange with Thea, he had been in a foul mood for the remainder of Wednesday afternoon. His black mood had not abated by the time he joined Lord Embry and Adam Paxton that evening at a favorite gaming hell of theirs. Determined not to dwell on Thea's response to his lovemaking, or the angry end to it, he was ripe for trouble. After one look at his hard face, his friends kept their mouths shut and his glass filled throughout the night. By the time they helped him home, dawn was breaking, and he was, indeed, thoroughly foxed.

When he woke, the thunderous pounding in his head reminded him why he no longer found excesses like last night's pleasurable. Like Thea earlier in the day, a bath and a meal helped restore him to some semblance of normality.

The argument with Thea yesterday was still on his mind, but he was no longer furious. And the more he considered all the aspects of what had occurred, her reaction shouldn't have surprised him. His mouth thinned. He really would like to get his hands on Hawley Randall. The bastard had not only done his best to ruin her life, but his atrocious behavior had not left Thea with much trust for the male of the species. Why the hell *shouldn't* she have questioned his motives?

Pouring his sixth cup of bitterly black coffee, he mulled the incident over in his mind, wishing for the hundredth time that he had not gone in search of her at Mrs. De Land's. *If I had waited in the parlor, like I should have, none of this would have happened,* he admitted sourly. And yet he could not be sorry for having made love to Thea. No, he would never be sorry for the pleasure she had given him. His only regret was for the timing and surroundings.

A peculiar feeling suddenly twisted in his gut. The next time they made love, she would be his wife, he thought. His wife. A foolish grin spread across his face.

"Sir?" inquired his butler, walking into the room where Patrick sat. "There is a, ah, gentleman to see you."

Patrick quirked a brow.

Chetham coughed delicately. "I believe it is the, uh, individual you saw several days ago. A Mr. Hackett."

Patrick frowned, then memory returned. "Of course. Send him in."

A pained expression crossed Chetham's austere features, and Patrick grinned. His butler was far more stiff-rumped about social niceties than he was, and he was quite certain that Chetham would have preferred that he not meet with Hackett at all, let alone in the breakfast room.

The individual Chetham ushered into Patrick's presence a few seconds later was certainly unprepossessing in his nondescript and decidedly *un*fashionable clothing. Hackett was a small man with hangdog features and habitually looked as if he had just come from the funeral of his last friend.

Today was no different; holding his black slouched hat in his hands, his soulful brown eyes met Patrick's. "Good morning, guvnor. Got that bit of information you wanted."

Patrick nodded and, indicating that Hackett should join him and help himself to the remains of the large repast that still littered the table, waited patiently until the little man had filled his plate to overflowing. Watching as Hackett savored his first bite of tender country ham, Patrick smiled.

A beatific expression on his face, Hackett chewed and swallowed. "Prime, sir, mighty prime."

"I am pleased it meets with your approval," Patrick replied, amusement dancing in his eyes. "Now what do you have for me?"

Never pausing once from shoveling into his mouth the ham, scrambled eggs, and kidneys in gravy that covered his plate, he reached inside his shabby jacket and brought forth a small packet. Handing it to Patrick, he said around a mouthful of kidney and gravy, "Think everything is there. Your man is clean. No flies on 'im that my friends could find."

Patrick had not expected news to the contrary, but he was still relieved that his stepfather did not appear to be in any financial difficulties. Reading the report before him, he shook his head. No. Lord Caldecott was in no need of money and had no reason to blackmail his wife. He regretted the necessity for prying into Caldecott's affairs, but he'd had to be sure.

Glancing again at the amount of private information that had been compiled, he raised a brow, and said, "I wouldn't have thought that this sort of information would be readily available. Your, er, employer must have sources and eyes everywhere."

Something that almost resembled a smile crossed Hackett's long face. "Indeed, guvnor. Why you'd be surprised what he can find out if he sets his mind to it."

Patrick did not probe deeper. Hackett would tell him nothing; he was merely the messenger.

Having paid Hackett and sent him on his way, Patrick left the morning room with the information in his hand and walked into the front parlor. A small fire burned on the hearth, and, standing before the orange-and-yellow flames, he tossed the packet he had just paid a very sizable sum to get into the fire. Watching the flames consume the pages, he felt a little less of a snoop.

The day was far advanced, and Patrick considered calling on Thea, but dismissed it. He had come to terms with his anger over yesterday's exchange, but he couldn't be sure of Thea's state of mind. Better to let her alone for a while than to run the risk of deepening the rift between them. He did not want to marry a woman on Saturday who has his *very* early demise on her mind. But neither did he wish to allow her to brood over the incident.

Making up his mind, he put on his high-crowned hat and left the house. His destination was an expensive jeweler on King Street. Entering the small, circumspect premises, he was greeted by the proprietor and head jeweler, Mr. Greenberg.

Once he had made his needs known, it did not take long to select a stunning set of topazes surrounded by diamonds. Having made his selection and leaving instructions for its delivery, Patrick left the shop feeling he had at least offered Thea an olive branch. What happened next was up to her. She might fling his gift into the gutter or, he admitted with a grin, his face, but he hoped that she would accept them as the peace offering that they were.

Finding himself with time on his hands, he wandered to Brooks and eventually found a table of gentlemen playing cards and joined them. Other gentlemen he knew drifted into the place, and since the news of his engagement still had the ton buzzing, he found himself to be a popular fellow.

Throughout the remainder of the afternoon and evening, he was toasted more times than he cared to admit. Not wishing to repeat last night's indulgence, he had only taken sips of the many glasses of liquor pressed upon him. By the time Nigel and Adam finally found him around midnight, he was still clearheaded.

"Been looking all over for you," Nigel complained as he took the empty seat next to Patrick. "Worried about you after last night. Been a long time since I've seen you that foxed. Didn't like it. You used to be able to hoist your glass with the best of us, but it ain't something I've noticed you doing very much these past few years. Worried me."

Patrick was sitting in a quiet corner of the club, having sought to remove himself from the throng of fashionable gentlemen who now crowded the various rooms. Paxton, lowering his elegant form into the deep leather chair on the other side of Patrick, grinned as he said, "He has been like this ever since he discovered you had gone out. We have searched for you in every den of iniquity that he knew." His golden brown eyes gleamed with amusement. "And believe me, he knows them all."

"I'm aware of that — I introduced him to half of them," Patrick said wryly.

"Never mind all that," Nigel said impatiently. "Discovered something for you." At Patrick's cocked brow he added, "Since you've been so damned interested in Ellsworth, thought I'd ask around. Gossip says that he and that cousin of his, Hirst, are caught in the toils of a moneylender — the worst bloodsucker of the lot, a fellow named Yates."

Patrick stiffened. "I believe I've met the gentleman," he said, "at Ellsworth's place the other night."

"Not surprised, if Ellsworth owes him money. Yates is a bad 'un. Aligned with the criminal element — not respectable at all. Even the most hardened gamblers avoid him, but there are those who have nowhere else to turn to cover their debts — like Ellsworth. Thing about Yates that makes him different is that, if one is late with a payment or cannot pay, he is not above threatening a fellow's family and friends. Been known to carve up the faces of wives and daughters or breaking the limbs and heads of the males — young or old. Don't matter to Yates. And if that fails —"

"If that fails," Paxton interrupted grimly, "he is not above using murder to get his point across. And because people in high places are indebted to him, no one can touch him. That and the fact," he added, "that Yates is very careful not to leave incriminating evidence lying around. He is both ruthless and clever, and he *always* gets his money or there is hell to pay. Not a man to be trifled with."

"He does sound a thoroughly nasty individual," Patrick admitted, his mind racing at the implications. Had it been Yates who had killed Hirst? Because he could not pay his debt? And had it been Yates and not Ellsworth he and Thea had surprised that night? He would have to think on it. Once his wedding was behind him.

To his friends he merely said, "I appreciate the information. I shall take care not to run afoul of Mr. Yates."

Nigel stared suspiciously at Patrick. "Now why don't I believe you?" He wagged a finger at Patrick. "I still say you're up to something."

Patrick shrugged. "Nothing for you to worry about. Now if you will excuse me, I think I shall find my way home." He grinned at them. "Last night's effects have not left me entirely, and I find myself longing for my bed."

Nigel snorted. "If you ain't careful, my

friend, you're going to turn into quite a respectable fellow."

"Better that than an old roué, laughed at behind one's back."

"Very good!" Paxton said, with a laugh. "A definite hit."

Nigel smiled ruefully. "Go seek your bed, Patrick. I shall consider the wisdom of your words."

Leaving his friends behind him, Patrick strolled to the entrance of the club. Bidding the porter good night as he stepped outside, he was surprised to discover that it was raining. When he had left the house that afternoon, the day had been sunny with a few clouds and he had dressed appropriately. Beyond the trip to King Street, having no other destination in mind, he had not thought to provide himself with transportation. Staring at the rain eerily revealed in the flickering light of the wall sconces at the club entrance, he grimaced, not relishing the notion of walking home through a downpour.

Deciding there was no help for it, he hunched his shoulders and descended the steps to street level. The sound of an approaching vehicle caught his attention and he raised an arm, hailing the black hackney that appeared out of the darkness. Shouting out his address, he leaped inside.

Chapter Thirteen

Powerful hands closed round Patrick's throat, strangling him, and, at the same time, a violent movement smashed his head against the rear of the carriage and knocked him half-unconscious. Dazed and fighting to remain conscious, spots danced in front of his eyes. His windpipe was being crushed, and he struggled to drag in a breath — to no avail. The fingers of his attacker dug into his throat, cutting off his air, and as he fought off another wave of dizziness, he knew that if he was to survive, he must break that grip. He was not afraid of dying, but the thought of never seeing Thea again, of dying at the hands of an unknown assailant, infuriated him.

He was acting on the blind instinct to live, and with his cocked arms surged upward and outward, wrenching apart the hands at his throat. The relief was instantaneous, and he eagerly gulped air into his straining lungs. His attacker lurched at him, and they grappled in the swaying coach, the dim light from the occasional lamppost giving Patrick a brief glimpse now and then of the big man he faced.

Outside, the rain beat against the roof of the carriage, the wheels hissing as they rolled over the wet pavement, the horses' hooves sending water spraying in all directions. Inside, inside away from the storm, a deadly battle was being fought, the odor of damp leather, old perfume, and stale tobacco mingling with the scent of danger.

Patrick could not see his assailant distinctly; his impression was of a hulking, lethal form — almost a giant of a man. It was not a mistaken impression. A fist that seemed the size of a ham came out of the shadows and slammed into Patrick's head, rocking him backward. Sparks exploded in his brain, and he desperately shook his head to clear it. His attacker struck again, only this time, Patrick managed to fend him off and struck out viciously at the other man. It was a lucky blow, and Patrick swore at the jolt of pain that traveled up his arm as his fist smashed into his assailant's face. The man groaned and half fell onto the other seat, and Patrick followed him, landing a few good punches of his own. The ache of his throat and the throbbing of his head made thinking nearly impossible — that and the fight itself — but Patrick had always thought on his feet, and he did so now. Considering the sheer size of the other man and the confined quarters of the coach, he was aware that he was not likely to win this fight. Thea's face flashed in front of him. By God! he swore. It was not going to end this way. He was going to marry Thea, and no one, not even this huge ox across from him, was going to stop him. He didn't like running from a fight, not even one he might lose, but while bravado had its place, it occurred to him that a hasty retreat might be called for about now.

A blocky shape hurtled toward him and Patrick kicked out with both booted feet, hitting the other man fully in the chest, slamming him backward. Without another thought, he flung open the carriage door and hurled himself out into the storm. He landed hard on the cobbled street, rolling and tumbling wildly before finally coming to a halt.

Suppressing a groan as tortured muscles made themselves felt, he staggered to his feet, prepared to continue the battle if necessary. To his relief he was alone, the lamp of the hackney rapidly disappearing into the night.

A quick glance around gave him his bearings, and mindful that his attacker might return, he wasted no time in reaching the safety of Hamilton Place. Whatever

Chetham thought of his master's bedraggled appearance when Patrick stumbled into the house, he kept to himself.

Taking in Patrick's wet and mud-splattered attire, he murmured only, "A rather nasty night, sir." Taking a second, longer look at his employer's battered state, he asked, "Shall I have a bath prepared?"

The hour was late, the majority of his servants abed, and though he longed for the comfort of a hot bath, Patrick shook his head. "No. I shall manage for tonight. The morning will be soon enough. See to it, will you?"

Patrick turned and began to ascend the stairs. Chetham delicately cleared his throat, and sighing, Patrick glanced back at his butler.

"Yes?" he asked wearily. "Is there something else you wish to tell me?"

"Cook has a fresh beefsteak hanging in the larder to age," Chetham replied. "If you like, I can bring it up to you."

"A beefsteak?" Patrick repeated.

"For your eye, sir. Unless I am mistaken, come morning, you shall have quite a, er, black eye."

Inspecting the orb in question in his shaving mirror, Patrick had to agree. He would indeed have a magnificent black eye come morning. He didn't remember the blow that had connected with his eye, but examining his other wounds, he guessed that some of them had occurred when he had leaped from the hackney. There was a long, wide scrape along the side of his face that was going to rival his eye for color if the livid bruise covering his cheek and temple was anything to go by. He grimaced. And he was going to be married in less than forty-eight hours. What a delightful sight he was going to present on Saturday to the many guests his mother would have coerced, ah, assembled to witness his vows to Thea. He grinned. No doubt half of them would be convinced that he'd had to be beaten into submission to actually marry his betrothed.

Chetham arrived with the beefsteak, and, after dismissing him, Patrick sank back onto the bed, the cool beefsteak resting on his battered eye. He ached in every bone in his body, and it occurred to him that he really was getting too old to be participating in such antics as he had tonight.

He frowned. Except that tonight he had been minding his own business, intent upon nothing more exciting than hailing a hackney to escape the rain. It wasn't, he reminded himself, as if he had been in a dangerous part of London, where such attacks could be expected. Brooks was, in the main, a respectable club. In a respectable part of town, too — unlike some of the rackety hells he and his friends had supported a decade or more ago.

Thinking about the attack, Patrick rose from his bed and, setting the beefsteak aside for a moment, dragged off his ripped and sodden apparel. Leaving them in a ruined heap on the floor, he walked to his dressing room. From the ewer on the gray marble washstand, he poured some water into the china bowl and gingerly began to wash himself, wincing whenever he touched a tender spot. Eyeing the purpling spots around his throat where his assailant had tried to choke him, he shook his head. Oh, but he was a lovely sight with his battered face and rapidly purpling body — every bride's dream. Shrugging into a wine-colored silk robe, he walked back into his bedroom and, lying down on the bed, picked up the beefsteak once again and placed it against his eye.

The hour was late, and he was tired, but sleep proved elusive, the events of the night running through his mind. Robbery and mayhem were not rare in London, but there was something queer about what had happened tonight. Using the hackney and the inclement weather to scoop up a target was clever, he'd grant them that, but it seemed rather catch-as-catch-can. Patrick could think of dozens of reasons why the scheme wouldn't work with any consistent degree of success. The culprits would have had to wait for a lone gentleman before putting their plan into action, and since most of the gentlemen left the club in pairs or crowds, they couldn't have been assured of definite prey. They also couldn't have known whether their target carried a great deal of money or not, nor could they have known whether the victim would be wearing any jewels worth stealing. And, of course, they couldn't have known if their prey would be sober or a rollicking drunk when he left the club at that hour of the night.

He could have been a random target, Patrick conceded, but he suspected not.

A scowl marred his features. But it *had* been chance that he had left the club alone. Chance, too, that he had not been well on his way to being foxed. But if it had not been chance that had brought them together, how had they known he would be at Brooks? Even he hadn't known his destination when he had left the house that afternoon . . . or rather the previous afternoon, since it was now the early-morning hours of Friday. It seemed unlikely that the hackney, its driver, and occupant had been waiting solely for him, and yet he could not dismiss the notion. Was he simply being unduly suspicious?

It was possible, but thinking back over the events of the past week or so, he was not convinced. There was a blackmailer at work. And he had interfered. Nor could he forget that it hadn't been too many nights ago that he had stood over Hirst's body, and it had not been long after that that he and Thea had tangled with the mysterious intruder in the same house that had seen Hirst's murder done. And what about this Yates fellow Nigel and Adam had mentioned this evening? The attack certainly had a criminal element about it, and since it was known that Yates had had dealings with Hirst and Ellsworth, was it possible that, for some unknown reason, Yates had entered the fray? It was something he would have to consider.

In fact, the more he thought about it, the more he became convinced that it had not been a coincidence. The blackmailer must have sought to eliminate the major obstacle that stood in the way of unlimited access to Lady Caldecott's purse. He had long assumed that it was the blackmailer who had killed Hirst — and if that were so, why would the fellow hesitate to kill again?

His impending wedding had pushed aside thoughts of Hirst's murder and, to a lesser extent, his mother's blackmailer. Unfortunately, at the moment he could see no way that he could accomplish anything in either direction until after the wedding. He frowned. He supposed he could find out if his most likely suspect, Ellsworth, had returned to town — Nigel would know.

Staring at his reflection in the mirror the next morning, Patrick decided that he more resembled one of the river pirates who prowled the wicked confines of Silver Street in Natchez than a respectable gentleman visiting London. He couldn't remember a time, even in his most decadant period, that he had looked quite so, er, colorful.

His eye was at half-mast, surrounded by a most impressive circle of black and purple, along his jaw ran a lurid bruise, and across his cheek there was a scarlet scrape that gave him, he told himself with a grimace, a rakish air. The livid prints of his assailant's fingers around his throat were hidden underneath his carefully tied cravat, as were the other more painful reminders of his frantic leap from the hackney.

The inclination not to venture forth and reveal to the world his battered features was strong, but there were things that he must do. And one of them, he reminded himself, was to find out from Nigel if Ellsworth had returned to town.

Seeing Patrick's face when he came to call, Nigel was horrified. Several minutes were wasted as Patrick assured him that he looked far worse than he felt. Barely.

"By Jove," Nigel muttered, when Patrick had finished an account of his travails, "if what happened to you isn't reason enough to remain safely drinking inside one's club with one's friends, I don't know what is!"

Patrick smiled — painfully. "At present, I can hardly argue with your sentiments."

"I would certainly think not!"

They were in the sitting room adjacent to Nigel's bedchamber — Nigel having struggled from his bed not many moments previous to Patrick's arrival. Gathering his thoughts, Patrick took a sip of his coffee. He was not in the mood for delicate probing or conversation — just as well, since Nigel appeared as if he could barely recall his own name.

Setting down his cup, Patrick asked, "Since you seem to know everything that goes on . . . have you heard whether Ellsworth has returned to town?"

Nigel's eyes bugged. Stupid he was not — even after a night of hard drinking. "Never tell me you think that Ellsworth had something to do with what happened to you!"

Patrick shrugged. "What makes you think that?"

Nigel snorted. "Because you ain't one to take that sort of thing without inflicting some sort of retaliation. And here you are bright and early the next morning wanting to know about that cawker Ellsworth. Even a fool could have figured it out. I ain't a fool!"

"Suppose I did think it was Ellsworth," Patrick murmured. "Would that surprise you?"

"Yes and no. Ellsworth is a dirty dish — told you that," Nigel replied with relish. "Worse — he's a coward." Nigel's eyes narrowed. "What happened to you sounds more like the work of Yates. And it wouldn't surprise me if Ellsworth hired Yates to take care of matters for him." His lip lifted contemptuously. "Just the sort of chicken-hearted thing he'd do."

Patrick nodded. "You may be right. But in order to hire Yates he would have had to see him — I don't think he'd be stupid enough to put such a request in writing. So do you know if Ellsworth has returned to town?"

"Not that I heard." He shot Patrick a look. "Why are you so interested in Ellsworth?"

"No particular reason," Patrick said carelessly.

"And I wonder why I have trouble believing you," Nigel said as he picked up his cup and took a long swallow. Setting aside the cup, he fixed Patrick with a stare. "You're up to something. Said so before. What is it?"

Patrick sighed. He and Nigel had been friends for a long time, he trusted him, and Nigel deserved some sort of explanation. Smiling wryly, Patrick said, "I cannot tell you — it is not my secret to share."

Nigel studied him for several seconds. "Thea? Is she in some sort of scrape?"

"No — not that it is any business of yours. And if I think about it long enough," Patrick drawled, "I might just take offense at your conclusion."

"Wouldn't matter if you did — I ain't about to let you provoke me into a meeting," Nigel said complacently, picking up his cup again.

Patrick laughed and rose to his feet. "Just as well — you are nearly as good a shot as I am."

Patrick was smiling when he left Nigel's home on Albemarle Street. Standing at the base of the steps, he glanced up and down the street, considering his next move. He supposed he should call on his mother and his betrothed. They both should have a private moment to get used to his rainbow-hued features before the wedding.

He kept his suspicions to himself and told his mother that he had been the victim of an attempted robbery. She had been appalled when she heard his tale, but he was able to leave her fairly convinced, even when she raised the issue, that what had happened had absolutely no connection to her blackmailer.

Dealing with Thea was not quite so simple. Standing before her in the small sitting room where she received him, Modesty seated on the sofa beside her, he told his story once more.

Her eyes never leaving his bruised features, when he finished she took a deep breath, and said, "It was the man who murdered Hirst, wasn't it? He tried to kill you, didn't he?"

Modesty gasped. "Of course! It had to have been."

Patrick grimaced. So much for hoping that they would dismiss it as merely a robbery gone bad. He should have known better. His darling was far too astute for her own good.

Sitting down across from them, he said,

"It could have been, I cannot pretend differently. But the important thing is that I was unharmed."

"This time," Thea said hollowly.

Patrick glanced at Modesty. "May I have a moment alone with her?"

"Oh, of course," Modesty exclaimed and, rising to her feet, exited the room.

Seating himself beside Thea on the sofa, he took one of her hands in his. "Sweetheart, we don't know that what happened last night had anything to do with Hirst's murder."

Her eyes searched his. "You don't really believe that, do you?"

Patrick started to lie, but staring into her intelligent features, the words died stillborn on his lips. "You don't, do you?" she repeated.

His expression wry, Patrick shook his head. "No. Like you, I think whoever attacked me has some connection to whoever murdered Hirst."

Thea's breath caught, and her hand tightened on his. "There is something I must say to you before we discuss this matter further." Her face averted and her voice low, she said, "I have thought of little else but what transpired between us at Mrs. De Land's Wednesday afternoon." She swallowed and her features pale and set, she continued, "It should not have happened, but once it had, I should not have implied that you acted as beastly as Lord Randall. I was unkind and unfair. I apologize."

Feeling lower than dirt, Patrick turned her face toward him. His eyes caressing, he murmured, "Sweetheart, it is I who should be offering you an apology. You were in my keeping — and I am, to my shame, far more experienced than you could ever dream. I should never have touched you. I am the one who is grievously at fault — not you. Never you." He smiled ruefully. "What I said then is the blunt truth — when I am with you, I cannot seem to keep my hands off of you . . . and knowing that, I should never have allowed the situation to develop as it did. What happened was solely my fault."

A smile peeped at the corner of her mouth. "If you continue to apologize so handsomely, I believe that I shall find you a most acceptable husband."

What could he do after that but pull her next to him and kiss her soundly? She returned his kiss enthusiastically, her arms winding around his neck. All too quickly Patrick felt passion rise and, with an effort, he slowly lifted his mouth from hers.

Her eyes were bright with desire and he groaned, pressing a swift hard kiss on her rosy mouth before setting her from him. "If you continue to look at me in that fashion," he muttered, "I shall not be responsible for my actions."

The most delicious sensations spreading through her, Thea was half-a-mind to throw convention to the winds and see just how strong his resolve really was. Only the thought that Modesty could return at any minute stopped her.

"I wonder if you shall show so much restraint after tomorrow?" she teased.

His eyes darkened, and Thea felt a thrill flash through her. No. He definitely would *not* show any restraint once she was his wife!

Looking down at her pale amber skirt, she said, "Your gift arrived yesterday afternoon. Thank you."

Patrick smiled. "What? You are not going to throw them in my face?"

She laughed. "I did consider just that, but I could not. Modesty thought you'd sent them because we'd had a quarrel — she knew something was wrong when I came home from Mrs. De Land's, but she has no idea what had really happened between us. She convinced me that the jewels were far too expensive to be tossed back into your face — or the gutter." She hesitated. "So I gave them to her."

Patrick choked. "You did what?"

"Well, you couldn't have expected me to keep them, could you? Not when I was furious with you?" she asked in such a reasonable tone that he had to grin.

"No, I suppose not," he admitted wryly, thinking of the small fortune he had spent on those topazes and diamonds. Lifting her hand, he dropped a kiss on it. "I trust in the future that when I buy you gifts that you will not give them away."

"Only if I am not furious with you at the time," she murmured, her eyes dancing. Her mood changed in an instant, and, reaching out, she laid a gentle hand on his bruised face. "Do you doubt what happened to you last night is connected to Hirst?"

He shook his head, sighing. "No. I am convinced that whoever was in that hackney was either the person who murdered Hirst — or our intruder."

"You don't think that they are the same?"

"Of course they could be, but we cannot simply assume that they are." With his mother's blackmailer in mind, he added, "It's possible that there are two different forces at work — and we, I, am caught in the middle."

Thea looked fierce. "We must expose whoever is behind all this." For a moment she considered sharing with him the contents of the note she had received prior to their visit to Mrs. De Land's. A pang of guilt smote her. Was she being unfair, withholding information from Patrick? Perhaps she should tell him.

A knock on the door interrupted her thoughts. Not waiting for an answer, the door swung open, and Edwina tripped into the room.

She looked charming. A wide-brimmed bonnet trimmed in lace and feathers sat upon her head; a few gold ringlets had been coaxed to dangle near her cheeks. Dainty rosebuds embroidered the white gloves she wore, and her rather plain blue-muslin gown trimmed with tambour embroidery called attention to her curvaceous body. She was smiling as she walked toward them, but her smile vanished the instant she caught sight of Patrick's face. An exclamation of alarm escaped her, and she rushed forward.

Sighing, Patrick stood up and quickly explained how he had fallen foul of robbers the previous night. Edwina was both outraged and fascinated by his recital. "You are to be congratulated on your near escape, sir," she said, when he finished. "Indeed you are most fortunate." She looked at him admiringly. "It was very brave of you to leap from the hackney. I am sure that I would have fainted dead away if I had been so confronted."

Patrick made all the polite replies and was relieved when the subject was finally dropped. Turning to Thea, Edwina said, "I did not mean to intrude. With Hirst gone from the city, I was feeling lonely this morning and thought to spend some time with you." Her lids lowered and she added in a mournful tone, "Of course, I see that you are otherwise occupied and do not need my company. I shall be on my way."

"Oh, don't be so theatrical," adjured Modesty, entering the room behind her. "Sit down and stay — after all, that was what you were angling for, wasn't it?"

For a moment it looked as if Edwina might take offense, but then she laughed, and confessed, "As always, dear, *dear* Modesty, you are perfectly right." Looking at Thea, she asked, "You truly don't mind if I stay, do you? I shall leave immediately if I have interrupted anything of importance."

Thea shook her head. "No. Patrick called merely to tell us of his misadventures last night."

Standing beside the sofa, Patrick said,

"And having discharged my errand, I think it is I who should be leaving. I am sure that you ladies have much to discuss." He grinned at Thea. "Wedding gowns and such."

"Oh, indeed, we do," agreed Edwina. "I went with Thea yesterday for a fitting at Mrs. De Land's — her gown is simply sumptuous — I am green with envy."

"You have no reason to be," Modesty said dryly. "Didn't your sister arrange for Mrs. De Land to make a ball gown for you at a later date?"

Edwina had the grace to look guilty. "Er, yes she did." She beamed a smile at Thea. "My sister is the dearest creature imaginable."

Edwina stayed only a few minutes longer. She had been gone for several minutes when Tillman came into the room. He looked uncomfortable. "Miss, I apologize for interrupting you, but this just arrived." He frowned. "It was delivered by a street urchin."

Premonition flashed through Thea, and, taking the folded piece of paper from the butler, she dismissed him. Aware of the other two watching her, she opened the note and read the contents. She blanched, and a gasp escaped her. Wordlessly she handed the note to Patrick. His face grew grim as he read:

> *You were unwise not to keep our appointment on Wednesday. Fail again and the next time your handsome husband-to-be will not escape so lightly.*

Chapter Fourteen

"And what," Patrick asked in a level tone, "appointment did you not keep?"

Thea swallowed and looked at Modesty.

Modesty held out her hand. "May I?"

His gaze never leaving Thea's face, he handed the note to Modesty.

"Oh dear!" exclaimed Modesty as she read the contents. "This is terrible." She glanced at Thea, her expression a mixture of commiseration and "I told you so."

Patrick cast a look at Modesty. "Apparently, I am the only one who does not know about the meeting the note refers to. Would one of you like to enlighten me?" A caustic tone crept into his voice. "After all, I did suffer the results of your failure to keep that meeting, so I think it is only fair that I understand why."

"Modesty wanted me to tell you when I received the first note, but I —" Thea stopped, filled with guilt and just a little uneasy at his manner. "But I didn't want to," she said in a low voice.

His expression giving nothing away, Patrick asked, "May I see the first note?"

Thea nodded and rang for Tillman. When the butler arrived, she asked that he have one of the servants bring her the small flowered porcelain box from her dressing table.

The three of them waited in silence. When Tillman returned, he handed the box to Thea and departed. Opening it, she gave Patrick the folded note.

Warily Thea and Modesty waited for his reaction. He was quiet for several moments as he considered the situation.

Looking at Thea, he finally asked, "Was there a particular reason why you didn't tell me about the first note? Other than the fact that you were simply being your usual foolish, headstrong, aggravating self?"

Thea's chin lifted. "I didn't keep the meeting — at least I wasn't that foolish," she flashed, temper sparkling in her eyes. "And since I did not keep the meeting, there was no reason to tell you about it."

There was a glint in his eyes that boded ill for the next few minutes. But apparently thinking better of whatever he had been about to say, he turned away and prowled the room for several minutes, fighting to get his temper in hand. It wasn't that her actions had resulted in his taking a beating last night that had him angry, so much as the fact that she had obviously not trusted him.

He took a deep breath. But then, why the hell should she trust him? She already thought he had trapped her into marriage, and she had only his word to go on that she had not killed Hirst. He also, he admitted with a grimace, had refused to share with her his own reasons for being at the scene of Hirst's murder. Considering everything, she had shown remarkable restraint . . . and trust. He smiled ruefully. Far more restraint and trust than he would have under the same circumstances.

He glanced again at the two notes in his hands. Walking back to where Thea and Modesty sat, he asked, "Did the first note arrive in the same manner as this one?"

Thea shook her head. "No, Wednesday morning countless people came to call. Tillman found the note after most of the visitors had left."

Patrick sighed. "Our culprit seems to leave us with no clues as to his identity." He looked over at Thea, his face softening. "There is no use repining over what happened." He slanted her a smile. "Believe me, sweetheart, I would far rather take any number of bruises from last night's villains than to have had you meet that coach on Wednesday afternoon."

Thea looked perplexed. "What do you

mean? The note only demanded money — I wasn't in any danger. Besides, I can stand the nonsense."

"No doubt you can, but I have a dislike of being plucked — whether I can afford it or not. And I find that I have an even stronger dislike of the woman I am about to marry being blackmailed — especially when I know that she is guilty of nothing more than a reckless nature."

"Thank you for that," Thea muttered, uncertain whether to be charmed or insulted.

Patrick frowned at the notes. "It appears, at least, that both notes were written by the same hand, but other than that, they tell us little." He glanced at Thea. "I really wish I had known about the first note."

"Which is precisely why I didn't want to tell you," Thea said. "If you had known, you would have done something every bit as foolish as you have accused me of doing."

He made a face. "Touché."

"So what are we going to do?" Modesty asked. "Pay the next demand? I think there is little doubt between us that there *will* be a next demand. It seems to pay it will be our only choice — unless, of course, we wish to run the risk of you suffering further harm."

Patrick sat down in the chair across from the two ladies. His long legs stretched out in front of him, he rubbed his chin. "At the moment I think we can do nothing but wait for another note. And depending on its demands, we shall see if we cannot expose the person behind all of this."

"I don't like it," Thea said, her hands tightly clasped in her lap. "I feel so helpless — and angry."

"I, too, sweetheart," Patrick replied gently. "But the notes tell us nothing. Although they do explain what happened to me last night."

A guilty expression on her face, Thea leaned forward, and said, "Oh, Patrick, I am so sorry I did not tell you about the first note. If I had, you would not have been attacked. It is all my fault!"

Modesty snorted. "Naturally. Who else's could it be? Certainly not the person who wrote the notes or who arranged for Patrick to be attacked. Of course we couldn't blame *him* — it would have to be you."

Thea flushed and stared down at her lap. "You are right to mock me," she said in a low voice, "but I cannot help but feel that if I had never been so foolish as to meet with Hirst, none of this would have happened." She looked at Modesty. "So you see, it *is* my fault."

Modesty's face immediately softened.

"No, chicken, it is not your fault. It is the fault of whoever murdered Hirst and set all these events in motion. If it will not offend your guilt-ridden conscience, you must realize that you are nothing more than a pawn in someone else's game."

"She's right, you know," Patrick said. "Your only fault is in having an impetuous nature — a fact our culprit is taking advantage of."

"If you both are finished showing me what a lowly, inconsequential, impetuous cog I am in someone else's machinations, I suggest that we work out a plan to deal with the next message. And we know that there will be a next message."

They discussed the matter for several minutes, but no particular plan was decided upon. What was decided upon was that the next time Thea received a message demanding money or anything else, and Patrick was rather obdurate about the "anything else" part, she or Modesty write to him immediately.

"Of course, a note will not be necessary," Patrick murmured, with a grin. "After tomorrow afternoon I do not intend to let my bride stray very far from my side."

Thea flushed again, this time for a very different reason, visions of lying abed with her new husband tumbling through her mind. She had barely recovered her composure by the time Patrick rose and took his leave a few minutes later.

The rest of the afternoon and evening passed in a whirl. There was an influx of well-wishers in the late afternoon, and early that evening she and Modesty went to Mrs. De Land's for the final fitting of the wedding gown. They left the premises with Mrs. De Land's firm promise that the gown would be delivered to Grosvenor Square by no later than ten o'clock the next morning.

Lady Caldecott had insisted that the bride and groom and several members of the family dine at her house that evening, and after the fitting, Thea and Modesty, joined by Edwina, had gone immediately to the Caldecott home. The evening proved pleasant, but Thea felt dazed and disoriented, hardly able to believe that by that time the next evening, her marriage to Patrick Blackburne would be a reality.

Time and again through the night, her gaze would touch on Patrick, and a queer thrill would go through her at the expression in those normally cool, gray eyes. He was acting very much the gentleman tonight and, despite the lurid hues of his bruised face, looked urbane and heartbreakingly handsome in his close-fitting dark gray jacket and black-silk knee breeches, his linen startling white against his bronzed skin. Every time their gazes met the coil of sweet anticipation in her belly tightened.

Wrenching her gaze away from him, she tried to concentrate on others. It was difficult, but eventually she was able to put Patrick and the pull he had upon her senses at a distance and observe some of the other guests.

Edwina was thrilled to find herself an honored guest in the home of one of the most exclusive and powerful leaders of society. She was dazzled to be moving in such select company; her dinner partner on one side had been a handsome young marquis and on her other side had been a dashing, newly married countess. After dinner, when most of the guests returned to the elegant blue saloon for coffee and tiny, delicate pastries, Edwina joined Thea, Modesty, and Lady Roland where they were standing near one end of the room.

Her eyes were shining, and there was a glow about her. Watching the glittering, titled assembly scattered about the handsome room, she gave a blissful sigh. "Oh, Thea, you are so lucky! Will you think me very wicked if I say that I envy you?" She shook her golden head. "Being here tonight has made me realize how much I wish that I had listened to you and Modesty when you warned me not to marry Hirst. My life would have been so very, very different."

"We all have excellent hindsight," Modesty said dryly. "The trick is to have clear foresight."

Edwina nodded. "You are right of course. And I promise you, from this moment on, I shall change my ways." At Modesty's skeptical glance, she added, "Haven't I agreed to follow Thea's advice and remove myself to the country? Doesn't that prove that I am trying to act responsibly?"

"Indeed it does," Thea said with a warm smile. "Removing yourself from London is a wonderful first step to recouping your fortune." Thinking of the effects of Hirst's murder upon Edwina when she learned of it, Thea continued, "Sometimes, the future may look dark, but believe me, in time the darkness does fade. And if you will be guided by those of us who love you, I swear to you that you shall have a bright and shining future."

"I intend to," Edwina replied, her lovely young features suddenly somber.

Patrick walked up just then, a wry expression on his dark, handsome face. Taking

Thea's hand in his, he murmured, "I am afraid, dear ladies, that I must take my bride from you. Mother insists upon another round of toasts before the evening ends."

Once the toasts were over, the party gradually broke up, and Thea was very glad to be leaving. Patrick accompanied the ladies home; Edwina had traveled with Thea and Modesty, and they saw her to her home first. Arriving at Grosvenor Square, Patrick escorted Thea and Modesty into the house.

Bidding Thea and Patrick good night, Modesty left them in the small sitting room, giving them a last moment alone before the wedding the next day.

Patrick smiled down at Thea. "By this time tomorrow evening, it will all be over — we shall be man and wife and hopefully no longer the cynosure of all eyes. I do not know about you, but all evening I have felt like a freak at a fair. Has it been very bad for you, my sweet?"

Thea laughed, looking fetching in a low-cut gown of pale amber silk. "You forget — I am used to being stared at — usually with condemnation, so finding myself awash in so many good wishes and looks of approval is a bit of a novelty. I have almost enjoyed it."

"And I trust you will enjoy being married

to me," he said softly as his mouth claimed hers. He kissed her tenderly, passion held in check. This was to be nothing more than a brief good-night salutation. Nothing more. It didn't matter that he had been tormented all evening by the scent of her perfume and by the knowledge that she would be his wife in less than twenty-four hours. He had sworn an incident such as had occurred at Mrs. De Land's would not happen again. But she was so sweet, so warm and tempting, as he held her in his embrace he wanted her so badly that all his good intentions went flying.

As he had wanted to do all evening, he yanked her slender body next to his, a muffled groan escaping from him as his lips feasted on hers, his tongue delving deep into the damp, wine-dark depths of her mouth. A flash fire of passion roared through him, and, intoxicated and blind with instant and urgent need, he very nearly jammed her against the wall and took her then and there.

Thea had never dreamed how swiftly desire could consume one, how swiftly a simple kiss could turn into something so much more. Denying him never occurred to her, not when her heart and body were crying out with one desperate plea for him to take her. Crushed next to his hard length, the rigid proof of his own hunger obvious, she tightened her arms around his neck, and kissed him back with equal fervor and yearning.

His hand tightened on the silky amber fabric of her gown at her hips, bunching it as he dragged the garment upward. Touching the warm feminine flesh of her thigh, he groaned again and, never stopping his urgent caresses, gradually walked her backward until the wall of the room stopped their progress.

With her back resting against the wall, she shivered when he was finally able to fumble through the layers of her gown and touch her between her legs, his fingers instantly finding the aching center of her. Thea moaned, waves of pleasure washing through her as he rubbed and tweaked that tender flesh, his kiss becoming harder, more demanding.

He was mad for her, desire to lose himself in her soft depths making him forget everything but the frantic need to possess her. Lifting one of her legs, he curled it around his hips, his hand tearing at the front of his breeches. He *would* have her, he would not be denied. The hell with restraint.

That thought sent a shaft of icy sanity through his brain, and, nearly choking on his frustration, he stilled his movements, gentling his kiss. He kissed her for several long moments, heedless of his own body's demands. She was aroused and ready, and deciding that at least one of them would have satisfaction this night, he slid down to his knees. Keeping her one leg over his shoulder, he kissed her intimately between her thighs, his tongue and lips drinking in the scent and taste of her. Holding her against the wall, with fingers and tongue he tortured her, the tensing and quaking of her body telling him louder than words that she was on the brink.

Assaulted with shocking, unthinkable emotions as each thrust of his fingers, each flick of his tongue hurled her toward some new plateau of pleasure, Thea's mind went blank. The pleasure, the achingly sweet sensations were so powerful that she was certain she could not bear them an instant longer. She had thought that what they had shared at Mrs. De Land's had prepared her for physical pleasure but she discovered that there were pleasures . . . and there were pleasures. Suddenly, her body clenched, tightening in sweet, sweet agony. The next instant ecstasy exploded through her.

Stunned, she slumped against the wall, only Patrick's hands keeping her from falling to the floor. He kissed that tingling flesh one last time and with a queer, satisfied smile on that knowing mouth, he stood up, her crumpled gown sliding into place.

His body was one long ache of unfullfillment, but knowing that at least one of them would sleep well tonight made the ache bearable. Barely.

With blind eyes, Thea stared at him, the clenching and unclenching of her body still sending small shocks of pleasure through her. It was the gentle touch of his fingers against her cheek that slowly brought her back to reality.

Her eyes were dilated, her features soft, and Patrick thought he had never seen anything quite so lovely and exciting. It was a look, he told himself, that he hoped to see often in the future. Only the next time his face would wear the same expression.

Smiling crookedly, he murmured, "I did not mean for that to happen . . . but I did warn you."

"Warn?" Thea croaked, her mind a mass of jumbled mush.

"That I cannot keep my hands off of you."

"Oh, that," she mumbled, flushing.

Patrick laughed. "Yes, *that!*" He kissed her, and said against her trembling mouth,

"And I intend for us to do more of *that* frequently."

Having assured himself that they were both put to rights, he kissed her again. "I had better leave now, before you prove too tempting again. I have bent my own vows far too much as it is."

How Thea made her way up the stairs and into her room, she never knew. Wrapped in a hazy glow, her body satiated and limp, she finally managed to take off her clothes and put on a nightrail of whisper-thin cambric. It had been a long, tiring day. Pleasurable in parts, to be sure, and she blushed as she recalled just how very pleasurable. But behind her smiles and outward composure, she had been aware of an inevitable strain and tenseness. Glad to seek her bed, she had been positive that sleep would not be long in coming.

She tossed and turned in her bed, listening with weary dismay to the sound of the clock chiming the hour in the hall outside her room. One o'clock came and went, as did two o'clock. When the clock began to chime the hour of three, and sleep still eluded her, she shoved back the covers of the bed and stood up.

Desperate for sleep, she wandered around her room, wondering if a glass of warm milk would help. Deciding that the trek to the kitchen and the time and effort it would take to stoke the kitchen fire to warm the milk would banish any notion of sleep, she dismissed the idea.

Walking over to one of the tall windows that overlooked the small garden at the rear of the house, she pushed aside the delicate drapery and stood there, staring down at nothing, her thoughts on Patrick and their coming marriage. The garden below was full of shadows, a half-moon shedding slivers of silver light here and there.

She was excited and fearful of the future. There was much about her husband-to-be that she did not know, much about their sudden betrothal that filled her with dismay, and yet . . . She smiled. And yet she would marry him and with gladness in her heart. Gladness, she admitted ruefully, tempered with reservation.

It was the stealthy opening of the main door to her bedroom that brought her out of her reverie. Startled, she half swung in that direction. Only faint, uneven moonlight lit the room, and she could barely discern the black shape of whoever had entered her room. She had the distinct impression that it was a man. A man who carefully shut the door behind him before he began to move in the direction of her bed. On the verge of calling out, of demanding the person's identity, her tongue suddenly cleaved to the roof of her mouth. There was something so furtive, so sly and ominous, about the intruder's movements that fright shot through her and stilled any idea of revealing her location.

From where she stood, half-concealed behind the curtains of the window, she could make out his shape, could hear his heavy breathing and his stealthy progress across the room toward her bed. Her breath suspended, she strained to pierce the shadowy darkness, her heart banging in thick, painful strokes.

Whoever had entered the room meant her harm — she knew that, but could not say how she knew it; she only knew that her life was in danger and there was no doubt in her mind of this. Afraid to give away her position, she stood frozen in the gloom, her mind racing.

It could not be one of their servants. They were all family retainers, and it was unthinkable that one of them would want to hurt her. But someone was even now creeping toward the bed where she should have been asleep. Who?

The person who had murdered Hirst! Her

mouth went dry. Whatever else was uncertain in her mind, she was certain that he had come to murder her. He must have, she thought sickly, broken in through one of the windows on the lower level. Something occurred to her, increasing her growing terror. How had he known which room was hers? Was it someone she knew? Someone familiar with her home?

Beneath her fear, anger began to burn. How dare this person creep into her house and think to terrorize her! Her hands clenched into fists. Swiftly, she considered and discarded dozens of ideas to end this ordeal. End it with the culprit in fast retreat.

The servants were all asleep on the upper floor; Modesty's room was nearby, but Thea did not think that Modesty's presence would count for much, and it would only place her in danger. Aside from making her feel a perfect fool, she did not think that screaming for help would gain her much either. By the time her screams woke the household and help arrived, she would be dead. Feeling frustrated and helpless, fury at the intruder having banished most of her fear, she sought for an advantage. Something occurred to her: the dueling pistol she had taken to the Curzon Street house. Only by chance, it was there, in her room, in the drawer of the table near her bed.

Suddenly the uneven moonlight flashed on an object carried in the person's hand. It was a dagger, and Thea gasped at the sight of the gleaming blade.

But her gasp had alerted the intruder and with the swiftness of a striking snake, the man swung in her direction and lunged toward her. She had no time to think or plan; instinct prompting her actions, she sprang forward from her position, grabbing for the silver candelabrum she knew sat on the corner of a bureau near the window.

Her move startled the intruder, and he hesitated. That precious hesitation was all the time she needed. Thea's hand closed around the heavy base of the candelabrum, and, with a fierce battle cry, she swung back to face her attacker.

Her full-throated shout startled both of them: the intruder freezing in his steps; Thea astonished that such a sound had come from her.

She recovered first and sprang forward, holding the candelabrum as she would a club. She said harshly, "Here I am, you miserable, stinking piece of offal. Let us see how brave you are now."

Fear mingled with fury and gave her boldness and strength she had not known she possessed. Striking with all the power in her slender body, a thrill of satisfaction went through her as the candelabrum made contact with his shoulder. It wasn't where she had aimed, but she had the pleasure of knowing she had struck him — hard.

He groaned and staggered backward and Thea shouted again, another stunning clarion call that rang through the room. Heedless of her own danger, she kept after him, striking and shouting with everything that was in her.

She'd had surprise on her side, but the intruder recovered and, with something between a curse and growl, leaped at her. With careless strength he knocked the candelabrum from her hand. Losing her momentum, Thea staggered backward. He was upon her in an instant, the pair of them tumbling and rolling to the floor.

Aware of the dagger in his hand, Thea wiggled like an eel, yelling and, yes, she was ashamed to admit, screaming at the top of her lungs. Time and time again she avoided the descending dagger by a mere hairbreadth. It was an ugly, desperate battle, the odds in favor of the attacker. He was bigger and stronger, but Thea had fury and fear on her side, and she gave as good as she got. Repeatedly she clawed at his face and used her feet and knees against him. His size worked to his advantage, and she had not only the dagger to avoid, but his fist as well — and he was not averse to using it, as she learned to her pain. But it was the dagger that Thea feared worst and a sudden sting at her shoulder, another along the side of her neck, then one on her wrist told her that if she lived, she would not escaped unscathed. She needed a weapon.

Her fingers found the fallen candelabrum and with renewed vigor she struck at his head. Cursing, he grabbed the candelabrum and ripped it once more from her hand. Fright made her desperate, and snatching at the hand that held the dagger, she bit him, the salty taste of blood on her tongue almost gagging her.

He let out a bellow of rage and, grasping a handful of her hair, yanked her head backward. Her hold slackened, but the side of one of her flailing hands struck him fully on the throat and he loosed his grip, gasping for air, his attack forgotten for the moment.

It was all the advantage she needed. Fear enabling her, she gave him a violent shove and, as his weight shifted, staggered to her feet. Stumbling, running, her breathing ragged, her body aching, she raced for the table near the bed. The drawer opened and she felt the cool comfort of the pistol.

It was primed and ready, and she swung back to confront her attacker. He had recovered enough from the blow to his throat to regain his feet and stood not more than six feet away from her, appearing only as a darker shadow in the gloom of the room.

"Stand!" she shouted. "I will shoot you dead if you move."

The door to her bedroom flung open and wondrous, bright golden light spilled into the area. Modesty, in her dressing robe, a long braid of hair hanging over one shoulder, stood in the doorway, a brilliantly lit candelabrum held in one hand. "My word," she exclaimed, "what is going on in here, the yelling and shouting — Oh, my God!"

Intent upon his prey, without a backward glance, the intruder sprang at Thea, the dagger poised. In that instant, she had an impression of twisted features, lips drawn back in a feral snarl, the dagger aimed for her heart. Instinct more than purpose guided her finger as she pulled the trigger.

The sound of the shot was explosive in the confines of the room. Thea's ears rang and her eyes stung from the cloud of blue smoke that erupted from the pistol. The distinctive scent of black powder was overpowering.

Modesty screamed. The intruder, an expression of utter stupefaction on his face, staggered backward, clutching his chest where a bloodred blossom suddenly bloomed. In horror Thea watched as he collapsed on the floor in front of her, the dagger still held in his hand. He twitched, groaned, and lay still.

Shaken and sickened, unexpected sobs racking her body, Thea sank down on the edge of her bed. Thunderstruck, Modesty stared at her, then at the body on the floor, then once again at Thea.

Without a word, she reached for the bell-pull and gave it several firm yanks. This was no time for the sensibilities of the servants — if any of them were still asleep after the pistol shot.

Putting down the candelabrum on a table, she came to Thea. Gently, she inspected Thea's bruises and wounds. There was silence between them as she continued her inventory, but her touch was soft and comforting. Blotting the tears with a corner of her dressing robe, she murmured, "Now, hush, chicken. It is all over. No one can hurt you now. You are safe."

The horrified exclamations from Tillman and a burly footman, who appeared in the doorway, made Modesty glance up from what she was doing. Looking at Tillman, she said, "We will need some warm water and some mulled wine." She glanced down at the body. "And remove this object from the house — take it out into the garden for now — do not let the other servants see what you are about. Oh, and after that send" — she glanced at the footman beside Tillman — "Eldon to Mr. Blackburne's, requesting his immediate presence here." She bent a stern look at Tillman. "And not a word of this to anyone else. Tell the other servants that Miss Garrett had a nightmare and fell out of bed in her fright." Her eyes hard, she added, "And any notion that they heard a shot is to be dismissed as nonsense. Do you understand me?"

His own face grim, Tillman nodded, and, as if by magic, he and Eldon disappeared, shutting the door firmly behind them.

Modesty sat down on the bed beside Thea, one hand rubbing comfortingly up and down Thea's back.

The worst of Thea's sobs had lessened and with a wobbly, teary smile, she muttered, "Has anyone ever told you that you would make a good general?"

Modesty beamed at her. "Do you know that is one of the nicest things you have ever said to me?" She took another considering look at Thea, noticing the bruises that were beginning to pop out all over her face and body. The bruises would fade and the knife slashes on her shoulder, neck, and wrist were not deep. With clever arrangement of scarves and gloves the knife wounds could be hidden until they healed. Thea's face was another matter.

"I suppose we should be grateful for one thing," Modesty said.

"And that is?"

Modesty patted Thea's hand. "You and your bridegroom will sport, I fear, identical black eyes for your wedding."

Chapter Fifteen

By the time Patrick arrived, the body had been removed and Thea and Modesty, both wearing dressing robes, met him in the small sitting room. Thea's wounds had been tended, and the cup of warm mulled wine Modesty had pressed upon her had helped to restore her shattered nerves.

Patrick entered the house like the blast of a storm front, brushing past Tillman as if he didn't exist. "Where is she?" he demanded, never halting in his forward rush. When Tillman told him, his long legs made short work of the distance that separated him from Thea. His dark face tight and set, he plunged into the sitting room and only the sight of Thea in a rose-hued dressing gown, sitting on the small sofa, halted his charge. She looked very small and unbearably dear as she sat there, her hands folded tightly in her lap, her big, dark eyes full of remembered terror. Dear God! She was safe. He never again wanted to experience the raw fright that had consumed him when he had been awakened by the news that one of her servants was downstairs in his house demanding that he come immediately to her side. His mind filled with monstrous scenarios, never had the distance that separated their residences seemed so great.

Standing a few feet inside the doorway, Patrick took a deep breath and fought to control his fierce emotions. She was alive and, it appeared, despite the purple marks on her face, unharmed. But the bruising on her face made his heart freeze, and a dangerous, inimical gleam leaped into his gray eyes. Crossing the room, he sank to one knee in front of her, his hands covering hers. His gaze on her pale features, he asked, "What happened? Your servant would tell me nothing but that I must come instantly." He smiled without humor. "I considered throttling him on the spot."

Thea sent him a shaky smile. "I think our intruder from Curzon Street came to pay me a visit." She swallowed and her chilled fingers tightened on his strong, warm hands. "I shot him. I-I-I killed him, Patrick."

"Just as well," he replied evenly, his eyes never leaving hers. "It saves me the trouble." His gaze roamed over her, taking an inventory of the wounds, his mouth growing grim when he noticed for the first time the cotton wrap around her right wrist. With cool efficiency, he undid Modesty's neat bandage. A muscle bunched in his jaw as he stared at the thin, red line that marred her soft, white skin. Tenderly, he kissed the scarlet laceration, the knowledge that only by chance he had not lost her that night clawing at his vitals. Fighting to master the naked fury against the man who had laid hands on her, he continued his careful scrutiny.

"I really am unharmed," she said. "He attacked me with a knife, and I have a few cuts, but nothing very serious."

"Hmmm, is that so?" Patrick asked, one lean hand deftly moving aside the collar of her dressing gown. That betraying muscle jumped in his jaw once more as he examined the slash on her neck and the second one on her shoulder.

Unnerved by his cool manner and embarrassed by the familiar way his gaze and hands were running over her, Thea muttered, "I am fine — really. I told you — he did no great harm. Ask Modesty — she already did a thorough examination."

Patrick's eyes swung to Modesty, and her quick nod gave him the answer to his unasked question.

"Indeed, just as you," she confirmed, "I had to assure myself that she was relatively unscathed." Her eyes twinkling, she said, "I can assure you, dear sir, that except for bruises and the three cuts, there is nothing to worry about." Wryly, she added, "She will live — no thanks to our intruder."

"Ah, yes, the intruder," Patrick murmured sinking back onto his heels. "And where might his, er, remains be?"

"I had the servants take the body into the garden. Would you like to see it for yourself?" Modesty replied.

Patrick nodded. Rising to her feet, Modesty looked at Thea, and said, "We shall not be gone long, chicken."

But Thea had no intention of being cosseted any longer. Her dark eyes still too big for her face, she stood up, and said firmly, "I will come with you."

Patrick and Modesty exchanged a glance. Modesty made a face and shrugged. Patrick stared for a long moment at Thea and nodded. It would be easier, he decided, to have Thea close at hand than to leave her alone.

It was damp and cool in the garden, wisps of fog drifting over the manicured shrubs and neat borders. The body was lying on a patch of lawn just outside the house; Eldon stood nearby, a flickering candle clutched in one hand.

Patrick and Modesty both carried double-branched candlesticks, and, in the golden glow of their light, they regarded the body. The dead man lay facedown, but Patrick could tell from the quality and cut of his coat and breeches that he had been no common housebreaker. The boots looked to be of good leather and, even in the wavering candlelight, their shine was apparent.

His face expressionless, Patrick used the toe of his own highly polished boot to tip the body on its back. Thea and Modesty shrank together at the ghastly sight of the gaping wound that had killed him; the footman, his face green, turned away.

Patrick studied the wound and then the slack features of the dead man. He did not recognize him, but he suspected he knew his name.

Glancing at Modesty, he asked, "Have you notified the proper authorities?"

Modesty shook her head. "No. I wanted you to be apprised of the situation first."

"Very quick thinking — my compliments." He looked back at the house. "Do we know how he entered?"

"Yes, that was another thing I had Tillman do while we were waiting for you to arrive — we checked all the doors and windows and discovered that the door to the tradesman's entrance had been forced. It was standing ajar when Tillman found it, and we assume that he entered the house from there."

Patrick frowned, his eyes on Thea. "Was there any sign of robbery?"

Modesty shook her head. "No. As near as we can tell, he broke in through the tradesman's entrance and went directly to Thea's room. None of the other rooms of the house appeared to have been touched. I had Tillman examine them all."

"He came to kill me, didn't he?" Thea asked painfully.

There was no hiding the truth from her, and Patrick nodded. "From everything that I have just learned, it would seem so, my sweet." He smiled, a smile that, despite the circumstances, made Thea feel warm and protected. "And you, my clever little darling, managed to beat him at his own game."

Thea shuddered. "It was only by chance that I am not the one lying dead. If I had been asleep . . ." She swallowed. "Or if I had not kept that dueling pistol in my drawer . . ." The words trailed off as the horror of the night washed over her.

In an instant Patrick's strong arms were around her, his lips buried in the black-silk hair at her temple. "Don't think of it," he urged. "It is over. You are safe." He lifted his head to look down at her. "And I will keep you safe. I swear it by the moon above."

Modesty cleared her throat, and they both looked at her. "At the moment, beyond ourselves, Eldon, the servant who came to your house, and Tillman are the only ones who know what happened." She looked meaningfully at Patrick. "They are both discreet and have an abiding loyalty to the family — especially to Thea. Eldon is Tillman's nephew, and Tillman has been with the Garretts since he was a young man, and his father before him. They will say nothing. However, if you think that it best that we notify the authorities, I shall send Eldon to do so."

Keeping an arm around Thea's shoulders, Patrick shook his head. "Not yet, if you please. I want him identified, and I know just the fellow to tell me."

If Nigel was astonished to be ordered from his bed and to come posthaste to Grosvenor Square, there was no sign of it on his face when Patrick met him in the hall of Thea's house. One eyebrow did quirk upward at the sight of the two women in their dressing gowns, but beyond that he betrayed nothing. In his dark blue jacket, buff breeches, and exquisitely tied cravat, he looked as if he were prepared to stroll down

St. James's Street instead of finding himself in the home of the notorious Thea Garrett as the hour approached five o'clock in the morning.

As he and Patrick strode down the hall toward the back of the house, he murmured, "I trust that you have an exemplary reason for having me dragged from my bed at this hour of the morning."

Patrick grinned at him. "Never tell me that you were actually abed?"

"For an hour only," Nigel said, quick to maintain his reputation for carousing.

"Then you couldn't possibly have been very deeply asleep, now could you?" Patrick said as he ushered his friend out into the garden. At the sight of the body, Nigel stopped, his blue eyes opening very wide, his composure shaken.

"Good Gad!" he exclaimed. "What the devil is going on here?"

"Oh, nothing very much," Patrick drawled, "only an attempt at murder, which Thea managed to thwart . . . and shoot the culprit in the process."

"My word, my word," Nigel muttered, walking carefully around the sprawled body. After staring for several seconds at the face revealed in the wavering light of the candle, he glanced over at Patrick. "You never met 'im, did you?" And at the shake of Patrick's head, he nodded. "Didn't think so. Well, allow me to introduce you to the, ah, late Mr. Thomas Ellsworth."

"I rather thought that was his name," Patrick said.

Nigel looked at Eldon hovering nearby. Motioning to Patrick to follow him, he walked a short distance away.

"How many people know about this?" Nigel asked in a low undertone.

Patrick shrugged. "The ladies, the butler, his nephew over there, and you and I."

Nigel made a vexed sound. "Six altogether. A large number to keep a secret . . . especially a secret like this!"

"Modesty has informed me that Tillman and Eldon, Tillman's nephew, hold a longtime allegiance to the family — they will say nothing." At Nigel's look of relief, Patrick added, "However, nearly all of the household knows that something happened tonight — Tillman sent them back to bed with a tale that Thea had been awakened by a nightmare and disoriented and frightened, fell in her bedroom, knocking over several items. They probably don't believe it — not when a pistol was fired in the house — but they can hardly call Tillman a liar to his face. They may speculate, but if we present a united front, we should brush through with a modicum of gossip."

"Damn and blast! In another hour it will be all over London! You know how servants gossip — even if they don't really know what went on."

"Once we report it to the authorities, what the servants say won't matter," Patrick replied, his eyes fixed on Nigel's face.

"Well, we ain't going to report it — and you know it," Nigel said, sending Patrick a fulminating look. "Thing is, we have to think this thing through before we do anything foolish."

"What do you propose?" Patrick asked, relieved that Nigel's thinking ran along the same path as his.

"I ain't proposing anything at the moment," Nigel complained. "But I'll tell you one thing that's as plain as a pikestaff — none of us needs to be connected to a dead man." He flashed Patrick a glance. "Especially not Thea! We know she is innocent, but do you think the rest of London will think so? Your unexpected betrothal and hasty wedding is causing enough gossip as it is — and the beating you received the other night only added fuel to an already-raging inferno of curiosity. The very last thing either one of you needs is a dead man laid at your feet."

Nodding, Patrick murmured, "Yes, I agree with you. The servants will not talk— Miss Bradford already confirmed that." He paused, running a plan through his mind. "You came by carriage?" At Nigel's nod, he added, "Then unless your coachman is not to be trusted, I suggest you have your coach brought to the back of the house and that we put Ellsworth in your carriage and take a ride out to Hounslow Heath. Ellsworth will have been the unfortunate victim of a highwayman."

"My coachman will keep mum," Nigel snapped, offended that Patrick would think otherwise. He considered the plan a moment. "It'll do," Nigel finally pronounced. "The main thing is that the body is not found *here*."

Returning to the ladies, Patrick told them the dead man's name and what he and Nigel intended to do with the body. "Why don't we simply notify Bow Street?" Thea asked, her huge dark eyes fastened on Patrick's face. "I *did* kill the man."

Patrick sighed and glanced across at Modesty. The three of them were alone in the small morning room: Nigel, Tillman, and Eldon were busy placing Ellsworth's body in Nigel's carriage at the back of the house.

Correctly reading Patrick's look, Modesty said from her position on the settee, "That may be true, my dear, but have you thought about all the implications of what happened? You have shot and killed a man in your bedroom on the eve of your wedding to Patrick — no one is going to believe that it was anything but a final assignation gone wrong. The gossip and scandal will utterly drown out the truth. The very worst connotation will be put upon your every action." Her eyes dropped, and she ended slyly, "And, of course, for Patrick it will be even worse — he will probably have to fight a half dozen duels defending your honor before you are married a fortnight. Poor fellow. If you insist upon notifying Bow Street, we must simply hope that your new husband will be as talented with the sword and pistol as his reputation declares."

Patrick might deplore Modesty's tactics, but there was no denying that they worked. Standing in his arms, at Modesty's last words, Thea quivered as if struck by an arrow, and he knew she was remembering another duel, a duel fought over a decade ago in which her brother had died.

"Modesty is making the situation sound much worse than it is," he murmured, "but there is some truth to her words. It would be better for all concerned if Ellsworth were found somewhere else."

Thea nodded, all the fight having gone out of her at the idea of Patrick on the dueling field. Her fingers digging into his jacket, crumpling his once impeccably pressed lapel, she half asked, half demanded, "You will be careful?"

A twinkle in his gray eyes, he nodded. "Sweetheart, believe me, nothing will prevent me from marrying you tomorrow."

"I didn't mean that!" She paused, her gaze moving painfully over his. "That man, Ellsworth," she began softly, "tried to kill me tonight. I-I-I would not want harm to come to you."

"Nigel will be with me — and I can think of no one else I would prefer at my side in a dangerous situation. Nothing will happen to me, sweetheart." Conscious of Modesty's interested look, he kissed Thea sedately on the forehead instead of that tempting mouth of hers as he yearned to. "I want you to go back to bed and try to get some sleep — I know it will be difficult. But you should rest easier now that we know that Ellsworth had to have been the person who murdered Hirst and hid his body — and I'm certain that it was also Ellsworth we tangled with the night of the Hilliard ball." He shook her gently. "It's over, sweetheart. Our mystery is solved. We may never know what happened between Hirst and Ellsworth to cause them to fall out, but I am convinced that is what occurred. They must have argued once Hirst regained his senses — long after you had left the house. Ellsworth killed Hirst. It is that simple." He grimaced. "Of course, we still have the problem of being the only ones who know that Hirst is dead. And unfortunately, we can't tell what we know without incriminating ourselves — particularly since we are going to make Ellsworth's death look as if it were the work of a highwayman." When Thea looked as if she would protest, he laid a finger against her lips. "I realize that the fact that Hirst is dead must come out and soon — for your sister's sake, if nothing else — but hear me out. Just as soon as is decently possible after our marriage, we will strongly encourage her to start inquiring after her husband's whereabouts." He shot a look at Modesty. "In fact, Modesty can start doing just that right away. Once your sister starts trying to locate him, it should rapidly become apparent that he never left London — or at least, never left it alive. A search will be instituted, and I am confident that a discreet hint in Bow Street's ear will have them taking a close look at Hirst's relationship with Ellsworth. It's going to be dicey, but between Nigel and me, we should be able to, er, guide the investigation in the direction we want." At Thea's still anxious expression, he could not help brushing a kiss against her mouth. "Put what happened out of your mind — tomorrow is our wedding day and I want no droopy-eyed bride! After Nigel and I have taken care of the body, we shall return to our homes and try to get some sleep ourselves."

From her expression it was obvious that Thea still had reservations about the entire affair. Sighing, she muttered, "You are no doubt right. But I —" She made a face. "I don't like it, but since everyone else seems to be satisfied, I have no choice but to concur with your plans." She sent him a level glance. "I would ask you one thing though: Do you trust Nigel to hold his tongue? You cannot have forgotten that he is a notorious gossip."

"Only when it pleases him to be so," Patrick replied evenly. "It amuses him to court that particular reputation, but when necessary, he is quite capable of keeping his mouth shut." Patrick grinned at her. "Besides, he is deeply involved in our plans — for all his faults, he is not likely to want his part in tonight's adventures to become known."

"That may be, but I want to know; are you going to tell him everything?"

Patrick's amusement fled. His eyes searching hers, he said, "I will tell him only as much as you allow."

Thea bit her lip. "You are certain he can be trusted?" And at Patrick's nod, she said, "Then tell him what you think he needs to know — he deserves the truth for proving to be our friend and risking his own reputation to help us."

Shortly thereafter, Patrick and Nigel were bowling down the London streets in Nigel's fine carriage with the body of a dead man propped up on the seat across from them. There was much that could go wrong with their plan, and neither one was happy that it all depended upon so many people holding their tongues. If even one person hinted at the truth . . . Patrick blocked the thought from his mind. No one would talk. There was no reason for them to speak of the night's doings, but if they did, he admitted grimly, there would be hell to pay.

Almost as if he knew what Patrick was thinking, Nigel said abruptly, "My coachman's lips are sealed, and Thea's people are loyal — they ain't likely to talk. But if the worst were to happen and someone did talk, if we all stick together and deny everything, we'll come about. Devil take it! I'm a bloody earl! No one would dare accuse me of lying."

They rode through the passing countryside without further speech, both conscious of the lightening sky and the fact that daylight was fast coming. Reaching a secluded section of the road, they made short work of depositing Ellsworth's body near an overgrown copse of trees and within minutes were driving back to London.

"Anybody sees us arriving home," Nigel said, "they'll think we spent your last night as a bachelor carousing."

Patrick swallowed back a huge yawn. "Better that than what we have been doing."

Nigel glanced at him. "What did Thea say about, er, moving the body?"

"She was inclined to balk, but Modesty and I made her see that it was a sensible solution."

Nigel was quiet a moment longer, then rubbing his nose, he said, "Er, don't mean to pry, old fellow, but don't you think it is time that you told me what is going on?"

Patrick sighed, staring blankly out of the window at the passing scenery. Thea was right, Nigel deserved some explanation, but he'd been hoping to avoid it. Yet, he could not deny that Nigel had come at a moment's notice and had asked no questions, not even when confronted with a dead man. Keeping back only his own reasons for being at the Curzon Street house on that fateful night, Patrick told him the tale.

When he finished speaking, Nigel regarded him in the shadowy confines in the coach for several minutes. "Rum tale," he finally pronounced. "Thing is, my friend, you never mentioned why *you* were there that night?"

Patrick groaned. "Nigel, my reasons for being there have nothing to do with what happened."

Nigel's gaze narrowed. "You're fair and far off there! Hirst and Ellsworth were a pair of queer coves up to no good — half a dozen people could confirm that fact. You want me to believe that you just happened to be there that night? It's all hum."

Patrick smiled. "It may be, but I'm not telling you anything else." He hesitated, then said simply, "Nigel, it's not my tale to tell."

"Hmm, like that is it?"

"Yes."

The subject was dropped and the outskirts of London came swiftly. The sun was up when Patrick was let down in front of his house.

"Fine day for a wedding," Nigel remarked, as Patrick prepared to shut the door of the coach.

"Indeed." Patrick cocked a brow. "And a memorable eve to mark my last night as an unmarried man."

Nigel gave a bark of laughter. "And the devil of it is, we can never share it with anyone. Why, I could dine out a year on tonight's doings."

"But you won't, will you?" Patrick asked with a deceptively sleepy look in his gray eyes.

Nigel shook his head. "Now don't come the ugly with me! If you'd thought I'd babble, you wouldn't have sent for me in the first place. Good day, my friend."

The wedding was less than eight hours away, and Patrick was certain he would not be able to sleep even for a few hours, but to his surprise, his head had hardly hit the pillow before he was asleep.

Thea did not find sleep quite so easily; but after some restless tossing and turning, she, too, managed to fall asleep. She did not sleep as soundly as did Patrick, fragments of weird and terrible dreams flashing through her mind.

She woke to the clatter of crockery and sat up to stare bleary-eyed at Modesty entering the room, a tray in her hands.

"Good!" Modesty said, looking disgustingly bright and cheerful as she put the tray down on Thea's dressing table. "You are awake."

"How could I not be with you playing housemaid — and not very well at that," Thea muttered, as she flung back the covers of the bed and stood up. She stretched and groaned as her sore muscles and many bruises made themselves felt.

Thea's cross mood did not bother Modesty. "Come along, chicken," she coaxed as she poured a cup of coffee from the pot on the tray, "drink some of this nice hot coffee — you'll feel much better."

Modesty was right, and, a few minutes later, Thea smiled across her cup at her friend. "Are you always right?"

Modesty pinched her chin. "Usually. Now come along, I've ordered a bath for you, and Mrs. De Land will be here within the hour for the last fitting of your gown. She said that she would do any final sewing and alterations here at the house."

There was no time for further conversation, and the next hours flew by, every tick of the clock bringing closer the actual moment she was to stand beside Patrick Blackburne and become his wife. Thea tried to stamp down the thrill of panic that went through her whenever she thought of that moment, a part of her excited and eager, another part absolutely terrified. As the morning passed, she wondered if she were mad. Had she really agreed to marry a virtual stranger? The answer was painfully apparent in the bustle and frantic rush going on about her as Modesty, Maggie, Mrs. De Land, and various maidservants fussed over each detail of her dress, her hair, her face.

Her face gave them all pause. The black eye Modesty had predicted last night had come to pass, along with a darkening bruise on her cheek, but it was not quite as bad as feared. A judicious use of rice powder hid the worst of the marks and it was hoped that the circles under her eyes would be put down to bridal nerves.

Mrs. De Land raised a brow at the tale of a nightmare fright and a horrific fall to explain the various purple-and-green marks on Thea's body. The cuts made by the knife were ignored.

Proving herself to be as discreet as reputed, Mrs. De Land made no comment, but crossing the room, plucked up a swath of the same silky material as the underdress.

She calmly ripped off the tiny puffed sleeves and, before their astonished gaze, magically fashioned a new pair of long, pleated sleeves for the gown that hid the bruises on Thea's arms — and the cut on her wrist. Putting in the last stitch, Mrs. De Land stepped back and surveyed her work. The long sleeves, she decided, were a touch of genius. They added so much more to the gown than the original puffed sleeves. But that neckline. . . . Lady Caldecott would be displeased if her son's bride walked down the aisle and all anyone noticed was the unmistakable knife slash on her neck and the mottled bruises that marred the soft white bosom. And Lady Caldecott would, no doubt, Mrs. De Land concluded, be willing to add a handsome gratuity to her already exorbitant bill when the circumstances were explained to her. Explained, very, very delicately, of course.

There was little time, and her eye on the gilt clock on the mantel, Mrs. De Land lifted off the bed a long scrap of Brussels lace. With practiced ease she added a few more rows of lace to those already adorning the square-cut bodice of the gown. By the time she was finished, the lace was halfway up Thea's chest, any obvious bruising having disappeared beneath the delicate lace.

Glancing at Modesty, Mrs. De Land murmured, "A modest gown is very important for a bride, don't you think?"

"Absolutely," Modesty replied, thinking that the changes did not detract from the original design of the gown in the least. In fact the changes were quite, quite fetching. She eyed the slash on Thea's neck. But it was all going to be for naught, she thought, if something wasn't done about that long, angry red laceration.

But Mrs. De Land rose to the occasion. One last piece of material was brought forth, and, with a twist of her clever fingers, Mrs. De Land fashioned a bow around Thea's neck from the rose-hued gauze of the overskirt.

When Thea was finally allowed to view herself in the cheval glass, she could hardly believe the stunning creature she saw reflected there. Her dark hair had been piled into a heap of careless curls on top of her head, a few wisps allowed to dangle near her ears. The long sleeves and higher neckline added an almost medieval look to the gown, and the dashing bow tied at the side of her neck, well the bow, she decided, saved the day. A faint smile on her lips, she touched the bow. It was possible that she would start a new fashion.

The carriage that would take them to the Caldecott home was waiting at the front of the house, and Thea was finally putting on the last touch to her wedding finery; a pair of pearl earrings. Mrs. De Land and the others, except for Modesty, had already left. Modesty, looking handsome in a new gown of gray-striped silk, was standing beside Thea.

A soft expression in her eyes, Modesty asked, "Are you happy, my dear? I know that yours has not been a conventional courtship, but somehow it seems fitting, doesn't it?"

Thea sighed, but her dark eyes were shining. "After w-w-what happened, I never thought to marry . . ." She glanced down at the gown, her fingers touching it almost with wonder. She looked at Modesty, her expression radiant. "Am I happy? Oh, yes!"

The door to the room was thrown open and Edwina rushed in, her blond curls bouncing. Wearing a frothy creation of sky-blue silk and lace, she paused just inside the threshold.

There was a stunned expression in her blue eyes as she stared at Thea. "Oh, Thea," she finally breathed, a smile curving her rosebud mouth, "you look beautiful!"

Thea laughed and dipped a teasing

curtsey. "Thank you, my dear."

"Are you riding with us?" Modesty asked. "I thought you had planned to go to Caldecott House directly from your own house."

Crossing the room and placing her arm in Thea's, Edwina said, "Indeed, that is what I planned to do, but then I realized that I would much rather arrive with my sister. We *are* family."

Ushering the two women from the room and toward the staircase, Modesty commented, "And you seem to remember that fact only when it suits you."

A pout appeared on Edwina's pretty face. Shaking her head, Thea glanced from one woman to the other.

"Ladies," she said, "it is my wedding day. Please, for me? Be nice to each other. And be happy for me."

Ashamed of herself, Modesty hugged Thea, and not to be outdone, Edwina did the same, both of them promising to lay aside their differences.

With Edwina on one side of her and Modesty on the other, Thea descended the staircase, in the knowledge that when next she came to this house it would be as Mrs. Patrick Blackburne. The thought was both exhilarating and utterly terrifying.

Chapter Sixteen

At Lady Caldecott's insistence the wedding was being held at Caldecott House in the grand ballroom. She had bullied and badgered everyone she knew, and some she didn't, who possessed a greenhouse into supplying her with the choicest of blooms. Under her expert hand the ballroom had been turned into a garden of paradise.

Great swaths of greenery hung from the high ceiling, and garlands of lilies and roses were draped in graceful curves along the walls. Potted palms and small trees in gold and silver pots were scattered along the edges of the room. A gleaming silver arbor covered in pink and white lilies arched over a large dais. Patrick, resplendent in a coat and knee breeches of a midnight blue, stood under the arch; the gloriously hued bruises on his hard face gave him a decidedly menacing appearance. Nigel, in his role of best man, was at his side. Beyond them, on the dais, waited a robed figure, his hands clasped loosely in front of him.

The two rows of hastily erected pews were adorned with white-and-green-satin bows and were crowded with members of the ton garbed in their finest clothes, all waiting for the bride. Modesty, Edwina, and other members of Thea's family sat in one of the front pews; in the other, Patrick's family and friends. Lady Caldecott looked as proud as a queen in her puce and pearls, her silver-streaked hair sculpted and curled to perfection; Lord Caldecott sat beside her, in a jacket and breeches nearly the same shade as her gown. Soft music from the hired musicians filled the room. All was in place. It was time.

Thea had been unable to choose between her two uncles to escort her down the makeshift aisle and so when the huge double doors swung open and she began her march down the aisle, Lord Hazlett was on one side of her, Lord Garrett on the other. Each man wore the identical smile — affectionate and proud and pleased. The sight of the ballroom made Thea blink. It was a fairyland of pink and white, silver and gold, and a ripple of delight went through her. It was beautiful.

She hesitated a moment at the entrance, suddenly uncertain. Then her eyes fell upon Patrick, and he smiled at her. The world, her uncles on either side of her, the avid stares of the ton, everything but Patrick disappeared. On feet that hardly touched the polished floor, a smile on her lips that glowed with the power of a thousand candles, she floated down the aisle, the knowledge that somehow she had been lucky enough, blessed perhaps, to marry this tall, commanding man flooding through her.

Patrick's breath caught in his throat as he stared at her. He had known that she exercised an extraordinary fascination for him, but he had never realized how much until this very moment. In her wedding finery, her eyes shining like opals, her smile dazzling, she was lovely, breathtaking. But it was more than mere physical loveliness that touched him, more than her slender body and intelligent features that made his heart behave in a most unrecognizable manner. It was simply Thea herself, something about her eager enthusiasm, her intrepid courage, as well as the endearing tilt at the corner of her mouth and the shimmering excitement in her eyes, that drew him, and he knew that he would never again doubt that love existed. He was consumed with it. For one particular woman. For Thea.

It was a simple ceremony, Patrick's voice carrying clear and bold as he repeated his vows; Thea's softer, but ringing out just as clearly to the assembled guests. And then it was over. They were wed.

Thea remembered little of the remainder of the day. She knew that the guests were invited out into the garden while the pews magically disappeared and tables laden with refreshments just as magically replaced them. She knew that she and Patrick were congratulated and exclaimed over, that they danced and drank and ate and laughed, but none of it was real to her. Only one thing was real — Patrick. Her husband. And as the afternoon progressed, she was so aware of him, so conscious of that tall, hard body standing next to hers, that she could not concentrate on what was being said around her. Conversations, comments, questions, kind or barbed, went right over her head, her whole focus being on the way her skin tingled whenever she brushed against him or the leap of her heart whenever their eyes met. She wanted, ached, she admitted, to be alone with him. To have him do again all those wanton things he'd already done with her. A shiver of anticipation went through her.

Remembering vividly the previous night, of her back pressed against the wall, gown tossed over his shoulders, as he had tasted and feasted between her thighs, a flush flew to her cheeks and she was conscious of sudden, embarrassing dampness flourishing between her legs. She was a shameless wanton! But she didn't care; all she cared was that he was her husband and she would lie tonight in his arms.

Because their wedding had been arranged so precipitously, no formal plans for a honeymoon had been made. Patrick had suggested earlier to Thea that they might spend the first few nights of their marriage in his London house. At the beginning of the week, they could decide upon a destination that would take them away from all the prying eyes that they were likely to encounter if they remained in London. Thea had concurred.

Of course, she had her own reasons for not wanting to leave the city immediately — her promise to meet on Monday with Edwina's terrifying gentleman, Mr. Yates. Preoccupied with the wedding and a dead man, Mr. Yates and that particular problem had been pushed to the back of her mind, but she had not forgotten about him. She might be Mrs. Patrick Blackburne now, but Mr. Yates was one last detail that she was determined to take care of herself. The enormous sum of money had already been withdrawn; all she had to do was elude her new husband for a short while on Monday and confront Mr. Yates at Edwina's house.

Thea was prepared to give Mr. Yates the money he had demanded from Edwina . . . this time, but she was determined to *strongly* impress upon him that, no matter what other debts he might claim Hirst owed him, no more money would be forthcoming. Ever. Modesty had urged her to consider that it might be wise to have Patrick meet with Mr. Yates, but Thea had dismissed that notion. Patrick might agree with her decision to pay the man . . . or he might not. If she involved him, and he decided *not* to pay Hirst's debt, as her husband, with control of her fortune, that would be his prerogative. And if he chose not to pay Mr. Yates, leaving her sister to fend for herself, Edwina would end up being dunned and hounded by a fellow who obviously frightened her. With Patrick holding the purse strings, Thea would be unable to help her. She did not believe that Patrick would prove to be so unreasonable, or unkind, but she was not prepared to take the chance. Better she handle this matter herself and worry about the consequences when her husband found out, as she was sure he would eventually, than to run the risk of Edwina being left alone to face Hirst's sins.

Thea didn't feel that she was precisely

hiding what she intended to do from Patrick; she viewed it more in the nature of cleaning up old business. Her business.

But at the moment, she wasn't thinking of Mr. Yates or the meeting on Monday; all her thoughts were on Patrick and how soon they could leave and be alone. A pang of guilt assailed her. Lady Caldecott had gone to a great deal of trouble to make the day and setting as charming and lovely as possible, and all Thea wanted to do was leave.

That moment could not come swiftly enough for Patrick, though from the polite expression on his face, no one could have guessed that he was impatient and eager to be alone with his bride. As physically aware of Thea as she was of him, Patrick had been in a semierect state since they had been pronounced man and wife. And with his skintight breeches, it created an awkward time for him. Time and again, as they moved through the crowd, he kept his lower body half-concealed behind Thea's gown and cursed his unruly member. She was simply too damned alluring. He didn't want to be here, smiling and talking to strangers. What he wanted was to be alone with his bride. Naked.

Though they were continually engulfed by well-wishers, all of his senses were concentrated on her. The mere sight of her slender form quickened his pulse, and the spicy scent that drifted up from her body teased him to find its source. As they accepted the good wishes of the guests, he was very aware of the silky softness of her hand and arm beneath his fingers and could not help caressing that tender flesh. The slight, seductive huskiness of her voice seemed to wrap itself around him, charming him and arousing him at the same time. And while it had been hours ago, the taste of their wedding kiss lingered on his lips, and he was avid to taste again the sweetness of her mouth.

His organ swelled at the images coursing through his mind, and with something between a groan, a curse, and a plea, he pulled Thea aside from the latest group of well-wishers, and muttered, "We have been here for hours — it is time that we depart. If we do not, I fear I shall do something shocking."

From across the room, Lady Caldecott observed the pair of them and smiled to herself. She may not have heard what her son had said to his bride, but she had a very good idea what was on his mind. She might be Patrick's mother, and considered long past the urgent mating commands of the body, but too well did she know the demands that desire could place upon one.

Lord Caldecott smiled, touching her hand with his, their eyes meeting. He lifted her hand to his mouth and brushed a kiss against the scented flesh. "Congratulations on a job well-done, my dear." He studied the ever-shifting crowd before them. "I did not think it could be done on such short notice, but you have made your son's wedding *the* event of the season. There will be much moaning and gnashing of teeth by those who were unable to attend . . . or not invited."

"Yes, I know," she replied, an amused gleam in her fine eyes. "Which was the whole point." The gleam vanished, and she looked again at Thea and Patrick. "Do you think they will be happy?"

He shrugged. "Perhaps, but if they are not, it is no fault of yours." He smiled. "Of course, there is the fact that by moving so swiftly you did not give him a chance to choose anyone else."

Lady Caldecott made a face. "Yes, I did do that, but I think, in the end, that I did the right thing. Who knew what those two would have gotten up to without a little push in the right direction." She gave a small shudder. "Agreeing to become his mistress! What was the child thinking of?"

"I do not think that a young woman of seven-and-twenty could be considered a child." A speculative expression on his patrician features, he looked at Patrick and Thea. "It might have been interesting to watch their courtship. It certainly would have been entertaining."

"And no doubt scandalous!"

He flashed her a sleepy-eyed glance. "Scandal serves its purpose, my dear."

Her fingers went to the pearls around her throat. "That may be, but I did not want my son or his prospective bride to be fodder for all the wicked tongues in London. And considering Patrick's reputation, as a rake, ripe and ready for any lark, and hers for, for — well, with her past, the ton would have fallen upon them like a pack of famished wolves. It would have been ugly. Enough so that it could have blighted the whole affair." She looked again at the newlyweds, her features softening. "She is the first woman who has ever touched his heart, and from what Modesty has told me, I believe that he is the first man to have deeply touched hers. I dared not let circumstances conspire against them." Her chin came up. "I have no regrets for what I have done."

"Bravo! And you should not, my pet. Regrets are for fools." Noticing, not for the first time, her nervous toying with the heavy strand of pearls around her neck, he frowned. "I thought you were going to wear your diamonds today."

She started, her hand dropping to her side. "Oh, I considered them, but decided that they were far too ostentatious for an afternoon wedding. The pearls were much better." She smiled at him. "Besides, they were a gift from you."

He bowed and kissed her hand. "Remind me to buy you the brooch that matches them."

"You are very good to me," she said.

"Yes, I am," he replied, his pale blue eyes caressing her.

Even at her age, Lady Caldecott blushed at the warmth behind his look. Her heart fluttered beneath her puce-covered bosom, and she wondered how she could be so fortunate, at her time of life, to be so besottedly in love . . . and loved in return. Her eyes flashed. And she was not going to let the past destroy her future. Her fingers went again to the pearls. Damn those letters! And damn the person who threatened her happiness.

During the next few hours, Lady Caldecott gave no further thought to her troubles. From across the room, Patrick signaled that they would soon be leaving, and she made her way to their sides. Pressing a warm kiss on Thea's cheek, she said, "Be happy, my dear." As she looked at her tall son, a lump suddenly formed in her throat. Hiding the emotion that welled up inside of her, she gave him a sharp tap on his cheek, and muttered, "And if you are not happy, it will be your own fault."

Patrick grinned at her.

And then in a flurry of laughter and ribald teasing, Patrick and Thea made a dash for the front of the house. And then they were gone. To start, Lady Caldecott hoped fervently, a long and happy life together.

After the departure of the newlyweds, the excitement ebbed and an hour or so later, Lord and Lady Caldecott were bidding the last stragglers good-bye. Ten minutes later, having giving the butler and the housekeeper their orders, Lady Caldecott was upstairs in her room, preparing for a quiet evening with her husband.

Having changed from her wedding clothes into an elegant blue-silk negligee trimmed with blond lace, Lady Caldecott dismissed her maid for the evening. Alone in her rooms, she was brushing her now-loosed hair, her thoughts on her husband's anticipated arrival, when her gaze fell upon the small silver salver sitting on the corner of her dressing table. There was an envelope lying there, and, putting down her brush, she stared at it for several minutes.

She told herself that the envelope contained nothing more than an innocuous message; a friend expressing regret for not being able to attend the wedding or a frivolous answer to a note she herself had written perhaps days ago. Whatever was inside that square envelope would have nothing to do with her blackmailer. But deep in her heart she knew differently.

The house had been crowded today with strangers; guests, delivery people, and newly hired servants pressed into service to help with the anticipated crush. The place had been a beehive of activity since early this morning, and if someone had wanted to leave behind a note anonymously, today would have been the day. She thought of ringing for Grimes and asking him when and where the note had been found, but she knew it would be futile. Whoever had left it had chosen the time and the place well. Grimes, or one of the other servants, had probably discovered it lying in a conspicuous spot sometime after the guests starting arriving. She would have been busy and preoccupied, and Grimes had probably had the note delivered to her rooms for her perusal later. No one would have given it any significance.

Looking at it as she would a viper, she reached over and picked it up and opened it. As she had suspected, it was from the blackmailer.

I find that my need is great and I can wait no longer. You must deliver to me, no later than midnight Sunday, the sum of ten thousand pounds. You know where to leave it.

She didn't, not really, but suspected the note referred to the house on Curzon Street. Setting the note down, she stared into space. Under the circumstances, and she surmised the blackmailer had already taken that fact into his plan, she could not ask Patrick to meet with this insufferable scoundrel. She frowned. She could take the money and go to the Curzon Street house herself, but something inside of her rebelled at tamely giving away a fortune.

It wasn't paying the money, she realized, that she objected to, so much as being shorn like a lamb. She had no doubt that if she met his demand, it would only be the first of many. And there was another reason she dismissed the notion of following the instructions of the note: She was not a fool, although she could not deny that she had acted the fool upon occasion, but she was long past the reckless age of leaping and thinking later. She had no intention of going alone to that particular house at that hour of the night. Especially not with ten thousand pounds! Of course, she could ask one of the servants to accompany her, but that was simply silly and might very well put *both* of them in danger. So what was she going to do? There was really only one solution, she thought with a sigh, and it was what she should have done in the first place.

Her expression set, she picked up the note and rose to her feet. Resolution in every step, she crossed the room to the door that separated her bedroom from her husband's. She gave a brief rap on the door and entered.

Lord Caldecott's bedroom was dark and empty, but the flickering light that came from the adjoining sitting room, gave her a clue to his whereabouts. Not giving herself a chance to change her mind, she walked toward the light, her heart heavy in her breast.

The letters had been written long ago, and they should not have mattered to her, but they did. Terribly. They showed that she had not always been the arbiter of virtue that she was today. Those letters revealed that once she had been wild and wanton and . . . and scandalous. She was not ashamed of the passionate emotions she had written of all those years before, but she did fear what her husband might make of them . . . that he might think less of her — that he might begin to look upon her with contempt.

Before they had married, Lord Caldecott had been a well-known roué and she the epitome of virtuous respectability. Their marriage had stunned the polite world, both of them coming from such very different parts of the ton. Both were wellborn and wealthy, but her world had been one of fashionable decorum; his the rakish sphere inhabited by hard drinkers, gamblers, and womanizers. Their respective pasts were not something they had ever discussed, the power and astonishing wonder of their love sweeping aside whatever their histories might have held.

Lady Caldecott had known her husband's reputation before they married, and, despite being confident that he did love her, she could not help thinking that perhaps part of her allure for him had been her very respectability. A gentleman could have all the mistresses he wished, but for a woman of her station to have embarked upon a torrid affair with a married man was something the polite world would not forgive. To discover that she was not quite the virtuous woman Lord Caldecott had thought her to be might very well undermine their very marriage. She knew she was being as fearful and silly as a green girl, but she could not help it. Her husband thought her above reproach, and she did not want to disillusion him — or have him look at her with disgust.

Entering the pleasant sitting room decorated in shades of blue and cream, she spied him sitting on one of the blue-damask sofas. He was wearing a sapphire blue silk dressing robe and apparently enjoying a snifter of brandy.

At her entrance, he put down his snifter and stood up. Walking over to her, he kissed her on the cheek. "Ah, my love, you are a sight to warm any man's heart. Especially this man's heart." He gestured toward the satinwood sideboard that sat against the far wall. "Would you care for something to drink? Some wine?"

She took a deep breath. "A brandy will be fine. A large one."

His brows rose, but he said nothing, merely crossing to the sideboard and pouring her a brandy in a snifter. Handing it to her, he said, "Have you decided that you needed something a little stronger after today?"

"It-it-it isn't because of today," she muttered, and sank down onto an identical sofa across from the one upon which he had been sitting. Holding the snifter in both hands, she breathed in the smoky bouquet. She took a drink, coughing a little at the bite of the strong liquor.

A faint frown in his eyes, he retook his seat across from her. Lifting his own brandy, he sipped it. "So what is it that has you forsaking your usual ladylike libations?"

She looked at him. "Do you love me?" she blurted out, her fingers gripping the snifter. Mortified at her outburst, her gaze dropped. She was a fool! What must he be thinking? That he had married a goose-brained ninny?

He appeared astounded. Putting down his snifter, he moved to sit beside her on the couch. He took her snifter away and after setting it down on the floor, pulled her into his arms. With her head nestled against his shoulder, he said, "Suppose you tell me what this is all about. And yes," he murmured, pressing a warm kiss into her temple, "I do love you. Never doubt it."

Lady Caldecott did not know where to

start, but eventually, her eyes fixed upon the sculpted blue carpet, she told him the entire story. Everything. He did not interrupt, and when she finished there was a small silence.

"Well, that certainly explains your son's many visits," he finally said. "I confess that I had wondered about them — he had never struck me as a young man who would be content to be dandled on his mother's knee." He turned her to face him. His blue eyes smiling, he murmured, "In fact, he rather reminded me of myself — before, of course, I met you and embarked upon a more respectable life."

Lady Caldecott flushed and looked away. With a gentle finger, he turned her face back to him. "I did not mean to tease you, my love. It is just that I find myself in a bit of a dilemma. This is not quite how I had planned for this to happen. You have surprised me — most agreeably, I will admit."

Puzzled, she stared at him. A whimsical expression on his features, he said, "You are not the only one with a confession. Wait here, I have something to show you." Leaving her on the sofa, he disappeared into his bedroom. Returning almost immediately, he handed her a small packet of letters.

Undoing the faded yellow ribbon bound

around them, with shaking fingers she opened the first one and read its contents. Her heart sank. It was her letters. She didn't know what to think. Her husband was her blackmailer? It seemed incomprehensible. She looked at him. "Why?"

Seating himself comfortably beside her, he said, "I wanted you to trust me."

"You wanted me to trust you?" she exclaimed, her voice rising incredulously. "And so you blackmailed me?"

"Er, no. Your, uh, original blackmailer was that fellow Ellsworth. I, er, stole the letters from him."

She shook her head, none of it making any sense. Her gaze fixed painfully on his calm blue eyes, she said, "Tell me."

For the first time, he looked a trifle discomposed. "My part is rather embarrassing and shows what a fool a man my age can be when he falls in love for the first time." He took one of her hands in his and kissed her fingers. "You see I do love you — beyond reason, and I am afraid that where you are concerned I am as vulnerable and foolish as any Nick Ninny." He kissed her fingers again. "Patrick's frequent visits aroused my suspicions." He shook his head at her expression. "No, I was not jealous of him, but I suspected that there was more than just filial affection behind his visits. Your actions only confirmed it — you may not realize it, but you have been obviously worried and anxious of late, distracted — I knew that something was bothering you." He made a face. "I hoped that you would come to me with whatever your problem was — if you will remember I have given you ample opportunity to do just that. But to all my lures, you turned away and turned instead to your son. It was not me, your adoring husband, but your son that you wanted to play knight-errant for you. Now *that* did make me jealous."

"You had no cause," she said huskily. "It was just that I —"

"It was just that you didn't want me to know," he said gruffly. His fingers tightened on hers. "Did you trust me so little?"

"Oh, it was never that! I was fearful that if you knew that I had not always been so-so-so virtuous that your feelings for me would change."

He gave a rough laugh. "You little fool! With my past? How could you think I would think any less of you? Haven't you been listening? I adore you! What do I care about some letters you wrote decades ago?"

A weight lifted from her heart. Her eyes as bright and glowing as a young maid's, she breathed, "Truly?"

He pulled her into his arms and kissed her. "Truly."

Her senses spinning, her head resting on his shoulder, she said, "Tell me. Everything."

"There is not a great deal to tell. Once I became aware that something was amiss, I eavesdropped shamelessly and from the bits and pieces I overheard, I was able to put most of the scheme together. Knowing that you were being blackmailed and that a certain house on Curzon Street seemed to be the blackmailer's place of business, I spent far more nights than I care to remember, lurking in that vicinity, watching and observing the goings-on. I even went so far as to break into the place, but I found nothing there to make me look in a different direction." He sent her a reproachful glance. "Not being privy to the whole side of it, I was left to scramble about on the fringes, hoping that luck would come my way." A pleased expression entered the blue eyes. "And one night recently I was very, very lucky. Like your son, I had discovered that the likely culprit had to have been Thomas Ellsworth. I was considering the best way to approach him, without," he said dryly, "stumbling over Patrick, when to my delight, what should happen, but for Ellsworth to come running right into my very arms. Of course I didn't know it was Ellsworth at the time — it was, I confess, very dark where I was lurking, but when I was suddenly confronted by a furtive fellow who wanted to hide in my alley, I guessed who he might be. Fortunately, I did not have to resort to violence — the silly fellow knocked himself senseless — giving me plenty of time to, er, root about his form. Having seen Patrick and Thea enter the house earlier, as well as Ellsworth shortly thereafter, I was pretty certain who my unexpected visitor might be, and upon searching him I confirmed his identity and discovered an interesting packet." He smiled reminiscently above her head. "I was not even certain what it was that I had found, but I dared not linger for fear that Patrick and Thea might come in pursuit of Ellsworth and stumble across me. It was only when I had returned home and had a moment to open the packet that all the answers became clear to me. I must admit that it was a grand piece of luck for me that Ellsworth actually had the letters on him when he bolted into the very alley where I was hiding."

She twisted around to look up at him.

"Why didn't you tell me?"

He rubbed his nose. "Well, you see, I had this ridiculous notion that I wanted you to come to me, to trust me with the tale — whatever it was. I wanted you to trust me with your troubles." He appeared uncomfortable. "My problem was that I hadn't thought far enough ahead — having finally gotten the damn things and realized what was going on, I didn't know what to do with them."

"You could have simply destroyed them — my blackmailer would have merely disappeared — ceased to dun me."

He shook his head. "No, you had to know that they no longer existed, that the blackmailing was over — for good."

She arched a brow. "So you decided to blackmail me yourself?"

"Not exactly. I was hoping that you would come to me. But if you didn't, I was simply going to leave the letters at the house for you to find tomorrow night."

"And the money?"

A devilish glint lit his eyes. "Oh, I suspect that over the next few months you would have found me lavishing you with the most extravagant gifts."

"Bought with my own money?" she inquired too sweetly.

He grinned and nodded. "What else could I have done with the blasted money — I certainly don't need it . . . as your son discovered when he had my finances investigated."

Lady Caldecott's mouth fell open. "He had you investigated?"

He cocked a brow. "You didn't know?" At the vehement shake of her head, the last of his anxieties disappeared. "Well, I must say that is a relief. It worried me that you might have known what he was up to and had concurred with his theory that I might be the blackmailer."

"He never breathed a word to me. That devious wretch! I shall have a thing or two to say to him the next time I see him." Something occurred to her and she frowned. "How did you find out that he had looked into your finances?"

"My dear, your son may be up to every rig and row in town, but you must remember that I have been around for a much longer time. I had my own sources, and when discreet inquiries were made into my affairs, I was informed of it."

"I see. Are you angry at his effrontery?"

He shook his head. "No. And I do not want you to be. He loves you, and he was determined to leave no stone unturned in trying to help you — even if it meant investigating your husband."

She snorted. "And do you think that it would have made me happy to find out that it was my own husband who was blackmailing me?"

"I sincerely hope not. But since it is a moot point, I suggest we leave it alone. And I would further suggest that you do not take your son to task for doing the very thing you asked him to do: find out who was blackmailing you."

"You are probably right." She glanced at him. "Whatever am I going to tell him now? Without the letters Ellsworth has no power over me and there is no reason for Patrick to continue his efforts in my behalf." She smiled. "Besides, he has a wife who will have first call on his time now." She hesitated. "Do you care if I tell him what happened? That you have the letters?"

"Ah, no. I think it would be better if I spoke with him and explained things." He slanted her a look and, with only a hint of reproach in his voice, added, "After all, I *am* your husband and as such I should have been the one you came to for help in the first place. Let me at least have the pleasure of putting an end to the affair." He kissed her. "It is my very great honor to serve you

— if you will let me."

"Oh, my dear, I so regret that I did not do so, but . . ." She glanced away. "But I was so ashamed and embarrassed by the whole incident. To think that someone of my age and in my position was being blackmailed. And by some foolish letters I had thought destroyed long ago. It was so ugly and horrid that I could not bring myself to tell you." She smiled wryly. "It was *your* knowing what a fool I had been that gave Ellsworth power over me — not necessarily the letters." A slight flush on her cheeks, she asked, "Er, did you read the letters?"

He smiled tenderly at her. "Only one and only enough to find out what had caused you such alarm. I did not relish my role of eavesdropper, and even less did I relish reading words that had been meant for another man." His lids drooped, and he flashed her a provocative look. "I must confess that some of what you wrote convinced me that I have been too tame in my lovemaking."

"Oh, really?" she commented. Putting her arms around his neck, she murmured, "Perhaps you would like to show me precisely what you mean."

He clasped her to him and kissed her. "Oh, I shall indeed," he muttered. And he did.

Chapter Seventeen

As Thea and Patrick raced away from all their well-wishers and to the intimacy of their waiting coach, Thea was astonished to realize that dusk was falling. The lamplighters were moving slowly down the streets, and purple shadows were beginning to fall. But then she had no time for other thoughts — the vehicle hardly began to move before Patrick urgently pulled her into his arms and kissed her.

They were both breathing hard when he lifted his head and carefully set her on the velvet seat across from him. Dazed and aroused, feeling as if a soft flame had brushed every inch of her body, Thea simply sat there staring at him. Her breasts and nipples tingled, her skin was flushed and warm, and between her legs she was throbbing and aching. Wide-eyed she continued to stare at Patrick in the gloom of the coach, her half-parted lips red and swollen from his kiss.

"Don't look at me that way, sweetheart," he murmured, "not unless you want me to finish what we just started right here."

"Well, we are married . . ." she said breathlessly, only half-teasing.

"Witch!" Patrick muttered, a carnal glint leaping to his gray eyes. "Don't tempt me too far. I am behaving with exemplary restraint — and only the knowledge that we are not many minutes from home is keeping you safe from a very thorough ravishment."

The drive was short, but the sexual tension between them was almost palpable by the time they reached Hamilton Place. Patrick helped her down from the coach and escorted her up the steps into his house.

Chetham greeted them, and after Patrick had presented his bride to him, the butler bowed low. A smile on his normally frigid features, he said, "It is a pleasure, Madam. I trust that you will be happy here and with the staff. Whenever you are ready, the housekeeper and cook are eager to meet you. They also wish to discuss any changes you might want to institute. Though we have been a bachelor's household, we look forward to the differences that having a lady in residence will bring. We shall serve you well — your wish is ours to provide."

"Th-thank you," Thea replied, charmed.

Patrick snorted. "Don't be fooled by his graceful manners. He is an old despot and tries to rule me with an iron hand — he'll do the same to you if you don't watch him."

Patrick grinned at the expression that congealed on Chetham's face. "Of course he would rather die than admit to a fondness for me."

Chetham drew himself up. His face disdainful, he glanced at Patrick, and said, "If you will follow me, sir. Cook has prepared a celebratory dinner for you and your bride." He coughed behind his hand. "In your rooms upstairs."

Patrick started to tease him further, but a swift poke in the ribs from Thea and the shake of her head stilled the words on his lips. Patrick grinned and meekly followed his wife and butler up the stairs to his suite of rooms.

After bowing low once more, Chetham left them at the door to Patrick's rooms. Pushing open the door, Patrick said, "Please come in, Mrs. Blackburne." He kissed the back of her neck, and murmured, "And let me assure you that your husband has every intention of continuing where he left off in the carriage."

A giggle rose in Thea's throat, only to die when she glanced at him and saw the intent expression in those gray eyes. Patrick did not give her time to think. Instead, he scooped her up in his arms and with swift, sure strides carried her into the room, slamming the door shut behind them with one shove of his broad shoulder.

The room was softly lit with only a few candles. The bed with its mulberry and silver bed hangings loomed up from the shadows of the spacious room. Opposite the bed stood a fireplace with a pale gray marble mantel. Drapery the same color as the bed hangings graced the narrow windows, and a thick rug in swirling shades of wine and gray lay upon the floor. A small table with a white linen cloth had been set up in one corner; another smaller table nearby held silver trays that contained several covered serving dishes. Three bottles of wine and one of brandy had been left on an oak stool next to the serving table. There were small bouquets of roses and lilies scattered throughout the room.

Seeing the flowers, Patrick commented, "The flowers are definitely my mother's touch."

"It was very kind of her," Thea said, her head resting on Patrick's shoulder.

Slowly setting her to her feet at the side of the high bed, Patrick shook his head. "But a wasted effort I am afraid." He reached out and plucked loose a curl from her elegant coiffure. His eyes darkened and his voice deepened. "We could be in a bower filled with the most exotic blooms in the world, and I am afraid that I would be oblivious to them all." He pulled her against him, and his mouth caught hers. His lips moved on hers, his teeth dragging sensually across her lower lip. Thea shuddered and her mouth opened for him. The taste of him instantly filled her mouth as his tongue claimed the wine-sweet darkness she offered. Leisurely, thoroughly he explored her mouth, his tongue a flick of fire against the sensitive surface, stoking the flame that already burned within her. His breath harsh and ragged when he finally raised his mouth from hers, he said thickly, "You see there is only one particularly lovely and precious blossom that catches my eye." His lips brushed hers. "You, my sweet. Only you."

He kissed her again, tipping her backward onto the bed. Piece by piece her beautiful wedding finery was whisked from her ever-increasingly heated flesh. First his hands, then his mouth traveled over her, nibbling, tasting, teasing, and arousing. By the time his own clothes had been ruthlessly dispensed with and her own were scattered across the wine-and-gray carpet, she was in the grip of such powerful hungers that her body was simply one long, yearning ache of desire.

Patrick felt the same. Having spent the afternoon in a state of near arousal, finally having Thea's slim, white body where he wanted it, only a brutal hold on his own desires kept him from taking her with all the finesse of a rutting boar. His lips nuzzling her soft pale breasts, he groaned as his rampant staff brushed against her slim thigh, the knowledge that she was his bride, his *wife*, the most powerful aphrodisiac in the world. Driven by needs as old as time, he touched the crisp, black curls between her legs, seeking the tender flesh they covered. Finding what he sought, he slid his finger deep into the hot, wet depth of her, stroking and thrusting, mimicking the motions of mating.

A moan was torn from Thea at that first invasion, her hips rising to encourage him, her fingers tightening on his naked shoulders. His tormenting mouth at her nipple coupled with the sweet sensation of his warm, sleekly muscled body half-lying on hers and the explicit rhythm of his hand at the junction of her thighs suddenly pushed her to the edge. The sensation that rippled upward through her was so intense, so powerful that her body arched like a tightly strung bow and she cried out in pleasure as a shaft of heat and ecstasy pulsed through her. Stunned by the force and fierce sweetness of her release, she sank back to the bed, feeling as if every bone in her body had turned to hot honey.

Patrick's head lifted from her breast, and a tight smile crossed his handsome face. Brushing a kiss across her cheek, he muttered, "And that is just the beginning, my sweet."

He kissed her again, his lips hard and demanding, his hands gripping her hips as he shifted and slid between her legs. He rested there several seconds, gently rocking against her, his rigid member sliding arousingly through the thick patch of curls that covered her mound.

Thea's arms went around his neck and even though gentle waves of pleasure were still washing through her body, she was eager for his full possession. She clasped him near, her legs tangled with his, bringing their bodies closer and closer to the alignment that would give them greatest pleasure. His kisses became more urgent, almost rough in their demand, and his grip on her hips tightened as he positioned her where he wanted and in one swift, sure stroke buried himself inside of her.

Thea stiffened, the sensation of being filled by an aroused male still new and unfamiliar. For one brief second she felt vulnerable and helpless and then Patrick moved on her, so sweetly, so gently that pleasure blossomed, driving away all emotion but those of wonder and delight . . . and love.

Patrick had felt that momentary rigidness and guessed its cause. With difficulty he fought the urges of his body and treated her with all the restraint he could muster, but she was so narrow, so hot and slick that he thought he would surely die of pleasure if he had to continue his lazy thrusts much longer. His body demanded a faster pace, the urgency to reach the ecstasy he knew awaited them overpowering.

The shy flick of Thea's tongue into his mouth and the winding of her legs around his hips were his undoing, smashing the frail hold he had on himself. A muffled groan came from him, and he began to thrust heavily, rapidly into her, his swollen-near-to-bursting shaft delving deeper and deeper with each stroke.

Thea held him to her, the blunt thrusting of his body into hers pushing her, driving her to a new level of pleasure. At this moment nothing in the world mattered but Patrick, and she was oblivious to anything but the mating of their bodies, the achingly sweet pressure of his broad invasion and the hungry, urgent demands of his kiss. The frantic intensity of their joining could not last, and suddenly Patrick's big body shuddered as he took them to that heaven known by lovers.

Pleasure spiraling through her, Thea's body clenched around his, her sheath convulsing and making him writhe in her tight embrace. She fought to sustain the fleeting bliss, and her slender form twisted beseechingly beneath his. But it was useless; awash in sensations so sweet, so piercing she could hardly bear them, inevitably the pleasure peaked and left her lying dazed and satiated in her husband's arms.

As shattered and replete as Thea, Patrick slid from her body. He felt boneless, the power and sweetness of their mating like nothing he had ever experienced. Hoisting himself up on to one elbow, he stared down into Thea's flushed features, his heart almost stopping at the shaft of joy that knifed through him as he looked at her.

Her disheveled hair was spread like strands of black silk across the glistening whiteness of the sheets, and her eyes were dark, fathomless pools, the dilated irises revealing the depth of the pleasure he had given her. He took masculine satisfaction in the knowledge that his woman, his bride, his wife had shared the intensity of the moment with him, and he marveled at how completely she had changed his life.

He, Patrick Blackburne, who had scoffed and scorned the notion of love, was wildly, deliriously in love — with this one, slender, dark-eyed waif. Tenderly, he ran a finger down her nose, lingering at the bow of her lips, thinking that he was a very lucky man indeed. And he had two conniving females to thank for it. He smiled to himself. He would have to find a particularly elegant gift for both his mother and Modesty.

Watching the emotions play across his face, Thea asked drowsily, "What are you thinking of?"

"You," he said simply, dropping a kiss on her nose.

She stretched luxuriously and grinned. "Hmm, I would hope so."

Patrick laughed and lay back down beside her, pulling her next to him and settling her head in the crook of his shoulder. One hand lazily running up and down her arm, he asked, "Have you given any thought about a honeymoon? Is there any place in particular you wish to go?"

Pleasantly tired, feeling warm and languid, Thea snuggled closer to him, marveling at how natural that action seemed. "I don't see the necessity of our going anywhere," she mumbled, suddenly hardly able to keep her eyes open. "Since I presume that we will be leaving for your home in Natchez soon, the sea journey can suffice for a honeymoon."

Patrick frowned. Because of the hastiness that the marriage had come about, there were many things he and Thea had not discussed, and the date of their departure for Natchez had been one of them. Obviously, she was still laboring under the mistaken impression given by his mother that the speed with which their wedding was arranged was to accommodate his impending return home. Which presented a slight problem, since his original plans had been not to leave England until spring. And in the time between his mother's announcement of their betrothal and their wedding he had not even thought once about arranging passage for the pair of them. Nor did he wish to. A sea crossing was not something one embarked upon on a whim, and since Thea was safely married to him, there was no need to keep up the pretense his mother had begun.

"Er, would you be disappointed if we postponed our journey to Natchez until, oh, say the spring?" he asked. "I find that I am not in such a hurry to leave England as I was, um, a few weeks ago."

Thea fought off the waves of sleep that threatened to overtake her. "What do you mean? Weren't we married in such a hasty manner because of your imminent departure?"

"Uh, that I'm afraid was all my mother's idea," Patrick answered truthfully.

Thea sat up and stared down at him, a little frown creasing her forehead. "Your mother's idea? What are you talking about? *Aren't* we leaving soon for Natchez?"

"Not unless you want to."

His answer startled her, and wide-awake now, she stared at him. "I was," she said slowly, "under the impression that the whole reason you rushed me into marriage was because of your plans to return to Natchez."

He touched her face lightly. "Plans can be changed, sweetheart. There is no need for us to leave England anytime soon, unless it is your wish."

She brushed his hand away, her eyes narrowing, suspicion rushing through her. "If your plans can be changed so easily, why couldn't you have changed them *before* you rushed me to the altar?"

"Well, you see," he began gently, "you might have figured out a way to wiggle out of marrying me, if I hadn't, ah, rushed you to the altar."

Thea's eyes widened. "It was all a lie, wasn't it? A trick?" At his guilty expression, she exclaimed, "I knew it! You lied to me! And your mother was in on it." She looked offended and wounded at the same time. "Why? Why go to all that subterfuge?"

"Would you have married me otherwise?" Patrick asked evenly, his eyes holding hers.

"Of course not!" she snapped. "Marriage to me is the last thing that any gentleman with any sense could want." Puzzled, she asked, "Is this all because I changed my mind about becoming your mistress? I told Modesty that I thought it was. Am I right?"

Patrick shook his head. "No, my foolish sweet, this has nothing to do with your refusal to become my mistress and everything to do with my very strong desire to marry you. If you will remember, it was your idea that you become my mistress . . . not mine." Dryly he added, "I had a far different position in mind — that of my wife."

Thea stared at him, openmouthed. "Your wife! But why?" she wailed. "You can't have wanted to marry me! With my reputation, no gentleman of any sense would marry someone like me. Have you forgotten that I was the cause of two men dying? Everyone knows that I am ruined — why would you want to marry me?"

Patrick sat up, his broad shoulders braced against the high headboard of the bed. Taking one of her hands in his, he bent his head and stared thoughtfully at the slender, restless fingers he held. Quietly he said, "Do you know that I'm becoming rather tired of hearing about an old, old scandal, one that happened when you were very young and one which has no bearing on the woman you are today. I think you enjoy punishing yourself for what happened, even though most people have come to realize that you were more sinned against than sinning."

Thea gasped in outrage and tried to jerk her hand away. Giving up the struggle when it became apparent that he had no intention of allowing her to escape, she glared at him, her dark eyes glinting with anger. "How dare you! You make me sound like one of those whining, maudlin, mutton-headed heroines in a gothic novel."

Patrick merely looked at her. Unable to sustain his calm stare, her gaze dropped. "I'm sorry you find me so silly," she said stiffly.

"Not silly," he answered gently, "but you do tend to wear your past like a very large, very formidable shield, sweetheart. You flaunt it every chance you get and throw it in the face of any man who might actually decide, scandal aside, that you are a very desirable young woman." His voice deepened. "A very, very charming and desirable young woman he might very much wish to marry."

"Of course," she said dryly. "And that is why I have been courted so assiduously these past years. Why poor Modesty has just had to beat my eager suitors away from our doors."

Patrick smiled faintly. "If you had dropped that formidable shield of yours for just a moment, that would surely have been the case. I'm grateful that you did not, because otherwise I would not have been the fortunate man to win your hand."

"You did not *win* my hand — you gained it by blatant sophistry," she muttered. Sending him a straight glance, she added, "I know who I am — what I am — and that I am definitely not the matrimonial catch of the season — any season." Frustration evident in her voice, she demanded, "So why did *you* choose to marry me?"

"Because I love you, you little goose."

Thea gaped at him. She blinked those magnificent dark eyes of hers, opened her mouth, shut it, and blinked again. Clearly that notion had never crossed her mind.

Wordlessly, she stared at him, her wondering gaze moving slowly over those features that had become so familiar and dear to her so swiftly that she had not even been aware of it happening. He loved her! Was it possible? Was he right? Had she been the one to drive prospective suitors away? Had she worn the decade-old scandal as a shield to protect herself? Her gaze dropped, and she bit her lip. She had been so terribly wounded and full of anguish after the horrible debacle that had led to her brother's death — and Hawley's, too — that Patrick might be right, she conceded reluctantly. She might very well have worn the scandal that had resulted like a proud banner, an impenetrable shield, determined to make certain that everyone knew just how ruined she had been. And she had done it all, she realized suddenly, because she had been afraid, afraid to risk her heart again. Terrified to take the risk that the next man who snared her affections might prove to be just as much a villain as Lord Randall, she had taken pains to make certain that no man would ever slip under the scandal-ridden exterior she presented to the world. No man would ever again have a chance to touch her heart. She sighed. But it had all been for naught because Patrick, a man she knew little about, a man she had no reason to trust, had so effortlessly slipped beneath her guard and made her fall in love with him. And if she could put away the past and believe him, it appeared that she was unbelievably lucky enough to have him love her.

A little flutter of hope sprang into her breast. Did he really love her? He said he did. Dare she take a chance and believe him? Trust him? Her soft gaze anxious and full of questions, she glanced at his still, dark face. Almost pleading, she asked, "Do you love me? Really love me?"

Patrick smiled and pulled her against his chest. "I adore you! And I have gone to great lengths to bind you to me." He turned her face up to his and his eyes steadily meeting hers, he murmured, "Thea, you little fool, I love you more than life itself. *That's* the reason — the only reason I married you."

"Oh," she managed weakly, her thoughts jumbled and chaotic. He loved her! And he had married her because he loved her. A tremor of delighted astonishment rippled through her. He loved her!

Watching her expressive features, his lips quirked. "Couldn't you put a little more enthusiasm into it, sweet? I have just declared myself. I have rather daringly left my heart lying defenseless at your feet." He kissed her gently. "I could use a little encouragement, you know." As she continued to stare at him, he gave her a little shake. "It is considered polite at this point," he murmured, "for the object of affection to return the sentiments."

Casting aside all her doubts, letting the love that was in her heart guide her, Thea threw her arms around his neck, and, her slender form melting into his, she breathed fervently, "Oh, I *do* love you!" Shyly she added, "It is why I married you." She flashed him a challenging look. "I could have run away, you know."

"Thank God you didn't," he said thickly, his mouth finding hers. "I wouldn't have relished searching all of England for you." He kissed her, all his love and longing evident in that one kiss. When he lifted his head, her eyes were shining. "And I would have you know, I would have searched England, the world for you, and I wouldn't have ceased until I had found you again. No matter where you had hidden, I would have found you," he muttered against her lips. "Never doubt that I do love you and only you." His gray eyes dark and compelling, he vowed, "I swear by the moon that I love you beyond life and that no matter how far or fast you would have run from me, you would still have ended up as my wife and in my arms."

"Oh, Patrick, I *have* been a fool, haven't I?"

"But a most adorable one," he murmured, the gray eyes teasing. He kissed her again, urging her naked body even closer to his. The kiss deepened, passion rising swiftly between them.

They made love. The powerful emotions that guided the fierce joining of their bodies were as strong and intensely pleasurable as their previous mating, but there was a new element in their lovemaking this time. This time the knowledge that they loved and were loved in return made their coming together all the more sweeter, all the more potent.

For a long time after desire had been slaked, they lay together, their arms around each other, their damp, naked bodies resting confidingly against each other. There were tender murmurings between them as they took delight in simply being together, in knowing that they had their entire lives in front of them and that the future glittered brightly with the promise of great joy. A joy they would make together; a joy that they would share.

It was several hours later before they finally managed to drag themselves from the pleasures of the marriage bed and actually eat any of the food that had been left for them. They tasted and nibbled at the various viands, but all too soon their desire for each other outweighed further thought of food. Like famished pilgrims they fell upon each other, their young, healthy bodies reveling in the physical pleasures they could give each other.

Her body still humming from Patrick's lovemaking, after their latest bout of lovemaking, Thea lay with her head resting on his shoulder, one leg thrown across his, her fingers moving idly through the pelt of black hair on his chest. Her body ached in places she had not known could ache, but she was happy, happier than she had ever been in her life. She was married. To Patrick Blackburne, and, best of all — he loved her!

Inevitably she asked the question all lovers do — "When did you know?"

A lazy smile on his face, Patrick answered, "That I loved you?" And feeling her nod against his shoulder, he said, "Well, it wasn't the first time I saw you — in the park, nor was it the second time when you catapulted practically into my arms. No, I wasn't in love with you then. . . ." He dropped a kiss on her dark head. "It was the third time that I saw you, that night I came to tell you that you had not murdered your brother-in-law, that I lost my heart."

Thea's eyes widened and she sat up, one pear-shaped breast peeking out from behind the sheet she held in front of her. "So soon? You knew then?"

Patrick nodded, his hard features content and full of love. "Hmm. I didn't know it at the time, but as I look back over our, er, courtship, I realize that it was that night when I actually spoke to you for the first time that you cast your spell over me and had me enthralled." He smiled reminiscently. "I'd come to your house, expecting to find a vulgar harpy, and instead . . ." His eyes darkened and his voice deepened. "And instead I found the love of my life."

"Oh, *Patrick!*" Thea cried distressed. "I didn't fall in love with you for ages after that . . . at least I don't think I did."

He smiled and pulled her to him. "The important thing is that you love me now. And you do love me, don't you?"

"I do — with all my heart," she murmured against his hungry mouth. And proceeded to show him in the ensuing minutes precisely how very much she did love him.

When Thea awoke the next morning, for a moment she was disoriented, but feeling Patrick's warm body pressed next to hers and the sight of her wedding finery spread decadently across the carpet brought the previous day's events flooding back. She was married. To Patrick. And he loved her! A smile of pure joy crossed her face, and she stretched luxuriously, wincing as well-used parts of her body made themselves felt.

Having wakened a moment or two previously, Patrick felt that slight wince and was aware of a twinge of guilt. He had not been able to keep his hands off of her last night, and it was no doubt his fault that she was sore.

Promising himself virtuously that he would show more restraint tonight, he kissed her shoulder, and murmured, "Good morning, my sweet. What would you like to do today?"

"A bath would be nice," she said. "And something to eat. Do you know I am positively famished?" She sat up and smiled at him. "I wonder why."

He grinned up at her. "I think you know very well why you are hungry, you insatiable little hussy. But I agree that a bath and food would make a nice addition to the day."

Leaving Thea in command of the larger of the bedrooms, which constituted the major suite of rooms in the house, Patrick went to the adjoining room and rang for Chetham.

An hour later, bathed and garbed appropriately, the newlyweds sat down to a large and varied breakfast in the dining room. Despite the grandeur of the room, with its high, carved ceilings and spacious size, there was an air of intimacy between the pair of them. Eschewing custom, they had their places set at one end of the impressive mahogany table and spent most of the meal with their dark heads bent together, feeding each other tasty tidbits off their plates and making plans for the future.

Several things were decided upon rather swiftly. Their honeymoon would be spent at Thea's country estate, technically now Patrick's, Halsted House. With her Monday meeting with Yates at the forefront of her mind, Thea suggested that they not leave for Cheltenham and Halsted House until Tuesday morning. Despite having justified her reasons for doing so, she felt a sharp pang of guilt at how easily Patrick was duped and concurred with her wishes.

The most pressing decisions made, they retired to a pleasant room at the rear of the house. It overlooked a surprisingly extensive garden, and although not at its best at this time of year, it made for a charming view, a few late-blooming roses adding a splash of vividness. Seated in a pair of wheat-colored satin-covered channel-back chairs, enjoying a last cup of coffee, they discussed at great length the timing of their journey to Natchez.

Smiling whimsically at her, Patrick said, "It is your choice, sweetheart. I find that it does not matter very much to me, where I am . . . provided you are within arm's length."

Across the rim of her fine china cup Thea regarded him with soft, glowing eyes. She resisted the urge to pinch herself, to see if this was all a dream. It was difficult to believe that she had ever possessed any doubts about marrying Patrick, and whatever doubts she may have had had been banished with his avowal of love and the tender way he had made her his wife. She didn't want to dwell on painful subjects, but it was impossible not to contrast the sheer joy that was in her heart this morning to the pain and humiliation that had been her companion on that terrible, terrible morning over a decade ago. Regret washed through her, dimming the glow in her eyes. Oh, but she wished that Tom were alive today to see her happily married to the man she loved. He would have liked Patrick, she was certain, and he would have delighted in being the one to give her hand away.

Seeing the slight dimming in her dark, expressive eyes, Patrick bent forward. "What is it, sweet? You look sad."

She smiled wistfully. "I was thinking of my brother, Tom, and how much he would have liked you and how proud he would have been to be the one to walk me down the aisle yesterday."

"You loved him very much, didn't you?"

"Oh, yes, I did. And I still miss him horribly. I suspect I always shall."

Patrick took one of her hands in his and pressed a kiss to it. "Do you know, I think we shall name our first male child after him. It will not bring him back, but I rather think that I would enjoy having a son named Tom."

"And I!" Thea exclaimed, her smile so dazzling that Patrick actually blinked at its brilliance.

"Perhaps we should go upstairs and commence work on the project?" he murmured, a distinctly carnal smile suddenly curving his full bottom lip.

Thea could not help the blush that stained her cheeks, but her eyes soft and shining with love, she leaned forward and brushed her lips across his. "Do you know, I can think of nothing that I would enjoy more."

Taking her to her feet, Patrick put her

hand on his arm and began to escort her from the room. "Well, never let it be said that I am a tyrant of a husband. Of course we shall do precisely as you wish."

Thea giggled and thought her heart would burst with all the love she had in it for him. "Oh, Patrick, I do love you," she said, her feelings evident in her face.

At the door, he stopped and caught her close to him. The normally cool gray eyes warm and caressing, he said huskily, "But not, my sweet, as much as I love you — remember, I have sworn it by the moon."

Chapter Eighteen

Monday morning came all too soon for Thea. She and Patrick had thoroughly enjoyed their first hours as man and wife, and it wasn't surprising that she had not thought once of the approaching meeting at Edwina's house.

But it was now eleven o'clock on Monday morning and Thea knew that in less than an hour she would be confronting Yates — a bully and a most unpleasant fellow. She was dreading the meeting for two reasons; it was bound to be ugly, and, more importantly, she was going to have to lie to Patrick.

Not for the first time she considered the notion of laying the whole of it at her husband's feet and letting him take care of the problem. Wandering around a small saloon at the rear of the house, Thea's nose wrinkled. Letting Patrick shoulder the entire burden seemed so, so, so very cowardly and she pushed that particular solution away. Yates's threats and Edwina's troubles were not something she felt she could share with her new husband at this time. They might be married and, wonder of wonders, in love with each other, but the fact remained that they had not known each other very long, and she had no way of predicting how her very new husband would react to the situation. No, it was far better that she kept to her original plan. She would, she told herself virtuously, explain everything to him . . . after the fact.

Thea had already withdrawn the seventeen thousand pounds she would need to pay off Yates — she had done that before her marriage, while her fortune, she thought with a wince, was still hers to command. The money was currently packed in her largest reticule, just waiting to be put in Yates's hands.

Which meant, she thought unhappily, that in just a short while she was going to have to think of an excuse to leave the house — alone. And that was a real problem, because any errand she could concoct, Patrick would no doubt either suggest sending a servant to do it or, just as bad, accompany her.

Fate, in the form of a message from Lady Caldecott, intervened. Patrick entered the room just then, a note in his hand and a frown upon his handsome face. Looking across at her, he said, "It is the most damnable thing, but my mother wishes to speak with me. Now." His mouth pulled at the corner. "She apologizes very prettily for interrupting me at such a time, but she has a matter she most urgently wishes to discuss with me. Will you mind if I leave you alone for a while? I should not be gone more than an hour."

Thea fairly beamed at him. "Why, no! In fact, it will give me an excuse to visit with Modesty and see how the packing of the rest of my things is coming along."

Patrick's face cleared. He had not known how his bride would react to his abandonment and was cheered that she was proving to be so understanding. He would not have blamed her if she had rung a peal over his head — not married forty-eight hours and already he was leaving her alone. His face twisted. To call upon his mother.

"Shall I meet you there when I am finished?"

"Oh, no!" she exclaimed, horrified at the idea. Gathering her wits, she said more calmly, "I mean that won't be necessary. I don't know how long I shall be and you would just be bored watching us go through piles of feminine fripperies. You wouldn't enjoy it at all. No. Take your time at your mother's, and I shall meet you here at home, oh, say, shortly after one o'clock?"

Crossing to stand in front of her, he kissed the tip of her nose. "I am fortunate to have such an understanding and thoughtful wife. Have I told you what an exemplary bride you are?"

Suppressing the shaft of guilt that went through her, she put her arms around his neck and brushed her lips against his. "Hmm, I don't remember you saying precisely that, but I do believe that you indicated very ably last night that I gave you great satisfaction."

His eyes darkened, and his voice grew husky. "Indeed you did, my love. So much satisfaction in fact that I can hardly wait to show you again." The note fluttered unheeded to the floor as he took her into his arms and kissed her hungrily.

Feeling as if she were drugged, Thea sagged against him, returning his kiss. Passion and desire entwined and instantly rose between them. For endless moments they were locked in each other's arms, and the world faded away.

With an effort Patrick lifted his mouth from hers. A febrile glitter in the gray eyes, he muttered, "You are a witch! I have to leave you now, but when I return . . ."

There was both promise and warning in his voice, and Thea shivered with anticipation. Oh, the things he would do to her. She giggled. And she to him!

She bid her husband farewell and not fifteen minutes after he had left was on her way to Edwina's. She had let Chetham tenderly escort her into the carriage and tell the coachman where she wished to go. It had been simple, a moment later, to countermand those orders, giving the coachman the directions to Edwina's less fashionable address.

Arriving at her sister's narrow-fronted house, after the footman had helped her down from the carriage, she smiled and said, "Come back for me at one o'clock, if you please."

The green-liveried young man bowed and rejoined the coachman. Thea glanced up and down the street at the row of houses, a slight frown marring her forehead. Though the address was an acceptable one, there was a faintly shabby air about the entire street, and she was even more determined to get Edwina away from this place. Her mouth curved unhappily. Once Edwina's widowed state was discovered. But in the meantime, there was Yates to be dealt with. Her shoulders ramrod straight beneath the purple pelisse, she took a deep, calming breath and marched up the few steps to

Edwina's door. She would deal forthrightly with Yates and before anyone ever knew that she had called upon her sister, she would be home and in her husband's arms — where she would tell him the whole tale. Resolution strong, she rapped smartly on the door.

But Thea was incorrect in believing that no one, except Modesty, knew that she was at her sister's house. She was intently watched by another pair of eyes as Edwina's door swung open and she disappeared into the interior of the house.

Not two houses down the street, John Hazlett was just stepping down from a hackney when Thea went inside Edwina's. Thea! What the hell was she doing here? Not that it really made any difference — his task still had to be accomplished. Thea was an added complication that he'd hoped to avoid. He'd been counting on her marriage and Blackburne to keep her well away from Edwina just now. He sighed. Obviously he had made a mistake. For several minutes he stood there frowning as he considered the situation, uncertain whether Thea's presence at her sister's house was a good thing or a bad one. Finally, he shook his head and motioned to another hackney clattering down the street. Well, there was only one thing he could do and it was what he should have done in the first place. *Trust Thea,* he thought, as he leaped inside the vehicle, *to bungle a perfectly good plan.*

Unaware of her cousin's scrutiny, Thea stepped into the main hallway of the house Edwina shared with Hirst. She was astonished to discover that it was her sister and not a servant who had opened the door for her.

"Edwina!" she exclaimed. "What are you doing answering the front door yourself? Where is your butler?"

Edwina smiled wanly. "I told you that we were in desperate straits — there are no servants — except when Alfred is winning — then we have servants aplenty, but only until, of course, the money is lost again. It is either feast or famine with us." Her expression wry, she added, "Mostly famine. I managed to ferret enough away from his last win to pay for a cleaning woman twice a week and a woman to cook most nights. But as for anything as grand as a butler . . ." She gave a bitter laugh. "The money for a butler or any other luxury has been squandered on the gaming table by my dear husband."

Thea didn't quite know what to say. She could hardly try to comfort Edwina by telling her that she didn't have to worry about her husband frittering away future funds — he was dead. But she was appalled to discover just how bad things were for her sister. Modesty was going to feel terrible for having said that Edwina might be exaggerating her situation. If anything Edwina had underestimated to what depths her husband had brought her.

Despite Edwina's claim of a twice-a-week cleaning lady, Thea noticed the slovenly air about the house. Nothing specific and nothing as obvious as filthy floors and dust-covered surfaces, but simply a feel of general untidiness.

Shoving aside her impressions, Thea put on a bracing smile, and said, "Are you ready for our meeting with Yates? After we have taken care of him, I am sure that you will feel much better. And perhaps I-I-I could lend you enough money to make things a bit easier."

Leading Thea toward the back of the house, Edwina glanced over her shoulder at her. "Do you think so? I wonder if your new husband would agree to spending money supporting another man's wife."

Thea bit her lip, wishing she had at least broached the subject with Patrick. She did not want to give Edwina false hope and make promises she could not keep. Patrick, she thought with a frown, had better prove to be as charming about money as he was about everything else. A soft smile suddenly lit her eyes. He would be generous to Edwina, she decided a second later, certain that she could not have fallen in love with a clutch-fisted tyrant.

Somewhere deep in the interior of the house, a clock chimed out the quarter hour. Realizing it was already eleven-forty-five, Thea said, "Where are we going? Shouldn't we be waiting for Yates? Noon was the hour set for his arrival, wasn't it?"

Edwina shrugged. "Don't worry about him. The important thing is: Did you bring the money with you?"

"Yes, I have it right here in my reticule. I will be glad to be rid it — even in broad daylight and in my own coach, I have been terrified of being robbed or of something dreadful happening."

Showing Thea into a small, stale-smelling room, at the very back of the house, Edwina murmured, "With your fortune you could always replenish it, couldn't you?"

"Well, yes," Thea replied, a little taken aback. "But seventeen thousand pounds is a small fortune — more than most people can ever expect to see in their lifetimes. My banker was most unhappy that I insisted upon such a large withdrawal. I am quite certain he thinks the worst."

"You are right, of course, it is just that I have known Hirst to lose that much or more during one night of gaming — once he lost fifty thousand pounds on the turn of a card. After a while, you tend not to think of it as an immense sum of money."

"Fifty thousand pounds!" Thea squeaked, aghast at the notion of throwing away a huge fortune in one night.

Seating herself behind a small cherry wood desk, Edwina looked up at her sister. "I don't see why you are so shocked — you knew he was a gambler before you let me marry him."

Sinking down into a balloon-backed chair covered in faded gold tapestry, Thea muttered, "I didn't let you do anything — you were determined to marry him."

Her blond curls framing her lovely features, Edwina fixed her big blue eyes on Thea. A mulish slant to her cupid's bow mouth, she argued, "But wasn't it your duty to protect me from fortune hunters like Hirst?"

"Edwina! I did everything in my power to stop you from marrying him," Thea protested. "You were determined — you ran away with him, remember?" An embarrassed flush stained her cheeks. In a low voice she said, "It is well that you actually married him — none of us wanted to go through a situation like mine again."

"It always comes back to you, doesn't it?" Edwina complained. "I have always been forced to stand in your shadow, always been made painfully conscious that you have a fortune much larger than mine and that the family is always ready to run to rescue 'poor Thea' — even if I am the one who needs help. They are all so anxious about you that not one of them would care if I dropped off the face of the earth. It is always 'Thea, Thea, Thea!' I'm sick of it!" A hard cast to her blue eyes, she added tightly, "If it weren't for you, I would have been able to make the grand match that I deserved. It is all your fault that I have to put up with a profligate husband and that I am reduced to almost hiding in my own home to avoid being dunned on my very doorstep."

Thea stared at her sister. She had never realized how very much Edwina resented her and blamed her for every misfortune. Perhaps Modesty was right and she had been too lenient with Edwina. Too willing to overlook her tantrums and wild accusations and blame herself for Edwina's misfortunes — misfortunes her sister often brought on herself.

Meeting Edwina's accusing stare, Thea said quietly, "I am sorry that you feel that way. I cannot change the past, but before I leave England with Patrick, I shall do my best to try to set things right for you. It is perhaps best that I shall be living across the ocean from you — with me no longer around to, er, ruin your life, mayhap you will start taking the responsibility for your own decisions. When misfortune strikes you will no longer have me to blame for it."

Edwina gasped and could not have looked more surprised than if Thea had bitten her.

Ignoring Edwina, Thea stood up and began to wander around the shabby little room. The house seemed very quiet, deserted, but suddenly Thea thought she heard a noise at the front of the house.

Looking at Edwina, she asked, "Did you hear that? It sounded like someone at the front door. Could it be Yates?"

Edwina cocked her head and they both listened. Silence enveloped the house. "You are mistaken," Edwina muttered, her blue eyes sullen. "Besides, I told Yates to come to the servants' entrance at the back of the house."

Thea listened intently for a few minutes longer, but hearing nothing else, continued her perambulations around the room. Running a finger idly over the top of a glass-fronted bookcase that sat against the wall, she observed the layer of dust that collected on her finger. There was a small gilt clock placed in the center of the bookcase, and, looking at the time, she realized that the hour of twelve o'clock had come and gone. It was now several minutes after the hour. Frowning, she glanced back at Edwina and murmured, "Shouldn't Yates have arrived by now?"

Edwina looked at the clock and nodded. "Yes, he should have. I wonder where he is?"

Yates's absence was not the only one being noted at that time. Whistling cheerfully as he left his mother's house, Patrick had been in a pleasant frame of mind. The news that Lady Caldecott had imparted had been excellent. There was no longer any threat of blackmail; the letters had been returned to her by, of all people, her husband! Patrick shook his head, smiling at the shifts Lord Caldecott had been put to in his endeavors to win the heart of his lady. *What we poor men will do for love,* he thought ruefully, trying to picture the elegant and suave Lord Caldecott crouching ignobly in a dark alley.

The meeting with his mother had not taken long and on a whim he had decided to ignore his wife's wishes and meet her at Modesty's. The news that greeted him at Thea's former home left him frowning.

Staring at Tillman, he demanded, "What do you mean Miss Bradford is not at home? My wife was to visit with her."

Tillman looked perplexed. "I cannot say, sir. I only know that Miss Bradford left, almost half an hour ago, on an errand." He cleared his throat. "She, uh, did not say where she was going or when she would be back." A flicker of anxiety in his eyes, he added, "As for Miss Th— er, Mrs. Blackburne, she has not called here today." He hesitated, obviously struggling with himself, took a deep breath, then offered, "Er, would it be of any use to know that Mr. John Hazlett called here not five minutes after Miss Bradford had left? He, uh, seemed quite put out that she was not at home."

Patrick thanked him for the information and, hiding his sense of unease, headed for his own house. There was no reason, he argued with himself, to feel such alarm. No one had any reason to harm his wife. Hirst was dead. Ellsworth was dead. The blackmail had ceased. He had no reason to feel such panic just because Thea was not where she had said she would be. She could have changed her mind about visiting Modesty and was even now waiting for him at their house. The tight knot in his chest vanished. Of course, that had to be the answer. His good mood restored, he hurried home.

But at the Hamilton Place house he was greeted with the news that his bride was not in residence. That she had left shortly after he had to visit with Miss Bradford. His face grim, Patrick stared at Chetham.

Chetham coughed and at Patrick's glare, murmured, "There is a gentleman, sir. In the library. He was disappointed to find you gone. He is, I believe, writing you a note. A Mr. John Hazlett."

With a sharp thank-you thrown over his shoulder, Patrick strode off in the direction of the library. Entering the library, Patrick found Mr. John Hazlett writing him a note.

Pleasantries, brief to the point of curtness, were exchanged. Rising to his feet from behind the desk where he had been seated, John said, "I am glad you are home. I have bad news" — he glanced down at the note he had been writing — "not the sort one wishes to impart in writing."

"What is it?" Patrick demanded, the knot of fear in his chest blooming once again. "Has something happened to Thea?"

John looked astonished. "Good Lord, no!

It is Hirst. Edwina's husband. He is dead. Murdered. His body was found concealed in an old chest and stuffed down an abandoned well in a small hamlet not far from Cheltenham. We only learned of it last night. Apparently one of the locals recognized him." His mouth twisted. "Or rather what was left of him. Though it has been rather cool of late, the corpse had begun to decay — the stench was quite distinctive. In trying to find the source of the smell, Hirst's body was discovered. He was identified, without question, by the calling cards that he carried in his waistcoat pocket. My father was the first to learn the news. As we speak, the other members of the family are being informed of the tragedy." He hesitated. "Considering your recent marriage, my father did not want you and Thea involved — at least not for a few days yet. He wanted, and I concurred, for you to have some time to yourselves before being plunged into this nasty business." He made a face. "I should have gone to Miss Bradford's first as I had originally planned, but I thought it might be wise to make certain that Edwina was home before seeing Miss Bradford. Even though Miss Bradford is not related to Edwina, she did help raise her, and we thought since we didn't want Thea involved just yet, Miss

Bradford should be with Edwina at a time like this. Once Miss Bradford was with her and she had been told of Hirst's death, I was to make arrangements to sweep her away to the seclusion and comfort of our family's estate." A wry expression on his face, he continued, "Thea's presence this morning at Edwina's threw me off stride. Hoping that Thea would be gone when I returned with Miss Bradford, I hurried away, but when I called at Miss Bradford's home, I had just missed her — she had gone on an errand." He smiled disarmingly. "I was at my wits' end. Since I could not talk to Miss Bradford, I decided to tell you what had happened and to let you decide how soon Thea should know of this tragedy." John grimaced. "She did not like Hirst very well, but even she would not have wanted him dead — especially not murdered." John shook his head. "It is a shocking, shocking thing to have happened. One does not expect one's relatives, even if connected only by marriage, to be murdered."

Patrick homed in on the only thing that mattered to him. "You saw Thea at Edwina's this morning?" he demanded, his gray eyes intent.

Taken aback at Patrick's manner, John replied slowly, "Why, yes, I had just arrived at

Edwina's when I saw her go into Edwina's house. Is something wrong?"

Patrick relaxed, realizing what must have happened. "It is merely a minor misunderstanding," he said lightly. "Thea had told me that she was going to visit with Modesty this morning while I undertook a pressing errand." He shrugged. "My errand did not take long, and I decided to join her, only to discover, as you had, that Miss Bradford was not at home. Thea must have discovered the same thing and decided to visit with Edwina instead." Even as the words left his mouth, Patrick knew that something was amiss with his conclusions. Tillman had stated quite clearly that Thea had not been there at all this morning. So how had she known that Modesty was not at home?

"Now that you know that Hirst is dead," John said, interrupting his thoughts, "what do you want to do? Conceal the fact from Thea for a few days, or shall you tell her?"

Patrick made a face. He could hardly tell John that Thea had known for some time that Hirst was dead. But he rather thought that it would be a good thing for the news of Hirst's death to be out in the open — Thea would no longer be plagued with worry about when and where the body would be discovered. His lips curved ruefully. Of course, that meant that he could kiss goodbye any thoughts of a honeymoon. Thea would want to be with her sister, and he could not blame her. No. It would be better if Thea found out now about the discovery of Hirst's body and was able to comfort Edwina. They would have time enough for a honeymoon — one that Thea would enjoy far more once this ugly business was behind her.

Glancing at John's anxious features, Patrick said, "I shall go with you to my sister-in-law's. I think that it is best that Thea be with her at this time." He smiled. "My wife is a strong woman. I think that she would rather hear the news of Hirst's demise now than at a later date."

"You know my cousin well," John said. He pulled a face and admitted, "Even with Miss Bradford there, I was not looking forward to telling Edwina about Hirst — she is prone to hysterics, you know. I know that it will disrupt your plans, but I shall be glad to have you and Thea at my side."

Patrick nodded as they walked to the door. Idly he asked, "Do the authorities have any idea who might have murdered Hirst?"

John shook his head decisively. "No. But it is not such a surprising occurrence when you think of it — and the manner of the man. He was a gambler of the worst sort, and his reputation was not savory." He sighed. "While none of us ever expected something this terrible to have happened, in a way, considering his way of life and his cronies, it is not so very shocking." He glanced at Patrick. "There is one odd coincidence though . . . Did you know that the body of his cousin, Tom Ellsworth, was found the day of your wedding? He, too, had been murdered. Shot. It makes you wonder if the pair of them weren't involved in something dangerous, doesn't it?"

"Er, that is one possibility," Patrick answered.

"It is a wicked thing to say," John muttered, "but I do not believe that Hirst or Ellsworth will be mourned by very many. I know that most of my family will not be sorry that Edwina is finally freed from Hirst. Several of us have been within Ames-ace of calling him out these past few months." He grinned. "That is, if we could first prevent Thea from breaking open his head. She loathed him."

When they reached the wide main entry hall of the house, Patrick rang for Chetham. A moment later, the butler appeared. At Patrick's request that the carriage be brought 'round, he bowed and departed on his errand.

The two gentlemen decided to step outside to await the carriage's appearance. The conversation between them was polite, but distracted, both of them busy with their thoughts as they scanned the street. Neither man was enjoying the prospect before them, although Patrick had less to worry about than John did. The news of Hirst's death would come as no surprise to Thea and would actually bring her a measure of relief. Their carriage had just turned the corner approaching the house when a smart Highflyer, pulled by a pair of matched grays, drove up. To Patrick's astonishment, Nigel jumped down and turned to help down his passenger, Miss Bradford. It took them but a moment to climb the steps.

Patrick took one look at Modesty's face and motioned to his coachman, who had just driven up behind the Highflyer, to wait.

"What is it?" he demanded, the most terrifying emotions roiling in his chest.

Nigel made a face. "You'll have to hear it from Miss Bradford. I am merely conveying her to you."

When Patrick looked to her, Modesty gave a sharp shake of her head. "We cannot talk here. Let us go inside."

Once more in the library, the three gentlemen stared at Modesty. She sighed. "I had hoped to avoid just this sort of scene, but Thea has left me no choice." She glanced at Patrick. "Did she tell you about Edwina and Mr. Yates?"

"Yates!" Mr. Hazlett interrupted. "What does that bounder have to do with Edwina?"

"Nothing with Edwina, but I believe that her husband owes him a great deal of money. Money that he is attempting to wrest from Edwina. Thea was supposed to have met with Yates this morning at twelve o'clock at Edwina's and paid him seventeen thousand pounds." At the expression on Patrick's face, she said defensively, "I told her to tell you, but I could not make her do so."

Patrick cocked a brow. "You did not feel it proper to perhaps write and tell me yourself?"

Modesty flushed and looked uncomfortable. "I felt that I had, uh, interfered in your lives enough as it was. And I was hoping that Thea would tell you on her own without my intervention."

"But you are intervening . . . what changed your mind?"

"Because I was afraid that Thea would do just as she has — gone to the meeting without telling you! I thought I had washed my hands of the matter, but this morning, not knowing what Thea had decided to do, I made up my mind to attend the meeting myself." Anxiety flickering in her blue eyes, she confessed, "I went to Edwina's and knocked on the door, but there was no answer." Her hands clenched together. "I did not know what to do. I knew that Thea had to be there, but the place seemed deserted. Certainly there was no answer to my knock."

Patrick turned and looked at Nigel. His face and voice deceptively mild, he asked, "And your part in this farce?"

"Oh, don't bully him!" Modesty snapped. "I had foolishly dismissed my hackney and was walking away from Edwina's when he drove by. He stopped to exchange greetings and when I explained my dilemma, he kindly offered me a ride."

"I must thank you, dear lady, for leaping to my defense," Nigel murmured. "When Patrick gets that sleepy look on his face, he's all the more dangerous." Glancing over to Patrick, he said, "It is clear that Thea has the bit between her teeth once again. The fact that Yates has entered the scene changes the whole concept of a sisterly visit. I think that we should go and rescue your wife, don't you?"

"If Yates is involved, she will certainly need rescuing," John muttered, his expression unhappy.

"I agree," said Nigel, his eyes meeting Patrick's. "Ugly things seem to happen to those unfortunate souls who run afoul of Yates. He is a very dangerous man."

Patrick's jaw hardened, and he smothered a curse. He should have known that the affair would not end so easily — especially not when Thea was involved! His reckless darling was meeting with one of the most dangerous men in London and probably completely convinced that she had the matter well in hand. Instead, her lovely little neck might very well be threatened — if not by Yates, he decided grimly, by her devoted husband. When he finally got his hands on his wife, after he had assured himself that she was unharmed, he thought that he might very well strangle her.

Modesty was staring at Nigel, her face white with horror. "Good heavens! We had no idea that he had such a terrible reputation," she said numbly as she turned to look at Patrick. "All we knew was that he had threatened Edwina, demanding his money. I thought she was exaggerating, as she is wont to do. Thea was going to pay him . . ." her voice faltered, ". . . and threaten him with the authorities if he dared to bother Edwina ever again."

Looking very much like a big, sleepy cat, Patrick purred, "In that case, I think that I should be at my wife's side when she faces this brute. I shall, er, lend credence to her threat." One brow rose as he glanced at Nigel. "Don't you agree?"

"Oh, precisely, my dear fellow. Precisely."

At that very moment Thea was glancing again at the clock on the bookcase. The minute hand had inched past the half hour several minutes ago and there was still no sign of Yates. She got up and took a turn around the room.

"Oh, this is ridiculous," she said finally. "Where is the fellow?"

"Oh, he'll be here soon," Edwina said, "Of that you can be assured. Seventeen thousand pounds is a powerful lure."

The words had just left Edwina's mouth when the sounds of approaching footsteps came to them. Both women stiffened and exchanged looks.

"That must be him!" Thea hissed. "How the devil did he get into the house?"

Her blue eyes so big they dominated her small face, Edwina stammered, "H-h-he told me to leave the tradesman's door unlocked and . . . and I d-d-did." At Thea's incredulous look, she said, "He is a terrifying man. I dared not disobey him."

Thea made an impatient sound but, preparing for battle, grasped the reticule that had been resting on the floor near the chair where she had been sitting. Chin up, shoulders back, she faced the door, her heart beating.

Chapter Nineteen

The man who pushed open the door and entered the room was a stranger to Thea. With Edwina's description in mind, she was a trifle relieved that he did not look particularly threatening. He was large and burly, it was true, but he also had the merriest blue eyes that Thea had ever seen, and she felt some of her unease ebbing. He was tastefully garbed, his dark blue coat and buff breeches were finely tailored, his boots gleamed, and his neckwear was clean and neatly tied. He was smiling as he came into the room and shut the door behind him.

"Ladies," he said in a pleasant tone, "I am sorry that I have kept you waiting."

Approaching Thea, he bowed with all the grace of a gentleman born. "Allow me to introduce myself: I am Asher Yates. You are, I believe, Mrs. Blackburne? Your sister has spoken of you often."

"Er, yes," Thea mumbled, trying to reconcile this charming fellow with Edwina's ogre.

"Oh, stop your playacting!" Edwina said nervously from her position behind the desk. "Take the money and do what I p-p-paid you to do."

Ignoring Thea's astonished expression, Yates glanced at Edwina. "So, you are still of the same mind?"

Not meeting Thea's eyes, Edwina nodded. "Yes."

Yates turned to look at Thea. He was smiling, and his eyes were just as merry, but she was suddenly conscious of being in danger. He reached out for the reticule she still clutched at her side, and said, "I'll take that, Madam. I believe it belongs to me."

"I think not," Thea said, stepping away from him. Fencing for time as she tried to make sense of Edwina's attitude, she faced Yates squarely. "You and I," she declared, "have several things to settle before I hand over this reticule to you."

He shook his head. "We have nothing to settle, Madam — my bargain is with your sister."

"And what," Thea asked, "is the nature of your bargain with my sister?"

He smiled, and Thea wondered how she had ever thought his smile pleasant and his eyes merry. They were the coldest, most calculating eyes she had ever seen in her life.

"A rather simple task," he said. "I am to

kill you and arrange for your body to be found far away from here." He looked soulful. "It will be a tragic accident, I think. Perhaps you shall be thrown from a carriage and your neck broken."

Thea glanced from one face to the other, her thoughts spinning wildly. It was difficult to credit Edwina with such malice, but it was obvious that her sister had indeed hired this smiling-faced villain to murder her. What astonished her most was that she accepted so easily the fact that Edwina was capable of such an act.

Edwina would not look at her, keeping her eyes downcast, her face averted. There was a flush on her cheeks and a sullen cast to her mouth. She looked, Thea thought dispassionately, just as she always did when she had been caught doing some mischief. Guilty and yet unabashed.

Thea did not doubt that Yates spoke the truth. Why would he lie? But she had to hear the words from Edwina herself. Quietly, she asked Edwina, "Is this true? Have you hired him to murder me?"

Edwina's gaze met hers briefly before skittering away. "I didn't want to," she said in a low voice.

"Then why?"

Edwina's lips thinned. "What does it

matter? Besides, why should I explain myself to you?"

"Since I am destined to die . . . and at your bidding, I think it is only fair that I at least understand why," Thea said evenly. When Edwina remained silent, Thea pleaded, "I am going to pay with my life for the information that only you and Yates can give me — won't you please grant me this, er, last request? You have nothing to lose — I am going to die, so I will not be able to repeat anything you tell me."

"The lady makes a persuasive argument," Yates drawled. "Why not tell her . . . why not let her see you as you are?"

"Shut your mouth!" Edwina shouted, throwing a vicious look at Yates. She glanced at Thea. "You are rather calm about this whole thing."

Thea made a face. "I doubt that hysterics would gain me anything." Trying to gain time and, in spite of the circumstances, morbidly curious, she took a deep breath, and asked, "So tell me: Why have you hired this gentleman to murder me?"

"I didn't want to," Edwina repeated, apparently having decided to grant Thea the explanation she had requested. "I simply had no choice."

"What do you mean — you had no

choice?" Thea exclaimed.

Edwina flashed her a petulant glance. "I was there that night — I heard what Hirst said to you. He was willing to desert me for money! It was obvious that he never loved me, that the only reason he married me was because he wanted to get his hands on your fortune."

"You were there? But how did you know of the meeting? It was supposed to be a secret," Thea said, surprised, and yet not, at Edwina's admission. Especially not when she recalled Edwina's unattractive habit of listening at keyholes and her own uneasy feeling that night of being watched.

Edwina gave an ugly laugh. "The same way I learned that Hirst and Ellsworth were blackmailers — I listened at the door. Ellsworth came to call, and Hirst told him all about the meeting he had set up with you. I already knew, from what I had overheard some days earlier of their scheme to blackmail Lady Caldecott, that they were using the Curzon Street house as their base. It was simple enough for me to leave home before my husband and to arrive ahead of both of you. Finding a convenient place to listen was not difficult." She gave a scornful laugh. "Neither one of you even suspected that I was there."

Thea managed to hide her start of surprise at the revelation that Hirst and Ellsworth had been blackmailing Lady Caldecott. Patrick's presence at Curzon Street that fateful night was finally explained. He must have come to the house to meet with his mother's blackmailer. No wonder he would not tell her why he had been there!

"Er, no, we didn't," Thea said lamely. She glanced at Yates, wondering at his part in what had happened that night. Hirst had been frightened that night. He'd been desperate to get the money from her. When he could not pay, had Yates murdered him?

Almost as if he read her mind, Yates shook his head. "No, Madam, it was not I who plunged those scissors into him." He nodded in Edwina's direction. "It was his dear, sweet, loving wife. I only, ah, disposed of the body for her and that sniveling coward, Ellsworth."

Revulsion flooded Thea. It had been *Edwina* who had murdered him in that ghastly way! She swallowed the bile that rose in her throat. Dear, sweet, innocent-looking Edwina. Thea looked at her sister in disbelief. "You killed him?"

Edwina shrugged. "I didn't mean to — I was just so furious and hurt. You have to understand — I had just learned that my husband never loved me — that it was only money that had drawn him to me. I was upset. I was coming down the stairs, intending to see how badly you had hurt Hirst, when a stranger arrived almost on your heels. I was horrified. My one thought was to escape, but he heard me trying to creep back up the stairs and came after me." She shivered. "I grabbed the iron doorstop to use as a weapon and hid upstairs in a big armoire. I was so frightened as I huddled inside that armoire hearing him move around the room searching for me. When he finally opened the door to the armoire, I didn't think, I just hit him with the doorstop. I didn't even look at him. I just hit him and ran." She sighed. "I was relieved when we returned later and found him gone. Whoever he was, I must have simply knocked him senseless."

"The lady," Yates interjected, "has a gentle heart when it comes to killing strangers."

Edwina shot him a glance of pure dislike. "Hirst deserved what he got," she ground out. "If he'd been an honest husband to me, I wouldn't have been there that night and Hirst and I wouldn't have fought and I wouldn't have stabbed him with the scissors."

"Is that what happened?" Thea asked gently, sick at heart, her own peril momentarily pushed to the back of her mind.

Edwina nodded. "When I came back downstairs, Hirst was on his feet, holding his head." Her mouth thinned. "He was furious to see me and started yelling at me, cursing me. I-I-I lost my temper and confronted him. We had a terrible fight. I didn't even know what I was doing — I simply snatched up the scissors from the desk and" — she swallowed — "and I stabbed him." Edwina buried her face in her hands. "It was awful."

Thea stared at Edwina's down-bent head. What could she say to her? Edwina had killed a man, and there was nothing that would ever change that fact. "And then what happened?" Thea asked softly. "You contacted Yates?"

"Oh, no," Edwina exclaimed, lifting her face from her hands. "That was Ellsworth. I fled home once I realized what I had done. Ellsworth was waiting here to learn of the outcome of Hirst's meeting with you . . ." She looked guilty and sly at the same time. "And to see me. He and I are . . . were close."

Thea did not misunderstand the expression or the words. "I see . . . you and

Ellsworth were lovers," she said flatly. She looked at Yates. "And it was Ellsworth who contacted you?"

He bowed. "Indeed it was, Madam. I provide many services to my clients."

Thea arched an elegant brow. "Are you the one who attacked my husband in the hackney?"

He bowed again. "A pair of my lackeys." He smiled that pleasant smile that was so misleading. "Your sister and Ellsworth didn't relish the notion of you marrying. They had their eyes on your fortune."

"That's not true!" Edwina said hotly. "It was your idea — never ours."

Ignoring the interruption, her eyes locked on Yates, Thea remarked thoughtfully, "Mr. Yates, you certainly seem to know a great deal."

"Well, yes, I do. I take a great interest in the lives of my clients," he admitted with a modest air. "It is all really quite simple. Hirst and Ellsworth both owed me a large sum of money — because of their debt to me, they embarked upon the scheme to blackmail Lady Caldecott. Ellsworth had found some incriminating letters amongst the effects of an old aunt of his and thought that they could put them to good use." Yates looked regretful. "Little did they know that

I might have been willing to write off their debt for the letters myself. The letters would have brought me in a nice steady bit of the ready, you understand?" Yates sighed for the lost opportunity. "But it was not to be. Instead, Ellsworth came to Hirst with the letters because they were relatives and Hirst had better connections to the ton. I didn't know of the scheme until Ellsworth came to me, frantic to get rid of Hirst's body. It was then that he divulged the blackmail and Hirst's plan to try to wrest some coin from you." He pulled idly on his ear. "Now I am a businessman, and I get paid for what I do. Hirst and Ellsworth already owed me a sizable sum. I wasn't about to get involved with disposing of a body for Ellsworth if I didn't know that down the road I'd be paid, and paid handsomely. That's when Ellsworth explained about your fortune. Hirst might have been dead, but I was still going to get my money, so I was willing to listen to his plan. I was even willing to help them — hence the attack on Blackburne."

Edwina gasped. "Why, you lying bastard! That is a damned lie. Don't listen to him, Thea, he is just trying to poison your mind against me."

"Oh, hush," Thea said, a frown marring

her forehead. "I'm afraid I'm a little confused about the attack on Patrick. If it was my fortune you were after, how would harming Patrick —" Thea stopped. She shook her head at her own folly. "Of course, how silly of me. You intended for him to die, didn't you? And if he were dead, then I could not marry him, could I? My fortune would be safe and secure." She looked steadily at Edwina. "That's why Ellsworth came to my room the night before my wedding. Having failed to kill Patrick, you thought to strike at me — before I married."

"It is all his fault!" Edwina cried, waving a hand in Yates's direction. "He demanded that we pay him, not only the seventeen thousand pounds that Hirst owed him, but nine thousand more to hide Hirst's body and to t-t-take care of Blackburne. Twenty-six thousand pounds. Thea! It was a nightmare. We didn't know which way to turn. Yates gave us no time to think. With Hirst's body lying on the floor almost at our feet, he demanded that Ellsworth sign over his London house and every penny he had in the 'Funds' that very night. He said he wouldn't move Hirst's body an inch unless Ellsworth paid up." Her mouth twisted. "He took all of my jewels and every piece of silver I had in the house. He told us that since we had been so reasonable, that he would give us a little time before he came after the rest of the money." Her eyes full of misery, she muttered, "That was why I wrote that note demanding the nine thousand — to redeem everything he had taken." Her gaze dropped. "We had to get our hands on your fortune, and that meant making certain that you did not marry Blackburne. When Blackburne escaped, we had to strike quickly. We couldn't let you marry him."

"Doesn't your friend Yates offer a refund when he fails?" Thea asked with apparent interest in the workings of murder for hire. "It seems to me since he did not, ah, perform as promised that you should have gotten your money back."

"It isn't amusing!" Edwina snapped.

"Believe me," Thea said in heartfelt tones, "I am finding none of this amusing. I am curious, though, why it was Ellsworth who attacked me. Why didn't you hire Yates to murder me that night?" There was a tense silence, and then Thea exclaimed, "Oh, how silly of me! Of course you were trying to save money and do the job yourself. Is that how it was?"

Before Edwina could answer they all heard a loud commotion coming from the front of the house. All three froze, listening intently. Thea's heart leaped as she thought she heard Patrick's voice above the fierce pounding. But then all noise faded, and there was nothing but echoing silence through the deserted house. What faint hope she'd had that a miracle had occurred and Patrick had somehow come to rescue her from her own folly faded. They remained as they were for a few minutes more as they waited to see if the assault at the front of the house would continue.

When it did not, Yates visibly relaxed, and remarked, "Whoever it was has gone away."

"No doubt it was an irate creditor wanting his money," Edwina muttered, a bitter curve to her mouth.

"You haven't answered my question," Thea continued as if the interruption had not occurred. "Was it to save money that Ellsworth came to my room that night?"

"Yes, damn you!" Edwina hissed. "Yates was bleeding us to death, and we simply could think of no other way. We didn't want to go deeper into debt to him. Ellsworth had already signed over everything he could lay his hands on to meet Yates's demands. Hirst had run my fortune into the ground, and Yates" — she shot him a look of hatred — "was dunning me to pay my husband's debts." She looked back to Thea. "We didn't have any choice! Your fortune was the only thing that could save us from ruin." Dully, she added, "You have to understand — I didn't want you to die, not really . . . but we, I, needed your fortune."

"Couldn't you have simply come to me and asked me for the money?"

Edwina's shoulders slumped and she looked away. "Oh, yes, I could have done that — at least for Hirst's gaming debts — especially once I had told you of Yates. I knew that you would come to my rescue." She swallowed thickly. "But you see when I k-k-killed Hirst it changed everything. I didn't want to hang! We had to hide the body and Yates was the only one we knew who could take care of that for us. And once he had his hooks into us, it just got worse." Tiredly she said, "Perhaps if we had hidden his body ourselves, things wouldn't have reached this stage. We didn't know what to do. Before we had time to think it through, Ellsworth had panicked and brought in Yates. Yates changed the stakes. Murdering you and gaining your fortune was *his* idea. He presented it as a solution to all of our problems. We were too frightened not to go along with him."

"You do realize," Thea said quietly, "that having Yates dispose of me will not be the end of your troubles. There is still Patrick to be dealt with. And of course, you understand, don't you, that if you continue to go along with Yates, you are handing him a powerful weapon." Thea glanced at Yates, who still stood in the center of the room, looking pleasant and totally at ease with the situation. Harshly, Thea said, "You will never be free of him. He will blackmail you and make you pay for the rest of your life, won't you, Mr. Yates?"

"Well, now, that's not exactly the way I would have put it," Yates murmured, "but I suppose from time to time that I should be happy to accept a small monetary gift from the lady. For services rendered, you understand."

Thea snorted.

Edwina stared at Yates in horror as the realization sank in that Thea spoke the truth. "Oh, God!" she cried. "What have I done? My husband is dead. My lover is dead. And all for naught."

"Now, now, Mrs. Hirst, that is no way to carry on," Yates said in a soothing tone. "Once I have taken care of your sister here, you can lend comfort to her husband and after a proper mourning time for both of you, you will marry him and gain access to his fortune, as well as your sister's. Just as we discussed, remember?"

Thea did not know whether to be appalled or amused. Briefly she wondered how much of this latest twist was Yates's idea and how much was Edwina's. But one thing was very clear; before any of it could be set into motion, she had to die. And while Edwina might suffer some remorse at her death, Thea had little doubt that her sister would not stop Yates from murdering her.

A soft, muted sound seemed to float through the house, and Edwina started. "What was that?" she asked fearfully.

His finger to his lips, Yates crept to the door. A wicked-looking pistol suddenly appeared in his hand, and he cautiously opened the door. Slowly, with great care, he glanced around the doorjamb, down the dark and gloomy hall.

Deciding she had nothing to lose and hoping against hope that Patrick had come for her, Thea filled her lungs and shouted as loud as she could, "Help! Help me! They're going to kill me!"

Yates turned and looked at her . . . and smiled. Her heart sank. Obviously, he had seen nothing to alarm him.

Shutting the door behind him, he walked back to the center of the room. "Now, now, my lady, that is no way to act. No one can hear you, and if you are going to prove difficult, I shall just have to silence you." His eyes danced. "And you won't like the way I shall do it."

From under her lashes, Thea studied Yates, wondering if there was any way that she could incapacitate him — if only for a second. If she could get him far enough away from the door . . . and if she could just nip around him . . . There was still Edwina to worry about, but Thea knew that Yates was her real problem, not Edwina. She could probably distract Edwina from her goal, but she didn't think that Yates would be thrown off the scent. He had arrived with the intention of killing her — if not here, somewhere nearby — and he was not going to be easily persuaded to change his plans. A last-minute rescue seemed improbable — only Modesty knew where she was, and Modesty had made it plain that she had washed her hands of the entire affair. Thea's nose wrinkled. *As I should have,* she thought unhappily. *Oh, Patrick, I am so sorry — and I was a fool not to tell you.*

"Killing me," Thea said in a steady voice, despite the painful banging of her heart against her ribs, "does not guarantee you success. My husband may not wish to marry Edwina. Have you considered that?"

"Oh, I wouldn't worry about that," Yates said, his blue eyes at their merriest. "These things can be arranged, and I am just the man to do the arranging. I can have a special license in my hands at the snap of my fingers. There is a fellow I know who will perform the marriage — even if the groom looks, ah, half-dead. And once the deed is done . . ."

Thea bit her lip and glanced around the shabby little room. *Oh, Patrick,* she thought mournfully, *what have I done? Not only my life is at stake, but yours, too.* A shaft of pain went through her at the knowledge of what her own stubborn foolishness had cost them. *I will not let them do it,* she vowed with a sudden invigorating burst of fury. *How dare they try to destroy our lives this way!*

Her chin lifted and she said coolly, "Well, you certainly seemed to have thought of everything, haven't you?"

Yates tried to look modest, and Thea's lip curled in contempt. She glanced around the room again, her brain racing desperately. Yates had already indicated the probable manner of her death. She was to be thrown from a carriage . . . after, of course, he had snapped her neck. She swallowed and looked at his ham-sized fists, imagining them closing around her neck. Patrick's face, his gray eyes tender as they looked at her, suddenly flashed across her mind. Dear God! She had too much to live for — she didn't want to die!

But how? How was she going to escape? She had no weapon. None except her large, heavy, money-filled reticule . . .

Yates never knew what hit him. One moment he was standing confidently in front of Thea, and, the next, Thea had taken a swift step forward and struck him in the face with the bulky reticule. Fright and fury mingled with all the power of her slender body and gave her an astonishing strength. Yates staggered back as if he'd been hit with a sledgehammer.

Thea didn't remain to see the effect of her desperate act; dropping the reticule like a hot brick, she picked up her skirts and sprinted for the door.

"Oh, no, you don't," Edwina growled. Leaping up from her place behind the desk, she whipped around it and grabbed Thea by the waist. The momentum of Edwina's body threw them both off-balance, and they went down in a flurry of flying skirts.

Thea recovered first and, wrenching free of Edwina's hold, gave her sister a facer that would have done Tom proud. Edwina shrieked as blood spurted from her nose.

Wasting neither remorse nor even a glance for Edwina, Thea scrambled to her feet and stumbled toward the door.

But the brief skirmish with Edwina had delayed her long enough. Yates had partially recovered and he lurched forward with a snarl, catching Thea by her hair just as her flailing fingers touched the doorknob. Brutally, he dragged her back against him, the pistol pressed into her jaw.

"Try that again, my lady, and I won't worry whether your death looks accidental or not," Yates snapped.

Edwina, a hand to her nose, dragged herself up off the floor and, half-leaning, half-standing next to the desk, glared at Thea. "Thank you, dear sister," she uttered thickly. "I shall have no regrets about your death now."

There was a soft whoosh, and Thea's heart swelled as the door swung open and Patrick, looking darkly handsome and oh, so beloved, stood in the opened doorway. His face very dark above his white cravat, his shoulders very broad beneath the elegant dark blue coat, he took in the situation in a glance. He was aware that there was still danger to be faced, but the brutal fist that had clutched at his heart these past several moments eased.

His gaze slid assessingly over Thea's slim form. Though slightly disheveled, a lock of midnight black hair dangling rakishly over one of her eyes, Thea appeared unharmed and, because of that, he decided, he might not kill Yates.

A lazy smile on his mouth, Patrick sauntered into the room, carelessly swinging an ebony-and-ivory walking stick. "Ah, here you are, my dear," he murmured. "I hope you do not mind that I have come to escort you home?"

Thea smiled at him, such a dazzling smile that Patrick blinked, strangely breathless and almost blinded by its brightness. He had never loved her quite as much as he did at that moment, but he had no illusions about what was at stake. Among the four of them, he, Nigel, Hazlett, and Modesty, they had put together an unpleasant scenario. And it looked as if they were not far wrong.

One thing had leaped out at all of them: Edwina had to be part of whatever was going on. It was possible that Edwina was innocent and that there was nothing more to this meeting than what she had originally told Thea. It was also possible, as Modesty had admitted, that Edwina could be helping Yates because it was in her own best interests to do so or because of something Yates held over her head.

Patrick didn't give a damn about Edwina's motives or the money Thea was supposedly paying Yates. He wanted his wife back. Now.

As he stared at the pistol held to Thea's jaw, dread constricted his heart. He'd known the situation was dangerous, but not *how* dangerous, when they had all returned and no one had answered Edwina's front door — God knew they had made enough noise to rouse the dead. Instinct had told him that something was very, very wrong — and he always trusted his instincts. He had been ready to tear the house down, brick by brick, and board by board. Only Nigel's suggestion that they find a less destructive way into the house had stopped him from battering down the front door.

His eyes still on the pistol held so menacing against Thea's fragile jaw, Patrick took grim satisfaction in knowing that his instincts had not betrayed him.

Recovering from his first start of astonishment at Patrick's sudden appearance, Yates growled, "Stop right there! As you can see, the lady will be delayed."

Patrick smiled sweetly. "But not for very long, I hope."

Yates gave a bark of laughter. "You have

pluck, I'll grant you that, my good fellow. But I'm afraid that all it has gained you is a meeting with old Mr. Grim."

"I beg to differ with you," Patrick returned, "but I have no intention of meeting death in the near future. I have just married that charming little baggage you are presently holding and plan to spend a long life with her." Patrick's eyes caught Thea's. His voice deepened. "We have great plans, she and I."

"Oh, have done!" Edwina said in muffled tones. She had found a dainty, lace-edged handkerchief and was holding it against her bleeding nose. Looking at Yates, she demanded fretfully, "What are we going to do now? We can't let him go, and if they are both dead, then there is no way for me to inherit any fortune at all."

"Ah, is that the point of all this?" Patrick asked with great interest. "Inheriting a fortune?"

Edwina cast him a glance, wondering how she had ever found him charming. "Yes," she said, "it is — and you have ruined it all." She looked at Yates again. "Well? What are we going to do?"

Yates looked thoughtful. "The first thing that needs to be done is for you to lock that damned door. I don't want anyone else strolling in."

Keeping an eye on Patrick, Edwina sidled out from behind the desk and locked the door, returning quickly to her previous position.

Yates nodded approvingly, and said, "This may work out for us, after all. I don't suppose that your sister has made a new will — not with her just being married and all. And if the new husband is not around to contest the will, you should inherit what you would have if your sister had not married." He cocked an eyebrow in Patrick's direction. "Am I right?"

Patrick shrugged. "I am not a legal scholar." He rubbed his walking stick lightly along his jaw. "I do think you are forgetting something . . . I did not come alone."

Yates snickered. "Very good, sir. I do admire a man with pluck and verve, but I'm afraid I'm too long in the tooth to be taken in by that bit of nonsense."

"Oh, Patrick! I am so sorry to have involved you in this," Thea cried, her distress obvious. "It is all a terrible tangle. Edwina killed Hirst! She admitted it. She and Ellsworth were lovers, and they hired this fellow Yates to hide the body."

Patrick looked over at Edwina. "An enterprising young lady, to be sure. Modesty said that you looked out for yourself."

"And you," Edwina snapped from around her handkerchief, "should have been looking out for yourself!"

"To be sure," Patrick replied equitably, "but since that also involved looking out for the woman I love, I'm sure you can understand my reluctance to simply stand by and allow her to fall into your tender clutches." He glanced at Thea, his gray eyes intent. "She has held up rather well, don't you think? Why, I would have thought that finding out her sister is a murderess and being confronted by a bully like Yates would have sent her off in a swoon."

"Not Thea!" Edwina muttered. "She is too strong-minded for that sort of silliness."

"No doubt you are right, but it certainly would have been convenient," Patrick murmured, his eyes still staring into Thea's.

Thea suddenly smiled, her gaze misty-eyed as she stared back at him. "Oh, I do love you, Patrick Blackburne — no matter what happens. You are such a clever fellow."

Patrick bowed. "Thank you, my dear, I treasure your opinion."

Yates laughed, and began, "If he is such a clever fellow — what the devil!"

Only a second before Yates had been holding a slim, firm body against his own; the next he was grappling with a form that seemed to have turned boneless as Thea swooned and went limp in his grasp. It was all the distraction that Patrick needed.

In a flash, the ebony-and-ivory walking stick revealed the small sword hidden within, and, with a flick of the wrist, Patrick brought it smartly across the hand in which Yates held the pistol.

A howl of pain burst from Yates as the pistol went spinning and Thea, magically recovering, grabbed his other wrist and bit down with all the fervor of a bulldog upon a bone. Before Yates had time to blink, Thea was out of his arms and standing next to her husband; Patrick's sword was pressed against his throat.

His breathing hardly disturbed, Patrick said in a deadly soft tone, "I am rather clever, don't you agree?"

"But not quite as clever as you think," Edwina replied.

Not moving his sword, Patrick glanced in her direction. Her face tight and grim, Edwina stood behind the desk, a small, dainty pistol leveled at Thea's heart.

"That does even the odds a bit," Patrick admitted. "We seem to have come to a standstill. I propose a bargain; you let us go, and we shall pretend that this morning never happened."

Edwina gave an ugly laugh. "Oh, you would leave me to Yates's tender mercies?" Her eyes narrowed. "I think not!"

Before anyone guessed her intention, she swung the pistol away from Thea and coolly shot Yates. The explosion of pistol fire was stunningly loud in the room, gray smoke and the scent of black powder instantly filling the small space. Yates, shot neatly through the temple, dropped to the floor without a sound.

"I never did like him," Edwina confessed. "Everything is all his fault. He deserved to die."

Patrick had shoved Thea behind him and, sword held loosely at his side, considered his next move. Edwina had just demonstrated that she was no stranger to firearms and he didn't think that he wanted another demonstration — not when either he or Thea was the target.

There was a furious pounding at the door, and Nigel's voice was heard. "Patrick, for God's sake, open the door. What is going on in there?"

His voice level, Patrick said to Edwina, "The bargain still stands. Let Thea and me go, and we will forget what has happened. Your husband's body has been found. John Hazlett was on his way here to tell you when he spied Thea coming into the house. He is with Lord Embry in the hall — they came with me. Modesty knows that we are here, too. You have only one shot left in your pistol. You cannot kill us all. It is finished." Gently, he added, "The game is lost. You cannot win. Give me the pistol."

Edwina's face showed that she realized that there was no way out except the one that Patrick offered. She would have her life, but little else. The family would close ranks behind her, but they would know what she had done. Her fortune was gone. Her lover was dead. She would never again be able to turn to Thea for help. Her life was ruined. She had, she realized, nothing to live for. Nothing at all. The long, bleak years of being the poor pitied relation stretched out unending before her.

"Edwina, Patrick is right," Thea said quietly. "It is over. You have failed. Give him the pistol and let this end here and now."

"Never!" Edwina cried, and, before their horrified gaze, she aimed the pistol at her own head and pulled the trigger.

Chapter Twenty

It was a lovely evening in April. A full, silvery moon was high in the sky, and Thea and Patrick had just finished dining al fresco in the charming gardens at Halsted House. Modesty, who had come to stay with them in late February, was dining this night with Lord and Lady Garrett at Garrett Manor.

The terrible and horrifying events of that Monday in late September seemed very far away, as indeed they were, since nearly seven months had passed since that fateful day. Thea was still haunted by Edwina's death. There was nothing she could have done to have prevented Edwina from taking her own life, but she fretted for months afterward, wondering how much she was to blame for the tragedy.

"If only I had not catered to her so much," she had said more than once. "Perhaps if I had listened to Modesty and the rest of the family and been sterner with her, she would not have taken the path she did."

Patrick would take her into his arms, and cradling her next to him, he would murmur, "What happened was not your fault. You cannot blame yourself for what Edwina did. And it is useless to speculate on the type of person she would have been if you had treated her differently. Hold on to the thought that you did the best that you could. Remember, Edwina made her own choices — as in the case of her husband, you counseled against it, but she ignored you and married the man of *her* choice. There is nothing that you could have done."

When Thea would have protested, he kissed her, and said against her lips, "You know that I am right, sweetheart. She made the choices — even the one to kill herself." He smiled down into her face. "The only thing you can blame yourself for is having a generous and loving heart — not a particularly terrible thing to possess."

Defeated, Thea laid her head against his breast and for a while was comforted. And as the weeks and months passed her bouts of guilt had gradually lessened, until these days she rarely pined or even mentioned Edwina's name.

Of course an appalling scandal had erupted when the bodies were found, which the family, closing ranks as they had a decade ago, did its best to temper. Edwina had hardly fallen dead to the floor behind the desk before Patrick had whisked Thea back to Hamilton Place, where Modesty was waiting anxiously. Having left Nigel and Hazlett to stand guard over the bodies, Patrick had swiftly returned once he had seen that Thea was safely in Modesty's keeping.

The three gentlemen had decided that the most expeditious way to handle the affair was *not* to handle it at all. No one except they and the loyal coachmen who had delivered them to her door had known of Thea's presence in the house, and no one was going to make that fact public. Their own presence would have been difficult to explain away, but they were confident that their first assault on the Hirsts' front door had not been noticed, despite the racket Patrick had raised. Their actual entrance into the house, through the same door that Yates had used, had been in a most clandestine manner. Just as Thea's presence had not been noted, it was unlikely that theirs had been either.

After a tense and hasty discussion, they agreed that the best thing to do was to get the hell out of the house before they were discovered standing in a room with two very dead bodies. Since the bodies told their own tale, they would leave them as they were — to be discovered at dusk by John Hazlett, when he ostensibly arrived for the first time to tell Edwina of her husband's murder.

All went as planned. Hazlett had rounded up a member of the watch to help him break into the house when his frantic pounding on his cousin's door roused no one. Together he and the watch discovered the ghastly contents in the small room at the rear of the house.

The family tried to keep the circumstances of Edwina's death a secret, but it was impossible. The fact that she had killed herself and, it was believed, her lover, the notorious Yates, was enough to cause a nine days' wonder amongst the ton. Hirst's murder only added fuel to the rampant gossip and speculation. Patrick's and Thea's sudden wedding was forgotten and all anyone could talk of that fall were the shocking deaths of the Hirsts and that Yates fellow.

As agreed, Patrick and Thea left for Halsted that very afternoon — before Edwina's body was discovered. His jaw tight, Patrick had said to Nigel, "I want Thea well out of it and the only way I can assure that she is, is to get her out of London — immediately. No one will think it strange — we had planned to leave for the country tomorrow anyway. As far as anyone is concerned, we just decided to leave earlier than expected. She can hear the news of her sister's death at Halsted as easily as she can here. At Halsted we can be sequestered and not intruded upon. She has enough to deal with, and I'll not have her subjected to avid stares and spurious gossip."

Thea had not argued; she was numb and horrified by what had happened and she had been as obedient as she was ever likely to be, not offering one objection to Patrick's plans. Like a small, delicate doll she had sat frozen in the sheltering curve of his arm as their coach bumped and swayed its way out of London and into the fading daylight, her thoughts dark and painful.

They would probably never know exactly all the facts surrounding what had happened. Whether it had been Yates who had first broached the idea of obtaining Thea's fortune or whether it had been Edwina who had put the notion forth would always be open to question. Modesty, who'd had no illusions about Edwina, rather thought that while Edwina might have wanted Thea's fortune, she never would have acted on that impulse without encouragement from Yates. Patrick was of a different mind; after all, he'd seen Edwina shoot a man down in cold blood.

Between themselves, Thea and Patrick had discussed Ellsworth's return to the

Curzon Street house the night after the murder.

"We know now that it was to get your mother's letters, but why didn't he take them with him the night of Hirst's murder? Why leave them there in the first place?" Thea had asked Patrick once.

Patrick had grimaced. "He probably didn't want Yates, or Edwina for that matter, to know where they were. With everything that was going on the night of the murder, I would guess that he was so panic-stricken, he never gave them a thought. Certainly with Yates and Edwina prowling about the house, there would have been no chance to retrieve them, so he simply waited until the next night."

But it had all happened months ago, and while they had speculated and surmised the subject to death in the beginning, just as Thea no longer went around with that heartrending haunted expression, the topic was no longer of much interest to any of them. Especially not on this pleasant evening in April, the full moon a mysterious, silver orb in a star-scattered black-velvet sky and the scent of early roses perfuming the air.

His arm around her waist, Patrick and Thea strolled down the wide garden path that cheerfully wended its way through the moonlit gardens. Deeply in love, looking forward to the future he and Thea would share, Patrick was a happy and contented man. He couldn't imagine a life without Thea, a day without looking into the lovely expressive eyes of hers or a night without her slim, warm body lying next to his. And while he would have preferred for Thea never to have been in danger and for events not to have ended so tragically, he would never be sorry that they had met under such unpleasant circumstances. Without the blackmail attempt on his mother and Hirst's attempt to solicit money from Thea, their paths would not have entwined so dramatically and he would not this evening be walking beside the only woman in the world for him. A woman whose gently rounded stomach told of the new life they had created together. The baby would be born in October, and they were both thrilled at the prospect.

Thinking of that, he dropped a kiss on her dark head. Thea glanced up at him and sent him that dazzling smile that still made him breathless. "What was that for?" she asked.

"Because I love you," he replied, his gray eyes warm and full of love. His hand dropped to her slightly protruding belly.

Caressing her stomach, he admitted, "And the babe, too." He grinned. "At the moment, I am so in love with you that there is nothing that I would not grant you."

She giggled. "That must be true — not many new husbands would be happy to have Modesty part of their households." Sobering, she asked, "You really don't mind her living with us?"

Patrick shook his head. "No. Halsted is a large house and as long as I can have my wicked way with you whenever I want, you may invite half of London to live with us if it gives you pleasure."

"Do you think Modesty will like Natchez? I was bowled over when you suggested she sail with us next month and she agreed to do so. I was certain she would want to stay with me until after the baby is born, but I was astonished that she accepted your offer of a permanent home with us." Thea frowned. "She has never liked the quiet of the country — which was one of the reasons why I bought the London town house. I worry that she will become bored and restless."

"The important question, my little love, is whether you think that you will like Natchez?"

Thea's face lit up. "Oh, I shall! I just know it. I am so looking forward to seeing your home and meeting your friends and neighbors. It shall be such an adventure."

Patrick's eyes danced. "Being married to you is adventure enough for me!"

"Unkind, sir!" She glanced down to where their child grew. "Do you hear that, Tom? Your father thinks that we are far too exciting for him."

"Oh, exciting is definitely a word I would use to describe you," he drawled. "And lovely, and charming . . . headstrong comes to mind, as well as, infuriating and terrifying." When Thea opened her mouth to protest, he kissed her, and added, "And most important of all — absolutely adorable!"

What could she do, but return his very agreeable sentiments? Arms twined, her head half-resting against his broad shoulder, Thea and Patrick turned and walked slowly toward the house. And high in the heavens, with its silvery light, the moon, as constant and enduring as their love, showed them the way home.